Semper Fi

Also by Keira Andrews

Contemporary

Honeymoon for One
Beyond the Sea
Ends of the Earth
Arctic Fire
The Chimera Affair

Holiday
Only One Bed
Merry Cherry Christmas
The Christmas Deal
Santa Daddy
In Case of Emergency
Eight Nights in December
If Only in My Dreams
Where the Lovelight Gleams
Gay Romance Holiday Collection

Sports
Kiss and Cry
Reading the Signs
Cold War
The Next Competitor
Love Match
Synchronicity (free read!)

Gay Amish Romance Series
A Forbidden Rumspringa
A Clean Break
A Way Home
A Very English Christmas

Valor Duology
Valor on the Move
Test of Valor
Complete Valor Duology

Lifeguards of Barking Beach
Flash Rip
Swept Away (free read!)

Historical

Kidnapped by the Pirate
Semper Fi
The Station
Voyageurs (free read!)

Paranormal

Kick at the Darkness
Kick at the Darkness
Fight the Tide

Taste of Midnight (free read!)

Fantasy

Barbarian Duet
Wed to the Barbarian
The Barbarian's Vow

SEMPER FI

BY KEIRA ANDREWS

Semper Fi
Written and published by Keira Andrews
Cover by Dar Albert
Formatting by BB eBooks

Copyright © 2014 by Keira Andrews
Print Edition

Dedication

To the veterans who have served
and sacrificed so much.

Acknowledgments

My eternal gratitude to Anne-Marie, Lisa, and Rachel for tirelessly helping me bring this story to life, and for loving Jim and Cal as much as I do. Thanks as well to Becky for beta work and support, and Dar Albert for creating a cover I want to frame.

This novel is particularly close to my heart because of the help my late father gave me in researching it. His incredible library of WWII books and passion for the era was invaluable in bringing Cal and Jim's story to life. Thanks, Dad.

PART ONE

CHAPTER ONE

1942

BELLOWING BLACK SMOKE in its wake, the train swayed as it crossed the Rappahannock River, the boisterous singing and chatter of the men inside muffling the creaking wood of the ancient cars. As Cal stumbled, a strong hand on his arm steadied him, and he smiled down at the man before flopping into the opposite seat. He held out a bottle. "Drink? It's allegedly bourbon."

A small smile lifted the man's lips. "Sure." He took the bottle and tipped it back. He tried to hide his grimace, but couldn't quite. "I've never really liked the hard stuff."

"Well, in defense of bourbon, this isn't exactly Kentucky's finest." Cal peered out the window past the sleeping man beside him, who drooled against the streaked glass. The sun splashed orange across the horizon as it sank out of sight. "Hard to believe we'll be in South Carolina in the morning. Assuming this dirty old pile of planks doesn't disintegrate along the way."

A pot-bellied stove in the middle of the train car belched, emitting only a small amount of heat in the January chill. Cal shivered against the competing drafts, wishing he'd brought a warmer jacket. But he supposed they'd all be trading their civvies for uniforms soon enough, and he'd yearn for the northern cold before too long.

"Let's hope we'll be shipping out in something a little sturdier," the man said before passing the bottle to the recruit beside him, who stopped screeching an Irish sea shanty long enough to gulp down a quarter of the swill.

"I'm Cal, by the way." Cal extended his hand. "Cal Cunningham."

"Jim Bennett."

If Jim noticed how smooth Cal's palm was in comparison to his own, he didn't let on. His neatly combed hair was a blond that probably lightened in the sun, and there was a general wholesomeness about him that indicated he spent significant time outside. Faded freckles dusted Jim's pale skin, and he wore a blue button-front shirt that couldn't match the brilliance of his eyes.

As most of the men around them launched into a recitation of a limerick about a man from Nantucket, a fresh waft of burning coal drifted on the air. Cal chuckled ruefully. "I think this is the Marine Corps' way of telling us not to expect many creature comforts where we're going." He reclaimed the bottle and took another swig. "Where do you hail from?" he asked Jim.

"Outside a little place called Tivoli, New York."

"We must have been on the same train down to DC. I'm from Manhattan." Cal thought he'd gotten a good look at everyone, but he'd definitely remember handsome Jim Bennett with the blue eyes. "How far is Tivoli from the city?"

"About three hours or so."

"Hey, we're practically neighbors."

Jim smiled. "I suppose so. I've never been out of the Hudson Valley before today."

Cal laughed before realizing Jim was serious. He ran a hand through his thick hair. "Uh, so what do you do? No, no, let me guess. Farming."

"Of a sort. My family owns an apple orchard. You?"

"I guess you could say I'm in the family business too. Truth is I don't do much of anything." He put a cigarette between his lips and offered the pack to Jim, who shook his head. Cal opened his lighter and struck a flame.

A few kerosene lamps shone through the car, casting shadows and light over the faces of the recruits. In the flickering glow, Jim's expression was placid. He seemed to be waiting for Cal to say more.

Exhaling a cloud of smoke, Cal leaned forward in his seat, talking quietly in the cacophony surrounding them. "After Princeton, my father just assumed I'd come work for him. Gave me an office and everything. Great view of the Statue of Liberty, but I've never had much to do. He doesn't trust me with anything important."

Jim took this in. "What's the business?"

"Banking."

"You don't mean…Cunningham Savings and Loan?"

"My father's pride and joy. My grandfather came over from Scotland and built himself a little empire. I'm Calhoun Cunningham the third, so I guess one day it'll all be mine."

Shaking his head, Jim laughed incredulously. "Geez, couldn't you have gotten a commission in the army or navy? How did you end up here?"

The wheels of the train shrieked as it rumbled south. Cal shrugged with a grin. "Couldn't think of anything that would piss off the old man quite so much as enlisting in the Marines."

Jim returned the smile. "I suppose that's one reason for joining up."

"Don't get me wrong. I'm all for fighting for my country and destroying the forces of evil. What about you?" He sat back, inhaling a lungful of sweet smoke and relaxing against the seat.

"After the Japs hit Pearl Harbor, I enlisted as soon as I could. My father's not doing very well these days, but my wife will look after him."

Disappointment flickered through Cal. Not that he expected clean-cut apple farmer Jim Bennett to be anything but a straight arrow. "Wife, huh? Did you get hitched before you left?"

"No, not long after high school. I took a few night classes at the local college and met Ann there. She worked at the café." He opened his wallet and handed over a picture of a pretty brunette and a young girl. "My wife and my daughter, Sophie."

"That's a real nice family you've got. How old is she?" Cal pointed to the child.

"Two and a half. She was actually born on my twentieth birthday." Jim gazed at the photo and smiled wistfully. "She's my special girl." He glanced around as another bawdy song began and tucked the picture away. "Are you married?"

Cal grinned. "Nope. In twenty-four years there hasn't been a woman yet who's been able to pin me down." He didn't add that there never would be.

The train shuddered alarmingly, wheels wailing as everyone held on. A recruit near the end of the car stood on his seat with arms out for balance. "All right, boys. We'd better all sing this train along or we won't live to see boot camp, let alone the war!" He launched into "Chattanooga Choo Choo" with a voice that wasn't half bad.

As they joined in the chorus, Cal and Jim shared a smile.

1948

CAL'S THROAT FELT drier than the dirt road as he steered his Cadillac past the painted sign reading *Clover Grove Orchard* in neat script above a faded red apple. Gravel pelted the undercarriage of the car, which had only ever driven down paved city boulevards. The laneway took a few gentle turns before ending at a two-story farmhouse. He pulled up next to a rusted gray pickup and killed the engine.

The white wooden house had a dark-blue door and a few small windows, and the shingled roof rose to a peak above the second floor. To Cal, it was exactly what he imagined a farmhouse should be. Simple and unadorned. Workmanlike yet homey. Off to the left was a small barn, its dark green paint peeling. A cow and two horses wandered a fenced-in area of brownish grass beside it, and a large storage shed stood nearby.

Beyond that the ground sloped down to the orchard, where row upon row of bare apple trees grew into the distance. Cal got out of the car and stretched, breathing the early spring air deeply. He caught movement at the top of the rise, and Jim walked over the crest of the gentle hill, his light hair gleaming in the sun. Breath caught, Cal forced his lungs to expand.

He should never have come.

Tall and lean, Jim had the body of a man who worked the land from sunup to sundown. The sleeves of his plaid shirt and light jacket were rolled to the elbows, and his dungarees fit his slim hips snugly. He walked with an even, measured stride—not too fast, not too slow. Steady as always. Or at least as he'd been when the war started, before…everything.

It was all Cal could do not to run to him. The longing burned his chest, and his heart thumped. In the past three years, Cal had almost convinced himself his feelings had faded. *Almost.*

A big shaggy brown dog bounded out of the orchard, barking loudly. Jim whistled and brought it to heel as he reached Cal. Smiling softly, Jim extended his hand. Cal tried to ignore the flare of excitement that skittered up his spine as their palms connected, keeping his smile relaxed.

They hugged briefly, slapping each other on the back. They were both just over six feet, with Jim a little taller, and Cal couldn't help but think of how perfectly they fit together. Jim's scent sparked a hundred memories that flitted through Cal's mind like a newsreel.

Concentrating on an easy tone, he stepped back and let the dog smell his hand. "I see you've got quite a guard dog here." After a cursory sniff, the animal licked Cal's fingers and rubbed against his leg.

"Oh yeah. Finnigan's a real killer. His bark is a heck of a lot worse than his bite, but he does keep the deer away from the trees."

"Deer give you trouble? Wait—you don't have any bears out here, do you?" Cal put on an exaggeratedly serious expression.

"*Tons* of bears. They love city slickers."

"They are known for their refined palate." Cal crouched down and scratched behind Finnigan's floppy ears. "This guy keeps the deer from eating your crop?"

"Yep, he patrols the orchard. I built him a little house out there, and he does a real fine job. Comes and sees us every so often throughout the day, but always does his rounds. Best employee I've ever had."

"You're my competition, huh, Finnigan?" The dog eagerly flopped on his back and Cal rubbed his tummy. "Which breed is he?"

"Your guess is as good as mine. He showed up one day a few years ago, limping and awfully thin. We couldn't turn him away."

"And now you've got another stray at your doorstep." Cal stood, grinning.

Jim grinned back. "I guess I do. Did you find the place all right?"

"Yep. It looks great, Jim." Cal waved his arm around to indicate the orchard. "This is all yours?"

"All sixty acres. It's not much, but it's home. I'm sure it's awfully…basic compared to what you're used to in the city."

"Hey, in case you've forgotten our jaunt through the Pacific already, I've roughed it with the best of them."

Jim chuckled. "True enough. Look, it's not the jungle, but are you sure you're up for this? Not that I don't appreciate your help, but I could find someone local. I don't want to put you out."

Cal clapped a hand on Jim's shoulder. "After being cooped up in New York and London, I'm ready for a little fresh air and hard work. Point me to the nearest shovel. Or whatever I need to take care of apple trees."

Jim's eyes twinkled. "Let me show you around first."

They fell into a comfortable stride as if no time had passed at all. Jim led the way into the barn past a small coop where several chickens clucked. The dim, hay-strewn interior of the building revealed farming equipment, several stalls for animals, and a well-worn ladder leading to a small loft.

It smelled of musky earth with the hint of manure but wasn't unpleasant. In fact, Cal's blood stirred as Jim leaned close to point out how the chickens' eggs were collected. It had only been minutes and simply being near Jim set him off. How was Cal going to spend hours a day with him and not humiliate himself?

"I know it needs a good cleaning. It's just been at the bottom of the list."

Cal realized he was frowning, and quickly smiled. "No, no, it's great. So the cow and horses live in here?"

As Jim explained the daily schedule for milking the cow, Mabel, and caring for the horses and chickens, Cal nodded and tried to pay attention. But his belly flip-flopped, and he felt like a schoolgirl going to her first dance. He truly had been a fool to think time and distance could change anything.

He followed along into the house through the kitchen door. Pale yellow curtains fluttered in the breeze over the sink, and a round wooden table fit neatly in the corner by the pantry. A gas stove stood in the other corner with a pot of something that smelled like oniony beef stew simmering on top.

Cal inhaled loudly. "Are you telling me you could've been whipping up gourmet delights all those years we were starving in the jungle?"

Jim feigned offense. "No one unwrapped a D-ration bar quite like I did. But I can't take credit for this." He motioned toward the pot. "Courtesy of Mrs. O'Brien. She helps out with Adam during the day and cooks dinner. She'll be meeting Sophie off the school bus now before she heads home. There's frozen applesauce too. You'll be sick of apples soon enough, but I thought you'd like it tonight. Tastes almost like ice cream."

"Sounds great." Dessert was swell, but at the mention of Sophie and Adam, Cal's stomach knotted. He hadn't spent more than five consecutive minutes with children since he'd been one himself. He hoped they wouldn't be too…complicated.

By the stove stood a starkly white refrigerator. Cal smiled. "Look at this. First electricity and now a refrigerator. Next you'll tell me you're getting a phone."

Jim's forehead furrowed. "Who would I talk to out here?"

"The rest of the world? People who might want to buy your apples?"

"I already have people to buy my apples. Wilson's grocery stores buy all the apples I can grow. I don't need the rest of the world. Besides, I had a shower head put in last year. Things are plenty modern around here."

"Very true. Although you could have talked to *me* on the phone."

"I wrote you letters, Cal. It's not my fault you're a terrible correspondent."

"*Moi?* I take offense at that insult to my fine, upstanding character."

Chuckling, Jim led him through a dining area and sitting room off the main hall. The walls were covered with faded floral wallpaper—small bouquets of pink, white, and yellow. A fine layer of dust covered the figurines displayed in a hutch by the dark sofa. Cal suspected the furnishings were Jim's mother's choices when the house was built after World War I.

Upstairs were three bedrooms. The first at the front of the house contained two small beds, with an open toy chest beneath the window. Several dolls spilled out, and Jim tidied them up as if embarrassed by the clutter.

Next was the neat and spare guest room. A double bed filled the center of the room, with a little table on one side. The oak dresser rested against pale blue wallpaper.

"Hope this'll be okay for you."

Cal smiled. "Of course. It's perfect. Nice big window and everything."

Next was the bathroom, and then the main bedroom at the back of the house. Jim's headboard was simple dark wood, and Cal breathed deeply as he took in the bed. Jim would be sleeping here every night. So close but so incredibly far away.

A cheval glass stood in the corner by the window, and two dressers of matching dark wood filled the rest of the room. The closest was Jim's, with a simple comb resting on top, alongside—

Cal's heart skipped a beat. Beside the comb was the gold watch. He swallowed hard. "You know you're supposed to wear that. It tells time and everything. That's why I gave it to you."

Jim's lips twitched. "Yes, I heard a rumor. But I don't want to get it scratched up out in the orchard. It's for special occasions."

"Guess you use the position of the sun to tell time, huh? Like Davy Crockett?"

Jim smiled. "Something like that."

Beside the watch sat Jim's battered dog tags, coiled neatly. Cal brushed them with his fingertips. In London he'd come close one night to throwing his tags into the Thames, but in the end he'd locked them away in a safe deposit box with his personal papers and Jim's letters.

Cal's eyes were inexorably drawn to the other dresser. Atop it sat several items on a yellowing lace doily. A velvet jewelry box that had probably never held anything like the diamonds and gold Cal's mother wore. A gilded brush-and-comb set, neatly arranged side by side. A small bottle of perfume that Cal guessed smelled of some sort of sweet bloom. A pot of face cream.

The remnants of a life.

Cal turned to Jim, who wore the stoic expression Cal had etched in his memory since boot camp—only his eyes betraying a weary sadness. "I'm sorry I couldn't make it back for the funeral."

"You were working in London. I understand." Jim tried to smile but didn't quite make it. He reached for the other item resting on the dresser, a silver-framed wedding photo.

Ann held a small bouquet and wore a simple calf-length floral dress and a lacy hat over her dark hair. She smiled widely on Jim's arm, her eyes crinkling. Jim stood ramrod straight in his suit, posing seriously.

Jim straightened the frame's position a fraction of an inch before stepping back. "I'm sorry you never got the chance to come out and meet her."

"So am I."

Cal's gut burned with shame. Standing in the woman's bedroom six months after her death, deep down he still prickled with jealousy and resentment. She'd had what Cal never would. Never *could*. Part of him still hated her for that, as unfair as it was.

As much as he'd shared with Jim in those three and a half years of the war, it could never be this. The truth was that Cal had hoped he wouldn't have to ever meet Ann, and had used every excuse in the book to avoid it. He'd often wondered what they'd make of each other. Now he'd never know.

He should tell Jim he'd made a mistake. Make his excuses and speed away from Clover Grove. Never, ever looking back. It would be best for both of them in the end. Cal would only mess everything up if he stayed, and Jim would understand if Cal left now. Jim always understood.

Squaring his shoulders, Cal took a deep breath. *No.* He wouldn't run. He'd stayed away this long for his own sake. Now he had to put Jim first. Even if they couldn't be together in the way Cal wanted, it would be enough. He hadn't been here when Jim needed him, and Cal wouldn't let him down this time.

"It's a beautiful home you've got here, Jim."

Jim exhaled. "Thanks." The door slammed downstairs, and footsteps echoed. Jim's solemn expression melted away, and his face lit up in a way Cal hadn't seen in a very long time.

"Come meet the kids."

CHAPTER TWO

1942

"You'll be sorree!"

The voices of Marines marching by rang in the dank air as the new recruits clambered off the truck. The Marines laughed heartily, and Jim had a feeling there would indeed be many moments he'd regret his decision. He was already missing Sophie more than he thought possible, not to mention his father and Ann, of course. He wondered what his mother would have said. He liked to think she'd be proud.

He and Cal fell into a haphazard line with the other men outside a red brick building identified by a large sign as the mess hall. A squat, barrel-shaped man of about fifty with a flat nose, square jaw and very little hair gazed at the murmuring group. He snapped his heels together, pulling his shoulders back, and the men fell silent.

"I am Sergeant Tyrell," he said with a gravelly drawl. "Your drill instructor, or DI. Welcome to Parris Island, recruits. The first thing you're all going to do is say a little prayer. Everyone now. Bow your heads."

Beside him, Cal muttered something Jim couldn't make out. He raised an eyebrow, and Cal leaned in, his breath hot on Jim's ear. "If they think saying our prayers is going to save us over there, the Japs have this thing all sewn up."

"What was that, recruit?" Tyrell was suddenly before them, eyes bulging. "Have something important to get off your chest?"

Cal smiled. "I was just saying—"

"You will speak when spoken to or you will shut your goddamn mouth! Do I make myself clear?" Tyrell roared, spittle flying from his lips.

Smile vanished, Cal nodded.

"I can't hear you!"

"Yes, sir."

Tyrell gazed around at the recruits. "What are y'all waiting for? Say your fucking prayers!"

Bowing his head, Jim closed his eyes and said a quick prayer for the safety of all the men around him.

"All right. Very good. Now I hope Jesus will keep your souls safe and sound, boys, because as of this moment, your asses belong to *me*. And I ain't gonna be kind to them! Now fall out and get some chow."

In the mess hall, Jim and Cal lined up for their food and sat at one of the long tables. Jim wasn't quite sure what the slop on his plate actually was, but swallowed small bites quietly. Cal screwed up his face in disgust. "What the hell are we eating?"

Another recruit piped up. "I think they're hominy grits."

"Hominy what?" Cal asked.

"Is there a problem here, recruits?" A voice barked from behind them. Sergeant Tyrell scowled down. "You northerners aren't complaining about our fine southern cooking, are you?"

Cal smiled winningly, and with his dark eyes, dimpled cheeks, and thick, almost black hair, Jim thought he wouldn't have been out of place in the latest Bogart picture.

"Complaining?" Cal asked. "No, Sergeant, we were just wondering if we could have the recipe to send home to our mothers."

For a long moment, Tyrell was silent, holding Cal's gaze. Then his thin lips curved into a smile that sent a chill up Jim's spine.

"I'll be sure to get that recipe for you, son." Tyrell turned on his heel and marched away.

They finished their grits in silence.

After breakfast, they were ordered to the quartermaster's shed for their uniforms, with Tyrell bellowing out the cadence as they marched clumsily. "Three-faw-ya-left!"

It echoed in Jim's mind: three, four, your left; three, four, your left…

Cal was just ahead in line. A few minutes after he went in, the door opened behind a corporal, and Jim glimpsed Cal naked as he stood before the quartermaster. His skin was creamy pale, his back broad over taut, round buttocks and powerful legs. Jim's throat was suddenly strangely dry, and he wished they'd been given their canteens.

When it was his turn, he was ordered to strip and then measured ten ways to Sunday by a team of men. Jim had never been ashamed of his body, and knew he was in trim shape, but he still flushed and shifted from foot to foot. When the flurry of activity was over, he was handed an armful of clothing with a pair of shoes and boots on top. In his new khakis, he was given a number—382749 USMCR.

United States Marine Corps. He couldn't help but hold his head higher.

But he was soon reminded he wasn't a Marine yet. First was a trip to the barber. Jim passed more laughing Marines as he went and reminded himself they'd likely only been at Parris Island a few weeks longer than he, and there was no need to be intimidated. Yet these men seemed so capable and confident.

As his hair fell in chunks around his shoulders, Jim wondered why the line for the barber wasn't far longer. There had been hundreds of men on that shuddering, filthy train, yet he could see only about a dozen waiting for their turn. He asked the old barber, who smirked.

"More than half of ya won't last the first day here. Already weeding them out. End up in the army, or worse yet, the navy. Those swab-jockeys'll take just about anyone."

When the barber was done, Jim's skull felt strangely light even though he'd never had long hair to begin with. Outside, he found Cal where the trainees gathered.

Cal rubbed a palm over his shorn head. "Guess we won't need to pack a comb when we ship out."

Finally the platoon of about sixty recruits were gathered, and Tyrell marched them off to the training field, roaring the cadence and threatening death and dismemberment to anyone who couldn't keep up.

The next morning, reveille sounded at zero-four-hundred hours. Everyone scrambled into their gear, bleary-eyed and disoriented. Everyone except for Cal, that was. His head remained buried under his thin pillow. Jim shook Cal's shoulder, earning a string of curses. He shook harder. "You're going to miss roll call. Come on."

"Go without me. Just five more minutes," Cal mumbled.

They were now the only two recruits left in the barracks. Jim tugged the scratchy wool blanket from Cal and grasped one of his ankles. With a great yank, he sent Cal crashing to the wooden floor.

"Jesus fucking Christ!" Cal rubbed his chin where he'd smacked it.

"Get up! We're late!"

"Why didn't you just say so?"

As Jim sputtered, Cal's face broke into a smile, and he winked. He pulled on his uniform in record time, and they raced each other to the parade ground, trying not to laugh too hard.

1948

ADAM RACED DOWN the hall, more steady on his little legs with each passing day. Jim caught his son and lifted him above his head as Adam laughed with delight. He nodded to Cal. "Adam, say hello to your Uncle Cal."

As Adam babbled a greeting, Cal chucked him under the chin. "Hi there, big man. Nice to meet you. And how old are you now?"

Adam held up two sticky fingers before thrusting them into his tangled blond curls, which were in need of a cut. Jim had insisted to Mrs.

O'Brien that he'd learn how to do it, but perhaps he should ask her to show him.

"Wow, that old already?" Cal asked. "You'll be driving before we know it."

Jim called down the hall. "Sophie, come say hi to Uncle Cal."

She remained in the kitchen doorway. "He's not my uncle."

Taking a deep breath, Jim kept his tone even. "Sophie. Come and say hello."

Smiling, Cal waved. "It's okay. I'm sure we'll get to know each other soon enough. You probably want to go play, right, Sophie?"

She scowled, tugging on the sleeve of her checkered day dress. "No. I'm not a *baby*."

"*Sophie*." Jim stared her down. As petulant as she could be, she hadn't bested him yet.

Grumbling, she shuffled toward them and addressed Cal. "Hi."

"It's nice to meet you, Sophie. Goodness, look how tall you are already."

She regarded Cal coolly. "I'm almost nine years old."

Cal smiled. "Duly noted."

Sophie twirled the ribbon holding back her dark curls around one finger. "Is that your car outside?"

"It sure is."

Her eyes narrowed. "It's a stupid car."

"Sophie!" Jim clenched his jaw. "You will apologize this instant. I don't know what's gotten into you today, young lady."

Cal laughed nervously. "No, she's right, Jim. That Caddy isn't exactly built for the country. I think your pickup is a lot more useful out here." He clapped his hands together. "I should go get my things. I happened to stop by FAO Schwartz on my way out of the city."

Sophie stared blankly, and Jim tried to place the name. "FAO…?"

"Oh, it's a toy store in Manhattan."

At the word "toy," Cal had Adam's undivided attention, but Sophie remained unimpressed. To Jim, she asked, "Can I go now?"

"First you can help Uncle Cal carry his things upstairs."

Her scowl deepened. "Upstairs? That's where we live. Why doesn't he stay in the cabin like Eddie did?"

"Because Cal is my friend. He's part of the family, and you'll treat him as such. Do you understand?"

"Eddie was *my* friend!" Sophie glared.

"I know, sweetheart, but Eddie had to leave." Jim hardened his tone. "Cal very generously offered to come and help us out, and you're going to give him the respect he deserves. Understand?"

She nodded, eyes downcast.

"Come on—let's help Uncle Cal with his bags."

Ten minutes later, Adam was flapping his pudgy hands, shrieking with joy as Jim and Cal set up his new train set on the floor of the kids' room. Sophie sat on her bed with arms crossed, a new doll untouched beside her.

JIM TOOK A swig from his bottle of beer as he walked away from the house. He found Cal leaning against the wooden paddock fence, gazing upward at the vivid canopy of stars.

Cal took a drag off his cigarette and whistled. "Let me tell you, the sky doesn't look quite like this in the city."

"I suppose not." Jim buttoned his jacket. The temperature in early spring still dipped quite a bit, especially when the sun went down, and their breath clouded the air.

Cal offered the pack of cigarettes, but Jim shook his head. Cal laughed. "I think you're the only man in the United States Marine Corps who got through the whole war without smoking."

"I told you I tried them once when I was a kid." Jim shuddered at the memory.

"Right, you swiped a pack from your father and smoked the whole thing in a couple of hours."

"Then I threw up all night. Never been tempted to try them again."

"Hey, why'd you call the orchard Clover Grove?"

"It was my mother's idea. She was Irish, and she thought it would be lucky. You know, four-leaf clovers and all that. Of course, she died two years after they bought the place, so I guess not."

"How old were you?"

"Didn't we ever talk about this?"

"No. I know she died, but that's all."

"I was five. She went in childbirth, along with the baby. I don't know if it was a boy or a girl. It was only me and my father after that, and he never spoke of it. Not once."

Cal exhaled a long puff of smoke. "Seems strange that I didn't know that, after everything. I guess over there, we didn't talk about home too much."

"No, not much." Jim took another drink.

Cal stubbed out his cigarette on the fence and took a pull from his own beer, his throat working as he swallowed. "The kids get to sleep okay?"

"Adam was out like a light. Sophie wanted to read her book. I told her she could read a chapter. She'll probably do five if I don't go back in a little while and check."

"I'm sorry if I upset her by coming here."

Jim shook his head. "It's not you. I'm sorry about the way she acted. There's just been so much change for her. First Ann, and then Eddie up and leaving not even a week later."

"Have you heard from him at all?"

"Not a word. I really don't get it, Cal." He blew out a long breath. "When my Dad took a bad turn in the summer of forty-two, he hired Eddie to do the hard labor. He kept on after Dad died, and when I got home I convinced him to stay. We were expanding onto the back twenty acres that used to belong to the Turners, and all that planting and tending to the new trees was a lot of work."

"He was keen to move on?"

"Yes. He and Ann had had a misunderstanding. She'd taken offense to some comment or other he'd made. I don't know why she was so worked up—it had all sounded harmless to me. It wasn't like her." He took a sip of beer. "Anyway, I really needed his help, so he stayed. Eventually he and Ann buried the hatchet. He kept to himself most of the time anyway. I invited him to eat meals with us at the house, but he preferred his cabin."

"Then he just left without any notice?"

"No forwarding address either. *Nothing.* His folks didn't know a thing when I wrote them. He'd always been so kind to Sophie, and it was tough on her, right on the heels of her mother…" He saw Ann in his mind, weary and sad. He wished he could remember her happier.

"I guess you never really know some people."

Jim sighed. "I suppose not. He'd always been so dependable. I should be grateful the harvest was almost over, at least."

"How did he get out of enlisting?"

"He was 4F-ed. Heart murmur."

Cal chuckled ruefully. "Lucky bastard."

"Yeah. He didn't see it that way, of course." They were silent as a brisk wind blew up, and Jim wondered if Cal struggled as much as he did not to dwell on the memories. After a moment he gathered his courage and asked, "It's strange, isn't it?"

"What?"

"Being here. Being back. You'd think I'd be used to it by now, but sometimes…"

Cal gazed at him, his dark eyes penetrating. "Yeah. Some nights I dream about—" He stopped abruptly.

"What?" Jim's neck prickled.

"Nah, never mind. We're here now." Cal tipped his head back. "I missed Ursa Major over there. The Southern Cross just doesn't have the same panache. Of course Orion's *bear* was something to behold."

Shaking his head, Jim laughed. "You're not supposed to remind me." He winced. "Lord, I was drunk."

"You were very certain it was a bear and not a dog. Despite the word 'canis' being in the name. Remember that night we convinced Smithy that Centaurus depicted a sexual position?"

Jim grinned at the memory of the boy craning his head to and fro with a furrowed brow. Then another image took hold, and Jim tensed, his smile vanishing.

Cal's voice was soft. "Hey, it's okay."

Jim swallowed hard. "It's not. How can I stand here laughing—even for a second—after what happened? It's like I forgot."

"We'll never forget. I wonder every day why the hell I'm here and they're not. Sometimes I close my eyes and all I can see are their faces."

As the recollections of friends long gone flickered through his mind, Jim nodded. "Me too."

Cal paused. "And I think of what happened on Okinawa."

Jim's stomach roiled now as he was flooded with remorse and images that were forever burned into his mind. He screwed his eyes shut, his breath hitching and heart suddenly racing as sweat broke out on his forehead. "Please…I can't…" It was like a vise had clamped down on his chest, squeezing tighter and tighter. His lungs burned.

"Hey, hey, it's all right. I'm sorry." Cal wrapped his arm around Jim's shoulders. "Just breathe."

Part of Jim wanted to shake Cal off and run until the memories couldn't catch him anymore. But he couldn't resist leaning into Cal just for a moment. Everything about his friend was so achingly familiar, from his voice to his warm grasp to his faint scent. After three years of impossibly close quarters during the war, Jim felt like he knew Cal inside and out. Lord, he'd missed him.

Cal squeezed. "It's okay," he murmured. "We won't forget, but we have to move on."

Taking a deep breath, Jim stepped away and nodded. He cleared his throat, willing his heart rate to slow.

Putting his hands in his pockets, Cal thankfully changed the subject, his tone light. "Think I'll make a good farmer?"

As everything returned to normal, the pressure in his chest lifting, Jim managed to smile. "Dunno if you're cut out for it, but we'll see."

"Why, you don't think I've got the look?"

Jim took in Cal's handsome features—those dark, twinkling eyes and the thick hair. "Well, you don't look much like a Marine now. I haven't seen your hair this long since that first night on the train."

"God, that rickety old train. It was pretty much all downhill from there. You know, that salty old bastard Tyrell never did give me the recipe for grits."

They both laughed, and Jim felt himself again. "You're sure your father can spare you until after the harvest? That's still at least six months away."

Cal's smile was sharp. "Don't worry about my old man. I don't think we'll be working together again any time soon." He snorted. "Not that we ever worked *together*. I'm through taking orders from him. I'm through taking orders from anybody. Except you, I suppose. You're the boss."

"Me? You're the one who made sergeant."

"Sergeant." Cal shook his head. "No one's called me that in a long time. Guess no one's called you Johnny Appleseed either."

Jim shoved Cal playfully with his elbow. "No, and don't go telling anyone around here that nickname. You know, I think the only person in How Company who actually called me my proper name was you."

Cal shrugged. "I had to keep you happy or you wouldn't have shared your rations with me."

"Have you had any rice since you got back?"

"Not a single grain." Cal grinned. "They put me off it for life, I think." He fiddled with his lighter. "Say, it's awfully dry up here for April, isn't it?"

"You're telling me. The driest spring in a hundred years. Good thing I had these Rain Birds installed last season." He pointed down at the ground in the orchard. "Probably can't see them too well right now."

Cal squinted. "Little metal nozzles, right? I noticed them earlier."

"They feed off the well and spray all the trees. They say it's just as good as rain, but I still prefer the real thing. Think the trees do too." He watched a rabbit sniffing around before hopping out of sight.

"Mighty advanced technology you've got, Jim Bennett."

Jim scoffed. "Plenty of farms and orchards are using them now. It was Eddie's idea, in case we have a dry season. Guess he was onto something. Still early yet." He took another swig of his beer. "Thanks for coming, Cal. It's good to see you again."

"It's good to be here."

"I've always been able to count on you." Jim hadn't known what he'd feel seeing his old friend again, and he was warm with a sense of relief and optimism. Things were always better when Cal was around. Everything was going to be okay.

Cal shrugged. "Nah, it's nothing. I could only take so much of London. Got enough rain in the jungle. And Manhattan's boring as hell these days."

"Right. The bright lights of Clover Grove are much more your speed."

"Crazy as this may sound, I think they are." Looking back up at the sky, Cal smiled, dimples creasing his cheeks.

Feeling warm and secure again, Jim gazed at the distant planets and smiled along.

CHAPTER THREE

1942

THE BRISTLES OF his stained toothbrush bent at impossible angles as Cal scrubbed the toilet bowl. He tried his best to keep the splashing to a minimum, but if he was going to get the latrines, sinks and showers clean by the time taps rang out across the base, he needed to put some muscle into it.

At least he wasn't marching or engaged in endless calisthenics. And he was actually alone for the first time in weeks, so that was something.

"Cal?" Jim called out.

His pulse spiked as Jim approached. Here was the one man in the platoon whose company he didn't mind at all. "The one and only. I wouldn't get too close if I were you."

Jim appeared. "I didn't see you in the barracks. I thought you might be sick." He took in the sight of Cal on his knees in front of the toilet and frowned. "Are you all right?"

"Yep. Just peachy." He held up the ruined toothbrush. "Partaking in a little light cleaning."

"Ah. What did you do this time?"

Cal nodded to the weapon leaning against the wall. "What's that?"

"What do you mean?"

"I mean, what is that piece of equipment right there?"

Jim examined it as if there was some trick he was missing. "It's a rifle."

"That's correct, recruit. Unfortunately, I made the unforgivable mistake of referring to it as my gun." Cal couldn't quite keep the bitterness from his tone. "But it is not a gun, it is a rifle. I have to carry the damn thing everywhere I go for a week. Even to bed." He lowered his voice, speaking from the back of his throat. "Because the rifle is a Marine's best friend."

After glancing over his shoulder, Jim laughed softly. "Careful. If Tyrell hears that impression—"

"He'll stick his boot so far up my ass I'll need a surgeon to get it out!" Cal growled, jutting his jaw forward.

Still laughing, Jim shushed him. "Aren't you in enough trouble?"

Cal dropped the impression and winked. "Trouble's my middle name."

"I thought it was Robert."

"No, no, it's trouble. It's right there on my birth certificate in black and white."

Jim's smile faded as he glanced at the row of toilets. "How many have you done?"

"Not enough." Cal went back to scrubbing, wincing as he angled the toothbrush under the stained rim. "At least I've had the place to myself." As with everything at Parris Island, there was no privacy to be found in the bathroom, and Cal didn't fancy having to clean while fellow recruits did their business.

"Can I help? You're going to miss chow at this rate." Jim kneeled beside him and peered around, as if looking for another toothbrush.

"Nah, you'd better not. Don't want to get you in the dog house. Go on and eat. I need to have this bathroom—no, I'm sorry, this *head*—clean by taps or God knows what other punishment Tyrell has in mind."

Although he was clearly reluctant to go, Jim stood. "Okay. See you later."

Cal couldn't resist watching him leave, admiring the way the uniform trousers showed off Jim's firm ass. Then he gave his head a shake and went back to his task. The last thing he needed was to get caught giving Jim the eye. He could only imagine what Tyrell would do then, and none of the options were remotely pleasant.

As if conjured by the mere thought, strident footsteps announced Tyrell's arrival. Lips narrowed, he watched Cal for a long moment before Cal remembered he was supposed to stand at attention. Hopping to his feet, he clicked his heels, stuck out his chest, raised his chin and snapped off a salute, toothbrush still in hand.

Seconds ticked by as Tyrell stared him down. Although he was shorter than Cal, he was a force of nature, his presence oppressively filling the corners of the room. Finally he barked, "At ease!"

Cal stood with his hands behind his back, the disgusting toothbrush between his fingers. Tyrell surveyed Cal's progress with steely eyes. He marched slowly from one end of the room to the other, steps so measured and exact that Cal was sure they were precisely six inches apart. He returned and stood so close that Cal had to stop himself from backing up. He kept his eyes focused on the wall.

"Cunningham, I ordered you to have this head clean by taps, did I not?" His drawl made the last word sound more like *nawt*.

"You did, sir."

"And I instructed you to use your toothbrush, did I not?"

"Yes, sir. I—this recruit has, sir." Cal held up the brush.

"It's chow time now. You're gonna miss it if you want to finish on time."

"Yes, sir." His stomach growled as if in protest.

"You hungry, Cunningham?"

Cal hesitated before going with the truth, since any answer he gave would undoubtedly be the wrong one. "Yes, sir."

Squinting, Tyrell leaned in even closer, his fetid breath on Cal's face. "Bet you had a maid to clean for you. Bet you never cleaned a damn thing in your whole sorry, useless life."

Even if Cal could argue, he wouldn't. "That's correct, sir." He resisted the urge to add that his family had a whole household staff, not just a maid. Even at Princeton, he and his roommate in the dorm had secretly hired a local cleaning woman.

"Finish the job or you'll be eating that there toothbrush, recruit."

Stomach heaving at the thought, Cal jerked out a nod. "Permission to get back to work, sir."

Tyrell's features arranged themselves into a smile. "Permission granted." He did an about face, pausing in the doorway. "Oh, and Cunningham?"

Cal braced. "Yes, sir?"

"Tomorrow mornin' you'll make sure this head is still gleaming before you hit the mess hall."

"Yes, sir."

Jaw clenched, Cal pivoted on his heel and started on the next toilet, thrusting his arm in and scrubbing. The tile was hard beneath his knees. He could sense Tyrell lingering in the doorway, so he pursed his lips and began whistling a merry tune. If Tyrell made any response, Cal didn't hear it.

As taps rang out a couple of hours later, he raced to the barracks. He'd scrubbed his hands raw, but still didn't think he'd feel clean for some time. In the darkness, he stripped off his sweaty, rank uniform and collapsed onto his bed, which he had to remember to call a "rack." He carefully pulled his rifle under the covers with him.

Moonlight streamed through the small windows, and he could see Jim watching him from the next bed. With a small smile, Jim pointed to Cal's pillow and mimed lifting it up. After a glance around, Cal pulled out a piece of bread and hunk of meat wrapped in a thin paper napkin. He grinned and wolfed them down before anyone was the wiser.

The last thought he had before falling into a deep sleep was how lucky he was to have a friend like Jim.

1948

THE ROOSTER HADN'T even crowed yet, but Cal was wide awake. He'd never had trouble sleeping, even after he joined up, and had always been able to go back under quite easily. But after the constant noise of war and a few years in civilization again, it was far too quiet in Clover Grove.

He watched the sky lighten inch by inch through the window, telling himself he should get another hour or so of rest. Yet his eyes remained stubbornly open. At the back of his mind was the constant reminder that Jim slept at the end of the hall.

Sighing, Cal rolled over. He wasn't sure why he continued torturing himself. Jim could have hired anyone to replace Eddie, but as soon as Cal had heard the man left, he'd insisted on taking over. First there had been business in London he had to finish, but Jim had seemed happy to wait for him. There wasn't as much to do around an orchard in winter, he'd said.

As much as Cal would have liked to leave his father high and dry, he'd given fair notice and trained his replacement. He didn't miss the job one bit. After fighting the Japs and watching too many good men die, the chicanery of international banking seemed so meaningless.

Of course his father had blown his lid when Cal told him he was leaving to work on an orchard. But he'd missed Jim so much, and maybe…

No.

Flipping onto his other side, Cal told himself sternly to stop thinking Jim could ever feel the same way. Jesus, Jim had just lost his wife, and more than that, he wasn't queer. Cal needed to go back to sleep and stop daydreaming.

Yet when he closed his eyes, the longing was an ache. After the war, he'd refused to allow himself the fantasies that had kept him going during the endless nights in the stink of the jungle. A few times beneath his blanket, with death all around, he'd taken himself in hand with thoughts of Jim running riot through his mind, clinging to scant moments of release and escape.

Now, under Jim's roof, Cal's body came alive and he gave up on sleep. He slept shirtless, and quickly kicked off his boxers before licking his palm and grasping his shaft. Just as he had on the islands, he turned onto his stomach, muffling his low moans as he stroked his swelling cock. Only this time there was a soft pillow beneath him instead of a folded-up raincoat.

He flicked his thumb over the head of his dick, sending a bolt of electricity through his body. Bracing himself on his left elbow, he thrust his hips, fucking his own hand. In his mind, it was Jim on his knees before him, mouth open wide, taking every inch of Cal and wanting more.

Groaning, Cal could almost feel Jim's fine hair as he reached out in his imagination, holding Jim's head, caressing him as he told him how good he was. Jim would pull off, a long string of saliva hanging from his lips. He'd suck his index finger and reach between Cal's legs, pushing it deep inside him as he took Cal into his mouth again.

With a gasp, Cal tightened his grip on his cock as the pressure built to a crescendo already and burst out, white hot. He took a shuddering breath as he came, imagining Jim swallowing it all. They would kiss, tongues stroking, and then Cal would get on his hands and knees, Jim thrusting inside him with his throbbing—

A cry pierced the air, and in his haze Cal froze. Had he made that noise? Then the rooster crowed again, and he slumped against the sticky sheets, wondering belatedly if Mrs. O'Brien did the laundry, and when would be a good time to sneak down and wash his bedding.

CAL COULDN'T FIND Jim when he went downstairs, although there was evidence of breakfast in the pile of dishes on the counter. He quickly ate a bowl of flaked cereal after skimming the cream off the container of milk in the fridge. He wasn't sure he'd ever tasted milk fresh from the cow before, but found he liked it.

Outside, Adam ran in circles, chattering to himself while Jim sharpened a machete with a leather strop. "I'm almost afraid to ask." Cal grinned as he approached.

Smiling, Jim nodded to another long blade resting by the paddock fence. "That's yours over there. We've got to get all the trees pruned. I've been doing it myself, but there are still a few acres left."

Picking up his machete, Cal tested its weight, swinging it through the air. "You sure our Ka-Bars wouldn't be better?"

At the mention of their foot-long fighting knives, Jim laughed. "We want to prune the trees. Not stab them in the guts."

Adam cried out gleefully, and Cal turned to see a woman he presumed to be Mrs. O'Brien pedaling up the laneway. She was about fifty or so, and her dark, graying hair was pulled back into a bun at the nape of her neck. Slightly stout and not unattractive, Cal imagined she had been a beauty in her youth. She wore a calf-length navy dress and sturdy shoes.

She leaned her bicycle against the side of the house and swept Adam up into her arms while he giggled. She smiled at Cal. "This must be Calhoun."

Wincing, Cal smiled back. "It's Cal. No one's called me Calhoun in…well, actually, I don't think anyone's ever called me that. Even my mother. A pleasure to meet you, ma'am."

"Did Sophie get on the bus all right?" Jim asked.

"Yes, it pulled up at the end of the lane just as I did," Mrs. O'Brien replied.

To Cal, Jim said, "I'll just go get the rest of the equipment from the barn." He loped off in that direction.

"Do you have far to come?" Cal asked Mrs. O'Brien.

"Oh no, not far. A mile or so." She lowered Adam to the ground and gave him an affectionate pat on his rear end. "Now that I can ride over with the snow gone, it takes no time at all, really." Her strong Irish lilt gave her voice a pleasant, singsong quality.

Barking happily, Finnigan raced toward them from the orchard.

Mrs. O'Brien scratched behind his ears. "I always give him the scraps when I'm cooking, and I swear he has an alarm that tells him when I'm due to arrive. Little scallywag."

Cal patted Finnigan. "It's very good of you to help out Jim like this."

"It's the least I can do for a neighbor. He's such a fine young man. Lost his mother far too young, and always took good care of his father. And his wife when she came along." She *tsked*. "Such a terrible business."

Cal had only heard the barest of details via telegram. "Did they ever discover why the car went off the road?"

"No. They said the brakes appeared to be in working order. The best they could guess was she'd just been going too fast, which doesn't sound like Ann at all. Of course who can say what she was even doing out on the road at that time."

"Was it very late? I'm afraid I don't know the details."

"Yes, quite late, apparently. It wasn't until dawn that she was discovered. There was nothing to be done for her by then."

Cal filed this curious information away. "It's a terrible loss." As much as he still envied Ann, he'd certainly never wanted her to come to any harm.

Mrs. O'Brien nodded sadly. "Jim survives that bloody war and not three years later his wife leaves him and the little ones behind. God has a cruel sense of humor, if you don't mind me saying."

"I don't mind at all." Cal reached down and ruffled Adam's hair as the boy tugged his trouser leg. "Well, it's still good of you to go out of your way to help."

"Oh, it's a pleasure. As long as my husband's dinner is ready when he comes home from the office he's happy. Gerald's a doctor in Tivoli, and he's an easy man, thank the heavens. I love the children, and mine are gone now. Theresa, she's off in Albany with her husband, starting a family of her own. I told her I'd never forgive her for having my grandchildren so far away, but they never listen, you know." She winked, and then her smile faded. "And Stephen didn't make it back from Europe."

Cal would have thought he'd be used to it by now, but he still found himself clearing his throat awkwardly. "I'm very sorry to hear that."

"He and Jim grew up together. Stephen was in the Airborne—jumping out of airplanes. Made it through D-Day, but not long after that. He was a hero, they said." Her gaze was lost on the horizon. "I'm sure they say that about all the boys who didn't make it home."

"They were heroes, ma'am." He had no doubt. Even if Stephen O'Brien had died in an instant, another senseless death amid the millions, he was a hero. More of a hero than Cal could ever be.

"Yes, well." She shook her head and clapped her hands together, addressing Adam. "Now what will we do today while your daddy and Uncle Cal are hard at work? Shall you help me peel the potatoes? I think you'll be very good at it."

Cal nodded goodbye as she ushered Adam toward the house. Picking up his machete, he squared his shoulders. Since the war's end, he hadn't done much but push paper and glad-hand bigwigs in New York and across the pond. Inhaling in the crisp morning air, he went to work.

As Cal tiptoed from the bathroom down the darkened hall, he stretched his aching shoulders. Pruning was damn hard work, but it had felt good to fall into bed exhausted and go out like a light. He was certainly looking forward to more shuteye before morning.

A muffled cry stopped him in his tracks. Cal looked back over his shoulder toward Jim's bedroom at the end of the hall, listening intently. Another cry—louder this time—echoed in the night, and Cal's gut twisted at the distress in Jim's voice.

Barely restraining himself from throwing open Jim's bedroom door, Cal twisted the handle and peeked in. Lying on his stomach in his pajamas, the sheets twisted about his legs, Jim whimpered and writhed, his eyes screwed shut. Cal closed the door behind him and hurried to the bed, shaking Jim's shoulder before leaning back out of reach.

Sure enough, Jim lashed out, limbs twitching as he woke gasping. Sweat soaked his hair and dampened his pajama top. Chest heaving, he gazed up at Cal, unfocused.

Cal kept his voice low. "It's okay. It was just a dream. Everything's okay."

Blinking, Jim peered around the room with jerky movements before coming back to Cal. With a shuddering exhale, he swallowed thickly. "I…" He ran a hand through his hair. He rasped, "I'm sorry."

Perching on the side of the bed, Cal smiled softly. "It's all right. Sounds like it was a doozy."

Jim nodded.

"The same as before?"

Nodding again, Jim pushed himself up against the headboard, clasping his knees to his chest. "I'm fine. It's nothing."

Cal hated that Jim was still haunted by the war. By that night. "Nothing" was the last word Cal would use. Jim still trembled, and Cal yearned to pull him close. Instead he went to Jim's dresser and pulled open a few drawers of neatly folded clothing before finding a fresh pair of pajamas. "Here. You'll feel better."

Jim went to work on his buttons with shaking hands. He managed to undo one before Cal sat beside him and reached over. "It's okay. I got it." He made quick work of the buttons and peeled the damp shirt from Jim's arms. In the bright moonlight, he could see the spattering of freckles and light hair across Jim's firm chest and barely resisted the urge to touch.

Forcing his mind to stay on task, he handed Jim the fresh pajamas and went to the window, imagining all too clearly Jim's lean thighs and tight buttocks. He started talking, the words tripping out. "Great view of the orchard from up here. What's beyond it?"

"The Turners' farm. Even though we bought part of it a few years ago, they still have a lot of land left."

"Ever think of buying more?"

"Sure. But I can't see it happening. At least not in the near future. The orchard's profits aren't high enough."

"If it's only money stopping you, I can—"

"Cal."

Raising his hands, Cal turned from the window and chuckled. "Okay, okay."

Jim managed a small smile. "I know you mean well." Breathing evenly now and redressed, he leaned back against the headboard. "Thanks for waking me. I'm sorry to have bothered you."

"It's no bother. I can stay for a while if you want."

"No, no. I'm fine. Go back to bed."

"Okay. Sleep tight." Cal wanted to go to him and brush down the piece of hair that stood askew atop Jim's head. But he walked away, closing the door behind him and returning to his own empty bed. This time, sleep didn't come.

CHAPTER FOUR

1942

"I'M BEGINNING TO think they're out of boats."

Jim kept his gaze forward and whispered, "What?"

As they marched on in close order drill in the gray afternoon, backs ramrod straight, legs striding in unison to the DI's cadence, Cal didn't turn his head either. "The only reason they could possibly have for marching us around this much is that we're walking to Japan."

Lips twitching, Jim fought a smile. "Right through the ocean, huh?"

"Yep. This rain is just a warm-up for the real thing."

"Plaatooon, halt!" Tyrell bellowed.

The men staggered to a stop, their rifles clattering together. Jim blinked the rain out of his eyes and waited to find out why Tyrell had stopped them. It could be safely assumed that the recruits had done something wrong. As always.

From the corner of his eye, he could see Tyrell slowly stride down the column of men, eyes sharp like a predator stalking its prey. Jim prayed he would pass Cal by just this once and pick on one of the other recruits. Not that Jim wished them any harm, but he hadn't gotten to know them. Everyone knew that once their six weeks of training was through, their platoon would be scattered throughout the Corps. No sense in getting attached.

But it was different with Cal. As much as Jim wanted the time to go quickly so he could officially be a Marine—and not stuck in this purgatory—he dreaded the day he would no longer have Cal at his side to raise a sardonic eyebrow or give him a hand, strong and sure, when he struggled at the top of the climbing wall during PT.

"Forrrward march!"

As they set out again, it happened so quickly that Jim wasn't sure if Tyrell tripped him or if Cal had unluckily stumbled. Jim could only catch the edge of Cal's rain poncho for a moment before Cal sprawled forward in the mud, crashing into the man in front of him, who staggered but remained upright.

"Plaatooon, halt!"

Shouldering his rifle, Jim sank to his knees beside Cal, who sputtered, wiping mud from his face as he glared up at Tyrell looming over them.

Tyrell narrowed his gaze on Jim. "Recruit! On your feet!"

The words were out before Jim could stop them. "He could be hurt, sir."

Jim had grasped Cal's shoulder, but Cal shook him off. "I'm fine." He hissed under his breath as he moved to his feet, "Get up!"

Clambering up as well, Jim stood at attention once more, eyes on the helmet of the man in front of him. They waited with bated breath for Tyrell's next move. The freezing rain pelted down, and all else was silent. Jim tensed from head to toe, wondering if Cal was hurt. Cal seemed to be standing fine beside him.

Finally Tyrell spoke. Instead of his usual red-faced roar, he addressed Cal with an eerie calm. "This is what happens when you don't stay in step, recruit."

"Yes, sir." Cal's voice was flat.

"You're filthy, recruit."

"Yes, sir."

"Get out of that disgusting uniform."

Cal hesitated. "Sir?"

With a swift intake of air, Tyrell unleashed at full volume. "Did I stutter? You're a disgrace to this platoon! You're not fit to wear that uniform, so get it off! On the double! Down to your skivvies!"

From the corner of his eye, Jim watched as Cal stripped, awkwardly shifting his rifle from arm to arm since he couldn't dare put it down in the mud. He hopped on one foot as he struggled to yank off his trousers over his boots. Jim clenched his fists, pressing his arms to his sides.

Once Cal stood at attention again, Tyrell inspected him. He barked, "Pick up those revolting pieces of clothing. You think I'm gonna carry them back to the barracks for you?"

Cal did as he was told, balling up his uniform and tucking it under his arm. "No, sir!"

"Forrrward march!"

They were off again. Jim caught glimpses of Cal's chest, the dark hair scattered across it matted down by the relentless, icy rain. As they marched on interminably, Cal began to noticeably shiver. Jim wanted to give him his own poncho and tell Tyrell to go to the devil, but knew it would only make things worse.

When they finally returned to the hub of the base, Marines laughed and hollered at Cal, whistling and breaking into a ribald song. Jim could see the stony set of Cal's jaw as he ignored them. They were finally dismissed for an hour to write letters, but Cal headed straight to the head.

Although he was eager to write home, Jim followed. The empty shower room was large and open. Still in his muddy boots, Cal dropped his gear and clomped over to one of the showers and turned on the water. His soaked white briefs clung to his buttocks.

For some reason, group showers always made Jim strangely bashful and uncomfortable, even back in high school phys ed. He'd seen Cal and all the other recruits naked by this point and didn't want to be labeled a prude. Yet there was something about the sight of Cal in his boots and see-through skivvies that made Jim flush and turn away.

He realized Cal needed dry clothes and hurried back to the barracks to retrieve Cal's spare khakis and towel. When he returned, Cal still stood beneath the spray of water, his legs parted and arms braced against the wall.

Jim croaked, "Cal?" He cleared his throat. "You'd better get dressed. Tyrell's likely to call off the personal time any minute and get us marching again."

With a nod, Cal turned off the water. A crooked smile lifted his lips when he saw Jim holding his spare clothes. "Thanks."

As Cal bent to unlace his boots, Jim made himself busy at the sink, scrubbing his hands even though they didn't need it. In the chipped mirror, he glanced at Cal toweling dry and dressing. When Cal swore under his breath, Jim turned around. "Okay?"

"Damn buttons." Cal had on his undershirt but struggled with his uniform.

Jim stepped closer and realized Cal's hands were shaking. He reached out and covered Cal's fingers with his own, wincing when he felt how cold they were even after the shower. "Here. Let me."

Although clearly wanting to argue, Cal lowered his arms to his sides. Jim inched closer but found his own hands clumsy as he tried to fasten Cal's shirt in the opposite way he was used to. "Wait, this'll be easier."

He moved behind Cal and reached around him, pressing against his back as he pushed each button through its hole. Cal seemed to be holding his breath and didn't move a muscle. When the last button was through, Jim stepped away and slapped Cal lightly on the back. "There you go. Ready for action."

Cal mumbled a reply, his face flushed. Jim was relieved the shower and dry clothes had done the trick, and that Cal was warming up again.

1948

"Jim?"

He glanced at Cal, who had walked back from the tree he was pruning and now eyed it critically. "Are these branches evenly spaced, or should I cut that little one off?"

From midway up his ladder, Jim gave the tree a once-over. "Cut it off. It's drooping too much. The branches should sort of look like the rungs of a ladder when you're done."

Cal nodded thoughtfully and took a gulp of water from his canteen after wiping his forehead. He'd taken off his jacket, and he and Jim both had their plaid work shirts rolled up at the sleeves. "Speaking of ladders, after those goddamn rope nets we had to climb to board the ships, I swore I wouldn't get on another ladder even if you paid me."

Jim remembered the treacherous climb after Guadalcanal, his limbs burning, the rope swaying and shifting as dozens of men scaled it. He gave the solid wooden ladder a pat. "These are a little easier to manage."

Cal climbed his and whacked at the offending branch with his machete. "Good thing, or I'd be liable to take off my own hand if I was swinging around like we did on those ropes."

Jim chuckled. He could always rely on Cal for a laugh. Not to mention all the other things he could rely on him for. Cal understood the nightmares and didn't say a word in the morning light. Jim hadn't felt so…settled in a long time. "Speaking of getting paid, we really need to discuss that."

Ignoring him, Cal hacked away.

"I know you can hear me."

"What's that? Gone partially deaf. I was in the war, you know. Lots of explosions. Hell of a racket over there."

"Har, har. Seriously, Cal. I'm paying you."

Cal pointed up. "Hey, is that a hawk?" He whistled softly. "Look at that wingspan."

Jim glanced at the bird soaring above the treetops. "Yes, it's a hawk, and don't change the subject."

With a sigh, Cal faced him, propping one foot up on a low branch, the other firmly on the ladder. "I'm not taking your money."

"Why not? You're doing the work, fair and square. So you should be paid, fair and square."

"I don't need it. I have more money than I know what to do with. Put it aside for the kids. Send Adam off to college one day. Maybe even Sophie. It'll do a lot more good that way. Just make sure they go to Princeton and not Yale." He winked.

Jim contemplated the notion. He knew Cal was richer than the devil himself, and that any salary Jim could pay him would be hopelessly paltry. But it didn't sit right, not paying a man for his work. "You need to be compensated. Even Mrs. O'Brien lets me give her a little every week. Fought me tooth and nail, but I wore her down."

"I am being compensated!" Cal waved his arm around. "Look at this place. It's paradise, Jim. Plus I'm getting room and board. I hated the bank. Sure, I had a lot more to do than before the war, but I'll never really make my father happy." He snorted. "Not until I get a wife and have a son to carry on the family name."

"Well, that's another thing. You aren't going to meet many women around here."

"On the contrary, my good man, just the other day I met a delight-ful woman who happened to ride up on her bicycle. Amazing cook."

"Aside from being two decades your senior, Mrs. O'Brien is happily married."

"Alas. Another heartbreak, but I'll persevere."

Jim chuckled. "But really, out here you aren't going to meet any-one."

"I don't want to meet any women," Cal muttered as he went back to the branch, hacking into it forcefully.

"You're thirty now. Not getting any younger." Jim kept his tone jocular.

"Oh, this handsome face will still be reeling 'em in for years to come, don't worry." He finished cutting through the branch with a flourish.

"I just hate to see you missing out."

Cal climbed up a few rungs and went to work on pruning another branch. He didn't meet Jim's gaze. "I'm not missing out on anything. I'm exactly where I want to be."

"But you'll make a great father, Cal. And you wouldn't believe how wonderful it is to have children. Until Sophie was born, I didn't know I could love another person that much."

"What about your wife?" As soon as the words left his mouth, Cal blanched. "I'm sorry. God. Forget I said that."

The ever-present guilt churned Jim's gut and dried his throat, but he kept his expression neutral. "Of course I loved Ann. She was a good woman."

"Absolutely." Cal ran a hand through his hair. "Geez, I'm sorry. I think I just woke up on the wrong side of the bed. Don't listen to me. What the hell do I know about any of this stuff anyway?"

With his good looks and gift of gab, women had always flocked to Cal, but since Jim had known him, Cal had never kept a lady around for long. As they went back to work, Jim wondered if Cal had ever been in love.

"PASS THE CARROTS."

Jim shot Sophie a reproachful look. "Pass the carrots, *please*."

She appeared ready to roll her eyes, and Jim's grip on his fork tightened. He didn't want to send her to bed without supper, but he'd had enough of her backtalk and attitude the past several months. Cal's arrival had unfortunately made it worse.

But she apparently thought better of an eye roll and grudgingly muttered, "Pass the carrots please."

Cal handed the dish over. "Here you go." He smiled, but Sophie kept her eyes downcast.

They sat at the round table in the kitchen. Jim's father had only used the dining room for special occasions, and Jim had kept up the tradition.

"This roast is delicious," Cal said.

"Mommy's was better." Sophie was clearly intent on disagreeing with everything Cal said, no matter how innocuous.

Before Jim could interject, Cal answered. "I'm sure your mom's cooking was really good. Say, how was school today?"

Sophie peered at him suspiciously before hitching her shoulders. "Okay."

"Just okay? You told me you got an A on your math test." Jim smiled at her encouragingly.

"Wow, that's great! I sure never got an A in math," Cal said.

"Why? Are you stupid?"

Jim dropped his fork with a clatter. "Sophie Elizabeth Bennett. Apologize to Uncle Cal."

"I was just asking a question," she muttered.

Exhaling heavily through his nose, Jim counted to three in his head. "I'm going to take my belt off in a minute. You apologize. Now."

Tears shone in Sophie's eyes. "I'm sorry," she mumbled.

"Now put your plate on the counter, go to your room, and get ready for bed."

Her wooden chair scraping on the linoleum, Sophie did as she was told, her little footsteps quick on the stairs as she raced to her room. Adam, aware that something was wrong, sat on his padded chair with wide eyes, mashed potatoes dribbling down his chin.

Jim reached over and swiped at Adam's face with his napkin, giving his son a smile. "It's okay."

"She's just acting out, Jim. Don't worry—I can take it." Cal chuckled awkwardly. "Not many women I can't win over in the end."

"It's not okay. Lord in heaven, I barely know my own daughter. She'd have never acted like this before…" Jim trailed off. Ann was gone, and there was no bringing her back. He was on his own.

"She lost her mother. Just give her some time. She'll come around." Cal patted Jim's shoulder.

No, he wasn't on his own, and Jim felt a wave of profound gratitude. "I'm sure you're right. Although in the meantime she won't be speaking to you or anyone else with that kind of sass. You'll tell me if she does when I'm not around, all right?"

Cal raised an eyebrow. "So you can take your belt to her? I have to say, I can't picture mild-mannered Jim Bennett worked up into such a rage."

"Well, the truth is I've only spanked her twice and never used my belt. But she's trying my patience and I don't want to spoil her. My father wouldn't hesitate when I was misbehaving. Didn't yours ever punish you?"

"Oh, he punished me. But his weapon of choice was a highly effective combination of concise verbal denunciation followed by a prolonged shunning that would make the Amish weep. But my nannies were damn skilled with the belt, let me tell you." Cal glanced at Adam, who was occupied with licking gravy from his fingers. "Darn skilled, I should say."

Jim smiled. "Good thing you didn't pick up the rest of the bad language we heard in the Corps." His smile faded and he pushed his plate away.

"Go talk to her."

"I have to get Adam cleaned up after he finishes his dinner."

"I've got it covered. Adam and I are old friends by now. Right, pal?" Cal ruffled Adam's hair, garnering a grin.

"If you're sure?"

"I insist." Cal took Adam's spoon and scooped up a bite of potatoes.

They were both laughing as Jim went upstairs, and he felt a bloom of warmth in his chest.

The door to Sophie's dark room stood ajar. Inside, she was curled toward the wall on her bed, the blankets pulled up tightly. Jim could tell from the way she was breathing that she was awake. He sat on the side of the bed and caressed her dark curls. "I know things haven't been easy for you."

She sniffled.

"A lot of things have changed, sweetheart. It's hard for everyone."

Sophie turned over. "I want Mommy to come back."

Her tearstained face and sorrowful expression was like a stab in the gut. Jim swallowed thickly. "I know, baby. But she's in heaven now. And there's nothing we can do to change that. Your grandmother died when I was only a boy. I know it's hard. We just have to do the best we can without her."

"I'm trying."

"I know you are. But you're being very rude to Uncle Cal. He came here to help us, and I want you to treat him nicely. He hasn't done anything wrong."

She pouted. "I don't like him."

"Why not?" The last person Jim knew who had disliked Cal this much was cranky old DI Tyrell. "Hasn't he been nice to you since he arrived? Didn't he bring you a pretty dolly?"

"I don't want it." She huffed, eyes skittering over to the corner of the room where the doll laid face down as if being punished.

"Uncle Cal just wants to be your friend. And I know for a fact that he's a darn good friend to have. I wouldn't be here if it wasn't for him. So try and be nice. At the very least, you're going to be polite."

Sophie's brow furrowed as she tensed. "Why wouldn't you be here?"

Images swam behind his eyes, and for a moment Jim could taste the blood in his mouth and smell the burning flesh. He swallowed hard. "It doesn't matter now. All that matters is that we're all here together, and we need to get along. Will you promise to be a good girl?"

Nodding, her eyes filled again. "I'm sorry, Daddy. Please don't be mad at me." She sat up and threw her little arms around him.

"I'm not mad anymore. I know you miss Mommy a lot. I miss her too."

Sophie's reply was muffled. "Do you?"

Jim's heart skipped a beat. "Of course I do. Why would you ask that?"

"Because."

"Because why? Come on, look at me. It's okay. I want you to tell me."

"Because you and Mommy never seemed to like each other very

much."

Jim focused on speaking evenly. "Why would you think that? We didn't argue."

"But you hardly ever smiled at each other. Not the way you smile at me, or Adam. Or *him*."

"Sophie, your mother and I loved each other very much." It was the truth. He had loved her, even if he hadn't loved her enough. "Now go to sleep."

"You'll always love me, won't you? Even if I'm bad?"

His chest constricted and Jim held her close, rocking her gently. "Always."

CHAPTER FIVE

1942

"HIT THE DECK and give me fifty!"

The recruits scrambled, heavy packs and rifles cumbersome as they dropped to the ground and started push-ups that Tyrell counted off. Cal had learned that in the Marines, the surface on which you were standing was "the deck," whether it was wood, tile, grass or dirt.

In this case, the deck was a muddy expanse of field on the way to the rifle range. They'd been marching for miles and this was the third time they'd been ordered to do push-ups. Cal's muscles protested, burning hotly as he heaved himself up and down. At forty-one, he saw Jim's hand slip on the mucky ground from the corner of his eye.

Tyrell pounced immediately, veins bulging in his neck as he loomed over Jim, screaming. "Did I say you could stop? You wanna nap, recruit?"

"No, sir," Jim ground out as he got his arm beneath him again and pressed up.

"What was that? I didn't hear you! I'll give you a nap!" Without warning, Tyrell's boot clomped down on Jim's back, shoving him to the ground. "Did I tell y'all to stop? Sound off!"

His blood boiling, the adrenaline got Cal through the rest of the push-ups. Jim struggled through them with the added weight of Tyrell's boot, his arms shaking. Cal bit his tongue, glaring up at Tyrell and quite sure he'd never hated anyone else this much in his life.

When they reached fifty, the men staggered to their feet. Cal kept his eyes on the helmet of the man in front of him, but a moment later felt Tyrell's stale breath on his cheek. "Got something to say, recruit?"

As he took a breath before giving the required response, another thought flickered through Cal's mind and barged out of his mouth. "Yes, sir."

The tension hung thick in the moist winter air. Tyrell stood still as a statue. "Don't keep us waiting, recruit."

"Permission to do another fifty, sir."

For a delicious moment, DI Tyrell was speechless.

Then, nostrils flaring, he screamed, "What are you waiting for, Cunningham? Hit the deck!"

As he pumped out the push-ups, Cal felt strangely light, a second wind giving him energy. The other recruits counted out the repetitions, hiding their smiles, while Tyrell could do nothing but watch.

When Cal was finished, he hopped to his feet and saluted Tyrell with a sharp snap of his wrist.

Tyrell pivoted on his heel. "Forrward march!"

Jim gave him a quick smile before whispering, "You know he'll make you pay for that."

Shrugging, Cal winked before turning his eyes front. One more black mark wouldn't kill him. He marched on, savoring his tiny victory.

The rifle range was a flat, rather barren area of grass and sand dunes beyond a small woodland. To Cal, it felt even more desolate than the rest of Parris Island, and that was saying something.

Along with a handful of one- and two-story buildings, tents were set up row upon row. Their sea bags, top-loading canvas sacks that closed with a drawstring, waited for them. Considering how cold and wet they were liable to get during the time they'd spend at the range, Cal was relieved to have some extra gear.

He was doubly relieved that he and Jim had been assigned to the same six-man tent, thankful that "Bennett" and "Cunningham" were close to each other in an alphabetical list of the platoon. Leading the way, he pushed back the flap of their tent and stooped to enter. The sun was setting, and in the gloom he squinted.

"I thought tents were supposed to have floors."

Jim ducked in behind him, shoulders hunched, neither of them quite able to stand upright even in the center. "I guess it depends on the tent."

"Think I should ask Tyrell for another?"

A recruit followed them in, chuckling. "I'd pay you to ask the son of a bitch. Of course, he'd make you sleep outside for the next two weeks."

"I have a bad feeling that this tent and 'outside' are not as far removed as we'd like them to be, boys." Cal dropped his sea bag on one side of the tent, his shoulders sighing in relief as he slipped the pack off his back as well.

Jim dropped his stuff beside Cal's, and the rest of the men marked their space. Not that there was much to go around. Soon they were called to the mess hall for chow, which they gobbled down. It was the same old slop, and Cal forbid himself to imagine what gourmet delicacies his parents and sister were eating at home.

In the tent at the end of the evening, Cal tried to make himself as comfortable as possible on the cold earth, spreading his rain poncho beneath him. "At least today we actually marched somewhere. Although I can't help but feel that we took the long way around this island."

Jim snorted. "Yeah, I got that feeling too. But it'll be nice to actually use our rifles instead of just lugging them around, so I'm glad we're here."

Heads cushioned by their sea bags, Cal, Jim, and the others settled in, rough blankets pulled up tightly to their chins. Despite his discomfort, Cal quickly dropped off into a deep sleep.

It was likely a couple of hours later when he woke, shivering from head to toe in the bitter cold. When the sun shone in South Carolina, even in the winter it never got too chilly. But under gray skies and rain, it could be a different story.

The cold leeched up from the ground, taking away every ounce of body heat and leaving Cal rigid, curled into the fetal position with knees to chest. In the darkness, he could hear Jim's teeth chattering.

Inching closer, Cal gritted his own teeth. "Christ, I thought the south was supposed to be warm."

Shuddering, Jim whispered back over his shoulder. "Feels colder than the barn in the dead of winter when I'm up early milking the cow. I'd have some gloves and a hat on, that's for sure. These uniforms don't quite cut it."

"Not quite." Cal shimmied closer. "Maybe we can share our blankets. Two's better than one."

In the murk, he could make out Jim's nod, and they edged toward each other, spreading their blankets. A warning bell sounded in Cal's mind as he pressed against Jim's back. Even through the layers of their uniforms and jackets, Cal already felt ten degrees warmer inside and out.

His mouth was inches from the back of Jim's neck, his senses filled with his friend's scent. The urge to close the final gap between them and press his lips to Jim's fair skin was overwhelming. The other recruits were shivering together in their corners of the tent, and in the dark, shapes had to be close to even be visible. No one would see.

It had been a happy circumstance that Cal had stumbled into Jim on the train, and with each passing day, he'd dreaded the end of boot camp and their likely separation. Who knew where they'd end up? Odds were one or both of them would die on the other side of the world.

At the thought of Jim cut down, Cal reflexively drew him closer, throwing his arm over Jim's waist. He waited for a protest, but Jim made no sound or movement. Spooned up behind him, desire heated Cal's veins, and he clenched his jaw, willing his body not to react. He didn't think Jim would take kindly to an erection nudging against him.

Soon Jim breathed deeply and evenly, and Cal allowed himself to creep just a bit closer before he faded away.

Reveille blared all too soon, as unwelcome as ever, but even more so because he wanted to stay curled up with Jim all day. But Jim scooted to his feet, instantly awake in a way Cal envied. Jim reached down. "Come on—up and at 'em."

Cal took his hand, and they were off.

1948

THE SMELL OF bacon cooking was always extremely welcome first thing in the morning, and Cal found himself bounding out of bed. He threw on his dungarees and navy work shirt, whistling to himself as he went downstairs.

Adam sat on the floor in the middle of the kitchen, his toy soldiers hard at battle. He glanced up and did a double take, grinning happily. "Hi!"

"Hey, buddy." Cal crouched and ruffled Adam's hair before joining Jim by the stove. "I don't think he quite grasps that I'm living here now. Still seems surprised to see me every morning."

Jim laughed softly. "Yeah, it takes a while to sink in sometimes. It's only been a week. He'll probably get it in a few days." He cracked an egg into the frying pan, where five eggs already sizzled in a layer of grease next to the bacon. "Sophie's in the barn milking Mabel. Why don't you give her a hand?"

"Ah, speaking of someone who is all too aware that I live here now." Cal poured himself a mug of coffee. "I don't think that's such a good idea."

"Things aren't going to change if you two avoid each other all the time."

"I'm not avoiding her!" Cal winced internally at his own defensiveness. *Of course I'm avoiding her.* "Come on, Jim. What the heck do I know about milking a cow? I'll break the damn thing."

Jim's lips twitched. "You'd have to try pretty hard to break a cow."

"Oh, I think I could do it. Farm animals and I are best left to our own devices."

"Sophie's never going to get to know you if you don't talk to her. I know she's been very rude, and I understand if you're upset with her, but—"

"Upset with her?" Cal interrupted. "No, no. I'm not holding a grudge against an eight-year-old. I just don't want to pressure her."

"Okay." Jim flipped the eggs over awkwardly with a spatula, seemingly resigned.

With a sigh, Cal gulped down the rest of his coffee. "What the hell. Might as well give it a shot."

Jim's face lit up. "Thanks. I just want you two to be friends."

The sun peeked over the horizon as Cal made his way to the barn. A couple of deer froze in their tracks at his approach before loping away. Normally Cal stopped and marveled at the wildlife, but this morning he was too busy giving himself a pep talk.

She's a kid. Nothing to be afraid of. You've faced scores of bloodthirsty enemy soldiers happily willing to die if it meant killing you. You can handle one little girl.

Taking a deep breath, Cal entered the barn. A lantern illuminated the cow's pen where Sophie perched on a stool, milking into a metal pail. Her hair in pigtails, she wore rubber boots to her knees and was remarkably small beside Mabel. Finnigan sat nearby, and turned to regard Cal with his tongue out.

As the door closed, Sophie glanced up, her hands freezing in mid-squeeze. "What are you doing in here?"

Cal put on his most winning smile. "Morning. I thought I'd come give you a hand."

Sophie sat up straight and regarded him suspiciously. "You want to help me milk Mabel?"

"Sure, why not?"

"Have you ever milked a cow before?"

"No, but I'm sure I can learn."

"Eddie already knew how to do it. He taught me."

"Well, that makes you the expert now. Maybe you can teach me.

You milk her every morning?"

"Yes."

"You really help out your dad a lot. It's great." Cal smiled again, shoving his hands in his pockets in an attempt not to fidget.

She didn't smile back. "It's just chores."

"You want to show me how you're doing that?"

With a put-upon sigh, Sophie stood and waited for Cal to take her place at the stool. It was very low, and his long legs barely fit in the stall with Mabel. He regarded the swollen udders with trepidation. "I just...squeeze?"

"Uh-huh."

"How hard?"

"Pretty hard."

Closing his fingers around the teat, Cal did as he was told, and was rewarded with an outraged screech from Mabel, who almost knocked over the bucket as she stamped. Finnigan barked sharply. "I guess that was too hard, huh?"

"I guess." There was an unmistakable smirk lingering on the edges of Sophie's expression. "You're stronger than me."

"That I am." With a deep breath, Cal took hold of the udder again and squeezed gently. Nothing came out. "Is she finished already?"

"No."

With no further advice forthcoming, Cal tried again, telling himself to keep his temper in check no matter how vexing Sophie might be. He squeezed lightly, increasing the pressure until Mabel objected once more. Sweat broke out on his forehead as he tried again. Surely if a child could milk the beast, he could.

Ducking his head down, he peered under the cow, trying to get a look at what he was doing wrong. He tried squeezing a different teat in his fist, and as Mabel hollered, a sharp pain exploded in Cal's temple. He toppled onto the wooden floor, hay scratchy under his palms as he scuttled like a crab out of the stall.

The arched wooden ceiling spun in his field of vision, and he felt the planks of the floor *thunk* beneath his head. He'd meant to stand up, but gravity apparently had other ideas. A moment later Sophie leaned over him with eyes so wide he could see white all around her irises.

She vanished, and Cal tried to call to her, but couldn't make any sounds come out of his mouth. The pain in his temple radiated over his skull and down his shoulder. He could hear Finnigan barking very loudly, and the dog's breath was hot on his cheek. Cal closed his eyes.

"Cal! Can you hear me?"

He tried to say yes, but it sounded strangely garbled. He looked up at Jim, whose face was pinched. Then it was dark again.

"No! Keep your eyes open. Cal! Focus." Jim pressed a soft wad of material against Cal's temple.

It was the sound of Jim's voice and the warmth of his hand against Cal's head that kept him tethered to consciousness. Despite the pain, he leaned into the touch, his eyes fluttering shut.

"Cal!"

He opened his eyes again. Jim was breathing heavily, and Cal was faintly aware of muffled sobbing nearby. Concentrating, he got a few words out. "Is Sophie all right?"

The sobbing grew in intensity. Cal tried to sit up, but Jim held him down with firm hands.

"Just stay right there." He glanced over his shoulder. "Sophie, you have to get Adam. Mrs. O'Brien should be here soon. You and Adam wait for her by the house, all right? It's okay. Everything's going to be okay."

Sophie's footsteps faded, Finnigan barking after her. There was something wet dripping down Cal's neck. His fingers probed his temple and came away bloody. "Huh."

Jim took Cal's hand, squeezing. "Don't." He applied pressure once more to the wound. "Looks like Mabel got you good. Don't worry, you'll be right as rain in no time."

"'M not worried. You're here."

Brushing back the hair from Cal's forehead, Jim exhaled, his voice tight. "God, Cal."

"Mmm." Before Cal could organize his brain to tell Jim everything was fine, Mrs. O'Brien bustled in.

"I hear someone's had a wee accident." She bent over Cal, clucking her tongue.

"We need to get Gerald. Has he left for work?" Jim asked.

"You know if you'd just get a telephone, we could call him. He said he didn't have any early appointments, so I might be able to catch him. I'll ride back straight away."

"Take my truck. The keys are in the ignition."

Mrs. O'Brien frowned. "Dear, you know I can't drive."

"It's just down the road. Please, we have to hurry." His voice rose in agitation.

"All right. I'll be careful. Gerald can drive back."

Jim nodded. "Thank you, Mrs. O'Brien. I'm sorry to put you out."

"Don't be silly, boy." She bent and gave Cal's arm a squeeze. "Good thing you have a hard head, eh? Back in a jiffy."

As Cal waited, flitting in and out of full awareness, Jim kneeled at his side, touching him every so often with fleeting movements—fingertips on his cheek, a palm on his thigh. Some of the fuzziness began to recede from Cal's mind, and the urge to sleep lessened. He cleared his throat. "Don't worry."

Jim huffed. "Of course I'm worried. It could kill you. Lord. If…" He trailed off, shaking his head.

Small footsteps approached, and Cal winced as he turned his head slightly. Holding Adam's hand, Sophie stood in the doorway. "Is he going to be okay?"

"Uncle Cal will be just fine. How are you, sweetheart? You're very brave." Jim went and hugged his daughter close, Adam clinging to his legs.

Sophie met Cal's gaze for a moment. Then she buried her face in Jim's shirt and wept.

★　★　★

A FEW HOURS later, Cal was ensconced in the guest room, propped up on pillows with a bandage wrapped around his head. The good news, as Dr. O'Brien had seen it, was that he suspected only a mild concussion. The bad news was the splitting headache would take days to go away.

As Jim peered around the half-open door, Cal chuckled. "I'm still alive. Don't you have some work to do?"

He shrugged. "It can wait." Perching on the side of the bed, Jim asked, "You still remember who the president is?"

"I do believe it's Mr. Harry S. Truman of Missouri. At least it will be until November. I don't like his chances, personally." Movement in the doorway caught Cal's eye. "I think we have company."

Jim called, "Sophie, is that you?"

After a pause, she appeared with a plate of cookies in her hands.

"Come in and say hi to Uncle Cal." Jim beckoned her. To Cal, he added, "She was too upset to go to school."

Sophie stepped just inside the room with eyes downcast.

"I promise I won't bite." Cal kept his tone light. "I thought I smelled cookies baking. That's real nice of you to bring some up."

In a rush, she placed the plate on the bed by Cal's feet and backed up.

Jim frowned. "Sophie, it's all right. It was an accident." He went to her and dropped a kiss onto her head. "You're not in trouble."

"But…" She trailed off, glancing at Cal, guilt written large all over her face.

"But what?" Jim's frown deepened and he eyed her carefully. "Sophie, you showed Uncle Cal the right way to milk Mabel, didn't you?"

Cal jumped in. "She did. It was all my fault, squeezing too hard. Couldn't get a drop out. I don't think I'm suited for milking. I'll stick to the apples."

"Sophie." Jim's tone was razor sharp. "Did you show Uncle Cal how to do it properly?"

Head down, she mumbled something.

"Look at me."

Tears swimming in her eyes, Sophie did as she was told. "I thought it would be funny. I didn't think she'd kick him like that! She's never kicked me."

"Because you milk her every morning and you do it the right way!" Jim's nostrils flared. For a moment, he just stared at her with his jaw clenched. Then he pointed to the door. "Go to your room. We'll discuss your punishment later."

A sob echoing in her wake, Sophie ran.

Cal's head throbbed. "Hey, don't be too hard on her. She didn't mean any harm. I probably would have done the same thing at her age. It was only meant to be a joke."

Jim shook his head. "I taught her better than that. I don't understand why she's acting like this."

"Hell, she's a kid. Why do kids do anything?"

"You could have—" Jim paced to the window and blew out a sharp breath, his eyes on the horizon. "You could have really been hurt."

"I'm fine." Cal couldn't help but be warmed by Jim's concern.

"If something happened to you, I…"

Cal's heart fluttered. "What?"

Jim was stock still, looking out the window. After a long moment he straightened up and cleared his throat. "After all this, if you're having second thoughts about…" He waved his hand. "This whole thing. I'll understand."

"What, you think I'm going to call it quits because of a little love tap from a bovine? You're not getting rid of me that easily, Bennett."

Smiling softly, Jim turned. "You sure?"

"Of course I'm sure. It's nothing."

Jim sat on the side of the bed again. "Thanks."

"Hey, in case I ever have to milk a cow again, was I not supposed to squeeze?"

"You have to pull down as well. Gently, though. Or else they get testy."

"Yeah, I heard a rumor." Cal reached toward the cookies and plucked one from the plate when Jim lifted it. "But like Mrs. O'Brien said, I've got a hard head."

"I'm just glad she was able to flag down her husband on his way to work. If she'd missed him, we'd have had to wait at least another hour, and if the kick had been harder, or you'd lost more blood, or—"

"But it wasn't, and I didn't. Jim, if the Japs couldn't get me, I'll be damned if Mabel will take me down."

Jim smiled. "It would make for a heck of an obituary, Cal."

"That it would." Cal took another cookie, grinning.

A few days later, a man from the telephone company arrived to install a line.

CHAPTER SIX

1942

Blinking away the sweat dripping into his eyes, Jim swiped his arm across his face. Grains of sand insinuated themselves into every pore and orifice, even burrowing into his ears. It was coarse and unrelenting on his tongue. For once he was glad of his shorn hair, since it was easier to brush the sand free.

"How the hell can it be so cold at night and this goddamn hot in the day?" Cal muttered. They were on their stomachs, practicing the prone position for shooting. He spit and wiped his mouth on his sleeve. "Christ, I've swallowed enough sand to vomit up my own desert."

A sergeant suddenly loomed overhead. "Just be fucking careful you don't get any of that fucking sand in your rifle, recruit!"

As the sergeant moved on, barking his way down the line of men, Jim couldn't help but wince at the foul language. At the rifle range, the supervisors had taken obscenity to a whole new level, with every other word starting with "f." Jim felt more of a bumpkin than ever, but had never heard such an unending string of curses in his life.

"If they don't want sand in our rifles, why did they put the range on a sand dune?" Cal whispered, shaking his head.

"Shh. You know how they feel about questions of logic."

They shared a fleeting smile before going back to their practice. Soon the sergeant's shout filled the air as he berated an unfortunate man down the line. "When will you get live ammunition? Is that what you're fucking asking me?"

They couldn't hear the recruit's undoubtedly cowed response.

"I bet you all want to jump right to fucking live ammunition and skip snapping-in, don't you? You fucking boots think you know better than the United States Marine Corps?" The sergeant's face was beet red, his hands in fists as he screamed. "You think you're good enough? Because you're not fucking good enough, so shut your fucking goddamn mouths and get back to it!"

Heads down, they worked on proper sighting and squeezing the trigger as they'd been taught. Tyrell surveyed the proceedings, but for the most part let the range sergeants do the hollering. It was unnerving to see him so quiet.

As the sun beat down, Jim found himself looking forward to the evening and the plunge of the mercury. All the men in their tent had taken to huddling up in pairs to get through the freezing nights. With Cal, it had become an unspoken routine, taking turns pressed up against each other. When Cal was behind him, his warm breath on Jim's neck was strangely reassuring.

Of course, it was a matter of practicality, nothing more. To function in the surprising heat of the day, they needed to get a good night's sleep and not let their body temperatures drop too much.

Jim's father had taught him how to shoot as a matter of course when he was a boy, but he soon learned the Marine Corps—as with everything it did—had its own way. The thin leather sling they'd been using to tote their rifles around were now instruments of torture. Jim found he was fairly comfortable in the standing and prone positions for shooting, but the sitting position was something else entirely.

As the day wore on, they were ordered to sit on the ground, cross-legged. They adjusted their slings until they created a small loop, through which they put their left arm until the loop was just below the shoulder. Jim followed along as the sergeant called out the instructions.

"Put the butt of your rifle against your right shoulder."

The loop around his left arm tightened painfully as Jim attempted to follow orders. He could imagine the goal, and how the sling would create a stable base as he pressed the right side of his face against the butt and took sight. He grunted as he strained to get the rifle in place, his left arm feeling as if it was about to be severed.

Beside him, Cal groaned. "This is impossible."

"Sure feels that way," Jim agreed.

Up and down the line of recruits, most of the men struggled with the awkward and excruciating position. Cal raised an eyebrow. "Are the Japs gonna give us time to sit down and set up before they attack? Would be mighty sporting of them."

Jim swallowed his chuckle as the sergeant appeared and concentrated on contorting his body into the required position. Above him, the sergeant yelled. "It's not that fucking difficult, boys! You've just gotta put your back into it!"

Without another word, he turned and sat across Jim's shoulders, the weight stretching the burning ligaments to the breaking point. Sucking in a ragged breath, Jim closed his eyes, certain his joints would snap. Then the fire subsided, and he realized the butt of his rifle was somehow nudged against his right shoulder.

The sergeant stood up. "There you go, recruit. Now was that so fucking hard?"

Jim had barely stuttered a response when the sergeant was already sitting on Cal, who swore loudly, garnering a hearty laugh from the NCO. "That's the fucking spirit, recruit!"

When the sergeant moved on to the next man, plonking his weight down with gusto, Jim murmured, "I guess that's why they call this snapping-in."

Cal laughed quietly, leaning over and nudging Jim's shoulder with his own. "As long as they're not snapping our spines."

As they left the mess hall after chow a few hours later, a runner appeared. "Recruit Cunningham? Drill Instructor Tyrell wants to see you in the administration building." He jerked his thumb over his shoulder.

"Now."

"I'll be right there." Cal glanced at Jim and muttered, "Here we go."

Jim watched him double-time it to the office, wishing he could follow and make sure Cal didn't do anything to get into more trouble. Although he couldn't think of anything Cal had done that day to upset Tyrell. But it was always something.

Instead Jim made his way to the tent. While the other men played a game of cards, he took out his pen and paper. He started his letter to Ann four times before giving up, his mind wandering back to Cal.

When the bugle sounded the end of the day, Cal still hadn't returned. As the last strains of taps echoed across the rifle range, Jim's stomach tightened. Tyrell wouldn't actually hurt Cal, would he?

He thought of Tyrell's face on the march to the rifle range when Cal had turned the tables on him. Fury had twisted his features. But surely there were rules? Even if Tyrell had a grudge against Cal, he couldn't do anything too bad to him. Could he?

Checking his battered watch every minute, Jim wound it repeatedly since the darn thing had a tendency to run slow. After an unbearably long hour, he creeped outside. Keeping low, heart pounding, he skirted around the row of tents, breath clouding in the cold night. Guards stood watch throughout the camp, but at the moment the one nearest the tents was turned away, fiddling with something Jim couldn't make out.

Not hesitating, Jim raced around the mess hall toward the sprawl of other buildings. He skidded to a stop as he made out Cal by the officer's barracks. Cal stood balanced atop a small wooden stool. He held his rifle above his head, arms extended high. His eyes widened as Jim dashed over.

"What are you doing out here?" Cal hissed.

"I…"

"What? If they catch you, you're in real trouble."

Jim felt foolish admitting his concern. He wasn't sure what had gotten into him, letting his imagination run away like that. Of course Cal was fine, albeit highly uncomfortable, no doubt. "How long do you have to stay out here?"

Cal grimaced. "All night. Tyrell claims he inspected our rifles during chow and there was sand inside mine. So now I have to learn the importance of caring for my rifle. Again."

"I have a feeling that when we're under enemy fire, there's going to be sand flying all over the darn place."

"Be that as it may, I have to keep my rifle above my head all night. Not allowed to smoke either, and that son of a bitch is going to check on me, so get the hell out of here. I don't want you getting caught up in this."

Jim glanced around. He didn't want to leave, but knew Cal was right. "See you in the morning."

Smirking, Cal whispered. "For once I'll be glad to hear that reveille. Now go!"

Jim darted his way back to the tent, hugging walls and somehow avoiding detection. The other four men slept soundly as he crawled in, two of them snoring. Jim pulled up his blanket. After a moment's hesitation, he spread Cal's blanket over him as well.

Still, as he tried to sleep he shivered, unable to get warm.

1948

EYES CLOSED DETERMINEDLY, Jim willed himself to fall asleep. Cal had been reluctantly laid up for several days, and Jim had been busier than ever finishing the last of the pruning that ideally should have been done by the end of March. Here it was weeks later, but at least it was finished now.

He was exhausted and it was after midnight, yet his mind stubbornly refused to turn off. Cal had informed him in no uncertain terms that he was done with his convalescence and was well enough to go back to work. Thank goodness he hadn't seemed to suffer any further side effects from the injury, aside from the nasty bruise on his temple.

But Lord almighty, when Jim had run into the barn, there'd been so much blood and Cal had been lying so still. Even now, Jim shivered at the memory. Dr. O'Brien had assured him head wounds simply bled more than others, and that Cal would be fine. Still, Jim would be glad when Cal's bruise faded and he was up and around again.

A low noise jolted him from his thoughts. Jim blinked in the darkness, his body rigid. There was only silence. The house creaked, and then nothing again. He knew he should turn over and go to sleep, but an instinct got Jim out of bed, easing into the hallway in his pajamas, feet bare. The door to the children's room at the front of the house stood ajar as usual. Creeping down the hall, Jim peered in to find Sophie and Adam fast asleep.

He'd given Sophie extra chores as punishment and she'd been sleeping more soundly than usual. Watching her now, lips parted, peaceful and innocent, a surge of love for her warmed his chest. He could hardly believe his little girl had done something so mean-spirited and careless to Cal.

As he tiptoed back to his room, he paused by the guest room door, which was usually shut, but had inched open a crack, likely due to the faulty latch in the knob that Jim had been meaning to fix for years. Leaning in, Jim put his eye to the crack to make sure Cal was sleeping comfortably.

His breath caught in his throat as he made out Cal, his bare skin pale in the moonlight. He was on his back, bent legs spread wide, his thick cock jutting up from dark curls. His head tipped back and eyes closed, Cal's lips were parted as he stroked himself.

Frozen from head to toe, Jim could only stare, his eye to the sliver of space between the door and the jamb.

As Cal arched his hips up, thrusting steadily into his fist, he teased his nipples with his other hand, pinching and twisting. He was silent but for little gasps that made Jim's blood run like lava through his veins. It was a hideous invasion of privacy, yet Jim couldn't tear his gaze away as his friend pleasured himself.

He knew it was unforgivable, but after so long dormant, Jim's own body came alive as Cal worked his to the brink. Jim hadn't moved an inch, let alone touched himself, but his cock tented his pajamas, a desperate urge humming through him, growing stronger by the second. He breathed shallowly, sweat beading on his forehead.

Cal caressed his balls, rolling them in his palm. He took some of the gleaming liquid from the tip of his cock on his fingers, and spit onto his hand. Then, spreading his legs wider, he pressed two fingers inside himself.

Jim watched in shock as Cal impaled himself on his fingers, his other hand stroking his cock again rapidly. He'd never imagined such a thing before, yet he quivered with a base desire to penetrate himself the same way. It was madness, but he couldn't stop watching.

With a whispered word Jim couldn't make out, Cal bit back a moan, coming over his hand and chest in long spurts that made Jim's own balls tighten. Of necessity, Jim's feet were finally able to move, and he crept back to his room, trembling. He eased the door shut and leaned against it, his heart hammering his ribcage.

Consumed with a want and need he'd never experienced, Jim tugged down his pajamas enough to free his leaking cock. It only took three strokes before he came, hand clamped over his mouth to muffle his cries as the pleasure flooded into every pore.

His legs gave way and he slumped to the floor. Closing his eyes, he said a silent prayer that whatever sickening weakness and depravity had gripped him would disappear as quickly as it had taken hold.

"WOULD YOU STOP?"

With effort, Jim kept his eyes on the road and his tone even. "Stop what?"

Cal laughed. "Stop sneaking looks at me every thirty seconds like I'm made of glass and going to faint dead away any moment. I told you, I feel as good as new."

As Jim turned the pickup onto County Road 78, he concentrated on keeping his voice flat and normal. "I'm not looking at you."

But his gaze had drifted to Cal all morning, seemingly of its own accord. Jim couldn't get the thought of what he'd witnessed the night before—Cal splayed wantonly, pleasuring himself—from his mind. It was disgusting and beyond the pale, invading Cal's privacy and feeling so…excited by it. *What's wrong with me?*

"Uh-huh. Jim, I'm fine." Cal reached out and patted Jim's shoulder. "You don't need to worry."

Even through his shirt and jacket, Jim felt like the touch of Cal's hand scorched his flesh, and his groin tightened. Good Lord in heaven. He cleared his throat. "If you say so."

"I say so." Cal glanced around as they entered the village, the country road becoming Tivoli's main street, Broadway. "So, this is where you went to school growing up?"

"Yep." Jim forced a laugh. "I'm sure Manhattan has nothing on Tivoli. Don't blink, or you'll miss it." They passed the bakery and the two-story Madalin Hotel before pulling up in front of the general store.

"It's nice. Peaceful. Is there a college here?"

"No. Bard College is just down the road, though. I took a few classes there after high school. Then my dad got sick and Sophie was on the way, and there just wasn't time. But Ann always wanted to go. They started admitting women during the war or else they wouldn't have had any students."

"I'm sorry she didn't get the chance."

Thoughts of Ann brought back the familiar shame, and combined with what he'd done the night before, Jim felt nauseated. "Me too. She'd wanted to go to one of the women's colleges after high school, but her parents wouldn't let her. She had to beg and plead to get a job."

"Where's her family from?"

"Up in the Catskills. They wanted her to marry the neighbor's son, but she ended up with me." He smiled ruefully. "I'm not sure they ever forgave me for it." At the thought of Ann's parents, Jim's stomach knotted further. "That reminds me, they're coming for lunch next Sunday. It won't be until after church, since they won't come to St. Paul's. They're Catholic."

"Aren't you Catholic too?"

Jim had to laugh. "No, Cal. I'm Episcopalian. It's not all the same, you know."

"Seems pretty similar from where I'm sitting, but then again I'm a Godless heathen. I'll catch up on my sleep while you and the kids get saved. Should I make myself scarce when your in-laws arrive?"

Jim blinked in surprise. "No. Why would you think that?"

"I don't want to intrude on family time."

"Don't be silly." In fact, Jim was glad Cal would be there to fill the silences since Mrs. O'Brien stayed home on Sundays.

As they walked across the sidewalk to the general store, Jim stopped in his tracks and sighed.

Cal raised an eyebrow. "What's wrong?"

Through the window, Jim could see Rebecca Graham perusing the candy counter. "It's Rebecca. She was Stephen O'Brien's girl, back before the war."

"So what's the problem?"

"The past few months, every time I see her, she's stuck to me. It's like she thinks because Stephen and Ann are gone, it's only natural that we pair up. I guess she doesn't have many other prospects."

As they entered the store, the bell above the door *dinged* and Rebecca's pretty face lit up. "Jim! What a lovely surprise."

"Hello, Rebecca." It wasn't that there was anything wrong with her—she was a perfectly pleasant woman—but she and Jim had never quite gelled. "How are you today?"

"Quite well, thank you." Her gaze went to Cal, standing a step or two behind Jim. She reached up and smoothed her coiffed blonde hair. "Hello. I don't think we've met."

"Cal Cunningham." Cal stepped forward and nodded a greeting.

"An old war buddy of Jim's."

"How wonderful. Are you here long?" She smiled widely.

"Until the harvest at least. I'm helping out at Clover Grove."

"That's so kind of you. Where are you from?"

As Cal answered Rebecca's litany of questions, Jim shifted his weight from foot to foot. He suddenly felt invisible. While he should have been glad to be free of Rebecca's undivided attention given how uncomfortable it always made him, watching her laugh and talk with Cal made him feel…he wasn't sure what. Jealous?

It didn't make a lick of sense. He'd never been interested in Rebecca, so why should he care now? As Rebecca and Cal continued chatting, Jim picked up items from his grocery list and stacked them on the counter, smiling at Mrs. Abbott, who leaned in and whispered, "What a nice couple they'd make!"

With a strained smile, Jim nodded.

He was crouched by the shelf of cereal, reaching for the corn flakes, when Cal squatted down and elbowed him playfully. "Thanks a lot! What happened to no man left behind?"

"You and Rebecca apparently had a lot to talk about. I didn't want to be in the way." He stood and glanced around the store, seeing no sign of her.

Cal furrowed his brow. "In the way? I was just being polite."

Jim kept his tone light. "Maybe you'll meet the woman of your dreams here after all." It was what he'd always wanted for Cal—why were the words so thick on his tongue?

"What?" Cal laughed. "I'm sure she's a wonderful lady, but I told you before. I'm not interested in a wife." He pulled the shopping list from Jim's hand. "What do you still need to pick up?"

It was unbearably selfish to not want happiness for Rebecca and Cal, but as they finished the shopping, Jim felt strangely relieved. While Mrs. Abbott rang up his purchases, several older women entered the store. One of them exclaimed, "Jim Bennett! How are you, dear?"

"Hello, Mrs. McBride. Ladies." Jim nodded. "I'm doing well, thank you." He introduced Cal, who greeted the women.

One of them beamed and said to Mrs. Abbott, "What an honor to have two heroes shopping in your store."

Mrs. Abbott nodded. "An honor indeed. Our country's finest men."

Jim cleared his throat. "We simply did our duty. Nothing more." He could sense the tension in Cal next to him.

"Oh, such modesty! You're our heroes, make no mistake," Mrs. McBride said.

"The heroes are the men who didn't come back." Cal spoke a bit too loudly.

Tension filled the air as the ladies glanced at each other. "Of course," one replied. "Well, we should be on our way. Just here to buy some wool. Do you have the new shipment, Mrs. Abbott?"

Jim quickly paid for the groceries and he and Cal made their escape. They silently loaded the paper bags into the truck and climbed in, heading back to the orchard on the county road.

Cal sighed. "God, I hate that."

"Me too."

"I know they mean well, but…"

"They just don't understand," Jim finished.

Their eyes met. "No." Cal turned to gaze out the window. "And how could they? But some days it makes my skin crawl, being reminded of it. At least they didn't ask what it was like. That's the worst."

Jim nodded.

"I mean, how can we answer that?" Cal looked to Jim, even though it was clearly a rhetorical question. "What was it like?" He faced the windshield, eyes on the horizon. "Starving and thirsty and sick as hell from every goddamn tropical disease in creation. A kind of tired you can't imagine. Watching your friends die, one after the other, blown up and mowed down and sliced open. Knowing you'd be next. Sometimes wishing you would be, just to get it over with."

"Cal."

But he didn't even seem to hear Jim as he rambled on. "Hoping that maybe when you got hit, it wouldn't kill you, or take your leg off, but would hurt you enough to get the hell out. To get a ticket home. Then you couldn't believe you'd think such a cowardly thing, that you'd want to leave your friends. That I'd want to leave you." He stopped suddenly, taking a shuddering breath. "Jesus, I'm sorry. I don't know what I'm saying."

"We all felt like that." He reached over and briefly squeezed Cal's shoulder, keeping him at arm's length. "It's okay. You're a hero to me, and don't ever think otherwise."

Swallowing hard, Cal nodded and turned his gaze to the fields they passed.

Jim kept his eyes on the road, both hands gripping the wheel.

CHAPTER SEVEN

1942

AFTER DAYS OF shooting with live rounds from dawn to dusk, Cal was certain his ears would never stop ringing again. He shouldered his Springfield rifle and eyed the target across the range, barely visible in the driving rain. When another recruit had suggested they wait to shoot for record until the weather cleared, he got such an earful that Cal wasn't about to complain.

His pulse raced. These were the scores that would count. If they passed, they'd be Marines. If not…Cal didn't want to think about the alternative. Sure, he'd only joined the Marines to piss off his father, but now it was a matter of pride. Damn it, he'd worked harder than he had in his entire life the last five weeks, and put up with pain and discomfort he hadn't known existed.

He was not going to fail now.

Lying in the muck, he tried to tell himself it was all just a game— that he was back in Connecticut at Andrew Boyle's country house, gunning for pheasants. Beside him, Jim was stoic as usual. The only time Cal had seen him really worked up was the night Jim had broken curfew to find him. The ache in Cal's shoulders and arms as he'd kept his rifle aloft hadn't been so bad after that. He'd even managed to smile at Tyrell when the bastard had appeared just before reveille.

The range sergeant bellowed, "All ready on the firing line!" After a pause he added, "Fire!"

The roar of their rifles exploded in the air. One target after the other, they fired from various distances. Once every recruit was finished, they lined up and waited while the scores were tabulated. It was Tyrell who approached each man and told him whether he'd passed, or perhaps even qualified as a marksman, sharpshooter, or expert.

When Tyrell stopped before Cal after telling Jim that he'd passed, the bottom fell from Cal's stomach. Tyrell looked so satisfied that Cal couldn't possibly have succeeded. He could feel Jim's gaze on him, but kept his eyes locked on the DI, who still said nothing. Cal wanted to scream at him to just spit it out.

Finally, Tyrell smirked. "Wouldn't you know it, we've got ourselves a marksman here."

Cal blinked. "Huh?"

At this, Tyrell actually smiled without malice. Just a small lift of his lips and flash of teeth, but a smile nonetheless. "That's right, Cunningham. Looks like we just might have made a Marine of you after all."

"I…thank you, sir." For the first time, Cal actually meant it.

After another moment, Tyrell continued on down the line, his customary scowl returned. When everyone who passed remained, he addressed them. "Now don't go getting all full of yourselves. Y'all are still the biggest bunch of screw-ups I've ever seen and I've got another week to whip you into shape!"

As they marched back to their barracks at the main base, puffed up with pride, Tyrell kept up the litany of shouts and curses, but all Cal could do was smile. Marching close together, Jim nudged his shoulder, and Cal nudged him back.

They were Marines.

A week later they climbed off the train at New River, North Carolina. The flat, tree-covered expanse of marshland, dotted with wooden huts, seemed to stretch to infinity under the fading light of day. Here they'd learn their fate and prepare to ship off to wherever the war should take them.

They marched to one end of a rectangular hut, waiting for their names to be called. Once men went in, they must have exited the other side, as none returned. As darkness settled in, Cal wondered if he'd ever see them again.

"Bennett!"

Jim gave Cal a nervous smile, and in that instant, Cal wanted to grab onto him, dig his fingers into Jim's flesh and hold him close. Instead he extended his hand. "Good luck."

Squeezing his palm, Jim nodded. "You too. Maybe we'll see each other once in a while, huh?"

"Maybe." But they both knew they were being fed into the war machine, with countless companies within regiments that would be spread out across the Pacific. "Take care of yourself." He still had Jim's hand in his grasp.

"And you." Jim looked like he wanted to say something else, and opened his mouth.

"Bennett! James Michael Bennett!"

He pulled away and double-timed it to the hut, disappearing inside. Cal took a deep breath, reminding himself that he'd known they'd be parted. They'd probably both get killed within a year anyway. As the minutes passed, he told himself it was for the best not to have a good friend in his company. Just gave him more to lose.

"Cunningham!"

Inside the hut sat a number of desks, each with a man interviewing the arrivals. Cal was pointed to a desk at the far end and sat in the chair opposite it. Not even glancing up, the man barked a litany of questions: name, serial number and personal details. Cal spoke, and the man recorded his answers, pen scratching across paper.

"All right. First Marines."

Cal went through the door at the end of the hut, and a sergeant shone his flashlight in Cal's face. "Well?"

"Uh, First Marines," Cal answered.

The flashlight beam swung over to a transport truck. It was a cloudy night, and Cal could barely see as he made his way over. There were other trucks and clusters of men, all being sent off to their new companies. He squinted, trying to catch a flash of Jim's golden hair.

As he neared the truck, the engine roared to life, and Cal hurried to clamber onto the back. A hand reached for his, pulling him up as the truck plodded away over potholes. "Hey, thanks."

"Anytime."

Cal blinked as he peered into the darkness. "Jim?"

In the black, he could just make out the gleam of Jim's teeth. They both laughed, slapping each other on the back as they lurched and dropped onto the wooden bench. Jim leaned in close, and Cal tried to ignore the flare of desire that skipped up his spine. "Looks like you're stuck with me after all."

"Looks that way."

As the truck lumbered off into the night, Cal couldn't wipe the grin from his face.

1948

GROANING SOFTLY, CAL touched himself with a firm grip. A growing callus on his palm gave his strokes a rough edge that sent a shiver up his spine. "Fuck," he muttered.

He woke almost every morning hard as a rock, aching for Jim. He couldn't even consider getting up before relieving the pressure. Some nights he couldn't sleep without jerking off either. He felt like a schoolboy again.

Sitting on the side of the bed with his legs spread, Cal closed his eyes. In his fantasies, Jim came to him with an easy smile and endless kisses. Cal went to his knees for him, sucking him off and swallowing every drop. Jim bent over and took Cal inside, begging for more as Cal slammed into him, hip deep, claiming him. Cal would make Jim scream and swear a blue streak.

Then in the jumble of Cal's fevered mind, it would be Jim fucking him face to face, Cal's legs up as Jim kissed him with his thick cock so hot and hard inside. Jim would stretch him, rocking in and out as he took Cal's dick in his spit-slicked hand, stroking in rhythm with his hips as they pistoned, driving his cock deeper and deeper and—

With a strangled gasp, Cal came over his hand, spraying the wooden floor at his feet. He slumped back on one elbow as he caught his breath. The last time he'd had sex was a few days before leaving New York. He'd met the man in Central Park. No names—quick and mechanical, up against a tree.

Perhaps he needed to go home for a weekend visit and fuck some of the tension away, because at this rate there was no way he'd last until harvest without throwing himself at Jim and ruining everything.

He wiped up his mess with a cloth and rinsed it out in the wash basin he kept on his armoire. After dressing quickly, Cal went downstairs, where Adam was facedown on the kitchen floor, screaming and banging his fists. Jim stood watching, his shoulders slumped.

Cal had no idea what to do. He bent over and awkwardly patted Adam's back. "Hey, buddy. What's wrong?"

Adam just wailed louder, squirming away from his touch.

"He wants his mother." Jim's voice was flat.

Jesus. "I'm sorry." He didn't know what else to say as he stood next to Jim.

As Adam continued screeching, tears streaming down his red face, Jim shook his head and spoke quietly. "He doesn't understand. I thought maybe…it was bad at first; he was always crying for her. Then he seemed to forget. But there's nothing I can do." He took a shaky breath, glancing away. "Not now."

"There was nothing you could do when it happened either. It was an accident."

Jim was silent, his arms crossed over his chest.

Cal squeezed Jim's shoulder. "You listening to me? It wasn't your fault."

After running his hand over his face wearily, Jim nodded. "Sorry about the fuss." He motioned to Adam's prone form. "He just needs to scream it out when he gets like this. If I try to talk to him or hold him, it just makes it worse."

"Jim, he's a kid. This is what they do. Stop beating yourself up— you're a great father."

Jim snorted. "If you say so. It doesn't feel like it much these days. Just look at my son, and Sophie's…" He shook his head.

"I'll go talk to her. Don't worry, I'll give Mabel a wide berth. And stop feeling guilty for that, too, okay?"

"I just don't know what I'm doing half the time. Ann made it look so easy."

"Hell, you're doing a lot better than I would be. I'd probably give the kid a beer and hope that would quiet him down."

At this, Jim smiled. "I might consider it in a few minutes."

With Adam's howls receding as he walked to the barn, Cal steeled himself to face Sophie. Jim had marched her into Cal's room to apologize for not teaching him the proper way to milk, and Cal had told her all was forgiven. Since then she hadn't been rude as she'd been before, but wouldn't meet Cal's eyes and clearly tried to avoid him.

Inside the barn, Sophie milked Mabel with practiced ease, her head resting against the cow's flank. Finnigan lounged nearby, and his tail wagged when he spotted Cal. Sophie was lost in thought, and Cal cleared his throat. "Good morning."

She leaped up, knocking over her stool. Mabel mooed and Finnigan barked sharply. Cal smiled. "Careful. Don't want to get on Mabel's bad side."

Eyes on the hay-strewn floor, Sophie asked, "What are you doing here?"

"Just thought I'd come down and see how you're getting on. Your brother's having a bad morning."

After a few moments of silence, she spoke. "Oh."

"Look, I know we got off on the wrong foot, but I'd really like it if we could be friends."

She glanced at him, her brow furrowed. "Why?"

"Why do I want to be friends?"

Sophie nodded.

"Because you're my best pal's daughter, and I'm going to be living here for months. I like you, and I think you'd like me if you gave me a chance."

"But…"

"Aw, I'm not so bad. I promise."

"But I am."

Cal blinked. "What?" He took a few steps closer, and she lowered her head. "You're not bad."

"I am!" With her shoulders hunched, she took in a shuddering breath.

"Hey, hey. It's okay." Standing before her, he wasn't sure what to do. "Uh…" Finally he crouched down and tipped her chin up so she'd look at him. Her eyes swam with tears. "Please don't cry."

"I was mean to you. But I never meant for anything bad to happen. I swear, I didn't."

"I know. Heck, when I was a kid, you should have seen the stuff I pulled with my new nanny. I liked the old one a lot more, and I tried every trick I could think of to make the new one leave."

She sniffled. "You did?"

"You bet I did. But you know what? Pretty soon I realized she wasn't so bad. In fact, she was pretty great." Actually, the woman had been insufferable and cruel, but Cal kept that part to himself.

"You really want to be friends with me still?"

"I really do. So how about we just forget all that other stuff and start over." He extended his hand. "Hi, I'm Cal."

After a moment, she put her little hand in his. "I'm Sophie."

"It's a pleasure to meet you, ma'am."

Sophie smiled tremulously. "You too." She swiped at her eyes. "Do you want to help me milk? The right way this time?"

"I don't know. You think Mabel will be my friend, too, or do cows hold grudges? Can you put in a good word for me?"

Giggling, Sophie nodded, and they went to work.

"GRANDMA, GRANDPA!" SOPHIE raced across the paddock and clambered over the fence.

Shading his eyes from the sun, Cal watched the rusted old pickup truck rumble up the drive. Ann's parents climbed out, wearing what had likely been their Sunday best for a decade, a dress and suit now rather threadbare. They must have been fairly young when Ann was born, as they couldn't be much older than fifty. Both had stocky builds and worn faces, and their dark hair was neatly combed.

From astride his horse, Jim waved. Adam sat before him, one of Jim's arms wrapped securely around him. Cal had just shuffled down for his morning coffee when they'd arrived back from church, and they'd quickly changed and headed out for some time with the horses.

Cal walked over and reached up for Adam, swooping him through the air and making the boy squeal before carrying him outside the paddock and setting him down on the ground. Jim dismounted and gave the horse a pat before going to greet his in-laws. Sophie chattered excitedly to them as they approached the paddock.

"Lorraine, Ron. Nice to see you." Jim pressed a kiss to Lorraine's cheek and shook his father-in-law's hand.

Ronald grunted, and Lorraine's smile didn't reach her eyes. "Thank you for the invitation. Always wonderful to visit our grandchildren." She bent and hugged Adam tightly.

"You know you're welcome anytime." Jim smiled and nodded to Cal. "This is my old friend Cal Cunningham. Cal, this is Lorraine and Ronald Shelton."

"Pleased to meet you." Cal shook with Ronald and nodded to Lorraine. He had a feeling kissing the back of her hand as he'd do with his parents' female friends would seem quite forward to the Sheltons.

Lorraine smiled politely. "And you. We're glad Jim has some help around the place again."

"Don't you have something better to do than farm apples?" Ronald's voice was gruff.

Cal laughed awkwardly. "No, sir. We've been working hard, getting ready for the growing season."

"Grandma, Grandpa, I made lunch. Are you hungry?" Sophie asked.

At this, Ronald smiled. "That sounds real good, honey. What did you make us?"

Sophie led the way into the house, and Cal glanced at Jim, who wore an apologetic expression. Cal hadn't expected Ann's parents to be particularly happy folk, not with their daughter's death so recent, but there was an unmistakable tension in the air he couldn't quite get a read on.

They sat at the formal dining table with Sophie playing hostess, albeit with Jim's help. Lunch was slightly crooked roast beef sandwiches and a potato salad Cal suspected Mrs. O'Brien had made the day before. He took a bite of his sandwich. "Mmm-mmm. That's delicious, Sophie."

She beamed as everyone chimed in with their agreement. Truthfully there was too much mustard and not enough tomato, but Cal ate his sandwich and reached for a second one. He addressed Lorraine. "Do you have far to come?"

She patted the corner of her mouth with her napkin. "A couple of hours. Not too far." She clucked her tongue at Adam beside her as he dropped a dollop of potato salad onto the polished wood table. Ronald grumbled something under his breath.

Sophie glared at her brother. "You're such a goober."

Jim's tone sharpened. "Sophie."

"Sorry," she muttered.

Jim went on. "Did you tell your grandparents about your math test? She got a perfect score."

"What does she need to learn math for?" Ronald asked with a frown.

Sophie glanced between her father and grandfather, hesitating. "I'm good at it, Grandpa."

He smiled kindly at her. "That kind of learnin' isn't for girls. You just need to cook and clean like your momma."

Jim spoke evenly. "Ann was good at school too."

"Don't remind me." Ronald glared. "Wanted to go to *college*." He spat the word out like it was a curse. "Should have stayed home with us."

Lorraine cleared her throat. "Now, now, let's not get into that. Sophie, that's real good that you're doing well in your classes."

Sophie nodded with her eyes on her plate.

After twenty more tortuous minutes of stilted talk, lunch was over and Lorraine and Sophie cleaned up while Jim helped Adam rebuild the train set in the sitting room, since Adam wanted to show his grandparents. Cal escaped outside and walked over to the barn to say hello to Mabel and get clear of any more loaded conversations.

He was sweeping up a stall when the floor creaked and Ronald appeared. The man put a cigarette between his lips and offered the pack to Cal. They both puffed away, and Cal desperately tried to think of something to say. "You're from up in the mountains? Beautiful country."

Ronald grunted, which seemed to be his favorite way of communicating.

"A dairy farmer, is that right?"

"Uh-huh. Best kind of farming there is." Ronald coughed and took another drag. "Apples." He snorted dismissively. "One bad storm and the whole crop's ruined for the year."

"I suppose every kind of farming has its risks."

Ronald watched Cal with a speculative gleam as he exhaled a cloud of smoke. Finally he said, "So, you're a Marine."

"I was. I stopped wearing my dog tags last year, but I guess I'll always be a Marine. That's what they say." The Marine motto echoed in his mind: *semper fidelis*—always faithful. He wondered if Ronald had fought in the first war but didn't ask. "How was your winter in the Catskills?"

"My only child died at the start of it."

Shifting his weight, Cal took a nervous puff. "I'm very sorry. I always heard wonderful things about Ann."

"She should have stayed with her family. Now she's dead and gone because of him."

Cal's hackles rose. "It wasn't Jim's fault. I can only imagine how difficult it must be for you—"

"Her mother talked me into letting her go work near that school. She got all those ideas in her head. Then she met him and stayed here in the *valley*."

He said the word with the same scorn he might direct toward the city, Cal suspected.

"She should have come home. The Johnson boy was all ready to marry her. Could have combined our land. But no, she insisted on Jim Bennett. Look where it got her."

"It was a terrible accident, sir."

Ronald tossed his cigarette to the floor and ground it out with the toe of his scuffed, lace-up shoe just as the hay ignited. "Wasn't no accident."

The tension in Cal's body increased tenfold. "Of course it was."

"Things were never the same once he came back. Annie tried to hide it, but we could see. He'd barely look her way, while she tried and tried to please him."

Cal frowned. That didn't sound at all like Jim. "I'm sure it was an adjustment for everyone when he returned home."

A grunt. "Last summer Lorraine came down for a surprise visit and there was our girl with a black eye. Gave some sorry excuse about opening a cupboard door too fast. I know it was him."

Cal's mouth dropped open before he inhaled sharply. "Jim would never hit a woman. Never."

"'Course you'd say that."

"Because it's true! I know him better than anyone, and I know he would never have hurt your daughter."

"Then what the hell was she running away from? Died all alone out in a ditch in the night. She must have been coming home to her mother and me! Just like we always wanted. I wish that son of a bitch had been killed over there. Annie would still be alive. We could sell this useless place and bring her and the children back home where they belong."

Cal's hands clenched into fists. "You've suffered a terrible loss, Mr. Shelton. I think you should go spend some time with your grandchildren and stop talking nonsense."

"I know the truth, and so does our Lord almighty. Jim Bennett will burn in the hellfire for what he's done to my daughter." With that, he stalked from the barn.

Cal trembled with rage. The man had some nerve spewing his poisonous accusations at Jim's own home. Outside of war, Jim wouldn't hurt a fly, let alone his wife. Of that, Cal was utterly certain. It wasn't even a question. He had half a mind to call out Ronald Shelton and tell Jim what had been said, but he couldn't see what good it would do.

Wincing as the smoldering end of his forgotten cigarette scorched his fingers, Cal quickly stubbed it out and went to make sure Ronald Shelton didn't cause trouble.

CHAPTER EIGHT

1942

"YOU ARE THE men of H Company, Second Battalion, First Regiment, First Marine Division. I'm your company commander, Captain Brown." The young captain walked along the line of men, surveying them carefully. Of medium height and build, with sandy hair and a snub nose, he was unremarkable, but carried an unmistakable air of quiet authority. "This is a machine gun and heavy mortar company."

They all listened intently as Brown explained their new training regimen. Jim had been assigned to be a mortarman, and Cal had quickly offered to be his partner. It was a relief having Cal there, and Jim thanked God they'd been lucky enough to be assigned the same company. It was silly, but he'd come to think of his friend as a sort of guardian angel.

"This is not boot camp. You are United States Marines, and you should be damn proud of that."

Jim stood a little straighter and could sense his fellow men doing the same.

"You are going to learn your new weapons inside and out. Before long, you'll be able to assemble your mortars and machine guns with your eyes closed. So let's get to work."

The days at New River began to blend together in a haze of firing drills and lessons on weapon parts and names. Jim and Cal worked with

60mm mortars. Over and over, they hauled the forty-five-pound tube, bipod and base plate and set up their weapon.

As Cal unfolded the bipod and snapped its legs into the base plate, he grumbled good-naturedly. "At least we can call this one a gun."

When the sight was snapped into place and the tube of the mortar pointed at a high angle, they mimed dropping the shell into the muzzle. Lining up the sight was an intricate business, and they learned how to use a compass to get a reading on their target area and line up their aiming stake in front of the gun.

With a young recruit named Greg Sullivan, whom everyone already called Sully, they rotated as number one and two gunners and ammo carrier, competing with other teams to be the fastest. When they moved on to using live ammo, Jim couldn't help but feel nervous. Cal was acting as number one gunner, and at his command of "Hanging!" Jim dropped the shell into the tube.

Cal shouted, "Fire!" and they all ducked their heads.

The shell soared right toward its target, exploding in a black cloud of smoke as deadly metal shrapnel scattered the area. They cheered loudly at their success. But as they walked back from the drilling grounds that evening in casual route march, Jim couldn't help but wonder what the shrapnel would do to a man.

Cal nudged him. "What's eating you?"

"Nothing."

"Uh-huh. Come on. There's something on your mind."

Jim relented. "I was thinking about that mortar. Wondering what kind of weapons the Japs will be lobbing back at us."

Cal frowned, silent for a few moments. "I haven't really thought about it. It's strange—most of the time the war still feels so far away. Doesn't it?"

"Yeah. It does."

"I mean, I know that's what we're doing all this training for. We wouldn't be here if there wasn't a war. You'd be on the apple farm and I'd be a useless bastard with a Princeton degree and a fancy car. But..."

He shrugged. "It doesn't seem real."

Jim slapped Cal's arm lightly. "Except you could never be useless."

"Oh, I think my father would disagree. Quite vehemently, in fact."

Captain Brown shouted, "Company! Atten-shun!"

This meant they were nearing the base, and they always entered looking sharp. As one, their slouches disappeared and the men marched in time, rifles straight and heads high.

A few hours later they were out on the local road, slouching once more. "Come on, give some fighting men a lift!" Cal stuck his thumb out as he shouted, but the car sped by them into the night. "Traitor!"

Jim and the others laughed as they walked along the side of the road. They'd been given free time, which after boot camp felt utterly foreign. A few other men in their company had decided the only thing to do was hitchhike to New Bern.

As another car zoomed by, Jim asked, "Why don't we just have a drink around here? There's a bar right down the street." Granted, it was little more than a shack, but surely it would serve their purposes.

One of the men answered, "Because there ain't no girls out here in the boondocks!"

Barely eighteen, Sully agreed vehemently. "I need to pop my cherry before I go face those Nips."

Cal slapped Jim on the back. "You may be a married man, but the rest of us aren't."

Soon they were piled in the back of a pickup truck that dropped them outside a dive bar in town. Sure enough, there were girls aplenty, and Jim spent the evening chatting with Cal and trying to avoid the women's avid gazes. He nudged Cal. "You don't have to keep me company. Like you said, you're not married. Go on and find a girl to dance with."

Cal drank his beer. "Nah, let the other guys have their fill." He gazed around. "It's strange, isn't it? Our superiors treating us with respect and letting us have time off. I don't quite know what to do with myself without that son of a gun Tyrell watching me like a hawk."

"I can't say I'll miss him." It was odd to think they'd likely never see Tyrell again, and that he was screaming at his new recruits now.

"No, can't say I will either, but I have to admit he knows what he's doing. I've never worked that hard in my life. I feel like a new man."

"So go dance. You don't want to sit here with me all night. I'm no fun." Jim smiled ruefully. "Can't dance to save my life."

"Did someone say dancing?" A blonde with red lips and a wide smile appeared at their table. "How about it?"

Before Jim could answer, Cal was already standing and edging away. "Sure, my buddy would love to dance with you."

Jim shot to his feet and tried to sidestep the woman, but her painted fingers grasped his arm.

"Come on, sugar. Won't you take a twirl with me?"

"Uh…I…" Jim hated to be rude, and quickly gave up the fight. "Of course, ma'am. It would be my pleasure."

Holding the woman at arm's length, Jim swayed awkwardly with her on the small, scuffed area of floor reserved for dancing. When the song ended, he tried to step away, but she edged closer and held on tighter. After another song went by, Jim offered to buy her a drink just to get off the dance floor.

Of course this led to a long conversation consisting of the woman rattling on while Jim nodded. He didn't want to hurt her feelings, but he hated small talk. When he spotted Cal and a local man by the door, he interrupted. "Sorry, ma'am, but I need to go with my friend. Cal!"

Cal jerked at the sound of his name, looking back with a strangely guilty expression. "We're just getting some air." The man beside him disappeared outside.

Jim hurried to the door. "But we should get going, right?"

"Nah, not yet. Stay and have fun. I'll be back in five. We're just smoking."

Gazing around at the thick haze in the room, Jim raised an eyebrow. "Not enough smoke in here?"

"Go on and dance with the lady again, Jim. I'll be right back." The door closed behind him.

"Oh yes, let's dance again! You're a marvellous dancer." The woman appeared by his side.

Jim's gaze kept finding the door, and four songs went by before Cal returned alone. He looked strangely flushed considering it was a mild night. With a winning smile, Cal took the hand of a woman sitting alone and joined them on the dance floor.

As the tempo increased, Cal whirled by in a blur, and Jim couldn't quite catch his eye.

1948

IT WAS LATE afternoon as Jim and Cal made their way back through the orchard. Jim was more than ready for a shower and a hot meal.

Cal wiped his hands over and over with an old towel. "You realize my hands are going to smell like shit for days? Even with the gloves."

Chuckling, Jim shrugged. "You said you were ready to do anything and everything."

"I'd like to revise my statement to exclude anything and everything having to do with fertilizer."

"Thought you were ready to get your hands dirty," Jim teased.

"It's a figure of speech, my friend."

"Not here."

Cal laughed. "No, I guess not. So, do you have any use for that now that Eddie's gone?" He jerked his chin toward the cabin.

The little wooden building was situated at the bottom of the last long slope before the house and barn, which were just out of sight over the rise. "Not really. I'll hire seasonal pickers this fall, but they're day laborers from the area with their own homes."

As they approached the cabin, Jim eyed it critically. About four hundred and fifty square feet, the one simple room was built of sturdy logs and had two small windows and a shake roof. A few of the shingles had seen better days, but it didn't really matter since the cabin stood empty.

Cal pushed open the door with his boot, and Jim followed him inside the musty interior. It was as Eddie left it: blankets folded at the foot of the narrow bed against the far wall, logs neatly stacked next to the wood-burning stove, and a bar of soap still resting next to the wash basin. An outhouse sat among the hickory trees skirting the orchard.

In the breeze from the open door, a blue ribbon fluttered across the floor. Cal picked it up. "That's strange."

Jim reached out and rubbed the velvet between his fingertips. Ann's face flickered through his mind, her hair pulled back at the nape of her neck. He blinked, pushing away the thought. "Must be Sophie's. She used to visit Eddie when her chores were done. He was good with her."

"Makes sense. I'll bring it back to her. We're friends now, after all." The ribbon disappeared into Cal's pocket.

Jim stepped outside the cabin, glad of the fresh air. "She told me you taught her a rhyme she's not allowed to repeat to anyone."

"Did she now?" Cal grinned. "Don't worry, I went with the tame version, and she doesn't even get it. She just likes having a secret. She assured me she's good at secrets, all evidence to the contrary."

Jim laughed. "I'm glad you're getting along. I know she didn't make it easy."

"I've been told I can be difficult myself once or twice over the years." He tilted his head thoughtfully. "Maybe just the once."

"Is that all?"

They shared a smile as they started back toward the house. Cal stopped and pointed. "What's that contraption?"

"Our old apple press. Eddie made cider from the bruised apples we couldn't sell."

The small press, standing waist high, rested against the cabin under the overhang of the roof. Cal cranked the handle of the metal grinder, which was positioned over one of two wooden baskets. He peered in. "So you just put the apples in here, and voila?"

Jim grimaced. "If only." He pointed to the other basket. The long, blunt-ended metal press hung over top. "First you grind the apples, and then you switch the baskets and press the ground-up fruit to get the juice."

Cal whistled. "That must be a hell of a job."

"That's why we don't sell much cider. Takes a ton of apples and a ton of work. Eddie liked doing it. Said it relaxed him. But my father always thought it was a waste of time."

Crouching down, Cal examined the press. "You know, my cousin in Philly works in hydraulics. I bet he could build something that would do all the work for you."

"Yeah, they have new mechanized presses now. But I don't think there's enough money in cider to invest. The Rain Birds cost an arm and a leg and I can't spare any more body parts."

"If it's just money, I can pay for it."

Here we go. "I appreciate the offer, but no thanks."

"Come on, it's nothing. It would be my pleasure."

"Cal, you won't even let me pay you. You're not buying me some fancy new apple press I don't even need."

Cal's face lit up and he went on as if Jim hadn't spoken. "Hey, you ever consider making the hard cider? Now that could rake in a profit."

"I don't know a thing about brewing. Clover Grove grows and sells apples. Maybe a bit of cider at the local market, but that's all. That's the way it's always been."

"But that doesn't mean it's the way it always has to be. I know a fella in the city in the bar business and—"

"*Cal.* You're not listening to me. Things are good the way they are."

For a moment, Cal gazed at him with an unreadable expression in his dark eyes. "Are they?"

Jim frowned. "Of course." He dropped his hand and turned away. "We should get back. Almost dinnertime."

"Sure. Okay." Cal fell into step. They walked in silence for a minute before Cal said, "I'm sorry if I was out of line. I just want you to have…everything."

Sophie and Adam appeared at the top of the rise, running toward them excitedly. "Daddy!"

Feeling very lucky in that moment to have two beautiful children and such a loyal friend, Jim patted Cal on the back. "I have enough."

CAL WHISTLED. "CORRECT me if I'm wrong, but it is spring, isn't it?"

Jim chuckled as he gazed out at the thin layer of snow over the orchard. Sophie and Adam shrieked with laughter as they tossed snowballs at one another before Sophie had to leave for school. He let the sitting room curtain fall back into place. "It'll melt by lunchtime. Sometimes Mother Nature just likes to remind us who's boss."

"It's not going to hurt the trees?" Cal asked.

"They're about to bloom, so we'd better hope winter is through. All these weeks of dryness, and of course now it snows." Jim tried to ignore the little nugget of concern in his gut. As long as it warmed up again, everything would be just fine.

"Maybe we should take the morning off. We can't spread any more fertilizer with snow on the ground."

"No, we'll have to wait until it melts."

Cal grinned. "Great. So what do you do for fun around here?"

"Well, I've been meaning to clean up the shed where we store the apples during harvest."

"I think you need to reassess the meaning of the word 'fun,' Jim." Cal sighed dramatically. "All right, let's get to it."

In the shed a few hours later, Cal leaned his broom against the wall and wiped his arm across his brow. "Looks pretty shipshape to me."

Jim glanced around, smiling. "Me too. I really let it go this winter. Thanks for your help."

"What are friends for? Now I think we need some fresh air. Come on."

Jim followed Cal behind the barn. The snow was indeed melting, but hadn't completely gone. His work boots squelched in the wet mess, and he breathed deeply as he gazed out over the rows of trees.

Suddenly a snowball thwacked the back of his head. Sputtering, he scooped up a handful of snow, packing it quickly and firing it back at Cal, who raced off into the trees with Jim in hot pursuit. Onward they ran, farther into the orchard and past the cabin, leaving the barn and house behind. Laughing and hollering, they dove into battle, each finding cover behind a tree and creating an arsenal of snowballs.

With two mighty weapons in his hands, Jim dashed out from behind his tree, zeroing in on Cal's position and tackling him to the ground. He mashed the snow onto Cal's head and down the back of his jacket.

Cal squirmed and yelped. "Kamikaze style, huh?" He reached for one of his snowballs and slammed it into Jim's face. "Take that!"

Laughter echoing in the branches, they wrestled in the wet snow, tumbling over until Jim finally got the upper hand. He straddled Cal's waist, holding his wrists down. "Admit defeat."

"Never!" Cal arched up, trying to buck Jim loose.

Jim tightened his grip, a smile splitting his face. It had been so long since he'd had such childish fun. Since he'd felt so free. Filled with gratitude for Cal in that moment, his chest swelling and tight, he leaned down and pressed their lips together.

Amid the snow, Cal's mouth was so warm, and Jim wanted to fall into him and never stop. But with a sickening sensation, his brain caught up to his body and he tore himself away, stumbling back into the wet snow like a crab. *What have I done?*

Cal sat up with a jerk, staring with his mouth agape.

Jim's throat was sandpaper. "I didn't…I'm sorry. I don't know what…I…" He lurched to his feet and ran, humiliation burning in his lungs as he struggled for breath.

Behind him, Cal called out, "Wait! Jim!"

I'm sick and wrong and now I've lost my best friend in the world. Jim forced his legs to move, slipping in the slush and mud. He tripped to his knees just as Cal caught up, reaching for him. Jim shook free and staggered to his feet, but Cal spun him around, gripping his upper arms.

"Just stop and listen to me." Cal gazed at him intently. "It's okay."

Panic flapped against Jim's ribcage. He cast about for some kind of explanation for his shameful behavior but had none. "No, it's not. Of course it's not! I'm sorry."

Cal's expression softened, and he smiled. "There's nothing to be sorry for."

How can he be smiling? "But…"

One of Cal's hands drifted up to cradle Jim's head. "It's okay," he repeated, his eyes alight. Leaning in, he whispered it again. "It's okay."

Then Cal was kissing him. His still-warm mouth pressed gently against Jim's. Jim felt strangely in his body and outside it as Cal touched him. One hand caressed Jim's hair, the other sliding down to his waist.

Cal pulled back an inch, his breath hot against Jim's lips. "It's okay."

Standing in the melting snow, Jim found himself kissing Cal back this time, their mouths moving, lightly stubbled cheeks rasping together. It was so different from kissing Ann, and he knew he should stop, but as Jim took a shaky breath, Cal's tongue reached out and touched his. It felt so right—so natural—and Jim leaned into Cal, wrapping his arms around his friend's back. A voice in his mind cried that this was wrong, but it felt so good.

A moan tore from his throat, and desire overtook him like wildfire. He rutted against Cal like an animal in heat, feeling a matching hardness there as Cal groaned into his mouth. Their tongues met with purpose as they panted and rubbed against each other. Jim wanted to have Cal against the nearest tree, wanted to thrust against him—*inside* him.

Tearing himself away, he staggered back, his head spinning. What were they doing? Good God in heaven, what had come over them?

His eyes beseeching, Cal reached out. "Jim, don't run away. Please."

His own voice sounded foreign to Jim's ears. "This is wrong. This is impossible."

"It's not. Please just stop. We can talk. We don't have to do anything else. Just talk to me."

Shaking his head, Jim ran. His lungs burned and his heart was going to explode. He didn't think he could ever stop.

CHAPTER NINE

1942

"YOU EVER GET a gal to suck on your cock?" Sully's face turned as red as his shorn hair as he blurted out the question.

Arms folded behind his head as he leaned back on his rack in their rectangular wooden hut, Pete smiled widely. "Oh, yeah. Plenty of times."

With his thick body and the flat nose of a bruiser, Pete wasn't particularly handsome, but Cal had no doubt the man had had his fair share of women. Cal wouldn't mind feasting on that meaty cock himself, but quickly steered his mind away from such dangerous territory and took a swig of beer. "Sully, you just need to find the right girl."

Guzzling his own drink, Sully leaned back against the hut wall, his bed creaking. "Believe me, I've tried. There was one girl at school who let me feel her up after a dance. But she wouldn't do anything more."

"Was she a nice girl?" Jim asked.

Cal blinked in surprise. Jim was usually quiet as a church mouse during their nightly down time, nursing a beer or two while the rest of the squad pounded them back as they relaxed on their racks. The conversation topics ranged from baseball to all the ways they were going to destroy the enemy, but returned time and time again to sex and women.

"Yeah. Real nice," Sully answered.

"You shouldn't ask nice girls to do things like that," Jim said. "It's disrespectful."

Joe, a big blond from Georgia, barked out a laugh. "Aw, come on. You sayin' your woman never gets on her knees?"

Jim inhaled sharply. "Don't talk about my wife."

As Joe continued laughing, tipping back his umpteenth beer, Sully asked, "Hey Cal, who was the first gal to do it for you?"

Cal opened a new bottle and settled himself again, leaning against the wall and stretching his legs out on the thin mattress. "Hmm, let's see. If you want to know the truth, it was pretty scandalous." Of course the actual truth was something considerably more shocking. Not to mention illegal.

Pete clapped his hands. "Hell yes! Let's hear it."

"She was the wife of one of my father's business partners. Eva Thorngood. We were all out in Connecticut for a weekend retreat at someone's estate."

"Well *la di da*," Joe drawled.

Cal ignored him. "I was snooping around upstairs in the library after dinner when she came in. Locked the door behind her, so that got my attention."

Sully listened, utterly rapt with wide eyes. "How old was she? How old were you?"

"She was about thirty-five. I'd just turned sixteen."

"Hot damn. Don't leave us hangin'!" Pete exclaimed.

"She made a little small talk about some book or other, leaning in real close so she could pull it off the shelf. It was like the air around us was electric, and my skin was on fire. I could have come right there in my pants at just the thought of her touching me."

Aside from the fact that it was *Michael* Thorngood who'd cornered him in the library that night, the rest was true. Cal went on. "She pressed me up against the bookcase and asked if she could do something for me. I nodded so hard I banged my head. Had a bump the next day, but it was worth it. Then she was kissing me and…"

He trailed off, lost for a moment in the memory of Michael against him, the feel of his rough stubble, his thrusting tongue, and his powerful hand gripping Cal through his dress trousers.

"And?" Sully swallowed hard. "Then what?"

"The next thing I knew my pants were undone and she was on her knees. Fuck, it was good. Her mouth was so wet and hot." Cal was acutely aware of Jim's gaze on him and forced himself to avoid it. It wouldn't do to start thinking of Jim right now.

"Lawd, I'm getting hard just hearin' about it." Joe whistled to Sully. "Come over here, boy, and do me a favor."

"In your dreams!" Sully called back, his face beet red. "Then what happened, Cal?"

"I think I was done in about twenty seconds. She swallowed every drop."

Pete grinned and took a drag from his cigarette. "Real nice. You ever do her again?"

"Oh yeah. We did a whole lot the rest of the weekend. A few more weekends over the years too. She was good to me, that's for sure."

"Wow." Sully finished his beer. "Pete, how about you?"

Cal grabbed his jacket. "I'll head over to the slop chute and get some more beer. It's my turn." He needed some air.

"I'll come with you." Jim reached for his boots.

"Don't worry—I've got it. Back in a jiff!" Cal escaped before Jim could respond.

The camp was quiet aside from gales of deep laughter echoing from other huts as the squads unwound. The forest spread out to his left, and Cal impulsively ducked into the trees, twigs snapping beneath his boots as he wandered into the darkness. He made his way in the wan sliver of moonlight, hands jammed in his pockets as he tried to relax.

Memories of Michael flitted around his mind. Michael had been a generous and enthusiastic teacher, and Cal looked back on their stolen moments fondly. It so happened that Eva Thorngood was a kindly woman, and Cal still felt a twinge of guilt for the things he'd done with her husband. But he hadn't been able to resist.

He was foolish for thinking on it at all when he was so pent up. He hadn't even had the privacy to jerk off since getting to boot camp, and the quick, furtive hand job with the local in the shadows outside the dive bar had done little to ease Cal's tension. But as he walked deeper into the forest, he realized he was truly alone. His body hummed and his dick twitched at the notion of release. As he reached for his zipper, footsteps crunched nearby.

Squinting into the murk, Cal held his breath. He hadn't done anything wrong yet, but felt like his hand was in the proverbial cookie jar. He was about to call out when another Marine stepped from behind a tree. He was short and about Cal's age, with light hair and a slim build. Their eyes locked, and excitement jolted through Cal like spurs to a horse's flank.

He knew that look.

The man drew nearer, glancing around. Cal licked his lips and closed the gap, and after another look of understanding, they gripped each other without a word, mouths opening as they kissed hungrily. Cal didn't waste any time in yanking open the man's pants and thrusting his hand inside. The hot, hard flesh pulsed in his grasp, the man grunting as Cal worked him.

They stumbled up against a tree, breath harsh in the still of the forest. It didn't take long for the Marine to come over Cal's hand, and Cal licked his fingers, his dick aching. The man sank to his knees and freed Cal's cock from his uniform before swallowing it almost to the base. Cal bit his lip to stop from crying out as the pleasure ricocheted through his body.

The Marine sucked him expertly, his tongue and hands working in tandem. Leaning back against the rough bark of the tree, Cal threaded his fingers through the man's fair hair, and in the darkness, he could almost imagine it was Jim at his feet—Jim's hot mouth tight around him.

A voice in his head shouted to stop that train of thought, but the images tumbled out of control and he gave in, letting himself pretend it was his friend sucking his cock. Balls tightening, Cal's knees trembled as he catapulted over the edge, Jim's face in his mind and Jim's name on his silent lips as he gasped for breath.

The man got to his feet, and they straightened themselves. With a nod, they went their separate ways, and Cal hurried to the slop chute to get the beer before it closed.

1948

AS HE PEERED out the window, worry gnawed Cal's gut. He glanced at his watch again.

"Where's Daddy?" Sophie stood in the sitting room doorway.

"Oh, he went out to check on the younger trees at the rear of the orchard. He'll be back any minute." Cal smiled in what he hoped was a reassuring fashion.

She stared back, solemn. "Then why are you so worried?"

"Worried?" Cal forced a laugh and patted Sophie's head as he made his way back to the kitchen. "I'm not worried."

"You look worried."

"Everything's fine." Cal glanced down at where Adam was making an unholy mess with his crayons, straying from his pad and dragging the colored wax onto the linoleum. "Hey, hey. Not on the floor, all right?"

Adam laughed in response. "I draw on the floor!"

"Yes, you do. But we don't want that. Not on the floor. On the paper." Cal grabbed a sponge and knelt to scrub off the marks.

"He's always back by now. Always." Sophie's face was ashen. "What if there was an accident?"

Cal hated to see her so anxious. He pulled out a chair and sat down, beckoning her over so they were on the same level. Taking her hands, he squeezed gently. "Your dad's okay. If he's not back soon I'll go get him."

"Promise?"

"Absolutely." The lid on the pot of green beans on the stove rattled as it boiled over. "I'll just finish getting dinner ready, okay?"

"Have you ever cooked before?"

"Sure. Plenty of times." He managed to drain the beans without scalding himself, which he considered a major victory. "See? I'm cooking." The fact that Mrs. O'Brien had prepared everything and he'd only had to turn on the burner and oven was beside the point.

A tiny smile played on Sophie's lips. "You better check the meatloaf."

"Can you clean up the crayon for me while I do?"

Sophie nodded and did as he asked while Cal opened the oven and peered inside at the nicely browning loaf. *What if something did happen to him? What if he fell and hit his head, or—*

The back door opened with a long creak, and Jim stomped his muddy boots on the mat.

"Daddy!" Sophie rocketed up into Jim's arms, clinging to him. Adam followed suit, yammering excitedly.

Cal regarded Jim evenly. "I told her how you had to go check to make sure the young trees weren't affected by the frost. Took a bit longer than you thought, huh?"

Jim pressed a kiss to Sophie's head. "It did. Sorry I'm late, sweetheart." He didn't meet Cal's eyes.

In fact, he didn't meet Cal's eyes all through dinner. Cal felt invisible as Jim laughed with Sophie and Adam and tried to act like everything was normal. Cal had let him run off the second time, not wanting to push, and now his best friend couldn't even *look* at him.

After dinner, Jim took the children up to bed. Cal stood at the sink washing the dishes, acid burning his stomach despite the meal he'd just choked down. His mind spun, trying to make sense of it all. He still couldn't quite believe it had happened.

When he'd felt Jim's lips against his, Cal had thought he was dreaming. But no, Jim had really kissed him. And when Cal chased him down, Jim had kissed him back, and he'd been unmistakably hard. They'd both wanted each other until Jim tore himself away.

He's been celibate for months on end. Any man would be desperate.

Had Cal taken advantage of that? Guilt gnawed at him. Perhaps he'd misconstrued an innocent display of affection. Yes, Jim had kissed him back, but he'd been through so much. He wasn't himself.

Cal had been light-headed with joy as Jim's tongue met his—as Jim had returned his kisses the way Cal always dreamed he would. But he should have known better. Jim wasn't queer. He was lonely.

The dishes were drying in the rack, and Jim still hadn't returned. Cal paced across the linoleum. They needed to clear the air, and he couldn't do that if Jim avoided him. But he'd never known Jim to be a coward, so Cal went outside and waited by the paddock, taking long drags from a cigarette.

He was on his third when Jim finally appeared. Cal ground the cigarette out with his boot. Jim stopped a few feet away, his gaze focused somewhere in the distance, and Cal cleared his throat. "Sophie was really worried when you didn't come back on time."

"I know. I'm sorry. Thanks for taking care of them."

He shrugged. "Of course." For the first time since the night they'd met on that train to South Carolina, Cal didn't know what to say to Jim. He took a deep breath and broke the uncomfortable silence. "I know you didn't want…what happened."

Jim's brow furrowed, his gaze still on the muddy grass. "It was my fault. I don't know what I was thinking. I *wasn't* thinking. You didn't want that either. We're just…bottled up."

"True enough." Cal had been bottling up his desire for Jim for years.

"We both made a mistake. It was wrong. That kind of thing is…"

Stomach churning again, Cal finished for him. "Unnatural? Sinful? Disgusting?"

"Yes." Jim nodded jerkily. "Exactly."

Cal forced the words from his dry throat. "Not to me."

"What?" Jim blinked, finally meeting Cal's gaze. "Of course it is."

"No. It's not. It's completely natural to me. It always has been." Cal shrugged. "Always will be."

"I…I don't understand."

"I'm queer, Jim."

"Of course you're not. That's ridiculous." Jim tried to smile, failing miserably. "Is this a joke?"

"No."

"Cal…"

Cal flicked his lighter open and shut, punctuating his terse words. "I'm a homo. A faggot, a queer, a poof, a cocksucker. I should have told you a long time ago, but…"

Silence settled over them again. Cal lit another cigarette, his fingers shaking. Jim simply stared at him, lips parted as he appeared to try to think of a response. He started to say something, but then shook his head.

Finally he said, "But you've been with so many women. You would tell us about them. Eva Thorngood when you were sixteen."

Cal had to laugh. "I can't believe you remember her name."

Jim barreled on. "And there was that girl in Melbourne. What was her name? Amanda? You ran off every day with her for a couple of months."

"*His* name was Adrian. And it was Michael Thorngood in the library. Eva's husband. The rest of it was true."

"Lord. That was…a man did those things? But you were still a boy. He took advantage of you. Mixed you up—"

"No, Jim. He didn't. He didn't do anything I didn't want. He didn't make me this way. If anyone did, it was your God."

"No. You're confused."

Cal inhaled smoke and held it in his lungs until they burned. He blew it out slowly. "I've never felt that way about women. It just isn't in me."

Jim took this in. "Have you ever been with a woman?"

"Kissed a few girls in junior high."

"But you've never…" He made a vague motion with his hand.

"No, Jim, I've never fucked a woman. I don't need to do that to know I'm queer. Believe me, I've been through this all from top to bottom. I didn't know what was wrong with me until I found out there were other men like me. Men who want each other the same way other men want women. You'd be surprised how many of us are out there, hiding in plain sight."

"Have you been to a doctor? Maybe there's something they could do."

Cal crushed his cigarette into the earth. "I'm not sick. I don't need a doctor."

"I just want to help you."

Then love me back. "Stop looking at me like I just told you I'm an ax murderer."

Jim blinked. "I'm sorry. I don't know what to do. What to say."

"If you want me to leave, I'll understand."

"No!" Jim lowered his voice. "I don't want you to go. What happened was a misunderstanding. We'll just forget about it."

"All right." Cal could live with it as long as Jim was still his friend. He couldn't stand the thought of losing that.

From the direction of the house, Sophie's voice rang out. "Daddy? Adam wet the bed. The sheets are up too high in the closet. I can't reach them."

Jim called, "I'm coming!" He turned to Cal. "It's fine. We'll just go back to normal." His smile was strained, and then he hurried away.

Cal put another cigarette between his lips. *Normal.* Whatever that meant.

AS HE DROVE the gleaming Cadillac along Tivoli's main street, Cal felt rather conspicuous. He should have taken Jim's truck, but considering he was escaping the tense atmosphere at the orchard, he hadn't wanted to ask. When he'd told Jim he was going into town, Jim had kept his eyes on the sprinkler head he was repairing and asked Cal to pick up some bread with false cheer in his voice.

Cal parked by the curb in front of the general store. He'd barely stepped out of the car when a lively voice called his name. He stifled a sigh and turned to find Rebecca Graham waving from across the street. He waved back and put on a smile as she walked over.

"Hi, Rebecca."

She brushed a strand of golden hair from her forehead as the breeze picked up. "What a nice surprise! What brings you to Tivoli?"

"Just picking up a few things." Cal jerked his thumb behind him at the store. "What about you?"

"I don't think I mentioned it when we met before, but I'm Dr. O'Brien's secretary. I'm taking my break. I was on my way to have a cup of coffee. Care to join me?"

A litany of excuses rattled through Cal's head, each sounding more pathetic than the last. He didn't want to lead her on, but being rude wasn't an attractive option either. "It would be my pleasure."

Her green eyes brightened. "Wonderful! There's a little coffee shop just down the street."

Rebecca led the way, chattering as they went. "How's your head? I heard what happened, you poor thing. Guess you don't have much call for milking cows in New York City."

"No, not much. I'm all healed, thankfully." Cal opened the café door for Rebecca. "I'm told I have a very hard head."

An older woman served them coffee at a small round table by the window. In the middle of a Thursday afternoon, the café was quiet, with the only other customers being a pair of old men engrossed in a game of chess.

Rebecca stirred a spoonful of sugar into her cup. "It's a good thing Dr. O'Brien wasn't too far away when it happened."

"It was indeed." Cal cast about for something to say. He was usually much better at small talk. "Do you like working for him?"

"Oh yes. He's a wonderful doctor, and he doesn't give me much trouble except with his handwriting, which is absolutely atrocious. But I've learned to decipher the code over the years."

"How long have you been his secretary?"

"For…gosh, I guess it's seven years now." She took a sip of coffee, her gaze faraway. "I thought he'd be my father-in-law." Shaking her head, she smiled sadly. "But life doesn't always turn out the way you planned."

"It sure doesn't. I can attest to that."

"Do you like it at Clover Grove? It's a beautiful place."

"It is. I like it a lot." *Except for the fact that Jim won't even look at me now.* "Have you been there often?"

"Before the war, Stephen and I used to visit some weekends. So long ago now. When Jim was overseas, I'd stay with Ann sometimes and we'd talk and talk long after we should have been in bed. But I haven't been out since she passed away." Her expression tightened.

"I'm sorry. Were you very close?"

"Oh yes. I miss her very much."

"What was she like?" Cal couldn't resist asking.

Rebecca pondered it for a moment, affection clear on her face. "She was a dreamer. I remember when I first met her, I never thought she'd stick around here for long. She had big plans, Ann Shelton. But then she fell for Jim, and it all changed. You know how it is, when you meet that special someone and everything else goes out the window." Her smile faded and she sipped her coffee.

"Is that how it was when you met Stephen?"

She nodded. "He was the one. I've tried to meet someone else. But after the war, there just aren't too many young men left." Lifting her hand to her mouth, she gasped softly. "What an awful, selfish thing to say! Please forgive me."

"No need." Cal smiled encouragingly, deciding he liked Rebecca Graham. "Have you considered leaving Tivoli? I bet I know a dozen guys in the city who would love to meet you." She was pretty and smart with a nice figure, and it was the truth.

A faint blush made her cheeks rosy. "That's very kind of you to say. But even if there were, my mother's not in good health. She relies on me for everything, and I could never leave her alone."

"I understand. That's very good of you, to care for her."

Rebecca shrugged. "It's just what people do, isn't it?"

Cal thought briefly of his parents and the army of servants catering to their every whim. "It's what some people do. Good people like you." A thought occurred. "Did you ever go out with Eddie?"

Rebecca went very still, and something flickered across her face. "Eddie?"

"I'm not sure what his last name is, but he worked at the orchard. He was unattached, wasn't he?"

"Of course he was!" She poured another spoonful of sugar into her cup, the metal clinking as she stirred. "But no, Eddie and I never dated." Her smile didn't reach her eyes. "Tell me about New York City. What's it like to live there?"

The seed of suspicion that had been quietly cultivating in Cal's mind bloomed. "Too bad Eddie wasn't your type. What was he like?" Cal asked, ignoring Rebecca's question.

She stirred in another spoonful of sugar. "We didn't spend much time together. He was a hard worker."

"Ann must have spent a lot of time with him."

"Ann?" Rebecca laughed too loudly. "Why do you say that?"

"Well, I know from experience that you don't get many visitors to Clover Grove, so you see quite a bit of the people who live there. It was just Jim's father, Ann, Eddie, and Sophie for a couple of years, right?"

"It was. But Eddie kept to himself, and Ann was so busy with Sophie."

"Why do you think he left the way he did? So suddenly after Ann's accident?"

Rebecca's gaze skittered away as she shrugged. "Who knows? I think he'd been planning to leave for a while."

"Really? That's interesting. Jim didn't know anything about that. It came as a complete surprise to him."

At this, she sighed. "Did it?"

"It did."

Painting a smile back on her face, Rebecca finished her coffee. "I'd love to visit the orchard one day. I know that Jim…well, I get the feeling Jim doesn't like me very much. Never really has."

Cal decided to let his questions about Eddie go for the moment. "Of course he likes you."

"Whenever I talk to him these days, it seems like he can't get away fast enough. But I'm sorry, I shouldn't be prattling on like this to you. This is probably why he doesn't like me. The prattling."

"It's not you. He's just having a hard time lately. What with…everything."

"Of course." Her eyes glistened. "I honestly just want to help. I love those children, and I know how much work they are. I'd be happy to come by sometime and entertain them for a few hours. I know Stephen's mother helps out, but many hands make light work, as my mama always said."

"I'm sure Jim would appreciate that. I'll suggest it to him."

"Thank you, Cal." She glanced at her wristwatch. "Goodness, I'd better skedaddle." She opened her handbag.

"No, no, it's on me." Cal quickly pulled a couple of coins from his pocket and slid them onto the table. "Let me walk you back."

As they neared the doctor's office, Rebecca slowed. "It was really nice chatting with you, Cal. When I'm not working I'm usually home with Mama, so I don't get the chance to just talk with a friend too often. I hope that's not overstepping the boundaries, to call you a friend."

Smiling, Cal replied, "Not at all," and meant it.

CHAPTER TEN

1942

"SPEEDY, IT'S YOUR turn!"

"Hell no, it ain't. I went last night."

Cal grinned. "But you're the fastest. I've never seen a man run as quick as you can with a bucket of oil without spilling a drop."

Speedy lit a cigarette and flopped down on his rack, crossing his skinny legs at the ankle. "And this is the thanks I get? It's Sully's turn."

"Me?" Sully squeaked. "No way. I went down with Joe to the slop chute to get more beer." He pointed to the stack of cases in the middle of the hut. "My duty is done. How about Johnny?"

It wasn't until all eyes swiveled his way that Jim realized they were talking to him. "Me?"

"Yeah, you. We need more oil for the stove. Come on, Johnny."

Their newest squad member, a shy blond boy by the name of Smith, spoke up hesitantly. "I thought your name was Jim."

"It is," Jim replied firmly.

"No, no!" Speedy shook his dark head. His skin was a rich tan color that seemed to indicate some Indian blood, although he'd almost punched Pete when Pete had asked about it. "This here's Johnny Appleseed. He grows apples up north. Now come on, Johnny. Fair is fair."

"Aw hell, I'll go with you." Cal hopped to his feet and picked up a couple of buckets, passing one to Jim. "Don't worry—we won't get caught."

With a sigh, Jim followed him into the night. "Famous last words," he muttered.

Each company in the battalion had its own supply of oil, kept in large drums. It had quickly become routine to sneak out under cover of darkness and pinch oil from other squads to keep their stove burning. Jim knew everyone did it, but that didn't make it right. "You know, if we'd stop stealing from each other, we'd all have enough oil."

"But where's the fun in that, Johnny?" Cal winked, scooting low and sneaking around the back of another hut.

They ducked under a lit window and crouched in the shadows. "This is not fun. And don't call me that!" Jim hissed.

"Okay, I won't," Cal whispered, his head close. "You know it only means they like you. Don't take it the wrong way, Jim."

"Then why don't you have a nickname yet?"

"Oh, I'm sure I'll have one before too long. Or maybe they just don't like me." He scuttled beneath the window. At the drum, he pried off the lid and dipped in his bucket.

"Don't be ridiculous. Everyone likes you."

"I am a pretty charming son of a bitch." Cal smirked. "Come on, fill up your bucket."

Jim did as he was told. "I feel like I'm back in school with all these silly games we play."

"This whole thing is one big game, and we're going to win. We're going to go over there and knock the stuffing out of the Japs. They don't know what they're in for."

Jim was about to respond when a flashlight beam blazed to life in the night. "Hey you! Stop!"

They didn't hesitate, flying back the way they'd come, spilling oil left and right as their pursuer squawked in outrage. Jim and Cal ducked out of sight into a darkened alcove where they squeezed into the tight space, chests pressed together, breath mingling.

Warm excitement surging in his veins, Jim had to admit it was fun after all.

The next morning was considerably less enjoyable.

"Off and on!"

At Captain Brown's barked order, Jim stifled a sigh and got off his rear end and onto his feet along with the rest of the platoon. They marched along the dusty road, finally reaching their destination an hour later.

Open, barge-like boats waited for them in a river that would take them to the ocean. After they clambered down, more than thirty men crammed onto each boat by Jim's estimation. Then the battalion commander shouted for attention.

"You are sitting in Higgins boats. These are going to win this war, gentlemen. You will also hear them referred to as LCVPs. Landing craft, vehicle, and personnel. Being a shallow boat, you can see it is a landing craft. It's built to carry a jeep if necessary. That's the vehicle. And obviously you men are the personnel. When this LCVP lands, the ramp at the front will lower, and you will move your asses. Understood? Good. Now try to make it through this exercise without puking your guts out."

Cal and Jim shared a glance. It was going to be a long ride.

Indeed, they hadn't reached the ocean before poor Sully was heaving into his helmet. Others followed suit, and Jim felt decidedly queasy as they reached the swells of open sea water. Cal, on the other hand, was just fine. "Doesn't it bother you?" Jim asked.

"Nah. Spent my summers sailing in the Hamptons."

"Of course you did." Jim smiled even as he fought a swell of nausea.

Suddenly the engine roared and the boat powered toward the beach. There was a sharp jolt as they landed, digging into the sand.

"Move, move, move!"

They plunged into the freezing surf swirling around their calves, rifles held high. On the beach they hit the deck, going through the motions of an offensive. Sand stuck in every pore, gritty on Jim's tongue and lips. When he rubbed his eyes, they burned from the saltwater residue.

When they had run through the whole routine, Captain Brown approached. "Very good, men. We're staying out here in the boondocks so we can practice these amphibious maneuvers. Smooth and efficient landings are absolutely vital to our success in the Pacific. Our camp is a mile down the coast. Let's get moving!"

"Something tells me our hut back at the base'll seem like the Ritz-Carlton in comparison," Cal muttered.

The tents they had to set up in a clearing in the forest weren't any better or worse than what they'd slept in at the rifle range on Parris Island. As they sat around a bonfire that night, men from several squads talking and laughing, Jim breathed in the scent of pine amid the smoky wood and felt utterly content.

Cal passed him the bottle of hooch going around the circle, and Jim cringed as the liquid burned his throat. Cal laughed and patted his back. "There you go. It'll put hair on your chest!"

Big Southern Joe, for all his crude bluster, had a shockingly fine singing voice, and he led them in a chorus of "Blueberry Hill." Surrounded by new friends, they sang to the stars. Cal's arm was a warm comfort across Jim's shoulders, and the war had never felt so far away.

1948

HOW STRANGE.

Jim didn't remember turning on the Rain Birds, yet as he walked down to the orchard, he could see them working, water glittering in the moonlight, arcing through the fresh, cool air. *Swish-swish-swish-swish.*

Somehow he remained dry as he walked amid the trees, down one row and then another, leaving the house and barn behind. He was looking for something, yet he couldn't seem to remember what it was. An owl hooted, and eyes glowed in the trees, the pheasants watching as he passed by.

Then as he came over a gentle rise, he found Cal.

His back turned, Cal was naked between the trees, skin glistening in the spray of water. Arms outstretched, his head was tipped back as if in some kind of ecstatic thrall. Lightheaded, Jim was rooted to the spot, even when Cal faced him.

Cal was hard, his thick cock jutting from his body. To his shame, Jim's own shaft swelled, and he was reaching out, desperate to touch his friend. Cal was suddenly right before him, a familiar smile on his lips.

"It's okay," he whispered.

When he wrapped his hand around Cal's length, a ragged moan filled the air, and Jim realized it was his own. As he stroked Cal's straining cock, he was overcome with the urge to kiss him and taste him—to run his tongue over Cal's wet skin. Jim was still fully dressed and painfully hard in his trousers, and Cal was completely exposed before him, beautiful and free.

Jim lunged for Cal's mouth, kissing him in a frenzy, his hand caught between their bodies, rubbing Cal and bringing him to the brink of—

Panting, Jim bolted up in bed.

The bedroom appeared as it always did. Nothing out of place. Jim listened intently for the children, but the night was still aside from his harsh breathing and the faint, soothing sound of the sprinklers in the orchard. It had been a surprisingly warm day, and he had left the window open. The curtain fluttered in the breeze.

Everything was normal. As normal as possible considering he was excited, and he'd been dreaming about…

With a long exhale, he stretched out again. It didn't mean anything. It was only a dream. He'd been under a lot of stress, and dreams were nothing more than jumbled nonsense. Yet when Jim closed his eyes, he could see it all so clearly—Cal in the orchard, naked and glistening. Hard and eager.

Grunting, Jim attempted to clear his mind and ignore the state of his body, although his blood still thrummed with sticky desire. He breathed deeply, willing himself to calm down and go back to sleep. It had just been a silly dream, and he needed to forget it.

After another minute, he opened his eyes. When Reverend Davis had come to school and taken the boys into another classroom, he'd told them it was a sin to touch themselves. Jim had resisted as much as he could growing up. When he'd given in to the need for release, he'd kept his mind purposefully blank.

Now he did the same as one hand skimmed beneath his pajama top, fingertips skating across his skin as he freed his cock with his other hand, kicking his bottoms free. He should think of his wife, but it felt wrong now that she was gone, and the thought of her sent guilt and shame spiraling through him anew.

Here in the surreal calm of the dead of night, he could admit that sex with his wife had never been the revelation other men talked about. Jim had always felt that physical acts between men and women were highly overrated, and that his buddies who crowed about their conquests exaggerated the enjoyment they experienced.

Sex was just a biological imperative that was largely awkward and provided only fleeting moments of pleasure and release. He needed that release now, and should just let friction take its course.

Unbidden, images of Cal flashed through Jim's mind, and his hips arched up as he spread his legs wider with his knees bent. He dug his heels into the mattress as he stroked himself faster, biting his lip. He told himself not to think of his friend—that it was sick and *wrong*. Kissing Cal had been a mistake and he was simply confused.

But now the vestiges of his dream clung stubbornly, so real in his mind. Cal's strong, glistening body in the moonlight. The pressure of his lips on Jim's, and his tongue in Jim's mouth. It should have repelled him, but want and need urged him on as he jerked himself faster and harder, hips lifting, moans low in his throat. He imagined it was still Cal he touched—Cal's thick heat against his palm.

Shaking, legs splayed, Jim came over his hand, splattering his pajama top. The intensity of the pleasure stunned him, leaving confusion and growing horror in its wake. As his seed dried, the disgrace settled in, and he crept to the bathroom to scrub himself clean.

BIRDS CHIRPED OVERHEAD, soaring through the clear blue sky. On a ladder, Jim examined the flowering buds. Soon the orchard would be resplendent with white blooms. "The trees don't seem any worse for wear after that snow last week."

"That's good." Cal squatted at the base of the tree, yanking on the weeds already sprouting up.

"Yeah."

Jim winced internally at their stilted conversation. Where in the past the words—and silences—had always come so easily, now everything was strained. Every time he looked at Cal, he felt a rush of heat, his skin prickling. It was madness. He didn't know what was wrong with him. He'd never felt such a keen desire for anyone, not even Ann.

Especially not Ann.

Banishing the thoughts with a mental shake, Jim climbed down and moved to the next tree, giving it a careful inspection. But again and again, his mind returned to Cal, like a magnet to steel.

He still couldn't believe that Cal was…what he was. Jim didn't even like to think the word. How was it possible? Cal had been his best friend for six years, and Jim hadn't known. And now that he did know, he couldn't stop thinking about it. Couldn't stop…wanting. Wanting things that were against God and nature.

He'd even considered whether the sickness was contagious, but that seemed a ridiculous notion. No, surely with the stress of losing Ann and caring for the children, Jim was simply overwrought. Finding out that Cal was a homosexual had put notions in his head that his subconscious didn't understand. Soon everything would be normal again.

But I kissed him first. And I liked it.

With a mutter, Jim pulled his knife from his belt. There was a stray branch they'd missed during pruning, and he hacked into the wood. It wavered but didn't fall. Gritting his teeth, Jim swung wildly at it, and the blade sliced into his left hand below his thumb. "Damn it!"

"What happened? You okay?"

Jim hopped down from the ladder, hissing as he yanked out the tail of his plaid shirt to wrap around the wound. "It's fine."

Cal came closer. "Here, let me see."

"It's fine," he repeated.

"If it's fine, then let me see." Cal took hold of Jim's arm.

With a burst of fury, Jim shoved him away. Cal stumbled onto the ground on his rear end and stared at him. Breathing hard, Jim got a hold of himself. "I'm sorry. It just…hurts. But it's fine." Jim turned away, pacing a few steps here and there. He should help Cal up, but he was afraid to touch him.

For a minute, Cal didn't say a thing. Then he slowly got to his feet, sighing. From the corner of his eye, Jim could see Cal hold something out.

"Here. Wrap this around it."

Jim took the handkerchief. "Thanks. Look, I…" He wished he knew how to explain.

"It's all right, Jim." Cal sounded so tired. "I understand."

The blood flow slowed, and Jim wrapped the cloth around his hand. "It's just a nick." He tried to laugh. "I was being a big baby, that's all."

"This isn't going to work."

Jim's heart skipped a beat. "No, it's fine." He lifted his hand. "See? Won't even need any stitches."

Cal didn't say anything for a few moments. When he spoke, it was with a terrible sense of defeat that made Jim's blood run cold.

"I can't stay here."

Jim croaked, "What?"

"We both know it. Hell, the kids know it. Things aren't right between us anymore."

"What are you talking about?" He peered intently at his hand, fiddling with the handkerchief. "Everything's fine. It'll be fine."

"You can't even look at me. You barely have since last week. It's best for everyone if I go."

"It was just a misunderstanding!" Sweat broke out on Jim's forehead. Cal couldn't leave. If he did, Jim knew with a strange certainty that he'd never see him again. Panic coiled inside him. "I don't want you to go."

Cal took a deep breath. "The thing is…I wasn't honest with you. What happened last week didn't happen just because I'm queer."

"What do you mean?" Jim's skin prickled.

"I've wanted to kiss you for a long time. Feels like forever now. Since boot camp. Hell, since the night we met."

Jim swallowed thickly. There was a buzzing in his ears. "I don't understand."

"I know you don't." Cal's dark eyes were kind, his expression ineffably sad. "I always knew you'd never feel the same way. I know it now, no matter how much I want to deny it."

"You're my best friend." Jim's voice was reedy. His chest was tight, and his stomach had formed a solid knot.

"I never wanted this to happen. I never told you how I felt because I knew it would ruin everything. But it's already ruined." Cal shook his head. "After the war, I made sure to stay away. I thought it would help. I fooled myself into thinking it had, but the minute I came here—the minute I saw you again—I knew I still wanted you just as much. Maybe more."

The words were molasses on Jim's thick tongue. "You…want me? *Me?*"

Cal nodded as he wrapped his arms around himself. "That's why I have to go. I know you don't feel the same. That you think it's wrong, what I am. Who I am. And I understand. But that's why I can't stay." He squared his shoulders. "I'll go pack my things." Then he was walking away.

Jim's head spun. His skin felt too tight, and he trembled. The way Cal was talking, it sounded as if Cal's feelings were about more than physical acts. That he cared for Jim the way men and women did for each other. Was it possible? Jim knew there were homosexuals in the world but had thought it was only about base desires. Could it be more?

When Jim was able to make his feet move, Cal was out of sight over the next rise. Jim called his name, racing through the orchard. Ahead, he glimpsed Cal disappearing into the house, and he sped up, arms pumping as he ran faster. Cal couldn't leave. Not like this.

In the house he shouted Cal's name, thankful it was market day and Mrs. O'Brien and Adam had gone into town with Mrs. Turner from the next farm. Cal didn't answer, and Jim took the stairs two at a time before bursting into the guest room. *Cal's* room.

Cal's suitcase was open on the bed, and he didn't look up from where he folded his shirts. "Don't worry. I'll help you find someone to replace me."

At those words, the panic and fear subsided like a wave receding from shore, and Jim could only stare, his chest heaving. Scattered pieces snapped into place in his mind––snatches of memory and images.

Cal's smile as he passed him the bottle on the train.
The warmth of his breath on Jim's neck as they huddled together during the cold, miserable nights.
Cal's arm around Jim's shoulders too many times to count.
His body protecting Jim as fire and death rained down.

Always there. Strong and steadfast.

Jim took a shuddering breath. "I could never replace you." In that moment, he saw things for how they really were. *How they'd always been.* He spoke that truth aloud for the first time. "I want you too."

Cal gaped. Finally he shook his head. "You don't mean it." He scooped up his clothes and tossed them in the suitcase, barely latching it shut before he brushed by Jim out the door. Jim made a grab for his arm, but Cal shook him off and pounded down the stairs, running now.

Jim gave chase. Outside, Cal slammed the door of his Cadillac, revving the engine. Not knowing what else to do, Jim stood in front of it, blocking the way since the car was backed up to the house. "Stop."

Muttering, Cal swore, his voice muffled inside the car. He shouted, "Move, Jim. You can't do this to me."

Frustration lanced through Jim, and he didn't budge. "You can't say those things and then leave. You can't just run away."

"Yes, I can!" Cal gripped the steering wheel. "It's finished. You don't know what you're saying. You don't mean any of it."

"Don't tell me what I mean." His heart thumped, and he smacked the Cadillac's hood with his palm. "I know what I'm saying. I want you."

Cal kicked open the door and stalked around the front of the car, keeping out of arm's reach. "No. Don't say that just to make me stay."

"I dream about you," Jim blurted, his breath shallow. "About…being with you. I can't stop thinking about it. About what it would be like."

Mouth opening and closing, Cal blinked. "Is that true?" His voice was soft, his question ending with a hopeful lilt.

"That's why I haven't been able to look at you since we…" He swallowed hard. "Since we kissed. Since I kissed you. It's not because I think badly of you. I could never. You have to know that."

Cal was very still. When he spoke, it was only a whisper. "Do you really mean it?"

"Yes." Jim moved toward him slowly, one foot in front of the other. He stopped a few inches away, his heart beating double-time. He reached for Cal. "I don't understand why I feel this way, but I do. I don't know what I'd do without you. Please don't go."

With a rush of breath and hands, they clutched each other, mouths together, kissing desperately. They were outside in broad daylight, but Jim couldn't stop. The dam burst, and they stumbled to the grass, Jim pressing his thigh between Cal's. Cal arched up, gripping Jim's ass as their tongues met and stroked.

They were both hard in their jeans, and Jim wanted desperately to feel the heat of Cal's skin against his own. But they were too far gone already, panting and rocking against each other, kissing with a need that Jim could hardly believe he'd kept tamped down. He realized the low grunts and moans filling the air were his, and Cal muttered against Jim's lips.

"Want you so much. God, Jim. *God.*"

The handkerchief tore free from Jim's hand as he scrabbled at Cal's shirt, unable to undo the buttons. Finally he just tugged it up and gripped Cal's bare waist as they rutted together, his blunt nails digging into Cal's skin. The pressure in Jim's balls intensified, his cock almost painfully hard as they clutched each other, mouths open as they gasped.

With a shout, Cal bucked up, head thrown back as he came. Jim was so close, and he buried his face in Cal's neck as he thrust against him, inhaling the scent of Cal's sweat. It was salty on his tongue as Cal wrapped his legs around Jim's, locking him in.

He held Jim's face in his hands and their eyes met. "Come for me."

With a final push, the ecstasy overtook Jim as he pulsed with his release, crying out. Nothing had ever felt so good in his life, and they still had all their clothes on. He sank over Cal, boneless, pressing his face to Cal's salty neck again.

Cal caressed Jim's hair softly. "It's always been you."

Lifting his head, Jim stared down at him. No words would come.

Cal froze, his fingers tight in Jim's hair. "Don't run this time. Promise me."

Nodding, Jim rested his head against Cal's chest, listening to the steady *thump-thump-thump* as Cal wrapped his arms around him.

He was finished running.

PART TWO

CHAPTER ELEVEN

1942

"WHERE ARE WE at tonight?"

"A hundred and seven."

They all groaned as Speedy slipped the thermometer back into his pack at the foot of his rack. They slept on canvas bunks strung up five high in the belly of the hulking metal ship powering its way across the Pacific. Cal was opposite Speedy on the bottom, and they shared a longsuffering glance as Cal wiped sweat from his brow.

Reaching up, Cal poked at Jim's back through the canvas. Only two feet separated each bunk, and in the sweltering, fetid heat, the claustrophobia made his skin crawl. At least he hoped it was the claustrophobia and not some unseen vermin. "Are you almost done with that book?"

"I will be if you stop pestering me. And if I could see to read properly."

The hold of the ship was murky, lit only from weak bulbs high in the ceiling. Cal smiled to himself. The truth was, he'd read the Kipling tale years ago at prep school. "I can just tell you how it ends if you want. So, Mowgli—"

"Cal, I swear…"

From above came Sully's voice. "You two are as bad as my folks."

This garnered several guffaws and agreement from the rest of the squad. Jim was silent as usual, and Cal kept his tone light. "Ah, but we have a distinct advantage over your parents."

"And what's that, Hollywood?"

"We don't have to suffer the indignity of such a little pipsqueak for a son."

"Yeah, yeah. I'll have you know I'm the pride of Mudforks, Mississippi."

"Remind me never to visit," Pistol Pete muttered.

Soon the conversation turned, as it usually did, to the war or women. In this case, it was both, as Speedy wondered aloud how long they'd go in the Pacific islands without encountering local girls.

"I bet you we're going to be tripping over buxom little beauties in hula skirts just dying to show their gratitude to the conquering heroes," Joe drawled.

"You really think there'll be natives there?" Sully asked.

"Unless we're fightin' over a whole bunch of empty piles of sand, there must be some natives somewhere," Speedy said.

Sully whined, "I can't sleep in this goddamned heat. Why can't they let us bring our bedrolls up top?"

"I guess the sailors don't want to be tripping over Marines all night," Cal answered.

"That's fair enough but at least there's a breeze up there. We're cookin' in this oven."

"Would you all just shut the fuck up and go to sleep?" Pete barked.

From farther down the hold, another Marine called back. "I second that fucking motion!"

Closing his eyes, Cal willed it to be morning.

The ever-present stench of smoke, paint, and grease that permeated the ship made Cal's stomach roil several hours later as he wavered in the chow line after a quick shave. Holding onto the wall of the gangway, he closed his eyes. He hadn't been seasick since he was five years old and he wasn't going to start now.

"You okay?" Jim stood behind him in line outside the galley.

Wiping his forehead with his sleeve, Cal nodded. "Yeah, yeah. Fine.

Just want to eat so I can get topside. Need some fresh air."

"Don't we all," big Joe noted, dragging the words out in his customary way.

Jim frowned. "You're drenched."

"Situation normal down here." They all dripped with sweat, adding to the constant stench.

"I know, but you look pale." Jim put his hand to Cal's forehead.

"Boys, we got our own Florence Nightingale here!" Pete snickered. "Johnny's gonna jump ship and join the Red Cross if we're not careful."

Jim pressed his lips together, shoving his hands in his pockets.

They were next into the galley, which was even hotter than the rest of the ship, if possible. Picking up metal trays with small compartments to theoretically keep different foods separated, they moved along the chow line as navy messmen haphazardly slopped a breakfast of dehydrated potatoes onto their trays.

Cal wanted more than anything to be able to eat topside, but it was strictly against the rules. So he took his place at one of the long folding tables where they ate standing up to keep the assembly line of men moving. Today it was fine by Cal, since he could only stomach a few ghastly bites before giving up.

"At least have some joe. That'll do you good." Jim nudged Cal's cup of steaming black coffee toward him.

Of all the smells in the squalid belly of the ship, this was the one that pushed Cal over the edge. He turned away from the table and puked, much to the vocal disgust of every man in the galley. Every man but Jim, who held Cal's shoulder with one hand and patted his back with the other.

"It's okay. Let's get you some air."

Letting Jim lead the way, Cal stumbled along, breathing deeply when they climbed up to the deck. He gulped in the clean air, which felt a million degrees cooler. Sailors and Marines milled around enjoying the breeze, and Jim navigated Cal through the crowd until they reached the railing at the stern. Cal gripped it, shaking.

"You've never been seasick before." Jim peered at him closely.

"And I'm not seasick now. This is something else. I don't know what, but I feel like my skin's on fire and my stomach's inside out."

Jim pressed the back of his hand to Cal's forehead again, and then his own. "You've got a fever."

"Tell me something I don't already know, Florence." Cal tried to smile.

"Come on. You've got to lie down."

"Oh Jesus, I can't go back down there."

"You're going to have to."

But as they soon discovered, the bug spread like wildfire, and before long their quarters were half full of fevered, nauseated men. Buckets were distributed throughout the hold. Cal heaved into his, thankful that at least his rack was closest to the floor.

Kneeling beside him, Jim held up a canteen and made him drink before going to clean out the bucket. When he came back, Cal muttered, "Don't bother. I'm just gonna puke in it again in a few minutes."

"It'll lessen the smell at least."

Cal had to smile. "Christ, this ship has never stunk so badly. One clean bucket isn't going to make a difference."

Jim shrugged, and sure enough, the next time Cal heaved, Jim disappeared and returned with the bucket clean. When it finally seemed like the worst had passed, Cal collapsed on his rack, shivering and exhausted. "Go get some air. I'll be fine." His eyes flickered shut.

When he woke again some time later, a wet cloth rested on his forehead, and Jim sat on the floor by the bucket. When Cal tried to speak, only a garbled croak emerged from his parched throat. On his knees, Jim lifted the canteen, his hand gentle on the back of Cal's head.

Cal gulped gratefully. "Really, Jim. Get topside. I'm feeling much better."

"Okay."

As Cal drifted off again, he was faintly aware of a fresh cloth on his forehead and a warm, comforting hand on his arm.

1948

"WHY ARE YOU smiling so much?"

Cal looked up at Sophie across the small kitchen table as he sliced into his pork chop. "I'm not."

"Yes, you are." She tugged one of her pigtails.

Glancing at Jim, who examined his plate as if it held the secrets of the universe, Cal shrugged. "I guess I'm just happy." *Ecstatic. Over the moon. Jubilant. Quixotic, even.*

"It's weird."

"Sophie." Jim frowned at her. "Don't be rude."

"I'm not! At least I didn't mean to be. He wasn't this happy at breakfast."

Cal put down his fork. "You want to know exactly why it is I'm so cheerful tonight?" As Jim's face blanched, Cal went on. "It's this broccoli." From the corner of his eye, he saw Jim exhale with a chuckle.

Sophie scrunched up her face. "Ew. I hate broccoli."

"Well, I love it. Can't get enough of it." He pierced a spear with his fork and ate it with gusto. "Puts hair on your chest."

"I don't want hair on my chest!" She giggled.

"What little girl doesn't want hair on her chest? Jim, can you believe this?"

Smiling, Jim shook his head. "I have to say, it's disappointing, Sophie."

Still giggling, Sophie lifted her plate and piled her broccoli onto Adam's. "Goober can have all the hair."

Adam, always willing to eat anything and everything under the sun, happily shoved a spear into his mouth before Jim could put the broccoli back on Sophie's plate.

"Uh-uh. You're eating your vegetables."

Heaving a great sigh, Sophie swallowed a small bite. Cal couldn't stop himself from laughing, and pretty soon they all did, Adam clapping his hands as chewed broccoli dribbled out of his mouth.

While Jim put Adam to bed after dinner, Cal helped Sophie with the washing up, drying the plates and cutlery as she placed them into the rack. They worked in easy silence, and Cal felt more at peace than he had in a long time. He'd been afraid Jim would freeze up and avoid him like the plague after what happened earlier that day, but he hadn't. Cal knew Jim was still mighty confused and unsettled, but at least he was meeting Cal's gaze.

It was like a dream, Jim saying the words Cal had wanted to hear for so long. Feeling the touch of his lips, and the weight of his body. It wasn't all one sided after all—Jim actually did feel something for him. When Cal woke that morning, the world had been a vastly different place. Now it was alive with possibility.

"You're doing it again."

Cal opened the cupboard to put away the clean plates. "Am I?"

"Uh-huh."

"I guess I'm just happy, then."

After a long moment, Sophie asked, "Can you make Daddy happy?"

Cal choked out a nervous laugh. "What?"

Sophie pulled the plug from the drain and peered up at him seriously. "He's hardly ever happy. Not really."

"Well, it's been tough, what with your mom's accident. Tough on all of you."

"I know. But…" She dried her hands, a crease between her brows.

"But what?"

"I don't think he's ever really been happy for as long as I can remember."

Struggling for something to say, Cal brushed a stray curl from her forehead. Finally he settled on the truth. "I'm going to do everything I can to make your dad happy."

"Thank you." Then she stepped forward and wrapped her arms around his waist. "I'm glad you're here, Uncle Cal."

He had to swallow hard over the sudden lump in his throat. Pressing a kiss to the top of her head, he hugged her back. "Me too."

Before long it was time for Sophie to go to bed as well, and Cal paced around the living room, the sounds of Jim reading a story floating downstairs from time to time. He poured himself a whiskey and went outside to wander by the paddock, inhaling a cigarette and playing with Finnigan. The dog soon ran off into the trees, barking at a threat either real or imagined—Cal wasn't sure which.

After his third cigarette, he went back inside. Standing at the bottom of the stairs, Cal listened. All was quiet. The wood seemed to creak more loudly than before as he climbed upstairs, and his breath stuttered when he saw Jim's closed door.

He listened for any sounds from the children down the hall and heard none through the partially open door. Steeling himself, he went to Jim's room, his knock barely more than a scratch. The door swung open a moment later. Jim still wore his jeans and white undershirt. After a tense moment, he stepped aside.

Cal closed the door behind him, the scrape of wood echoing in the silence. The lock sliding home seemed as loud as a gunshot. "I waited for you outside," he whispered.

"I shouldn't leave the kids alone."

Cal didn't point out that they'd gone outside in the evenings plenty of times, and the children had been just fine. "Sure. Okay."

"We can't…" Jim waved his hand between them. "Not here." Jim hurried to the door, brushing Cal aside. He listened intently, his shoulders high.

As Jim turned, Cal stepped close, lifting his finger to Jim's lips. "Shh. It's okay." He kissed him softly. "We just have to be quiet. They're fast asleep by now."

Jim's body was rigid from head to toe. "We shouldn't."

Cal pressed kisses to Jim's neck, one hand skimming up under his undershirt. "Just relax," he murmured.

Inch by inch, Jim unclenched. Cal took his time, kissing and caressing, teasing and coaxing until Jim dragged his undershirt over his head, breath coming in shallow gasps as he tugged Cal closer. Cal bent and took one of Jim's nipples into his mouth, flicking it with his tongue before grazing it with his teeth.

Jim's harsh moan filled the air, and he froze. Chuckling, Cal kissed him again before covering Jim's mouth with his hand. "Shh."

As he went back to Jim's chest, licking and sucking, his other hand drifting lower with light caresses, Jim's forceful exhalations tickled Cal's palm. When he lowered the zipper on Jim's jeans, Jim arched his hips, his cock tenting his drawers. Cal took his hand away from Jim's mouth and kissed him deeply, sucking his tongue.

Then he dropped slowly to his knees. Jim actually *whimpered*, and Cal glanced up, smiling wickedly. He felt powerful. He'd waited years for this, and he was going to make Jim fly apart. Make him come so hard. Show him how good it could be.

He kissed Jim's flat belly as he pulled his drawers and jeans down. Jim lifted his feet one at a time, and Cal tossed the clothing aside. Jim's cock stood up, flushed red and already leaking. When Cal tasted a salty drop on his tongue, Jim swallowed a low groan, his hands tightening into fists. Cal licked along the underside of the shaft, his hands moving to Jim's hips. He knew Jim likely wouldn't last tonight, but he wanted to make the most of it.

For so long, Cal had fantasized about how Jim would feel and taste in his mouth. As he sucked the head of Jim's cock between his lips, he had to muffle his own groan of pure pleasure, sparks skittering up his spine. Breathing deeply through his nose, he took in more, reveling in the musky scent.

Jim tangled his fingers in Cal's hair, and Cal glanced up. With eyes closed and lips parted, Jim panted silently. His skin was flushed all over, and he was the most beautiful thing Cal had ever seen. Cal kept his gaze up as he licked and sucked, one hand moving to stroke the sensitive skin behind Jim's balls, which were tight and heavy.

Jim's cock throbbed in Cal's mouth, making his own dick ache. He increased his tempo, using strong suction and teasing with his tongue.

Caressing Jim's balls in his palm, he watched Jim's breath hitch, his whole body seizing. Jim tugged on Cal's head, but Cal stayed latched onto his cock, swallowing deeply as Jim came with a strangled moan.

He milked every last drop as he stroked Jim's trembling thighs. Panting, Jim leaned back against the door, his eyes closed. Cal's cock strained against his fly, and he got to his feet and kissed Jim, slipping his tongue between his lips.

Eyes snapping open, Jim tore his mouth away, one hand pressing roughly against Cal's chest. He swiped the other across his lips, grimacing. "I can…taste it."

Cal smiled uneasily. "Well, I know. I can taste it too."

"I tried to warn you so you wouldn't have to." Jim wiped at his mouth again.

"But I wanted to." Jesus, he'd only dreamt of it for years.

"You really…like that?"

Cal tried to ignore the hot prickles of something akin to shame. "I really do. You seemed to like being on the receiving end."

"I…yes. I just…" Jim reached for his discarded drawers and tugged them on.

"What?" Cal took a deep breath, telling himself to be patient.

"I don't know." Jim ran a hand through his hair before gesturing to Cal's crotch. "I should…you're…"

"Nah." Cal forced a smile. "It's been a long day. I think we should both hit the hay." At Jim's sharp look, he added, "Separately. I need to have a shower anyway. 'Night." He turned the doorknob.

"Cal."

He waited.

"I don't know how to feel. This is all new."

Cal looked back, and this time his smile was real. "I know. We'll figure it out."

Jim nodded and closed the door behind him. Cal tiptoed to the bathroom and turned the shower on, making the water as cold as he could stand it.

WHEN CAL CAME down for breakfast, Jim said good morning as usual but kept his eyes on his cereal. Adam babbled happily and Sophie told them about the book report she was writing. As she ran the water for the dishes, Jim cleared his throat.

"Cal, do you think you can drive to Buffalo today? I ordered some new chemicals to spray on the trees. Pesticide, it's called. They say it'll get rid of the maggot flies. Maggots ruined nearly a quarter of the crop last year. Anyway, I need to pick it up and it's a six-hour drive."

Cal's laugh was forced. "Trying to get rid of me already, huh?"

"No! Of course not." Jim glanced at the children by the sink and gave Cal a warning look. "I asked him if he could deliver, but it would take weeks. He's got a backlog of orders, but if I go pick it up myself, he'll make an exception. It would really help me out if you went."

"Hey, you're the boss. Whatever you need." Cal told himself it didn't mean anything. "When did you talk to him?"

"A few days ago. I wasn't sure about trying it, but I've made up my mind. I'd go, but I don't want to leave the children overnight. It's too much to drive in one day."

"How much am I picking up? Think it'll fit in the Caddy's trunk?" Cal tried to tell himself it was just business—that Jim wasn't pushing him away.

"Should do. You can take the truck though. Don't want to mess up your car."

"No, it's fine. It'll be good to put some miles on her. Brush off the cobwebs. I'll get going." He pushed his chair back and swallowed the last of his coffee.

"You don't have to rush off."

Cal ignored him with a wave of his hand and said goodbye to Adam and Sophie before going upstairs and quickly throwing a change of clothes into an overnight bag. He strode out to the car, trying not to let the hurt get the better of him and failing miserably. He fished out his keys.

"Cal!" Jim hurried over. "Would you wait a second?"

"Why? What more is there to say? I got the message loud and clear."

"Message?" Jim exhaled, clearly exasperated. "This isn't because of...*that*."

"Uh-huh." Cal knew he was being petulant, but couldn't stop.

"Whatever this is…" Jim glanced around. "Whatever this is between us, it's a lot to take in. I need some time. But I'm not denying it. I really do need you to pick up the pesticide. I know the timing stinks."

Sighing, Cal ran a hand through his hair. "Okay. Just don't talk yourself out of anything while I'm gone. I know this is new for you." He wanted to take Jim's hand, but resisted, simply stepping in close instead. "We could have something good. We *do* have something good. We always have. But it can be more. Just remember that."

Jim nodded. "I will."

"See you tomorrow."

"Let me know how much the hotel costs and I'll reimburse you. For gas and meals too."

Cal chuckled. "I'm going to leave before we get into another fight about money."

Jim smiled softly. "Drive carefully."

As Cal drove down the laneway, he watched Jim in the rearview mirror, standing there with his hands in his pockets and an unreadable expression on his face.

TWO DAYS LATER they were back at the breakfast table, the children chattering as Jim and Cal listened and nodded.

Jim finished eating and wiped his mouth with his napkin. "Cal, can you rake up any old leaves in the orchard while I check on the newer trees?"

Cal concentrated on a light tone. "Sure. Worried about anything in particular?"

Jim had been perfectly friendly, and had looked Cal in the eyes since his return the previous evening, but there'd been no hint as to how he was feeling. Cal had let him off the hook after dinner and claimed a headache as an excuse for an early night. Still, he'd waited and hoped that Jim would come to him once the children were asleep. He'd finally drifted off alone.

"Apple scab fungus. It can spread to the healthy young apples as spring warms up."

"Well, we don't want that."

"Uncle Cal, guess what?" Sophie bounced in her seat.

"Mabel started making chocolate milk?"

Sophie giggled. "Noooo!"

"You said to guess."

Everyone laughed, including Jim, and Cal felt a little better.

As the morning went on, he raked forcefully in the shade of the orchard. He still struggled to put the look of disgust that had creased Jim's face the other night out of his mind. He thought back to the first time he'd tasted semen. He'd licked Michael Thorngood clean and had asked for more. Tasting himself on Michael's lips later had sent an erotic charge through his veins.

That doesn't mean Jim has to feel the same way. It's okay if he doesn't like it. He's not me.

"I know he's not me," Cal muttered.

"They say talking to yourself is one of the first signs of insanity."

Cal chuckled as he turned to find Jim several feet away. "I'm sure I display more than just one sign." Even after so many years, a thrill of attraction whipped through him at the sight of Jim, with his blond hair gleaming and jeans hugging his hips. His plaid shirtsleeves were rolled to his elbows.

Jim smiled and lifted up a basket. "I brought lunch. Made your favorite."

"Peanut butter?" Cal's stomach growled.

"What else?"

"And you actually made this sandwich? Or did Mrs. O'Brien?"

Jim sat on the freshly raked grass beneath the nearest tree, crossing his legs. "I'll have you know I slaved over this for a full two minutes."

Laughing, Cal took a seat beside him, leaning back against the tree trunk. "My apologies to the chef."

They ate quietly, drinking from their canteens as the sun blinked out from behind a cluster of clouds. Rabbits scurried by in the distance, Finnigan barking after them. When they were finished eating, Jim tidied up the basket and leaned back against the tree beside Cal.

He inched closer, pressing their shoulders together. "I'm sorry for the way I acted."

"You don't have to be sorry. You were honest. That's all I can ask for."

"But you deserve so much more."

"Jim—"

"Let me say this, all right?"

"All right." Cal tried to relax.

Jim took a deep breath and blew it out. "This is all…new. Obviously whatever this is between us, but everything else too."

"Everything else?"

"With Ann, it was never…she never…" He waved his hand in the air. "In the bedroom, it was very…basic. I remember the guys talking about the wild things they did with women, and I thought they were making it all up."

Cal smiled. "Most of them probably were."

"But Ann and I—it was never anything like the other night. I've never felt like that. The way I feel with you."

Cal tentatively rested his hand on Jim's denim-clad thigh. "How did you feel?"

"Connected. So full of need I could hardly stand it." After a quick glance around, he covered Cal's hand with his own, threading their fingers together. "I can't believe I'm feeling this. For you. *With* you.

Nothing seems real. I keep expecting to wake up."

"Me too." Cal's pulse spiked as he leaned in and kissed Jim's neck.

Jim took a shuddering breath, squeezing Cal's hand. "It scares me. Not like in the war. A different kind of fear. But still terrifying."

"We don't have to do anything you don't want." Even though it would nearly kill him to turn back now, Cal couldn't bear the thought of Jim being unhappy or frightened.

"But I do. I *want*. I want things I didn't know were possible. That's what really scares me. I shouldn't want this."

"It's okay. I promise."

"How is this happening? How does it feel so…right?"

Cal caressed Jim's face with gentle fingers. "It's not wrong. I don't care what anyone else thinks. Love isn't wrong."

Jim swallowed hard. "Love?"

"Of course." Cal smiled. "I love you. You must know that."

Jim squeezed his eyes shut, and Cal's heart thumped. He'd gone too far, too fast. He was about to take it back when Jim looked at him.

Eyes glistening, Jim reached with both hands to cradle Cal's face. "God forgive me." He pressed their lips together.

Cal's head swam with pure joy, and they were lost, kissing deeply as time fell away. All Cal knew was the stroke of Jim's tongue against his own, and their mingled breath. Their hands gripping each other. When Jim broke the kiss, Cal followed, groaning at the loss of contact. His chest rising and falling rapidly, Jim smiled shyly and popped open the button on Cal's jeans. He took a deep breath, pausing.

Although he ached for Jim's touch, Cal reassured him. "There's no rush. You don't have to."

"I want to. I really do." He appeared surprised by his own admission.

Leaning back against the rough bark, Cal watched as Jim fished into his pants and pulled out Cal's stiff cock. Jim's eyes darted back and forth between Cal's crotch and his face as he stroked tentatively. Cal lifted his hips, thrusting into Jim's grasp. "Oh. Yes. Like that."

Every guttural moan and murmur seemed to give Jim confidence, and he twisted his thumb over the head of Cal's dick, teasing the leaking slit. Cal was so heavy and hard in Jim's hand, all his nerve endings zeroed in on the slick pressure. Sweat gathered at Cal's brow as the pleasure coiled low in his belly, ready to strike.

Birds sang overhead, the leaves swaying gently in the late spring breeze, new blooms in the air. Cal panted as he arched his back, Jim's hand tight around him. His cock pulsated, so heavy and full, and he could hardly believe Jim was actually touching him—bringing his fantasies to life.

Breath hot on Cal's ear, Jim whispered, "Let me see you come."

His balls drawing up, Cal shot over Jim's hand, crying out as he shuddered. The pleasure waved through him, and he felt complete peace. He yanked Jim close to kiss him hard.

They jumped apart at a sudden noise, and stared at Finnigan several yards away, watching them with head cocked. The dog barked again, and they burst out laughing, flopping back against the tree.

"It's okay, Finnigan," Cal called out. "Just don't tell anyone what you saw, all right? I'll buy you a nice juicy bone."

Jim's smile faded. "We really do have to be careful. No one can know about this. *No one.* This isn't a game."

"I know. We have to hide, but we won't be the first. Won't be the last. We'll make it work."

Jim nodded. "Okay." He lifted his sticky hand, peering at it curiously.

"Here, I think I have a handkerchief." Cal rummaged in his pockets and passed over the cloth.

Jim wiped off most of his hand, and then paused and lifted his index finger to his mouth. His tongue flicked out. He raised his eyebrows, and then took his finger into his mouth, sucking it clean. "Hmm."

Cal licked his lips and reached for Jim's fly, pretty sure they weren't going back to work any time soon.

CHAPTER TWELVE

1942

I T WAS STILL night when they climbed from the belly of the ship and fell into line on deck. No moon was visible, and clouds obscured their view of the southern stars. Sporadic firelight flickered on Guadalcanal Island in the distance. The sun would be up soon, but until then the world was only shadows.

Jim swiped at a bead of sweat on his forehead as he adjusted his pack and secured his rifle over his shoulder. Beside him, Cal smiled unconvincingly.

Leaning in, Cal whispered, "Look how many ships we have. All these men. The Japs don't stand a chance."

Nodding, Jim squinted at the island—a dark, mountainous shape looming before them, populated by an unseen enemy. He realized he'd never actually met a Japanese person. Now he'd kill these men or be killed.

Captain Brown's voice was loud and confident. "Moving out! Over the side and down the nets!"

One platoon at a time they did as they were told, clambering over the edge of the ship one man after the other. Jim threw his leg over and caught hold of the cargo net, putting his foot on one of the squares of rope. The net swayed—shaking with the exertions of the men who'd gone before him—and he thumped against the hull of the ship, which rocked in the swells of the ocean.

Peering down, he could barely make out the Higgins Boats waiting below. A heavy boot landed on his fingers and he bit back a cry as he forced himself to keep moving, gripping the vertical ropes to avoid being stepped on again.

About three feet above the waiting vessel, the net stopped short. Fear of plunging into the murky depths gripped Jim, but there was no time to hesitate. He stepped off and landed safely with a thump on the bottom of the boat. He let out the breath he'd been holding. His equipment must have weighed fifty pounds, and he wasn't sure he'd have been able to make the surface again if he'd missed the mark.

Cal steadied him, and they all took their places as the boats moved into assault formation, wave after wave lined up and fanning out toward Guadalcanal in the impending dawn. Crouching low below the gunwales, they kept their heads down. The boat vibrated beneath their feet as the engines kicked in, and they surged forward.

"Here we go," Cal muttered.

They'd trained in the boats so many times that the spray of salt water on Jim's face was strangely familiar and comforting. They each knew exactly what to do when they landed, and he could already imagine the gritty sand that would coat his tongue and sting his eyes as they stormed up the beach.

But this time, it wouldn't be NCOs waiting to critique their performance and offer a hand up or an encouraging clap on the back.

Icy terror coiled in Jim's stomach as the boat cut through the waves. For a desperate moment, he closed his eyes, praying to the Almighty that this was only a dream and he was safe back in Clover Grove, or even in the troop ship, where the war was still a mythical, faraway thing even as they steamed ever onward toward it.

"Hey. It's okay." Cal's voice trembled for the briefest of moments, belying his words. He cleared his throat. "We're going to be okay." He leaned in a little closer, and their helmets clanked together.

Jim nodded. He reached down with his left hand between them and grasped Cal's fingers for just a second. But when he would have let go, Cal held tight. Jim squeezed and moved his lips in a silent prayer, pleading with God to keep him and Cal safe. Him and Cal, and Sully and Speedy and Joe and Pistol, and their whole platoon and all the men in the boats around them.

Jim had tried not to think much of home since going to Parris Island. It only made him yearn to see his child and his land. But now Sophie's sweet face filled his mind and heart, and he imagined he could feel her chubby arms around his neck as he lifted her. A surge of panic tightened his chest. Would he see her grow? Would she ever really know him, or would he be nothing but a faded photograph on the wall?

With a sharp stab of guilt, he belatedly thought of Ann. Good, kind Ann. In these moments as he rushed toward his fate, he could admit to himself that there was a sadness in her eyes, and a longing in her soul that he didn't think he could ever fulfill. If only the Lord would spare him, he would try to be a better husband.

And Cal. Cal had to be saved. He clutched his friend's hand, opening his eyes to meet Cal's warm, steady gaze. As the rising sun began to lighten the sky and the clouds seemed to evaporate, they shared a final glance.

With a last squeeze, Cal let go. "See you on the other side."

Blood rushed in his ears as Jim eyed the shore, looking for any sign of the enemy. With a lurch, they hit ground and the men leaped over the side of the boat as one, splashing to land and dropping onto the beach. Everything was sound and movement, and Jim caught a glimpse of palm trees overhead as he propelled himself forward.

The order that had been drilled into them echoed in his mind, screaming in his ears to get off the beach. They were sitting ducks out in the open, and he pushed himself to the tree line, keeping low, his part of the mortar gun a heavy load. His line of sight became a tunnel, focused solely on the coconut grove beyond the beach.

Chest rising and falling, rifle at the ready and clutched in his hands, Jim made it to the trees and flopped onto his stomach. His helmet had slipped down his forehead and he pushed it up as he jerked his head left and right. He caught sight of Cal a few yards away. He exhaled in a rush and said a prayer of thanks that Cal was uninjured.

It was only then he realized it was far too quiet. No explosions split the air. No bullets screamed toward them. He and Cal shared a glance, looking around at the rest of their platoon in wonder. They'd taken the beach unopposed. The Japanese had turned tail and run.

Sully laughed out loud, and soon they were all smiling. As the minutes ticked by, the sun rose, birds chirped, and they gathered in the shade. Speedy grinned as he whacked open a coconut with his Ka-Bar. Soon more men followed suit, and Jim reached for one, eager to taste something other than salt and sand.

The sweet milk felt wonderfully cool as it slid down his throat. He passed his coconut to Cal, who tipped his head back and drank. His tongue darted out to swipe at a stray white drop on his lip. Jim felt a strange flutter in his belly and hoped the milk wouldn't make them sick.

Sully spoke up. "So…what are we supposed to do now?"

Big Joe slurped from a coconut shell. "Only been ten minutes. Don't worry, pipsqueak, they'll find something for us to do real soon."

Sully grinned. "That wasn't so hard. I reckon this war's gonna be a piece of cake."

1948

"ONE, TWO, THREE…"

A nail in his mouth, Jim looked up from the broken railing of the paddock fence and rested his hammer against his thigh for a moment. He watched as Cal spun in a circle near the barn, his eyes closed while the children ran and hid.

The bursts of affection and little thrills of desire that sparked across Jim's skin in Cal's presence left him perpetually distracted, but no matter how many times he chided himself to stop acting like a lovesick schoolgirl, all he could do was smile.

"Eight, nine, ten! Ready or not, here I come!"

Cal raced toward the barn. Adam was still too young to really understand the concept of hide and seek, and within seconds Cal cried out that he'd found him, and Adam's giggles floated out on the breeze. Jim had spotted Sophie ducking into the house, so the game would last for a while.

He went back to repairing the fence, humming to himself. Before long, Cal emerged from the barn with Adam secure on his shoulders, Adam laughing uproariously as Cal trotted toward the house. Jim waved as they went by, and Adam flapped his arm in return. Cal gave Jim a smile that did nothing to stop the giddiness Jim felt.

A voice in his head warned him for the umpteenth time that they had to be careful. At church that morning without Cal, Rebecca had commented that Jim seemed happy. Not that there was anything wrong with being happy, but folks would wonder. It hadn't even been a year since Ann's accident. Now the familiar litany of remorse settled over him heavily.

What if she was alive? Would I still feel this way for Cal? Why didn't I ever feel this for her? I should have been a better husband. Has this sickness always been there? It must be a sin, but I can't stop myself. Even if I could, I can't bring her back.

The thoughts tumbled through his mind endlessly. He pulled another nail from his pocket and hammered it into the railing as he told himself not to go any farther down that road.

Instead he thought of church, an equally uncomfortable topic. Jim knew he was sinning, but he couldn't help himself. Going to church had been part of his routine his whole life, but he had to admit he often daydreamed during services. He'd barely listened to a word the reverend had said that morning, instead wishing he was home with Cal. *If I'm going to hell, might as well skip church.*

He laughed out loud at the thought, and then looked around as if someone could have heard him. Sophie's muffled shriek from the house was followed by her bursting out of the kitchen door with Cal and Adam in pursuit.

"You can't catch me!" she yelled, heading toward the orchard.

Watching Cal with the children, Jim felt a fresh swell of affection. He'd always thought Cal would be a wonderful father, but now he knew why he hadn't married. All these years he'd been ignorant of Cal's true desires, and Jim couldn't help but feel foolish. He supposed Cal had hidden it well.

There was no hiding now. They stole moments together whenever they could, far out in the orchard, on the ground, or up against trees. Yesterday they'd come together in the dark recesses of the barn, kissing frantically as they stroked each other. It was always furtive and rushed, even when Jim knew there was no one about. They'd made a rule to never touch in the house, and obviously never when the children were present.

"Daddy, Daddy!" Sophie came around out of the trees, screeching as Cal swung her up into his arms and tickled her. Adam toddled along behind them clapping in delight, and Finnigan barked in the distance as he raced over.

"Daddy can't save you now! The monster caught you!" Cal roared.

Shaking off his thoughts, Jim put down his hammer and ran over to join in the fun as his children's laughter filled the air.

"WAS THIS THING even built in this century?" Cal eyed the tractor critically from the doorway of the barn.

Jim patted the rusty Fordson. "Nineteen-eighteen, I think."

"How much horsepower?"

"Twenty."

Cal climbed up on the seat. "Feels sturdy enough, I suppose."

The two back wheels were much larger and wider than the front, providing a secure base. "Of course it is. It works just fine."

"You know, I could buy a new one. It wouldn't cost much."

Jim snorted. "We have differing opinions on the relative value of 'much.'"

Cal smiled as he hopped down. "Fair enough. All right, I'll get the sprayer ready."

Jim sat on the tractor and started the engine, which belched to life. "See? Runs like a dream." He couldn't help but cough as a plume of smoke rose.

"Uh-huh." Cal passed him the jug of pesticide attached to a hose. "You know, it occurs to me that there were gas masks for this kind of stuff in the war. You sure we should be spraying this on the trees?"

"They say it's a different formula, and it's safe. Everyone's starting to use it, and I can't afford a plague of insects."

"All right. I'll go to town and pick up those other supplies we need and meet you out there in a couple of hours."

"I'm starting at the far end and I'll make my way back." Jim drove off through the sun-dappled orchard, going a few miles per hour. The spraying was straightforward enough, and he'd done three quarters of the trees by the time he spotted Cal walking toward him in the distance with a lunch basket in hand.

Jim left his pesticide supplies and drove away from where he'd been spraying. Cal stood against a tree, waiting for him with his legs crossed at the ankle. It was almost the end of June, and they both wore simple white T-shirts and jeans for work every day. Cal's trousers hugged his slim hips and lean thighs, the cotton of his T-shirt stretching across his firm chest.

When he'd arrived at Clover Grove after sitting behind a desk for a few years, he was still in good shape, but the manual labor and time in the sun made him look just as Jim remembered him in the Marines, save for the haircut. Cal smiled slyly as Jim turned off the tractor and hopped down.

"Like what you see?"

Jim flushed. "Was I that obvious?"

"Mm-hmm. But hey, I'm not complaining." Cal reached out and

tugged Jim against him, kissing him soundly. "Not complaining at all." He nuzzled Jim's neck, finding the spot under his ear that never failed to make Jim's knees weak.

Sighing, Jim ran his palms up Cal's sides. "We shouldn't. We're too close to the house."

"Mrs. O'Brien's busy polishing the silver and keeping Adam occupied." Cal reached down and rubbed Jim's cock through the rough denim. "Besides, I'm hungry."

"Did you bring sandwiches?" Jim shivered, leaning into Cal's touch.

Grinning wickedly, Cal ran his tongue across Jim's bottom lip and whispered, "I'm hungry for *you*."

Jim groaned, his cock twitching at the thought of the things Cal could do with his mouth. He hadn't had the nerve to do it to Cal yet, but Cal seemed to love sucking him, and it was irresistible. "I can't get enough of you," Jim muttered.

Cal murmured in Jim's ear hotly, "I'm all yours."

Jim steeled himself and stepped back. "Later this afternoon. We'll go check on the young fruit. No one will come out that far."

"I suppose you're worth waiting for." Cal kissed him softly.

They ate their sandwiches in easy silence, listening to the birds chirp. When it was time to get back to work, Cal clambered onto the tractor. "My turn to have a go. It's not often you get the chance to use an antique." He winked.

Chuckling to himself, Jim turned away to pack up the basket. Suddenly his ears rang with an explosion, the air sucked from his lungs as he flattened himself on the ground, arms over his head. The sunlight disappeared and it was the black of night, mud beneath him, cries all around as the fire and flesh rained down.

There was blood in his mouth, and Cal was there, saying something Jim couldn't understand, his hands on Jim. He breathed in acrid smoke, his lungs seizing, the burning filling his senses. His heart was going to burst, his blood pumping in his veins too hard, and oh God, oh God, oh God—

"Jim!"

He squirmed away, the mud squelching beneath him, getting into his mouth and mixing with the coppery blood, choking him as more explosions rent the air. There were cries all around, his own throat hoarse, and he realized he was screaming too. Then he was rolled over with a forceful push, and he held his hands out, waiting for a bayonet to end him—for a blade to carve into him.

"Open your eyes!"

Blinking, Jim saw snatches of sunlight and blue sky. Branches with green leaves. Cal's pale face. Cal—*Cal's all right, thank God*—was saying something again, and Jim shook his head, trying to clear the rushing in his ears. He gasped as his burning lungs expanded.

"It's okay. You're okay. Just breathe. Breathe." Cal brushed back Jim's hair. "You're all right. You're home in the orchard. It's over. You're home."

Taking a shuddering breath, Jim swallowed thickly. *Home.* He felt the grass beneath his back. No mud. No bodies. No bombs or gunfire. Just the trees and fresh air. He focused on Cal's pinched face. *I'm okay. He's here.*

Jim panted, sweating and tingling as the panic subsided. "She was…she…I couldn't…" He closed his eyes, trying to banish the memory.

"Shh. It's over." Cal caressed Jim's cheek and kissed his forehead. "It's over. You're here. You're safe." He held Jim close, lying beside him and touching him gently.

"I'm sorry." Tears prickled Jim's eyes, and he screwed them shut.

"The tractor backfired. Scared me too. It's okay."

Jim breathed deeply. *In and out. In and out.* "It's like I was there somehow. It was all happening again."

"We're never going back. It's over. I promise."

Jim clung to him, praying he was right. After a few more minutes of soothing caresses and whispered words of comfort, Cal grabbed his canteen and Jim sat up to drink with Cal's arm solid around his back.

Jim gulped down the water and swiped the back of his hand over his mouth. "Thanks. I'm fine. We should get back to work."

"Work can wait. Let's rest for a few more minutes. Come on."

Cal scooted over and leaned against the nearest tree, tugging Jim along. Jim didn't argue and stretched out perpendicular on his back, resting his head on Cal's thigh. Cal ran his fingers lightly through Jim's hair.

"Now will you let me buy a new tractor?" he asked, smiling softly.

Jim had to laugh. "I guess it's something to consider."

The breeze stirred the leaves overhead, and Jim closed his eyes. "Sometimes I can't believe we're really here. Both in one piece."

"There were times I thought it was impossible." Cal paused. "And I never thought I'd be here with you like this." He rested his palm on Jim's chest.

Eyes still shut, Jim reached up and covered Cal's hand with his own. "I'm so glad you're here." He wanted to say more but wasn't sure how to put his feelings into words.

Before Cal could reply, a cry rose on the wind. "Hello!"

It was Mrs. O'Brien's Irish lilt, and Jim shot up, he and Cal both on their feet in seconds. Jim peered around but couldn't see her anywhere. A moment later she and Adam appeared at the top of a gentle hill, coming from the direction of the house. She waved, and Adam charged forward.

Jim and Cal exhaled in unison. "It's all right. She didn't see anything," Cal said.

Jim nodded, his heart still racing. *Everything's fine. I'm okay. I'm okay.* Opening his arms wide, he put on a smile and swept up Adam. Mrs. O'Brien chatted with Cal as Adam babbled on to Jim, telling him something about carrots that Jim didn't quite understand. He caught Cal's gaze for a moment, and Cal smiled.

They were okay.

CHAPTER THIRTEEN

1942

A TRICKLE OF water from Cal's upended canteen dribbled onto his tongue. Despite the dense and oppressive jungle that oozed moisture, they hadn't encountered so much as a pond of fresh water as they hacked their way into the heart of Guadalcanal.

"Here." Jim offered his canteen.

"No. That's yours." Cal swatted at mosquitoes. It had been hot on the troop ship, but the jungle had a clammy humidity that soaked their uniforms and bloated their skin.

"I'm not thirsty."

Cal had to laugh. "Oh, really?"

Jim rolled his eyes. "We'll find water soon. Drink." He thrust the canteen into Cal's hand.

"If you insist." Cal took a grateful swig, careful not to drink it all, although his body screamed for him to drain it greedily. He'd never known such thirst.

Joe puffed on his cigarette. "Where d' y'all reckon we're headed?"

Pistol Pete shrugged. "Hell if I know." He called over to the clump of worried-looking officers crouched around a map. "Hey, where we goin'?"

One of the lieutenants called back. "Another part of the island."

Cal screwed the cap back on Jim's canteen. "That's specific. Good to know we're on the right island at least."

Sully's fair skin was flushed as red as his hair. "Man, I wish we could just get it over with. Let's go find the Nips and kick their asses."

"Easy as that?" Jim asked.

"Hell yes. You saw our navy out there! Even when the slant-eyed bastards came, they couldn't catch us." Sully puffed out his narrow chest proudly.

"We were lucky to get off that beach without casualties," Jim quietly replied.

"Lucky?" Pete winked at Sully. "It was all skill. We're US Marines! Japs don't know what they're in for, the poor bastards. Now come on, fellas. A little humidity ain't gonna get us down. Let's buck up."

Soon they were slogging through the jungle again, and as much as Cal wanted to buck up, it wasn't until he heard the unmistakable sound of running water that he got a spring in his step. Appearing as if by magic beyond a thick stand of trees, a river flowed swiftly amid the blooming vegetation. Speedy whooped and splashed in without a second thought. "Come on, boys! The water's fine!"

Abandoning their rifles and equipment on the bank, they charged in, splashing, laughing, and drinking desperately from cupped palms.

Jim tried to stop Cal with a hand on his arm. "We should use the purifying tablets."

"Uh-huh." Cal took another swallow, the cool water irresistible.

Beside him, Jim's resolve crumbled and they both drank deeply, kneeling in the current. Even the officers didn't bother with the tablets. Water had never tasted so good, and in that moment, Cal didn't care if it was poisoned by the Japs or carrying some tropical disease.

Laughing, Joe hauled Sully over his broad back, and soon most of the men roughhoused and played around in the water like they were at a picnic on a summer's day. Before Cal knew what was happening, Jim tumbled him back into the shallows by the riverbank, their legs entwined.

Jim pressed him down, their faces inches apart. He smiled mischievously as he caught Cal's wrists in his hands. "Say uncle."

Pulse thrumming, Cal's breath caught in his throat. The splashing and laughter of the other men faded around them, until all Cal could see were Jim's blue eyes and pink lips, his exhalations faintly tickling Cal's face. If only he could wrap his legs around Jim's hips and lift his head to capture Jim's mouth…

A furrow appeared between Jim's eyebrows, and his smile faded. His gaze fell to Cal's lips, and he licked his own—

"Moving out! Now!" His hands clenched, Captain Brown stood on the riverbank. "Christ almighty, you're sitting ducks making a racket they can probably hear clear across the island! Get up and move your sorry asses!"

Jim scrambled off Cal as if he'd been burned. With a shaky smile, he tugged Cal to his feet and clapped him on the back. "Next time I'll make you beg."

Cal tried to laugh as he gathered his gear and fell into step, willing the desire coursing through him to fade.

They marched on, the day never ending. As darkness settled in, the rain began. They set up a perimeter and waited—for what, they didn't know.

"Where are the Japs anyway? What're they waiting for?" Smith whispered.

Cal readjusted his poncho, which did little to protect him from the driving rain. "I guess we'll find out, Smithy." The boy rarely spoke, and Cal gave him what he hoped was an encouraging smile.

Jim shivered beside him, and Cal passed him a piece of dried meat. The rain leeched into them with a tenacious chill, and it was hard to believe they'd been so hot only hours ago. It was Parris Island all over again, but so much worse.

"Thanks." Jim nudged Cal's shoulder.

Cal nudged him back and kept his eyes peeled. The sounds of the jungle at night made them all jump and grip their weapons, but time and time again no enemy emerged. Water dripped endlessly from the canopy of leaves high above, and the jungle was alive, hissing in his ear. Sleep was an impossibility.

Yet as the hours ticked by, Cal's eyes finally grew heavy, and he curled up on the muddy ground…

Ka-boom.

Heart in his throat as the earth trembled, Cal bolted up. Above them, the sky was red, and for a moment Cal thought it was surely their blood—that the Japs had come and eviscerated them in their sleep. Beside him, Jim stared with his mouth open. His pale skin was bathed in crimson as the flares glowed in the night sky.

Planes roared overhead, and from a distance, explosions rumbled, shaking the ground. Light flashed in the darkness, accompanied by great claps of thunder, and for a moment, Cal wanted to believe it was only a storm, Mother Nature displaying her might and putting them all in their place as they huddled together.

It went on and on, and they could only watch.

When dawn broke, they made their way down the jungle slope and through a field of kunai grass that reached to their shoulders with its razor edges. Hours passed with the sun fiery overhead.

"Didn't we just come from the beach?" Pete grumbled. "Why are we goin' back?"

But onward they marched. When they passed another battalion going inland, the others barely acknowledged them despite H Company's friendly greeting. The other men's eyes were hollow as they trudged on in filthy uniforms. Cal and Jim shared a glance, and Cal's stomach clenched.

As the beach came into view, Cal relaxed at the sight of a supply vehicle. They could all use more cigarettes already. Beside him, Jim inhaled sharply, and Cal lifted his gaze beyond the sand to where the fleet was docked.

A few wrecked ships still smoldered in the shimmering blue water stretching from Guadalcanal to Florida Island. Cal struggled for words as he took in the destruction of the naval force that had seemed so mighty only the day before.

Jim's voice was steady as ever, but barely more than a whisper. "They're gone."

Cal shook his head. "What are we going to do?"

A sergeant's bark cut through the air. "Forward march!"

One by one, they fell into line.

1948

CRICKETS SERENADED THEM through the open door of the barn, the night settled in and the half moon peeking out from the clouds. A lantern on a metal hook cast a soft yellow glow over a new worktable, where Jim sanded a plank of wood as Cal took the measurements of a finished piece.

"I think you missed your calling."

Cal glanced up. "Hmm?"

"I never knew you were such a good carpenter."

"I wouldn't go that far." He examined the plans he'd drawn and checked the measurements. "I loved making model planes and ships when I was a kid. Building a dollhouse shouldn't be too different. Aside from the fact that we have to make the pieces instead of them coming in a box."

"At least we have until the end of August to work it out." Jim rubbed down the ragged edges of the wood.

"Still have to figure out what to get you for your birthday."

Jim chuckled. "Me? No, no. It's Sophie's day now."

"Just because you two share a birthday doesn't mean you don't get a present."

"I have everything I need. Besides, she was the best gift I could ever ask for." He smiled fondly. "She'll love this dollhouse."

"Let's hope we can keep it a secret. I wouldn't put it past her to do some snooping."

Jim laughed. "Me either. But she and Adam were out like a light, so at least we're safe for tonight. Besides, it's just a pile of wood right now. We'll have to be careful once we start putting it together."

They worked in comfortable silence, and Cal double checked his calculations. After a while he found himself watching Jim sanding. They'd both changed into light cotton button-front shirts when they'd cleaned up before dinner, but now Jim wore just his sleeveless white undershirt. Freckles dotted his arms from all the time spent in the sun, and his lean muscles flexed as he worked the wood.

Jim glanced up and smiled hesitantly. "What?"

Cal put down his pencil and slowly rounded the table. "You work too hard."

"Do I?" Jim turned to face him.

Cal took the sandpaper and stepped in closer. He kissed Jim's neck, and Jim tilted his head eagerly, his hands dropping to Cal's waist. Cal chuckled low in his throat. "You like that?"

Jim nodded, and Cal went back to kissing, pushing him against the sturdy worktable as he teased Jim's tender skin. God, how he wanted to bend Jim over it and feel his heat. Make him moan and writhe.

He took a deep breath. *Slowly. Slowly.*

"Can I ask you…"

"Hmm?" Cal sucked at the juncture of Jim's neck and shoulder as he caressed his back through the thin undershirt.

"It's…" Jim trailed off.

"Ask me anything." Cal licked a bead of sweat from the hollow of Jim's collarbone.

There was only silence for a long moment, and then Jim mumbled, "Does it really feel good to…" He trailed off.

Cal lifted his head. "What?"

Jim wouldn't meet his eyes. "To…put things…*there.*"

It took Cal a moment to understand what he was asking. He smiled widely. "Oh, yeah. It sure does." He skimmed his palm over Jim's ass. "When you're ready I'll show you how good it can be."

"I watched you," Jim blurted. His cheeks reddened. "A few nights after Mabel kicked you. I heard a noise and I went to make sure you were all right, and you were…"

"You were watching?" Cal thought back, remembering his open legs and his fingers twisting in his ass as he jerked his dick. His smile only grew wider, desire coiling in his belly.

"I'm sorry. I know I shouldn't have." Jim shook his head. "I don't understand what's wrong with me."

"There's nothing wrong with you." Cal bit back his frustration at Jim's ever-present sense of shame. Kissing him softly, he wrapped Jim in his arms. "*Nothing.*"

"But—"

"No buts about it." He kissed him again, and then whispered in his ear. "Did you like it?"

Shivering, Jim nodded.

"Did watching me finger myself make you hard?"

Another jerky nod and strangled breath were Jim's reply. Cal reached down, pressing the heel of his hand against Jim's swelling cock. He rubbed through the denim. "How long did you watch?"

"Until you were done," Jim mumbled.

A groan escaped Cal's lips as he imagined Jim hard and wanting him, secretly watching. He met Jim's mouth, plunging his tongue inside as he took his hand away and pushed his thigh between Jim's. "Did you jerk yourself off after?"

His breath catching, Jim rocked his hips against Cal's. He nodded.

They kissed again, panting into each other's mouths as they ground their cocks together through their jeans. Pulling back, Cal put his finger to Jim's lips. Jim opened his mouth and Cal dipped it inside. After a moment of hesitation, Jim sucked on it.

"Jesus, you're a natural," Cal muttered.

He pulled his hand away and slipped it down the back of Jim's jeans, lightly caressing along his crack. When Jim tensed, Cal kissed him again slowly. "It's okay. Relax. Trust me."

Exhaling, Jim nodded. Eyes closed, he leaned into Cal, shuddering when Cal teased his hole. Cal wished he had some lubricant, but he wasn't going anywhere at the moment, so they'd have to make do. Lifting his hand again, he spit on his fingertip before rubbing it into Jim's opening. Jim was rock hard against him as Cal pushed the tip of his finger inside.

Kissing Jim's neck again, Cal stroked gently with his free hand, up Jim's side and across his back, keeping him relaxed as his body opened. Slowly and surely, Cal worked his way inside with his index finger. When he pulled it out, Jim gasped, frowning. Cal just smiled and unzipped Jim's pants before turning him around to get a better angle. Cal pushed his finger in slowly as he kissed the back of Jim's neck.

Jim was so tight and hot, and Cal moaned hoarsely, imagining his cock buried inside. The sound seemed to loosen something in Jim, and Cal inched his finger in farther. He began moving it slightly, and Jim pushed back as he braced his hands on the table and made needy little sounds in the back of his throat. Patiently, Cal went deeper, reaching around to rub Jim's cock and pull it out of his drawers. He stroked it roughly and Jim rutted into his hand.

Then Cal crooked his finger, finding just the right spot, and Jim gasped, shuddering. Cal pressed the little gland again, and again, and again as he jerked Jim's cock harder. Crying out, Jim came in a rush. His ass clamped down on Cal's finger.

Cal turned Jim's head to kiss him messily as his own balls tightened. "Jesus, Jim. So good." Cal freed his cock and jerked himself, his moan echoing off the rafters as he spilled over his fist.

Kissing tenderly, they caught their breath. As Cal gently pulled his finger out of Jim's ass, he smiled. "That's just a taste of what it can be."

As the pleasure receded and reality returned, this was when Jim usually withdrew into himself. Cal tapped under Jim's chin, focusing Jim's gaze on him. "Don't be sorry, all right?"

"All right." Jim smiled and exhaled an uneven breath.

They kissed a last time and stepped away from each other to

straighten their clothes and clean up. Cal ran a hand through his hair, smoothing it down. "I'll go check on the kids while you finish up."

"Thanks." Jim's hands were shaking as he picked up the sandpaper again.

At the door, Cal turned. "By the way, you can watch me anytime you like. In fact, I strongly encourage it."

Jim's warm laughter followed him into the night.

CAL WAS JUST finishing washing up and changing into a clean shirt and khakis when he heard Sophie barreling up the stairs. "Uncle Cal!" She skidded to a stop in the doorway of Cal's room, her pigtails swaying.

"How was your last day of school?"

She grinned and thrust a piece of paper toward him. "Look at my report card."

Cal unfolded the paper and scanned the rows of grades—A, A, A, A, A—except for one B-plus in geography. He whistled. "Beauty *and* brains, huh?"

She giggled. "Yep."

Jim's voice rang from downstairs. "Sophie! Set the table, please."

"Come on, we'll do it together." Cal gave her a squeeze and they went down.

He found himself looking forward to their dinners around the kitchen table. After a hard day's work outside, it was relaxing to sit down together and ask Sophie questions about school. Adam was talking more and more each day, and Cal wondered what kind of boy he'd grow up to be.

Jim swallowed a bite of the roast beef Mrs. O'Brien had prepared. "I spoke to your grandparents yesterday."

"About what?" Sophie asked.

"Now that school's over, we thought it would be nice for you and Adam to stay with them for a few days. Would you like that?"

Adam looked to his sister, waiting for her response.

Sophie nodded. "Grandpa said he'd take me fishing this summer!"

Adam nodded along. "Fishing."

Jim chuckled and wiped a dribble of mashed potato from Adam's chin. "Glad you're in agreement."

Anticipation sparked up Cal's spine. "When are they going?"

"I'm driving them up tomorrow afternoon. Ron will bring them back on Sunday. It'll give Mrs. O'Brien a few days off as well."

"Sounds good." Cal kept his tone casual despite his excitement at the thought of four days alone with Jim.

"Can I bring a suitcase, Daddy? I've never used a suitcase before." Sophie's face glowed.

"Sure." Jim smiled at her, and then his gaze met Cal's. They both looked away quickly, and Cal counted the hours until they'd be alone.

The next evening he waited under the waning sun, leaning against the paddock fence. He'd smoked six cigarettes, had two beers, and played fetch with Finnigan for more than an hour. He glanced at his watch again. Eight o'clock. Jim said he'd have dinner with the Sheltons and then drive back. Which meant he should be back any minute, since it was roughly a two-hour drive and they surely ate supper early on a dairy farm.

Finnigan barked, nudging Cal's leg with a stick. Cal dutifully tossed it near the barn. The green paint was starting to peel off quite badly in some places, and Cal wondered if he could get some fresh paint in town as a surprise for Jim. Finnigan bounded back with the stick, but before he reached Cal, he dropped it and looked toward the lane with ears perked.

A moment later, Cal heard the rumble of the pickup, and he shuddered with anticipation. While Finnigan ran to greet his master, Cal leaned back against the fence and picked up his beer bottle, taking a long pull. He watched Jim climb out of the truck and crouch down to pet Finnigan before walking over to the paddock.

The setting sun cast a pink glow over the orchard into the distance, and Jim's fair hair shone. Cal's breath caught in his throat. "Everything go all right?" he asked.

"Yeah. They didn't want me to leave when it came time for it, but they're settled now. It'll be nice for them to spend some time with their grandparents. Nice for Lorraine and Ronald too."

Cal could hardly keep still. "And nice for us."

Jim nodded, his gaze intent as he stepped closer. "Yeah." He leaned into Cal and brushed their lips together. Then he seemed to suddenly get nervous and glanced around.

"It's just us." Cal smiled and called over his shoulder. "Mabel will keep our secret, won't you, girl?"

They both looked at the cow, who stood near the edge of the paddock away from the horses, chewing lazily and regarding them with a dim expression.

Jim laughed. "I think we're safe with Mabel. Finnigan will keep her in line. But I don't know—the horses tend to tell tales."

"Better give them a good story, then. C'mere." Cal kissed him slowly, sliding his tongue into Jim's mouth.

Jim kissed him back and they sighed into each other as the stars twinkled into sight. For long minutes they just kissed, their tongues exploring and sliding together, wet and deep. Cal's skin tingled from head to toe, and he moaned into Jim's mouth at the thought that they would have the whole night alone together, not to mention the next several days.

"Let's go to bed," Jim muttered, his voice gravelly.

"I thought we weren't allowed to do anything in the house," Cal teased.

Jim squeezed Cal's cock through his trousers. "No rules this weekend."

Cal could only nod, and they stumbled to the house, kissing and touching as they practically ran inside and kicked off their boots. Cal led the way upstairs, going straight to his room. Ann's presence still lingered in Jim's bedroom, and Cal wanted this to be a fresh start.

They peeled off their clothing with sharp movements, and Cal felt like a nervous teenager again. The rising moon shone through the gauzy curtains, and the desire that took hold as Cal looked at Jim's naked flesh stole the breath from his lungs. Without another word, he dropped to his knees at Jim's feet, swallowing Jim's cock between his lips.

He could suck Jim for hours with the heavy heat of that shaft on his tongue, but tonight he needed more. He released Jim with a wet *smack*, and Jim moaned at the loss, fingers grasping at Cal's hair. Cal walked Jim to the bed, urging him onto his back. Straddling Jim's hips, he bent over and they kissed.

Although he wanted nothing more than to impale himself on Jim's hard cock, Cal took his time, kissing his way down Jim's chest and licking his nipples.

Jim was practically vibrating. "Please, Cal. I need…"

Lifting his head, Cal smiled. "What?"

Jim pulled him up, kissing him hard. "You. I need you."

Cal reached for the small jar of petroleum jelly he'd left on the side table. He knew Jim didn't have any experience with men—hell, not much experience with women from the sound of it—so Cal took the lead. On his knees, he reached back with slick fingers and pushed one into his hole. His eyes fluttered.

Jim watched avidly as Cal worked himself open. Reaching up, Jim caressed Cal's chest, teasing Cal's nipples with his fingertips. "I love looking at you like this," he murmured.

Excitement humming in his veins, Cal worked a second finger inside himself, and then a third. Then he couldn't wait any longer and pulled out, scooping up more jelly to slick onto Jim's proud cock. He edged forward on his knees and positioned Jim at his hole.

Cal lowered himself, keeping steady as the head of Jim's cock pushed against him. "Breathe," he whispered. In the moonlight he could see that Jim was holding his breath.

Jim's Adam's apple bobbed. "I don't want to hurt you."

"You won't." Cal lowered himself farther, Jim's cock inching into the tight ring of muscle.

"Are you sure? It feels so tight." He moaned. "*So good.*"

Spreading his legs, Cal relaxed and slid down, the sweet friction as Jim filled him bringing a groan to his lips. "Wanted this for so long. Wanted you." He couldn't believe it was really happening.

Jim bucked up, his eyes dark with lust and lips parted. "It feels so good. I didn't know…I didn't think…"

His thighs flexing, Cal began to ride Jim's cock, reveling in the burn and stretch as Jim filled him from root to tip. "God, Jim. Oh fuck. *Fuck.*" Obscenities tripped off Cal's tongue, his cock jutting out as waves of pleasure washed over him, building the fire in his belly with each down stroke.

Jim gripped Cal's thighs, rocking his hips up and fucking Cal with low groans and gasps, their eyes locked together. Sweat gathered on their skin, shining in the pale light as they grunted, moving faster and harder, Cal slamming down onto Jim's cock as Jim surged up into him.

When Jim hit the right spot, Cal cried out. "Yes. There. *There.* Again." He reached for his cock, jerking it in time to Jim's thrusts, desperate for completion even though part of him never wanted it to end. But the animal desire drove him on, overpowering him.

With a cry, his balls drew up and he exploded, spurting onto Jim's chest, splattering his chin. Limbs trembling, Cal shook and gasped Jim's name as the pleasure coursed through him.

Jim was so stiff and ready, and Cal squeezed down. With a shout, Jim came, his head tipped back and eyes closed as he shuddered. His release was hot and wet deep in Cal, and Cal wanted to keep him inside for as long as he could. Panting, he leaned his palms on Jim's chest as the aftershocks faded.

With a shaky hand, Jim cupped Cal's face. "Thank you."

After kissing gently, they held each other close, and Cal imagined their hearts beat in unison.

CHAPTER FOURTEEN

1942

MOSQUITOES BUZZED INCESSANTLY, and Jim batted them away from his face. As the early rays of dawn penetrated the jungle canopy, the flies came to life in the squalid heat. The stench of the dead invaded Jim's nose, and he breathed shallowly. It was no longer such a shock—the sight and smell of bodies—but Jim hoped he'd never get used to it.

The river, no more than thirty feet across, was littered with the Japanese, who had kept coming, wave after wave. Too close for mortars, so Jim, Cal, and Sully had fired on the enemy with their rifles and what little ammunition they had, thankful for the machine gunners.

Beside Jim, Cal cleaned his rifle silently. Sully, feverish and likely infected with malaria, leaned against a tree with his arms wrapped around his knees. He muttered, jerking restlessly, and finally Jim asked what he was saying.

"Wanted to die."

Cal raised his head, and he and Jim shared a glance. Cal cleared his throat. "What's that, buddy?"

Sully didn't seem to hear, his eyes fixed on some faraway point. Jim took a candy bar from his sodden pack and crawled over to the boy. "Here, have some breakfast." He unwrapped the chocolate and held it up to Sully's mouth. "Go on. You're fine. We're all fine."

"I know." Sully took a bite, chewing slowly. "It's those crazy bastards. It was like they wanted to die."

"Not that they wanted to. They just weren't afraid to." Cal spoke quietly.

"For what? I mean, what the hell are we doing here?" Sully's sunburnt skin flushed even redder.

"We're protecting the airfield," Jim answered. He knew that wasn't what Sully was asking, but he had no other answer to give.

Sully didn't say anything else, but at least finished the candy bar. After he tossed the crumpled wrapper toward the river, he blinked. "Where'd that come from? All they've given us is that damned rice."

"I had it from before. Don't really like chocolate." Jim could feel Cal's eyes on him, and willed Cal not to call out the lie.

"Thanks, Johnny. That hit the spot." Sully wiped his stained sleeve over his forehead. He closed his eyes and fell into a fitful sleep, still sitting up.

When Cal arched an eyebrow, Jim just shrugged. "He needed it more," he whispered.

Cal was about to reply when their attention was drawn to a fellow Marine splashing into the fetid water, wading straight to the bloating corpses of the enemy. When he reached the first, he yanked open the man's mouth.

Joe's drawl drifted across the water. "What'cha doin' there?"

The Marine, who Jim didn't recognize, grinned. "Lot of these bastards got gold in their teeth." He held up a pair of pliers. "I'm gonna go home a rich man."

Jim's stomach churned. He'd heard others talking about collecting souvenirs, and many of the men were desperate for an officer's saber. He could understand the satisfying feeling of triumph such items could bring, even though the thought of robbing the dead didn't sit right. But this was something else entirely.

Cal shook his head. "All yours, pal."

Joe snorted. "Not all of us got your kind of money, Hollywood." Yet he didn't move from his tree stump.

As the Marine continued from body to body, the rain began. At first it was a welcome relief from the heat, but the short bursts of rainfall had been getting longer. Cal sighed and shrugged his poncho over his head. "Ever feel like we're never going to be dry again?"

"Absolutely." Jim put on his own poncho, not that it did much good.

"My uniform's starting to rot. If we don't get the chance to dry off soon we're going to be fighting the Japs stark raving naked."

Jim chuckled, even though the thought of Cal naked made him feel a strange surge. He shuddered. "Not enough quinine for all of us either. If the Japs don't get us, these mosquitoes will."

"Silly place to have a war if you ask me. Most uncivilized," Cal said before glancing at Sully, who slept with his mouth open. Cal inched closer to Jim and lowered his voice. "We'd better keep an eye on him."

Jim nodded. "How long do you think we'll be out here?"

"Hard to say. Let's just hope the Japs give up on that airfield sooner rather than later."

The rain didn't deter the gold hunter, who continued on, tossing bodies aside once he'd yanked out their teeth or determined them to be of no use. Some of the men cheered him on. Cal leaned into Jim's side, and Jim was glad of the warm pressure.

"What's that?" Joe pointed upriver.

Jim squinted into the driving rain. "What?"

"It's water, Joe. Lots of it," Cal replied.

"Ya don't say, Hollywood." Joe harrumphed, but smiled. "In the water. Coming toward us."

Moving onto his knees, Jim peered intently. After a moment he made out a V shape. "I see it. Yeah, coming this way."

Twenty feet from where the Marine mined for gold in Japanese mouths, one of the bodies suddenly shook wildly and then disappeared beneath the murky surface. Intent on his hunt, the man continued on, not noticing amid the pouring rain.

"What the fuck was that?" someone cried out.

Cal shot to his feet. "Jesus Christ, it's a croc!" To the Marine in the river he shouted, "Get out of the water!"

"There's another one!"

"Holy cow!"

"Get your ass back here!"

Cries rang out, and the man splashed back to shore, whooping as if it was a game. Jim's gaze was riveted to the carnage as the crocodiles ripped into the corpses. He heard the exclamations of the other men and the triumphant crowing of the gold hunter safe and sound, but couldn't look away.

"Could be us. Probably will be. Gonna be me," Sully muttered, awake again and trembling.

Jim tore his gaze away but swore he could still hear the crunching and tearing flesh.

Cal sat beside Sully and threw his arm over the boy's shoulders. "Nah, those crocs aren't interested in you, kid."

A ghost of a smile teased Sully's lips. "Why's that?"

"You kidding? You're all gristle and bone! They're meat eaters! You're safe as can be." Cal patted his own stomach, which was as lean as any man's in the unit. "Now me, I'm in trouble. I bet I'd taste absolutely delicious. Especially with a good merlot, but I don't think those bastards are too picky."

Sully laughed, and Joe joined in, talking about how tasty he'd be to the crocs as well. But Jim had to close his eyes, overcome by the notion of Cal being torn apart by one of the beasts. He hated the thought of Cal dying here with the flies and maggots devouring him as efficiently as the crocodiles might.

"Jim?" Cal's hand grasped his arm. "You okay?"

Forcing a nod, Jim opened his eyes. Cal peered at him, his brow furrowed, and Jim resisted a wild urge to reach up and smooth it out. "Yeah. Fine."

Over the rush of the rain and splashing of the crocodiles at feast, a growing drone settled into their bones and filled the thick air. A voice called out, "Christ, in this weather? Give us a fucking break!"

"If they wait for a day without rain we're gonna be stuck in this jungle forever!" someone answered.

As one, they gathered their equipment and hurried away from the river, back into the slit trenches farther into the jungle. Jim urged Sully in first, grasping his arm when Sully stumbled. Then Jim dove into the muck, Cal right behind him. Their bodies were pressed close, and Cal's arm slid about Jim's waist as they ducked their heads. The approaching aircraft grew louder, the whine of the bombs masked by the rain. Yet there was no mistaking the shudder of the earth as the explosions began.

1948

As Jim stirred, he became aware of a heavy warmth against his side, and a leg thrown over his own where he was sprawled on his back. The memory of what he and Cal had done flooded back with a spark of desire that sent blood rushing to his cock. He opened his eyes to find Cal watching him with his head propped on his hand.

Smiling, Cal caressed Jim's chest. "Morning."

"Morning." The pale light of dawn brightened the horizon through the window. "I think this is the first time you've woken up before me."

Cal chuckled. "Probably." He leaned over and brushed their lips together. "But I like watching you sleep."

Jim would likely have been embarrassed to hear anyone else say that, but he only smiled. While he'd considered Cal his best friend for years, now that he'd been *inside* him there was a new intimacy that made Jim's heart soar. "I don't mind at all."

"Good, because I'm not planning on stopping."

"Enjoy it while you can."

Cal's smile faltered, his hand frozen where he'd been tracing lazy circles on Jim's chest. "Are you sorry? I thought…I thought we both—"

"No, I didn't mean it like that." He took Cal's hand, threading their fingers together. "I just wish it could always be like this. Waking up together. But when the children are back…"

"Right." Cal exhaled heavily. "I know. It's the way it has to be. We'll make it work." His smile returned.

Jim had to swallow hard over the lump in his throat. "I don't know what I ever did to deserve you."

"I'm the lucky one." Cal kissed him again. "Feeling okay?"

Jim nodded. "Better than okay." He touched Cal's chest, playing with the dark hair scattered there. "I didn't think it could be like that." It was positively surreal to be lying naked in a bed with Cal and for it to feel so *right*.

Cal kissed him lightly. "All that and much, much more. We're only getting started."

"It was…okay for you? I'm a bit out of my depth." Cal had certainly seemed satisfied, yet Jim couldn't help but worry.

"Better than okay. I told you, you're a natural. It's different with you, Jim. So much better."

The question that had quietly been circling Jim's mind for some time tripped off his tongue. "There hasn't been anyone else?"

Cal frowned. "I haven't been living as a monk the last three years, but…"

"No, I mean anyone else you cared for. You didn't think we'd ever be together, so was there anyone else you thought might be…special?" Now that the question hung in the air, Jim wasn't sure what he wanted the answer to be.

"Would it bother you if I said yes?"

The thought of Cal with another man stabbed him to the core with jealousy. "Yes. But I know that's not fair, and I'd never want you to be lonely."

"The truth is, I've been with other men over the years. But I knew a long time ago no one else could hold a candle to you. I tried to forget you. Tried to move on." He traced Jim's lips with his fingertips. "In my wildest dreams, I never thought you'd want me back."

Jim's heart clenched at the thought of how painful it had been for Cal keeping his feelings bottled up for so long. *Feelings for me.* "I want you so much. Truly."

Then they were kissing again, and Jim spread his legs and tugged Cal on top of him. Their tongues met, mouths open as they explored each other. The feel of skin on skin, of Cal's body against his, was dizzying. He touched every part of Cal he could reach.

They were both fully hard before long, and Jim reached between them and grasped Cal's cock. "I want this. Nothing between us ever again."

"You sure?" Cal licked his lips.

Part of him wasn't sure at all. He stroked Cal's throbbing dick with his hand, feeling all around it. Would he like it inside him? Would it hurt? Jim was sure it would, and the anticipation was edged with anxiety. But the greater anxiety came from the thought that he might miss his opportunity. He nodded.

"We don't have to. There's no rush." Cal brushed Jim's hair back from his forehead.

Jim ran his fingers up and down Cal's shaft. "I've waited long enough. I want to know how it feels. I want to know how you felt last night. I want everything. I want you to…" He trailed off, knowing Cal would get the idea. He let go of Cal's cock and pulled him closer.

Cal's lips curved up. "What? What do you want me to do?" He squeezed his hand down below Jim's balls, teasing the sensitive skin and nearing Jim's hole.

"You *know*."

"Sorry. I'm really not sure what you're after."

Jim groaned. The devil was really going to make him say it. "I want you to…do that."

"Ohh, *that*." Cal put on a contemplative expression. "Although I'm still not crystal clear." He circled Jim's opening with his fingertip. "I want to hear you say it."

"Cal! For goodness' sake." Jim pushed back against Cal's finger. "*Please.*"

"Hmm. I think I have a notion of what you're asking for." Cal ducked his head, his lips at Jim's ear as he teased his hole. "Do you want me to fuck your tight little ass with my thick, hard cock?"

The dirty words sent a bolt of desire gasping through Jim. He nodded vigorously. His throat was dry, and he took a breath, gritting the words out. "*Fuck me.*"

Cal lifted his head, grinning. "Why didn't you just say so?"

Jim's response was swallowed by Cal's playful kiss, and they both laughed as Cal reached for the jar on the side table. But as he knelt between Jim's thighs and pushed a slick finger inside, their smiles faded, and they kissed with purpose.

"Breathe," Cal murmured as he edged in a second finger.

It burned, and Jim didn't think he'd ever felt quite so vulnerable as he did with his legs splayed, ass lifted, Cal easing him open with his fingers. He concentrated on breathing in and out, his eyes locked on Cal's.

Cal leaned over to rub their noses together. "Trust me."

"I do."

Cal kissed him tenderly. "I won't hurt you." He slicked himself and lifted up one of Jim's legs, hooking it over his shoulder. The head of Cal's cock nudged Jim's hole. "Try to relax."

Jim nodded. The burning sensation returned as Cal began to push in. Cal had seemed to get such pleasure when Jim had been inside him, but at the moment Jim couldn't imagine how. The stretch was undeniably painful, and when he glanced down he was shocked to see Cal was barely inside.

"Look at me."

Jim's gaze flicked back up to Cal's face. Cal leaned down to kiss him, and as he did, he pushed farther in. Jim gasped at the burn, but as Cal coaxed him open, pleasure returned in flickers. Cal steadily inched in, kissing him softly. The slow progression continued until amazingly, Jim could feel Cal's wiry hair against his ass. Jim's erection had flagged, and Cal took him in hand, stroking lightly.

Jim had never felt so *much*. He struggled to breathe.

"Okay?" Cal pressed little kisses to Jim's forehead and cheeks.

"I am. I'm okay." Cal throbbed inside him, and Jim experimented with squeezing his inner muscles, making Cal moan. Jim could feel the strain in Cal's body—the struggle to go slowly and stay in control.

"Need to move," Cal gritted out. "You're so tight. God, Jim."

As Cal began to rock into him, pulling out a few inches and thrusting back in, the pleasure increased. Jim found the rhythm, moving with Cal, relaxing and taking his cock deeper inside him. The need was primal, and his whole body blazed with it, sweat dripping down his forehead.

He'd felt the same way the night before as Cal rode him, and now as Cal filled him—*completed* him—Jim cried out. He bent his leg around Cal's waist and dug his heel into Cal's back. His other leg was still hooked over Cal's shoulder, and Jim felt like he was being turned inside out.

"Yes, yes," he muttered.

"Like my cock stretching you?"

Gnawing his lip, Jim nodded.

"You like being fucked? You want me to come inside you?" Cal asked as he thrust in and out.

"Yes," Jim gasped. He felt utterly wanton as Cal opened him, and he never wanted it to stop. "I want it all. All of you."

They both moaned, panting as they approached the edge. Cal jerked Jim's cock roughly, kissing him messily and muttering and moaning as they rocked together. Then Cal hit a glorious spot that somehow made the world spin, and Jim's pleasure overtook him. He called out as pure bliss sang in his veins, washing over him in waves.

Cal thrust several more times before letting go, painting his seed deep inside Jim. Marking him forever. This was the kind of love Jim hadn't thought existed, and oh yes, he loved Cal. He may go to hell for it, but Jim knew the truth. Accepted it.

With a final groan, Cal collapsed, and Jim let his legs flop down to the mattress. He wrapped his arms around Cal. Jim was flushed from head to toes—warm and *safe*. They kissed slowly.

The sun was up and there was work to be done, but Jim pulled the covers over them and held Cal close, alone in their own private world for just a little while longer.

As HE TURNED the pickup onto the wet county road, Jim felt the press of Cal's hand on his thigh. He raised an eyebrow. "Should I pull over?"

Cal barked out a laugh. "Well, I wouldn't say no. But I guess we should get *some* work done today, even if it's only buying groceries. Just wondering how you're doing."

"I was fine this morning, and I'm still fine." Cal's concern gave Jim a warm glow in his chest to accompany the flutters he felt in his stomach whenever they touched. He supposed that would go away eventually, but he hoped not. "More than fine."

"Not too sore?"

Jim shifted on the seat. "Just a little. But—" He hesitated before forging on. "I like it. It's as though I can still feel it. Feel *you*."

Cal dipped his hand farther and caressed Jim's inner thigh. "Keep talking like that and you'll definitely need to pull over. Somewhere with a lot of trees and no people. In this rain, no one will be around."

The desire flooding Jim's groin sent a shiver up his spine. "Extremely tempting." Ahead, the rooftops of Tivoli came into sight. "But we should wait until we get home."

With an exaggerated sigh, Cal removed his hand. "Always playing hard to get, Jim Bennett."

Jim chuckled. "This time I'll only make you wait an hour or two instead of six years."

Cal reached out again, taking Jim's hand off the wheel and squeezing briefly. "It was worth the wait."

The warmth in Jim's chest spread, and he smiled as he pulled up to the curb by the general store. When he turned off the engine and looked at the sidewalk, he groaned. "Great."

"What?"

"Rebecca." He pointed to where she walked down the street in their direction holding a floral umbrella. "She's bound to talk our ears off. So much for being home before long."

"What's your problem with her?" Cal frowned.

Jim blinked. "I don't have a *problem*. I'm just eager to get home." He glanced around, even though he knew no one could hear them inside the truck. "Eager to be with you. We only have a few days alone."

But Cal's expression didn't soften. "No, that's not it. What is it about her?"

It was Jim's turn to frown. "I don't know. Why does it matter?"

"I just feel badly for her. She's lonely, Jim. She wants a friend. It's not like you to be unkind."

"I never said I didn't like her! I just…" Jim grasped for the right words, but nothing came. "And how do you know she's lonely? You met her for, what, five minutes?"

"Actually, we had coffee last month one day when I came into town."

Jim was taken aback. "Oh. Why didn't you mention it?"

"I didn't think I had to."

"That's not what I meant." Jim was adrift, not sure how things had suddenly become so tense.

"I'm going to say hello." Cal opened the door and waved to Rebecca as he hopped out.

Jim hurried to join them on the sidewalk under the general store's awning, which protected them from the rain.

Rebecca smiled brightly. "Good afternoon, Cal. Jim."

"You look lovely today," Cal said.

In her light blue summer dress that complemented her blonde hair, she did indeed look lovely. But what was Cal doing? *Is he trying to make me jealous?* Jim cleared his throat. "Yes, you're looking well, Rebecca."

"Thank you, gentlemen. I've decided I'm not going to let a little rain dampen my spirits today. Jim, how is Sophie enjoying her summer vacation so far?"

"She's visiting her grandparents. I'm sure she and Adam are having a nice time." With a flare of guilt he realized he'd thought of little else but Cal and himself since he'd driven back from the Catskills.

He hoped they were getting along all right with Lorraine and Ronald, and weren't missing home too much. He should call to make sure. He should have called first thing in the morning but had been too distracted. A flush traveled up his neck.

"I'm sure. That'll be nice for them to spend some time where their mother grew up."

The previous warmth in Jim's chest now burned hollowly, the thought of Ann increasing his guilt tenfold. He cleared his throat. "Yes."

"And nice for you two to have some time to yourselves, I'm sure."

The bottom of Jim's stomach dropped out, and he forced his lungs to expand. "What do you mean by that?"

Blinking, Rebecca opened and closed her mouth before saying, "Just that I'm sure you could use a break. The children must keep you so busy. I didn't intend any offense."

Cal patted her arm. "Of course not. It is good to have a bit of a break, isn't it, Jim?" Cal glared at him.

Jim's mind whirled. When he and Cal were alone he'd felt so certain of his feelings, but now he wasn't so sure. He'd allowed himself to be swept up into this…whatever *this* was with Cal, and he was struck by the notion that Rebecca somehow knew—that her eyes bored straight into him and saw the sickness inside. Frank Bell and his wife passed by on the sidewalk, and their gaze felt hot on Jim's face.

They all know.

"Jim?" Cal stepped closer.

His heart pounding, Jim jumped back. "I have to go." He resisted the urge to run. The shame choked him as he escaped inside the store, not waiting for a response.

He grabbed a basket and tossed in items, reaching blindly for cans on the shelf. Through the window, he could see Rebecca and Cal talking. What had Cal told her when they'd had coffee? Surely he hadn't said anything about his feelings for Jim? *Does she know?*

"All right there, Jim?" Mrs. Abbott asked.

He jerked his gaze to the front counter. "What?"

She smiled kindly. "You're looking a little peaked today, dear."

She knows. She sees what I really am. His voice was little more than a croak. "There's nothing wrong with me."

Mrs. Abbott frowned, and the bell *dinged* as Cal entered the store alone. Jim continued filling up the basket as Cal exchanged pleasantries with Mrs. Abbott. When Cal came over, he pitched his voice low. "Is it any wonder Rebecca thinks you don't like her? What's gotten into you?"

Jim could only shake his head in response.

Cal clasped Jim's arm with a frown. "Hey, it's okay. You're shaking. Did something happen…are you thinking about Okinawa?"

Squirming out of Cal's grasp, Jim jerked his head around. They were alone, Mrs. Abbott having disappeared into the stockroom, where he could hear her humming. "They know," he whispered.

"Know what?" Realization flickered across Cal's face. "No. You're being paranoid."

"I can tell. They all know. You told her," he accused.

"Jim, you're wrong. You said this morning that you trusted me. So trust me now. Everything's okay."

At the thought of the morning and what they'd done—Cal moving inside him, stretching him open and filling him—shame and lust battled within. Lord in heaven, it had been so good, and he wanted to do it again and again. He wanted to fuck Cal and be fucked by him, and a little voice inside said it didn't matter who knew. He couldn't stop.

Cal eased the basket from Jim's grip. "Let's finish this and get back home." He peered inside. "I don't think we need seven cans of applesauce considering you have a never-ending supply in the icebox."

As Jim breathed deeply, the panic began to subside. He stood there uselessly while Cal finished the shopping and made small talk with Mrs. Abbott. He let Cal propel him out to the truck, and he climbed into the passenger seat, his eyes unfocused as Cal drove them back toward Clover Grove.

Halfway there, Cal turned onto a side road and pulled off. He twisted the key and the engine stopped, rattling a few times before going quiet. The rain had intensified, and even through the trees it beat down on the truck, drumming on the roof as they sat in silence. For a moment Jim could have closed his eyes and been back in the Pacific.

Finally Cal spoke. "I know you're ashamed of how you feel. Of what we're doing together. I understand why, even though it hurts me."

An iron band circled Jim's chest. "The last thing I want to do is hurt you."

"I know. I understand that it's all new for you. But no one can tell, Jim. Believe me, I know a thing or two about hiding who I am and how I feel."

Jim took a shaky breath. "I wasn't thinking straight. All of a sudden the thought was there and growing out of control. I can't explain it." Tentatively, he reached for Cal's hand on the seat between them. "I'm sorry. It's all so new. I feel so much. It scares me."

Cal turned his palm up and clasped Jim's hand. "It's okay. Jim, I didn't say a word to Rebecca. I wouldn't."

"I know. I don't understand what happened." He groaned. "You're right—she's really going to think I don't like her now."

Cal peered intently. "What is it with her?"

Jim shrugged. "I only really knew her by sight before Stephen asked her out. Then she was everywhere. Stephen always wanted to bring her along, even when we went fishing. She was always there, hanging off him. Stephen and I were never alone anymore."

"Ah." Cal smiled softly.

"What?"

"You were jealous."

"Jealous?" Jim sputtered and yanked his hand free. "Why in heaven's name would I be jealous?"

"Until he met her, I bet it was just you and Stephen together most of the time, huh?"

"Well, yes. When you grow up in the country, you spend the most time with your neighbors. We went to the same school. He was a good friend."

"Then Rebecca came along with her red lips and silky hair and big tits. She was everything you weren't."

Jim shifted uncomfortably. "I don't see what that has to do with anything."

"And Stephen wanted to spend time with her instead of you."

"Of course. He was completely smitten with her." A light bulb went off, and Jim sat up straighter. "Wait—if you're trying to say I had feelings for *Stephen*, you're way off base."

"Mm-hmm." Cal's smile had taken on the gleam of a smirk.

"Cal, that's ridiculous! Stephen was my friend. Nothing more."

"I was nothing more until recently."

Jim shook his head. "That's different."

"Uh-huh."

"But…" Jim had to admit he'd resented Rebecca for no good reason when she'd come into Stephen's life. "I didn't mind her so much after I met Ann."

Cal wasn't teasing now. "Why was that?"

"Because she and Ann would talk each other's ears off, and…" He swallowed hard, the truth dislodging. "And I had Stephen to myself again."

"I get it, Jim. Believe me, I get it. But none of it was Rebecca's fault. So give her a break, okay? She's a good woman."

Jim shook his head, amazed by his own obtuseness. "You must think I'm ridiculous."

"No." Cal brushed Jim's hair back from his forehead. "Sometimes we all need a push to see things clearly."

Stephen had been a good friend, and Jim still mourned his death. But whatever his buried, confused emotions had been all those years ago, they didn't hold a candle to what he felt for Cal, which was so deep inside him he knew it would never shake free. "It was nothing like this. Like you and me. A crush, maybe. With you it's so much more."

Cal's eyes darkened and he tugged Jim over, kissing him hard. The staccato beat of the rain on the roof matched Jim's heart as their mouths opened, tongues questing as the spark blazed to life. Jim clutched Cal's plaid shirt, desperate to feel his strong body.

The drone of an engine and squelch of tires filtered through Jim's consciousness just as Cal sprang back behind the wheel, breathing hard. Through the pouring rain, Jim couldn't make out the driver of the other truck as it passed, and was fairly certain the person couldn't see them clearly either.

As the truck disappeared around a bend, Jim met Cal's eyes. They burst out laughing, and all the tension and dread Jim had felt dissolved. "Let's go home."

With a grin, Cal turned the key and revved the engine.

CHAPTER FIFTEEN

1942

"SPEEDY! CAN WE borrow your blanket?" Jim's whisper was almost lost in the midnight downpour.

Speedy crawled over the tree roots. "Sure thing. It's not doing me any good."

Cal took the blanket and added it to his and Jim's, already spread out over Sully. Sully's teeth chattered, and he murmured almost constantly, the fever and chills wracking his increasingly slight frame. Cal gave Sully's head a pat, wishing there was more they could do. "There you go, pal. It'll warm you right up."

Jim sighed. "How could they send him back to the line? At least in the aid station he could keep dry."

"Said there was nothing else they could do for him," Speedy whispered. "They needed the bed. I heard a couple boys from Dog Company got their legs blown off. Couldn't move 'em out right away. Guess we're lucky up here."

The company was closer to the airfield now, on higher ground. "Poor bastards." Cal laughed humorlessly. "At least they're off this godforsaken island."

Speedy kept his voice low. "Did you see some of the other guys in the platoon got nailed yesterday?"

"Yeah." As more men died around them, Cal found himself creating a distance between the dead and the living in his mind. Once they were gone, he tried not to think of them at all.

Sully shook, coughing and writhing. Speedy whistled. "Pistol," he hissed. "Pass over your blanket."

"Won't do him any fucking good," Pete grumbled. But he still tossed over the sodden bundle of cloth.

Jim piled the blanket on top. Jim murmured to Sully, "The fever'll break soon. You'll be okay." To Cal, he added, "He won't get better out here. We're a three-man mortar team. He could barely hold himself upright today, let alone the gun."

Cal shrugged. "We'll make do. He's got both his legs. That's something, I guess."

Speedy piped up. "Remember when the rain used to actually stop sometimes?"

They all grumbled. Plopping down beside Jim in the muck, Cal fiddled with a ruined cigarette. Keeping their mortar rounds dry was the priority, and even tucked deep in his pack, cigarettes got soaked.

He ran a hand over his head, glad for his shorn hair. None of them wore their helmets when they didn't have to because they felt more claustrophobic than ever. Now in mid-November the downpour was an unrelenting misery as rainy season was upon them.

"At least we're on higher ground now. The river must be overflowing. Those crocs could be anywhere down there," Speedy said. "They should move the galley tent."

Cal smirked. "I don't think the crocs want our wormy rice."

"Corpsman says we should eat the worms. Good protein," Jim noted.

"I wouldn't listen to anything that son of a bitch has to say."

Speedy snorted. "Aw, Hollywood. Don't hold a grudge now. You know that ulcer was infected."

"That may be, but I don't want that rusty scalpel anywhere near my leg again." Cal poked at his right shin, wincing.

Jim caught his hand and pulled it away. "Stop that. You're going to make it worse. Talk all you like, but you sure don't want flies hatching in your leg. The corpsman did you a favor."

There was movement in the foliage, and they tensed as one, rifles at the ready. Then Big Joe's low voice drawled, "Looky what we found." He appeared with Buster and Smith. "Killed all those slit-eyed fuckers yesterday and now we're gonna drink their hooch."

Pete shot to his feet, more animated than Cal had seen him since New River. "That's a fucking beautiful sight."

Cradling an enormous bottle in his arms, Joe struggled to sit. They all formed a circle and passed around the container of sake. It was so big they could barely lift it, and they laughed as they took turns slurping from the bottle. The wine was too warm, but Cal didn't care, gulping it greedily.

Grimacing, Jim drank, and after a while he swayed slightly, nudging Cal's shoulder, clumsy with the bottle. Buster's laughter rumbled. "Johnny, you'd better stop. If those Nips come tonight we need your level head on straight or we're fucked."

Jim scoffed, slurring slightly. "Me? Nah."

"To Johnny!" Speedy heaved up the bottle and tipped the wine down his throat before passing it on.

They drank a few more rounds, and Jim leaned heavier onto Cal. Cal's head spun. "Time to hit the hay."

He tugged Jim away from the circle, back to where Sully still shivered in the grip of his fever in the shallow trench. They settled in nearby, Jim pliable in Cal's arms as Cal arranged them on their sides, spooning up behind Jim's back the way they had those freezing nights out on the rifle range at Parris Island.

Cal was parched, and he gulped water from his canteen before pressing it into Jim's hand. "Drink or we're going to have a hell of a headache. That sake's drier than my father's favorite vermouth."

Jim swallowed obediently before settling back down, squirming closer to Cal. They'd dug the slit trench with a makeshift drain on the downhill side, and the water poured over them, but at least they weren't swimming in it. Of course they were still swimming in mud, and Cal wasn't sure which was worse.

But one thing was wonderful, and that was Jim, warm and lean and pressing against him. Cal pillowed Jim's head with his arm, Jim murmuring and drunker than Cal had ever seen him. He could feel Jim's lips moving against the skin of his forearm, and Cal imagined those lips on his own. On his body.

Of course this was an exceedingly dangerous train of thought, and Cal's prick twitched.

God, how he wanted to roll Jim onto his back and kiss him until they were breathless, hard and wanting, hips thrusting together. They'd sink into the mud and no one would find them. They could stay there forever, bodies entwined.

"Cal?"

"Hmm?"

"If I don't make it off this island, you need to do something for me."

"Shh. Go to sleep."

Jim gripped Cal's wrist. "I mean it. Promise."

"Okay. What's on your mind?"

"I told my little girl I'd get her a horse. Had to sell ours a few years back when things were tight. I swore when I got home she'd have one."

"Sure. But you'll be able to get her that horse yourself. You're going to go home to your family safe and sound. I'll make sure of it."

Jim exhaled audibly, his breath hot against Cal's forearm. "You're the best buddy a guy could have."

"You should get drunk more often. It's good for my ego." Cal resisted the urge to press a kiss to Jim's head.

After mumbling something Cal couldn't make out, Jim went quiet. Just when Cal thought he'd gone to sleep, he spoke again.

"She won't even know me."

"Of course she will."

"We could be out here for years. If not Guadalcanal, then some other island. We could die tomorrow. Tonight. I might never see her again. Even if I do, she'll be so big."

"You're her daddy. Nothing's going to change that. I promise." Cal murmured reassurances as the rain fell, his lips close to Jim's ear long after Jim snored softly.

1948

AS CAL EKED out the detail on the last of the dollhouse's shutters, he leaned closer to the lantern. His hair was still damp from a shower, and he hadn't bothered to put on even an undershirt over his jeans in the sultry evening. He'd considered coming out in just his boxers.

The pickup rattled in the distance, and Finnigan barked happily when Jim returned to the barn. Cal chuckled. "He missed you. But I fed him a few treats, so he didn't miss you *too* much."

Finnigan barked as if in agreement, and Jim scratched behind his ears. "So fickle, eh boy?"

"In his defense, I do give out delicious treats." Cal carved the small block of wood carefully. "Everything okay at the O'Briens'?"

"Yeah. I managed to help Mrs. O'Brien talk Gerald into going to the hospital. Doctors make the worst patients."

"Is it serious?"

"No, the cut only needs a few stitches, but he insisted he'd do them himself, left-handed. Put up a fuss about driving himself in, because he's *not a damn invalid*."

Cal chuckled. "I'm sure Mrs. O'Brien appreciated your help."

"It's the least I can do." Jim gave Finnigan a final pat and stood before peeling his shirts over his head to bare his chest. "Hot one. At least the kids should be cooler in the mountains."

"I'm sorry, were you saying something?" Cal leered.

Jim rolled his eyes, although he still blushed. "You're looking pretty good yourself." He came over to the worktable and kissed Cal lightly before running his fingertips over the gabled roof of the dollhouse. "And wow, this is looking great, Cal. She's going to love it. You're a born carpenter."

"Thanks. At least I'm a born something. Nice not to be completely useless."

Jim frowned. "You could never be useless."

"I think my father would disagree with you there."

"I wish you wouldn't do that."

He picked up the block of wood again. "What?"

"You know exactly what. Run yourself down. You've never been useless since I've known you." Jim stepped close and kissed him softly. "You're worth more than you could ever know."

Cal kissed him back and tossed the wood aside. "If you say so."

"I do." Jim nipped at his lips and splayed his hand on Cal's back. "Did you miss me too?"

Shaking his head, Cal couldn't quite keep a straight face. "Nope. Not a bit. Pretty sick of you now. A man can only fuck so much."

Jim fought a grin. "That's strange—I haven't heard you complain once this weekend."

"Now if you'll excuse me, I've got work to do."

In a blink, Jim snatched up Cal's carving tool. "Not without this." He grinned, and the chase was on.

Finnigan's barks mixed with their laughter as they raced through the barn, Jim ducking and weaving and staying just an inch out of Cal's grasp. Jim made it to the loft ladder and clambered up, Cal hot on his heels. At the top Cal dove and toppled Jim into the hay with a triumphant yell.

They wrestled, sending rough hay scattering everywhere until finally they gave in to their laughter, kissing lightly. Jim reached for an old blanket he tossed over the hay before pushing Cal down. Cal kissed him thoroughly, exploring Jim's mouth with his tongue until they were both panting.

"First time you showed me this barn I fantasized about this. Having you here."

Jim's eyes were dark, and he rolled his hips into Cal's. "Just the first time?"

"No. Just about every other time I've been in here."

"What did you think about?"

"Plenty of things. Like right now, I'm thinking of me on my hands and knees with you inside me."

Jim's breath stuttered and his lips parted. "We don't have anything. It'll hurt."

Cal gripped Jim's ass as he ground his hips up. "Yeah. It'll be rough with just your spit to ease the way. But you won't stop. You'll just keep pounding into me, and it'll be tight and—"

Groaning, Jim thrust his tongue into Cal's mouth, and they kissed, teeth clashing. Then Jim sat back on his heels and jerked open his belt, and Cal scrambled onto all fours. He tore his jeans open and tugged them down with his drawers to his ankles, too impatient to unlace his boots. Even with the blanket, the hay scratched his skin, but it only excited him more, and he inhaled the musk of the barn deeply.

Breathing hard, Jim hesitated as his hands closed over Cal's hips. Cal reached back and tugged Jim's hand forward, licking it and sucking on Jim's fingers sloppily before letting go. Without being told, Jim stroked himself with his wet hand.

Looking over his shoulder, Cal nodded. "Now spit in me."

Jim hesitated, but then Cal could feel Jim's lips on his skin as he leaned close, his fingers parting Cal's cheeks. He spit several times, and Cal wanted to beg Jim to use his tongue, but didn't want to push too far. Yet a few moments later there was a fleeting wet pressure on his hole, and Cal moaned. "Christ. *Yes*. Please, do that again."

Tentatively, Jim kissed and licked at Cal's hole, seeming to grow more confident as Cal pushed back, the thrills of pleasure making his dick leak. His balls hung heavy between his legs, and he shuddered as Jim licked him wetly. "Yes, like that. Feels so good. Gonna make me come so hard."

He moaned in protest when Jim moved away, but then he felt Jim's hardness against his ass. They were both sweating in the sweet warmth of the summer night, and Jim licked along Cal's spine before positioning himself. Cal could hear him spitting again, and his cock nudged inside. Cal spread his legs as far as the jeans around his ankles would allow and relaxed his muscles.

It burned as Jim inched inside, and Cal grunted. "More. *More.*"

Jim hesitated, but then he took hold of Cal's shoulders and slammed in farther, thrusting with little strokes until he was all the way inside. His chest rose and fell as he pressed across Cal's back, his fingers tangling in Cal's hair.

"Not too much?" Jim gritted the words out.

Lips parted, Cal shook his head. "Fuck me hard, Jim."

Groaning, Jim did as he was asked, pounding into Cal. It was rough and deep, and Cal moaned loudly, his thighs trembling as Jim worked his ass. Jim's cock was so big and full inside him, and the burning gave way to ripples of sensation as Jim brushed against the right spot. Cal reached for his cock, jerking it unevenly as the pressure built.

They strained together, panting and muttering, moaning and grunting until Jim's hips stuttered and he came with a shout. Cal looked over his shoulder, watching Jim tip his head back, his eyes closed and mouth open as he shot deep into Cal. Stroking himself harder, soon Cal was coming, Jim's name on his lips.

They collapsed onto the blanket, Jim heavy on Cal's back in a way that made him want to stay like that forever. He could still feel Jim's softening cock inside him and seed dripping out of his hole.

Jim pressed kisses to Cal's neck and shoulders, and Cal closed his eyes, sighing. Crickets sang in the night, and he didn't think he'd ever been quite this happy. Jim's breath fanned across Cal's neck, and even though they were messy and hay stabbed through the blanket, Cal didn't want to move. Possibly ever.

A faint rumble grew. Jim stirred, and Finnigan barked from below. With a sinking sensation, Cal realized it was a vehicle.

In a burst of panic, they disentangled themselves. Jim leaped to his feet and pulled up his pants, scurrying down the ladder without a backward glance. Cal was right behind him, zipping up his jeans as he went. Cal ran his hands through his hair, trying to dislodge the hay as Jim yanked on his undershirt. He tossed Cal his short-sleeved work shirt, and Cal's fingers stuttered as he shoved the buttons through the holes.

Finnigan raced from the barn and Cal glimpsed headlights on the laneway. He pulled Jim out of sight behind the barn door. "The O'Briens?" he asked as he brushed hay from Jim's hair.

"Maybe. Kids aren't back until morning. How do I look?"

Jim's cheeks were red from Cal's stubble, and his lips swollen from kissing. "Like you've been fucking in a hayloft. It's dark. Try to stay in the shadows."

"Daddy!" Sophie's voice rang out.

Jim's eyes widened, and he rushed outside. Cal quickly followed, dousing the lantern and closing the barn door behind him. The Sheltons' truck idled on the drive with Ronald behind the wheel. Lorraine got out, trying to keep hold of a wriggling Adam as Sophie raced to Jim. She threw her arms around his waist.

"Sophie, what happened?" Jim held her. To Lorraine, he called, "Are they all right?"

Lorraine approached and let Adam go. Adam ran on his little legs to his sister and father, wailing. "They're fine. She's coming down with something. Been insufferable since before dinner. Whining about coming home. Ronald finally had enough."

Indeed, Ronald still remained in the truck with the engine running. He puffed on a cigarette, and smoke wafted from the window. Cal couldn't make out his expression but was sure it wasn't a happy one.

Jim crouched and felt Sophie's forehead. "Are you sick, sweetie? You're a little warm."

"I just wanted to be home with you and Uncle Cal. I missed you."

Lorraine huffed. "She's coming down with something, mark my words. I told her I can take care of her just fine. Took care of her momma after all."

Jim stood. "I'm sorry for the trouble, Lorraine."

She sighed. "It's all right. Maybe they can come up again later in the summer. It's real nice having them. Livens up the old place."

"Of course. We'll work out a time."

"I don't want to live there." Sophie shook her head, her waves of dark hair whipping around her face.

Jim frowned. "Of course you're not going to live there, sweetheart. You're only visiting Grandma and Grandpa. You're always going to come back here. This is your home."

Sophie's voice was barely a whisper. "That's not what Grandpa said."

Cal inhaled sharply through a flash of anger and had to bite his tongue. He kept back, knowing he'd only make things worse if he got in the middle. He glared at the truck, part of him wishing Ronald would come out and say what was clearly on his mind.

Still calm, Jim addressed Lorraine. "What's this about?"

"Heavens, it was only an idea. Ronald just thought it would help if Sophie and Adam came to live with us for the summer. That way they wouldn't be underfoot with all the work you have to do."

Jim's tone was even, but steely. "That's a kind offer, but not necessary. You and Ronald are always welcome here, but this is the children's home. All year round."

"He didn't mean any harm." She glanced back at the truck and lowered her voice. Her eyes glistened. "They're all we have left of her. Surely you can understand."

Softening, Jim nodded. "We'll set up that other weekend. Perhaps you and Ronald can come down for the Fourth of July. I think the children would love that. Wouldn't you, Sophie?"

Blinking back tears, Sophie nodded and went to her grandmother, hugging her tightly. "I'm sorry. I just got homesick."

Lorraine kissed Sophie's head. "That's all right, child. I understand. That sounds like a real fun day in July. We'll see you then." To Jim, she added, "Ronald won't want to drive back that night, so we'll stay in the hotel in town."

Cal stepped forward. "You can have my room. I insist. I'll stay out in the cabin."

"Then it's settled." Jim smiled, although his shoulders were still tense. "Kids, say goodbye to Grandma." He walked to the truck and spoke to Ronald through the open window.

Cal could imagine that was an enjoyable conversation. As Lorraine returned to her husband, Cal swept Adam up and smoothed his palm over Sophie's hair. "Good to have you both back."

It surprised him a bit to realize that, despite the end of his idyll with Jim, he meant it.

THE CREAK OF the floorboard penetrated Cal's fuzzy dream, and he opened his eyes to find Jim standing by his bed in an undershirt and pajama bottoms. Cal reached for his hand. "What time is it?"

"Late. After midnight."

Cal stretched and scratched his bare belly. His boxers sat low on his hips. "Couldn't sleep?"

Jim shook his head.

"C'mere." Cal tugged and shifted over, holding up the sheet so Jim could climb in.

"We can't do anything. I shouldn't be in here."

"I know." Cal kissed Jim lightly. "Just stay for a minute."

"Just a minute." Jim snuggled close, their heads together on the pillow.

"They both sleeping?"

"Adam was down for the count right away. Sophie took longer, but I just checked and she's out."

"It's nice to have them back."

"Even though it means we can't…"

"Don't underestimate our powers of creativity." Cal waggled his eyebrows. "We'll still find ways to do plenty of things while we're out in the orchard on our own."

Jim grinned. "I don't think I've ever looked forward to working this much before." His smile faded. "What do you make of Ronald and Lorraine?"

Cal pondered it. "I think they love their grandchildren and miss their daughter. And I think we have to be very careful around them. If they even suspected, Ronald would have our asses in jail before we knew it."

Jim nodded with a grim expression. "It makes me nervous, him wanting them to live there for the summer. They're my children. He's not taking them away from me."

"He won't. We won't let that happen. It's all going to be fine."

"I hope so."

Jim traced a pattern over Cal's back with his fingertips, and Cal nuzzled closer, his lips grazing Jim's throat. A light breeze blew in through the open window, and the crickets still chirped. As Cal closed his eyes, he wondered if they ever got tired…

"Daddy?"

With a sickening jolt, Cal woke.

Blinking, her damp curls mussed, Sophie stood at the foot of the bed. "Daddy? I couldn't find you."

Jim bolted to his feet, staring at his daughter dumbly. When he spoke, his voice was a croak. "I was just talking to Uncle Cal. Are you sick?" He went to her and kneeled before feeling her forehead.

She nodded. "I threw up on the floor. I'm sorry, Daddy."

"Baby, don't be sorry. Come on, let's get you cleaned up and back to bed." Jim scooped her into his arms and carried her out. He didn't even glance back.

Cal rubbed his eyes and reached for his watch. Three o'clock. Cal remembered holding Jim close and listening to his heartbeat, and then dreaming of the orchard. *Christ. Thank God we were dressed.*

For eternal minutes, Cal paced his room. When the waiting became unbearable, he crept down the hall. The children's door was ajar, and he peeked in. Jim sat on Sophie's bed, leaning back against the headboard with Sophie sprawled on his lap, sleeping with her lips parted.

Jim looked up, and icy dread washed over Cal.

Anger and guilt warred in Jim's eyes, and Cal felt sick to see it. He wanted to tell Jim that it would be okay—that Sophie didn't see anything wrong—but he couldn't. He knew it was too late. Still, he whispered a plea. "Jim."

With infinite gentleness, Jim rearranged Sophie and edged out from beneath her. On quiet feet he passed Adam, still dead to the world and flopped on his back with limbs splayed. As he reached the entry to the children's room, Jim kept his gaze on the worn wooden floor. Without a word, he closed the door on Cal.

CHAPTER SIXTEEN

1942

IN THE DISTANCE, the *rat-tat-tat* of gunfire echoed. Then there was an answering barrage, and Cal was already shouldering the mortar tube when the lieutenant shouted orders to move. Sully was weak, struggling with the bipod, but at least hadn't had a fever in days. Jim hoisted the base plate and fell in beside Cal as they slip-slided down the hill with the other men in the blackness. The rain had eased to a drizzle for the moment.

Captain Brown, who they hadn't seen in weeks, barked commands as they took cover. "Mortars!"

The enemy approached below across a ravine, surging toward them in the night. Even with Sully not at full strength, the three of them worked seamlessly as they assembled their gun under a craggy rock overhang. One by one, they loaded the mortars into the gun's muzzle, ducking their heads to the familiar refrain of "Hanging! Fire!" as they rained shrapnel on the enemy.

The ground rocked as the Japanese answered with shells of their own. Jim, Cal, and Sully edged back, trying to keep their cover. The other mortarmen along the ridge got it, too, and the battle seemed to go on for hours, each side launching round after round as the enemy tried to gain precious inches in the steaming jungle.

By morning's murky light, it was over. As the sun rose, Jim sighed in relief, wiping the sweat and dirt from his cheeks. He opened his mouth to say something to Cal when he caught the expression on Sully's face. "What?"

Sully stared at something, and Jim turned to follow his gaze. Black smoke wisped from a crater in the hillside about twenty feet away. Before Jim could stop him, Cal was on the move, keeping low. Jim and Sully followed.

They halted a few feet from the smoldering mess of metal and flesh, and Jim struggled to make sense of what his eyes saw. He held his hand over his mouth and nose; bile rose at the stench of charred flesh. Big Joe and a few of the others approached from the opposite side. Joe shook his head.

"Speedy and Buster and Smithy."

"Direct hit," Cal added quietly.

Crouched low, they were all silent as they took it in. Just like that, their squad was decimated. Jim bowed his head in a silent prayer for his friends. It was all he could do, and it didn't feel like nearly enough. Just the night before at chow time, Speedy had given Jim his extra rice with a smile. Jim blinked at the charred mess that had been good men. Smith had been so quiet that Jim had hardly spoken to him, and now he was gone.

Sully sniffled beside him, and Jim reached an arm around him.

One by one, they all went back to their weapons, but Jim's feet felt stuck in the soft ground. He'd started to think that since they'd been lucky so far, maybe that luck would last. Maybe his squad would get out unscathed. He laughed harshly.

Then Cal was there with a hand on his shoulder. "Hey. We've gotta move."

"Uh-huh."

Cal sighed. "Nothing we can do for them now."

"Just like that. They're…gone." Jim's throat was dry, and he swallowed thickly.

Cal held out his canteen insistently until Jim drank. "I know. We've been tripping over bodies all across this island, but it still didn't seem quite real somehow. But Speedy and those guys...they were real."

Jim nodded. It was a comfort at least that Cal understood. Like always. "If it was you..."

Cal squeezed Jim's shoulder. "We just have to keep our heads down and do our job. It's all we can do."

It was the truth, and finally Jim turned his back and trudged through the jungle.

As they went, Sully muttered, "Wish those bastards would just make their move once and for all. How long is this gonna go on?"

A few nights later they had their answer.

The seismic quakes had them huddled in their holes, but soon enough curiosity won out and they crept up to the ridge of the hillside on their bellies. There in the distance, spread out before them, the great warships battled. Sully squeezed in between Jim and Joe, and then ducked as a tracer illuminated the night.

"It's miles away," Joe told him, not unkindly.

The arcs of light from the tracers were followed by the red explosions of the star shells, bright enough to show the enemy's position perfectly. On opposite sides of a great circle in the sea, the ships blasted at each other, the thunder of their guns sending shivers up Jim's spine.

They'd become as accustomed as one could be to the aerial dogfights that broke out most days over the island, but the terrible rage of the warships was unlike anything Jim had experienced. It seemed that the very stars in the sky were exploding, with others collapsing in on themselves in great bursts. The ground vibrated, and for a moment Jim imagined the sea might open up and swallow them all whole.

On Jim's other side, Cal's shoulder and hip pressed into him. Cal watched the battle unfold with wide eyes, fear and wonder warring in his expression. He whistled softly as another mighty blast split the air and flames climbed to the sky.

"Jesus. This has to be it."

Jim winced at another explosion. "Can you tell who's winning?"

Cal shook his head. None of them could, and they were left to watch with horror and pray their boys came out on top. The barrage went on, and they waited. The harbor was vividly bright. From this distance, Jim could almost believe he was back on the riverbank in Tivoli at the town picnic, egg salad sandwiches in his belly and a cold beer in his hand as he watched the fireworks with one eye on Sophie's tiny awed face.

"Hey, go wake up Speedy! He's missing it," Sully muttered.

Jim and Cal shared a look before Jim pressed his hand to Sully's forehead. "Maybe you should go back to bed, huh?"

Sully quivered, the fever returning in a flush that overtook him in minutes. "No way. I ain't missin' this."

He wouldn't be any better off in his hole, so they didn't argue, and big Joe slithered down the hill and returned with blankets to throw over Sully.

"You really should get Speedy," Sully mumbled. "He won't wanna miss this."

Jim wasn't sure if it was the malaria, or if Sully's glassy stares and flights of fancy were his mind's way of protecting him. Either way, Jim didn't see the point in correcting him.

As quickly as it began, the battle was done, and darkness settled back over Guadalcanal. They slunk to their holes to wait for dawn, and Jim doubted any of them would sleep but Sully, who whimpered and shuddered violently as the fever worsened. They hissed for the corpsman, who came and shoved aspirin down Sully's throat. With an apologetic shrug, he disappeared back into the jungle.

When the sky lightened, the hum of the planes on the airfield came to life. Joe let out a mighty whoop. "We still got the field! We won!"

Jim and Cal shared a grin as they leaped to their feet, cheering the planes as they roared overhead. Cal called out, "Go sink the rest of that fleet to the bottom of the sea!"

One by one, their planes zoomed off in pursuit of the retreating Japanese. Although they were still wet and hungry and so very tired, the men celebrated, and renewed vigor flooded Jim's veins.

They'd won. Perhaps the worst was over.

1948

IN THE FIRST rays of dawn, Sophie slept fitfully. Her forehead was still hot, and she'd cried out from a nightmare earlier and shivered in Jim's arms before dropping off again. Her hair was damp with sweat, and every time Jim tried to pull the sheet over her, she kicked it off.

On the other side of the room, Adam was still fast asleep. On one of his passes as he paced, Jim put the back of his hand to Adam's forehead. Still cool, and Jim blew out a long breath. Sophie rolled over, whimpering, but didn't wake. He wondered what nightmare haunted her fever dreams.

Maybe the sight of her father in bed with his best friend.

Stomach roiling, Jim cringed. What had he been thinking? It had only been a matter of time before they were caught. He was supposed to protect his children and put them first. Instead he'd recklessly brought sin into their home.

But was it truly a sin?

He would worry about God's judgment when the time came, but the law was another matter. Nothing in Jim's life had ever felt so natural and right, but what he and Cal had done was illegal, no matter how good it made him feel. His mind spun as he walked to the window and looked at the expanse of treetops. A flash of movement caught his eye—the barn door opening. He glimpsed Cal disappearing inside.

After checking to make sure the children still slept more or less soundly, Jim forced himself to go to Cal. There was no sense in delaying the inevitable. He felt like he'd swallowed an iron ball as he made his way across the dewy grass.

When Jim walked into the barn, Cal glanced over. He was milking Mabel, and a steady flow streamed into the bucket. "How's Sophie feeling? I didn't think she'd be up for milking this morning."

"She's feverish still. I have to go back in a minute and check on her. But you don't have to do that." Jim gestured at Mabel. "I can."

"Nah, I don't mind. Mabel and I are old friends now, aren't we, girl?" He patted her flank.

Jim tried to smile. "You've been such a help around here. You really have."

With a sigh, Cal sat back on the stool. "It's okay, Jim. You don't have to say it."

"Cal…" His head was light as nausea washed over him. "We can't do this."

Cal stood. "I know."

Selfishly, part of Jim wanted Cal to fight with him. *For* him. He wanted Cal to tell him that they'd make it work—that it didn't have to end. He shook his head. *Enough daydreaming.* "I have to put them first. I can't…*we* can't. I let myself believe that it wasn't hurting anyone. That no one had to know."

"Do you really think it would hurt her? Or Adam? That we feel this way for each other?"

Jim scrubbed a hand through his hair. "It's wrong, Cal. Despite what you say, deep down you know it."

"No. I don't." Cal clenched his jaw. "No preacher will ever convince me. No one will."

"What about the police? It's a *crime*, the things we've done. We could go to prison. My God, think of the shame it would bring to our families."

"We're not hurting anyone. There have been men like us since the dawn of time. The law just needs to catch up. People need to catch up."

"That's never going to happen. We'd spend our lives living in the shadows."

Cal took a step forward, beseeching. "But we'd be *together*. It wouldn't be perfect, but we could make it work."

"What about the children? Think of how confusing it would be for them. I can only pray that Sophie didn't understand what she saw—that the fever means she won't remember. How could she ever understand? How could I ever explain it? I still can't explain it to myself."

Cal's shoulders drooped. "I don't have the answers. All I know is that I've never been so happy as I have been here with you. With Sophie and Adam. All of us together. And I know you feel the same way. I know it."

Jim took a deep breath and blew it out. "It doesn't change anything. It doesn't change the world. We've been dreaming, Cal. Fooling ourselves. I let myself get swept up. I've been selfish, and it has to stop. My children have to come first."

"I would never want to hurt them. I'll miss them more than I ever thought I could."

Panic flapped in Jim's chest. "But you don't have to leave. We could just go back to how it was before."

Cal smiled sadly. "We can't, and you know it." He closed the distance between them, but stopped a foot away. "If it has to end, then I have to leave. I know you need help here, but school's out, and maybe some of the older boys will want work."

Jim clenched his hands, fighting the urge to reach out. "We've done most of the hard jobs now. The crop is growing, and I hire people for harvest. I'll ask a few to start early. It'll be fine. We'll get by."

"If you need anything—money, or anything else, just call. You have a phone now, after all." Cal's tone was teasing, but his eyes glistened.

Jim's throat was painfully dry. "I owe you so much. My life." Cal opened his mouth to say something, but Jim barreled on. "Not just on Okinawa. Here. You helped me see clearly for the first time. For so long I couldn't—*wouldn't*—admit my feelings. My…desires. They're wrong, but at least I know them."

Cal stepped closer. He was only inches away now. "I just want you to be happy."

Jim swallowed thickly. "I have to do the right thing."

Nodding, Cal moved away, but Jim reached for him, catching his lips in a fierce kiss. They pressed their mouths together as they gripped each other with fingers that would leave bruises. After several heartbeats, Cal broke the kiss and pushed away, stepping back out of Jim's arms.

"Adam will wake up soon. You'd better get back. I'll finish with Mabel and get packed. It shouldn't take long."

The panic returned, and Jim felt as if he was choking on it. "You don't have to leave right away!" He cleared his throat. "Sophie's sick, and we have to break it to her gently. Give her time. At least a day or two."

It seemed as though Cal would argue, but after a moment, he relented. "All right. I'll go tomorrow." He forced a tight smile. "You'd better get back. I'll finish up the chores."

Jim shoved everything else he wanted to say way down deep and left the barn. This was the way it had to be. He repeated the words like a mantra as he went to check on the children.

CAL STOOD AT the kitchen sink with the water running. He was dressed in his city clothes—slacks and a nice shirt, although when he turned Jim saw he wasn't wearing a tie. Jim wanted to press him back against the counter, kiss him senseless, and tear off those fancy clothes.

After turning off the tap, Cal put his coffee cup on the counter. "I should be going."

"Right." Now that the moment had come, Jim couldn't believe it would end like this. That Cal was going to walk out of the house, get in his car, and drive back to the city. That it would simply be over.

"It's for the best." Cal recited the words hollowly.

Jim nodded. "For the best." If he took only a few steps, they could be in each other's arms, yet it felt like miles separated them rather than several feet of scuffed linoleum. He cleared his throat. "She won't come down."

"It's okay. I understand. Tell her goodbye for me."

Jim could hear Adam outside, playing with Mrs. O'Brien. He took a step. "Cal…"

"Let's not make this any harder." Cal rubbed his face, looking as if he'd slept as little as Jim had. "There's nothing else to say."

All night, Jim had paced his room, his hand on the doorknob a hundred times to go to Cal. Then he remembered Sophie standing at the foot of the bed, lost and confused, and the shame burned him from the inside out. No. He had to get control of his desires. Should never have given in to them in the first place.

Yet watching Cal now, his hair slicked back the way it had been that night on the train to Parris Island, Jim didn't care what the Bible or the law said. The urge to touch was overwhelming. He wanted to crush Cal to him and kiss until they couldn't breathe. The sin was locked in his heart, pumping through his veins.

But he remained rooted to the spot, and no words escaped his lips. With eyes down, Cal brushed by him, and Jim reached out too late. His fingers only grasped air.

Outside, Cal kissed Mrs. O'Brien's cheek and hugged Adam tightly. He lifted his suitcase into the trunk of the Cadillac, and it was really happening. He was leaving.

As Jim approached, Cal extended his hand. "I'll see you."

God, *would* he see Cal again? His head swimming, Jim took Cal's hand, trying to ignore the flare that ignited his body. He had to believe this wasn't the last time. "Thank you for everything."

Their eyes locked, and Cal gripped his hand. Jim wanted more than anything to kiss him again. Just one more time. Instead he could only squeeze back.

"No!" Sophie's face was red, and her hands were balled into fists as she stormed out of the house in her nightgown. "You can't go!" Her eyes shone, and she dodged out of Jim's reach, leveling Cal with a furious glare.

"Sweetie, we explained to you last night why Cal has to leave." Jim reached for her again, but she squirmed away and crossed her arms over her chest.

"Sophie, I really wish I didn't have to leave, but my father needs my help in the city. I'd give anything to be able to stay, but…sometimes things just don't work out the way we'd like. I'll send you presents every month," Cal said.

"I don't want your stupid presents! I want you to stay!"

"*Sophie.* That's enough. Uncle Cal has to leave. Now say goodbye nicely."

Mrs. O'Brien had Adam in her arms, and she gave Jim a sympathetic look before addressing Sophie. "I'm sure Uncle Cal will come back and visit, darling."

Tears slipping down her cheeks, Sophie backed away. "I don't want him to visit! I hate him." She screamed at Cal, "I hate you!" Turning tail, she raced into the house. The screen door slammed behind her, bouncing off the wooden frame.

Before Jim could say a word, Cal had the car door open. "You'd better go after her."

There was so much Jim wanted to tell him, but it was too late now as the Cadillac purred to life. Cal disappeared around the bend in the driveway, leaving only a faint cloud of dust in his wake.

PART THREE

CHAPTER SEVENTEEN

1942

"Hoo boy," Joe exclaimed. "I sure wish someone had told me how many dames there are in Australia! Wouldn't have wasted so much time playing around on Guadalcanal!"

Laughing, Cal waved to the people of Melbourne, who crowded along the railroad tracks, cheering. Beside him, Jim waved politely, and Cal elbowed Sully, who only watched silently with hollow eyes. Being in the hold of the transport ship in rough seas hadn't helped Sully's symptoms, but at least there'd be more medicine where they were going.

Soon they marched off the train and into a sports stadium. Pete snorted. "A football field? That's the best they can do?"

"I think it's a cricket ground, actually," Jim noted.

"Cricket? Pansy-ass idea of a sport. Either way there's no goddamn roof." Pete grumbled to himself as they continued on inside.

The tiers of seats had been replaced with their bunks, and despite the open air, Cal stretched out happily. "Feels like luxury to me."

Jim smiled from his rack nearby. "Now we just need a shower."

"Do you ever." Pete grinned.

"That's an outrageous claim, Marine. Private First Class Bennett smells like roses on a summer morning. As do I, of course." Cal grinned himself.

"Oh yeah, and I'm a bucket of fucking daisies." Pete laughed.

They were given some of their back pay in Australian dollars—along with strict orders not to leave the cricket ground that night. As darkness set in, Cal nudged Jim's arm. "Come on, Pistol found a way out."

"But we're not allowed to go."

"What are they going to do? Throw us all in the brig? Who's going to fight the Japs?"

Jim waved a hand at his uniform. "We're filthy."

"Who cares? This is our first night back in civilization in what, a year? Since I don't count New River as civilization. We're right downtown. We are seeing the sights, my friend."

Even Sully perked up. "Think we can meet some girls? I'd sure like to meet a girl."

"Damn right we'll meet some girls," Cal said, smiling.

Jim raised an eyebrow. "I'm married, in case you forgot."

As if he could forget that. "You're still coming for moral support."

Off they went, along with half the men quartered in the stadium, and probably most of the officers too. The streets of Melbourne teemed with Marines and Australian women. The bars had closed at six, but a drunken corporal slurred that the hotel up the street was still serving.

They crowded into a booth and drank round after round. Jim stuck to beer, but it wasn't long before he was flushed and loose limbed, his knee knocking into Cal's beneath the table. Cal jammed his hand in his pocket so he wouldn't reach for Jim's thigh.

Back on the street, they ate meat pies and sang rousing choruses of any song they could think of. Soon they broke off to pursue the women giving them shy looks—or in some cases, rather bold glances. By an ice cream stand, Sully ogled a young brunette who giggled with her friends.

Joe swung his arm over Sully's shoulders. "Go an' buy her a treat. Maybe she'll give ya one too."

When Sully shambled off in her direction, Jim frowned. "We should take him back. He needs his sleep."

"For fuck's sake, Johnny, he hasn't looked this good in months. Let the kid have some fun," Pete muttered.

Cal cleared his throat. "As much as I hate to say it—seriously, don't get used to it—Pistol's right. Let him have a night out."

"Have another drink, Johnny," Joe drawled, brandishing the bottle he'd lifted from the hotel. He took a swig and passed it to Jim. "Jesus, lighten up."

"Fine." Jim grabbed the bottle and lifted it to his lips, gulping rapidly.

"Whoa, not too much." Cal reached for it, but Jim ducked away.

"No, Joe's right." Grimacing, Jim took another swig. "I'm going to lighten up."

"If you insist." Trying not to worry, Cal fell into step as they left Sully and his girl behind.

It was long after midnight when they stumbled into a park and flopped down on the grass. Sprawled out, Pete snored loudly, while Joe sung slurred verses to himself as he sat against a tree. Jim dropped next to Cal, leaning on his hands with his legs splayed carelessly. He tilted his head back.

"There's the Southern Cross."

"Indeed it is. Nice seeing the stars again after all that rain and being holed up on the ship."

Jim leaned closer, still looking up. His shoulder pressed against Cal's. "What's that one there?"

"I think it's Canis Major. One of Orion's hunting dogs." Cal breathed deeply and closed his eyes for a moment, leaning back into Jim.

"Huh. Don't see a dog."

Cal opened his eyes. "No?"

Jim's gaze was still locked on the night sky. "Nope. A bear maybe."

"A bear? With a tail?"

"Yeah. Why not?"

Chuckling, Cal shrugged. "Sure. Okay. It's a bear. Definitely."

Jim turned his head, and they almost bumped noses. "Now you're just humoring me."

Cal swallowed hard. "Me? Humor you? Never."

Laughing again, Jim's breath fluttered across Cal's face. It was warm and smelled of whiskey, and Cal wanted to dive into Jim's mouth and taste him. They stared at each other for long moments—too long. The look in Jim's eyes—Cal could almost convince himself Jim returned his feelings. Maybe…

"Cal? Can I ask you something?"

He nodded, not trusting his voice.

"Do you ever—"

But before Jim could say another word, Joe vomited loudly in the grass, and Jim jerked away and jumped to his feet. "We'd better get back. Reveille is in… Lord, too soon."

"Let me just piss." Swallowing the disappointment, Cal disappeared into the bushes. He was out of his mind, thinking even for a moment that Jim could ever feel anything for him but friendship. "Wishful fucking thinking," he muttered as he pulled out his cock and pissed.

"What is, mate?"

Cal nearly jumped out of his skin. He glanced to his right, where a man leaned casually against a tree. They were hidden from sight by thick bushes on all sides. Cal said, "I thought I was alone."

"Apologies. Didn't mean to startle you." The man was a few years older, with broad shoulders and what looked to be light brown hair. He was handsome, and his gaze didn't falter.

A thrill shot up Cal's spine. He returned the appraising look boldly. When he finished pissing, he didn't zip up. Instead he stroked his cock lightly, giving his audience the show he clearly wanted. "Shouldn't you be off at war?"

The man grinned, dimples creasing his cheeks. "I was. Got enough of my leg blown off that I don't have to go back." He knocked on his left shin, which reverberated hollowly. He pushed off the tree, limping slightly as he stepped toward Cal. "How long are you here for?"

"Cal?" Jim's voice echoed in the night.

Feeling strangely guilty, Cal tucked himself away. "Coming!"

The man smirked. "Not yet. But meet me here tomorrow night and we'll see what we can do."

Cal nodded. Maybe it was just what he needed.

1948

WHEN THE FIRST explosion rocketed into the night, Cal jerked, and his breath caught as his eyes popped open. He rubbed his bleary face and blinked at the bursts of color—red, blue, green, pink, and yellow— reflected in the windows across his office.

He could hear the distant cheers of the crowds as the fireworks continued. Pushing his chair back, he got up and walked around his desk to the window. The explosions sparkled and shimmered over the water with *pops* that echoed, fading along with the trails of color.

Before he could stop himself, he thought about bringing Sophie and Adam next year—how they could have a picnic in Central Park beforehand and ride the carousel, and maybe he could convince Jim to ride it too.

He wondered what the Fourth of July fireworks in Tivoli were like. Surely couldn't compare to New York City, but he wanted to be there so badly his chest burned. He leaned his forehead against the glass, the bursts of light visible even with his eyes closed, licks of flame around the edges of the darkness.

"Oh! Mr. Cunningham."

Cal turned to face the plump, older woman in the doorway. "Hello, Audrey."

"I didn't think anyone else was still here." She pushed her glasses up her nose. "You gave me a fright."

"Sorry." He frowned and glanced at his watch. "You should've gone home hours ago. Not to mention that you shouldn't have been at work at all today."

She held up a folder and smiled. "I was just going to leave this for you on your desk. I had some files to finish up for your father. And I could say the same to you. I thought you'd be at your family's barbecue on the beach."

Cal stepped forward and reached for the folder. "Didn't feel like the Hamptons today. All that fresh air and sunshine." He exaggerated a shudder.

Audrey smiled wryly. "Yes, what a trial it must be. Why don't you go out with your friends? It'll do you good."

"I was just getting ready to leave." Cal put the folder on his desk and shrugged on his suit jacket. "See you tomorrow."

"Goodnight, sir."

When Cal was alone again, he leaned against his desk. He'd had no real reason to come into the office, but his Fifth Avenue apartment had felt suffocating since he'd returned to the city two weeks before. He took any excuse to go out. His nights were restless as he tossed and turned and dreamed of freckled skin and warm lips.

He nodded to the security guard on his way downstairs and braced himself for the blast of humidity once he was out of the building. He had Wall Street to himself as he made his way uptown. The air was ripe with the smells of the city, especially the lingering scent of garbage that never quite disappeared in the summer. He could have taken the subway, but that would just get him home to his empty apartment faster.

By the time he reached Greenwich Village, his tie was in his pocket and his jacket slung over his shoulder. He approached a bar and thought about going in for a drink, but hesitated by the door, remembering another establishment a couple of blocks away.

Maybe it'll do me good.

He found himself walking again, turning down a dim alleyway behind a row of shops that were closed for the holiday. As he approached the battered red door, he felt that familiar old rush of adrenaline, even as the pang of guilt hit. He wiped the sweat from his brow, pausing at the threshold.

There was no sign, or markings of any kind. Just a bright door with chipped paint and a handle that creaked as he twisted it. The hinges were rusty as Cal swung the door open decisively. Inside, a bare light bulb hanging from the ceiling illuminated the staircase leading down. If he'd thought the humidity outside was bad, it was nothing compared to the lush, thick air he practically had to push aside as he descended.

Most men with money would go to the Everard on West Twenty-Eighth, but Cal cringed at the thought of running into anyone he knew. The last thing he needed was Nicholas Bourne wanting to go for drinks after a fuck, or even Michael Thorngood, eager to relive their past.

The young man in the booth at the bottom of the stairs glanced up, his head resting on his hand. "Sixty cents." He slid a thin folded towel across the counter along with a basket. Cal dropped his wallet, keys, watch, and spare change inside after taking out two quarters and a dime.

"Room seventeen."

Cal nodded and continued to the end of a short hallway. Once through the door, the steam and smell of sex hit full force. Men of all ages were spread out across the open shower room—some literally spread, being fucked and moaning hoarsely.

Along the wall were small rooms with faded curtains for doors. Cal didn't bother pulling the curtain behind him as he entered seventeen, which was empty but for a low cot and hooks on the wall for his clothing. He stripped off and slung the scratchy towel over his shoulders. Making his way slowly through the main shower room, Cal perused the clientele, falling back into his old routine. Hands reached for him, touching here and there, but he didn't stop.

Finally he saw a young blond waiting his turn outside the small steam room, glistening and hard, with dog tags around his neck. Cal joined him, turning on the smile he knew few could resist. The boy blinked and stepped close, his hand reaching for Cal's cock as he leaned in. Cal turned his head, avoiding the kiss.

Closing his eyes, he willed himself to relax. The boy's hand was smooth—*too smooth*—but he stroked Cal expertly. Cal returned the favor, keeping his face averted as he began to get hard. The boy nipped at Cal's neck, making little sounds—*too high*—and Cal fought to clear his mind. To just be in the moment.

What would Jim think of this place? Think of me?

The guilt reared its head again, and Cal swore under his breath.

The boy's movement faltered. "Is it okay?"

Cal nodded and dropped to his knees on the hard, gritty tile. He swallowed the boy's dick, breathing him in desperately. Sucking roughly, he stroked around the base of the stranger's shaft with his hand. But it was all wrong.

When the boy spurted into his mouth, Cal spit it out and wheeled away, ignoring the stares and the boy's calls. In his room, he yanked the curtain behind him, gasping for breath. He leaned a hand on the wall and spread his legs, stroking himself harshly. If he could just forget…

But his mind filled with Jim's smile. *His laughter. The taste of his skin. The gasps he made when he came. The feel of his touch. His breath in Cal's ear. The thump of his heartbeat. The reassurance of his quiet presence. The twinkle in his eyes when he made a joke. The firmness of his body. Cal's name on his lips—*

With a choked gasp, Cal's balls drew up and he shot over his hand. Any pleasure was gone in a blink, and he stroked himself harshly, spending as much as he could until he had to stop, hollow and empty. He wiped himself with the towel and tugged on his clothes, getting his socks wet and not caring as he shoved his feet into his oxfords.

He practically ran up the stairs and outside, choking in the humid air. As he walked on, weaving over to Fifth Avenue, the tension that had taken root since he left Clover Grove only felt tighter.

"CAL."

"Father." Cal closed the office door behind him and sat in one of the chairs opposite his father's desk. He waited.

It was almost a full minute before Calhoun Cunningham the second put down his pen and leaned back in his chair, folding his hands over his round belly. He was impeccably dressed, and his graying hair was trim and brushed back with pomade. "What can I do for you?"

Cal cleared his throat. "I was thinking that with everything going on in London, it might be smart for me to go back over and take care of a few things."

His father only watched him with a steady gaze, barely even blinking.

"There's uncertainty, and I can help ease the transition as we open the new branches."

"Can you now?"

Cal stopped himself from fidgeting by digging his fingers into the armrests. "Yes."

His father stared a while longer, and Cal swallowed the resentment burning in his gut. Yes, his father had taken him back at the bank with no questions asked when he'd suddenly returned. But he'd known the silence only meant his father was biding his time before saying what was on his mind.

"What's to say you won't abandon your post again?"

"I didn't *abandon* anything. I waited months to come home and made sure everything was running smoothly. But with the new acquisitions, the situation has changed. I think the company will be better served with me back in London."

At least with the Atlantic between them, Cal wouldn't be tempted every day to get in the car and drive back to the orchard, even only for a visit. The best thing was to get far away.

"And what happens when your *girlfriend* has another crisis?"

Cal's breath caught. In all his years—in all his battles with his father—it had never been addressed. But now disdain and disgust dripped from his father's tongue.

"You know it was my war buddy who needed help," Cal said.

His father laughed, a bark that echoed off the polished wood surfaces around them. "Oh, I know a lot more than you think. I'm not such a fool as you like to imagine. What happened? Lover's spat?"

Struggling to breathe evenly, Cal shifted in his seat. "No. It wasn't like that."

"I don't want to know what it was like. I've put up with your filthy predilections for far too long. You were useful after the war. It did you good, going over there. Toughened you up." He paused, emotion flickering in his eyes. "I was proud of you."

Despite himself, something small and young inside Cal rejoiced at hearing those words.

Then his father went on. "But if you go to London this time you'd better not come back unless it's with a wife."

"That's not going to happen."

"Why the hell not? Plenty of your kind fake it. Your apple farmer did."

Cal clenched his jaw. "Don't talk about him."

"Oh, is it true love? I guess not since you came running back here with your tail between your legs. Did he have enough of you? Can't blame him really."

Cal leaped up. "You don't know anything."

"I know that you're a disappointment of a son, and that your sister's idiot husband is going to have to carry on my legacy here unless you finally decide to be a man."

"You know what? I don't need you, or this job. Grandfather left me my inheritance free and clear. I don't know why I ever worked for you." He laughed humorlessly. "I've been trying to please you and spite you in equal measure ever since I can remember. I don't know why we go on this way." He shook his head as the anger drained away. "Enough's enough."

His father sighed. "I agree, son."

"I'll pack up my things." Cal turned to go.

"Your mother expects you next weekend for her charity event. Don't disappoint her."

Cal nodded and closed the door behind him once and for all.

CHAPTER EIGHTEEN

1943

"SULLY, I THINK we should go."

Shivering, Sully blinked. His gaze focused blearily on Jim. "Huh?"

"We should get back."

His pale skin a deathly white, Sully ran his hand over his shorn hair, which looked a starker ginger color than usual. "Nah, it's still early."

Jim glanced around the street, hoping for a glimpse of Joe or Pete, but they'd disappeared with two women they met at the bar. Not for the first time, Jim wished Cal was with them. But Cal was off with Amanda again, and Jim had to swallow the strange bitterness he felt. He should have been happy for his friend, and he was. Of course he was.

He refocused on Sully, trembling on the bench beside him. Jim knew, and Sully knew, that the malaria that had been blissfully dormant the past few weeks was rearing its ugly head again for another attack. But Jim also knew from the stubborn set of Sully's chin that the boy wasn't about to acknowledge it.

"I'm not feeling well. Will you come back with me?"

Sully blinked again, his brow creased. "You sick, Johnny?"

"Yeah, it's my stomach." Jim rubbed his belly, wincing. "That sausage didn't sit right."

"Where's Hollywood? He'll take care of ya."

There it was again, that strange pang at Cal's absence. "He's with his lady friend."

Sully's lips twitched. "Oh right. Sounds like a bonzer gal. A top sheila."

Jim sighed. Sully delighted in picking up Australian slang, and was likely to burst into a round of "Waltzing Matilda" once he got going. "Yes, I'm sure she is. Look, Sully—"

"You ain't met her yet, Johnny? Even Pistol brought his girl around. Well, before she told him where to go."

Again, Jim tamped down the surge of discontent. He'd asked Cal numerous times to meet Amanda, but Cal always had one excuse or another. It seemed there was some reason Cal didn't want Jim to meet her, but Jim told himself he was being paranoid. "She's very busy at her parents' shop. Cal wants time alone with her."

Sully snorted. "I bet he does. Surprised Hollywood doesn't have girls lined up for each day of the week. Did I tell you about my girl, Johnny?"

"Why don't we catch a taxi, and you can tell me on the way?"

"Hell, I ain't got money for that. We can just walk."

Jim painted on a distressed expression. "Sully, I really need to get to sick bay. I'll pay."

"Shit, Johnny. Sure. Why didn't you say?" Sully lurched to his feet and tugged on Jim's arm. "I'll get you fixed up right."

Rain splattered the windshield as the taxi drove them back to the cricket ground in the gathering dusk. Sully's whole body was wracked with tremors now. "Almost there," Jim murmured.

Sully closed his eyes and leaned his head against the window as he shook. "She was a great girl, Johnny. I never should'a kissed that other gal at the dance. But she was so pretty and smelled so nice."

Jim patted Sully's arm. "It's all right. You'll find another girl."

"We been here almost three months. You think maybe we can just stay until the war ends?"

"That would be nice, wouldn't it?"

"Sure would. It can't go on forever, right?"

It had been more than a year now since Jim boarded the troop train south to Parris Island. Christmas had come and gone in the stifling heat on the other side of the world. There had been no snowmen or Christmas trees at the cricket ground. No presents or stockings, or turkey and stuffing. He thought of Sophie and home with a powerful pang.

He hoped his father was feeling better, but it sounded as if his hip was only getting worse. At least he'd agreed to hire that fellow to help out. Jim tried to remember the name. Oh yes, Eddie. That was a comfort at least.

As usual, thinking of home made his stomach churn, and he shook his head, muttering to himself to not dwell on it. Sophie, Ann, and his father were just fine, especially now that they had Eddie to help around the place.

Sully jerked and took a shuddering breath. "Hey, Johnny?"

"Yeah?"

"I better come with you to sick bay."

"Okay, buddy."

By the next morning, Sully was fast asleep in his cot in sick bay, and Jim returned to his own bunk in the stadium stands. On his way, he spotted Cal up ahead on the grass, which put a spring in his step. "Hey!"

Cal turned. He was unshaven, and his uniform was wrinkled. He smiled as Jim caught up. "Hay is for horses. That's what my mother used to say."

Jim chuckled. "How's Amanda?"

"Swell."

This was the standard answer whenever Jim asked about her. While the others would talk up their girls all day if you'd let them, Cal's answers were always short and vague. Maybe he really cared for her and didn't want to gossip. "Is it getting serious?"

Frowning, Cal's steps faltered. "Serious?"

"Heck, you spend more time with her than you do here. I thought maybe she's the one."

There was a look on Cal's face that Jim couldn't decipher. Finally he laughed softly. "No. She's not the one."

"I was thinking I could come with you next time. If she's working, we could drop by the store. Wouldn't have to stay long. I'd like to meet her, even if you're not going to whisk her back to America after the war and make an honest woman of her."

As they reached the stadium steps and climbed to their bunks, Cal said, "The truth is she's finished with me."

Jim stopped. "I'm sorry. What happened?"

Cal shrugged. "Swept off her feet by some swab-jockey from Oklahoma. It's the ultimate indignity, really." He slung his arm around Jim's shoulders. "Guess you're stuck with me. Now come on, let's get some chow."

Jim found himself smiling as Cal led the way.

Their respite in Melbourne screeched to a halt the next week as they were ordered to move out to a camp south of the city. Jim had gotten too used to the freedom of the cricket ground, and his helmet felt unbearably heavy. His rifle and pack strained his shoulders as they marched along the pavement, boots thudding.

Beside him, Cal laughed derisively. "This again. For a while there, I forgot."

"Me too."

They left civilization behind with the broiling sun high overhead. Local dogs followed their progress, tails wagging as they ran up and down the line of men. Soon the heat got the better of the animals, and they rested along the roadside as the Marines marched on.

"Guess they're gonna whip us back into shape, huh?" Sully asked, struggling to keep up.

"Looks that way," Joe answered. He grabbed Sully's pack and hauled it over his shoulder along with his own.

Sure enough, the night marches began. They trudged along, one of the lieutenants fighting with the compass and map in the cloudy darkness. By dawn, they'd covered thirty miles. They collapsed in a pasture to sleep, huddled together in loose clumps. A few hours later,

Jim woke to the lowing of the nearby cattle, and watched the rise and fall of Cal's chest beside him.

He had the strange urge to rest his palm over Cal's heart and feel the steady beating. Cal's lips were parted, and he was peaceful, the tired lines on his face smoothed away in sleep. Jim found his hand moving, closing the distance between them to cover Cal's chest.

"Company 'tenn-shun!"

As the sergeant's voice rang out over the field, Jim yanked his hand back as if he'd been burned. They all scrambled to their feet, and Cal slapped on his helmet, giving Jim a smile. Then they were moving again.

Although they were still safe on Australian soil, with each step Jim knew they got closer to the front lines across the sea.

1948

JIM SHIELDED HIS eyes from the sun, peering past the paddock as he heard the car rumbling up the laneway. His heart foolishly skipped a beat, and he hated himself for the disappointment that coursed through him when the Cadillac didn't appear. Instead an old blue Ford Model A came to a stop by the house.

When Rebecca climbed out, Jim reminded himself to be polite. Sophie was already running over with Adam in her wake, his chubby legs flying faster than ever. Jim followed, forcing a smile on his face. "Good morning."

Rebecca hugged the children and kissed Sophie's cheek. "Happy birthday!"

"You remembered!" Sophie beamed, swinging her arms and bouncing on her toes.

"Of course I remembered. I might have even brought you a little something." She smiled and leaned back into the car.

It was a hot and humid August day, yet her red dress was neatly pressed and her lipstick perfect. Rebecca had always put her best foot forward, and Jim smiled to himself as he remembered how crazy Stephen had been for her. Cal was right—Jim had held a needless and unfair grudge, but that was going to change.

Rebecca hoisted a large, rectangular box wrapped in colorful paper from the car and handed it to Sophie. "Just a little something for your special day."

Sophie wheeled around to face Jim. "Can I open it?"

"Sure, sweetheart."

Kneeling on the grass, she tore off the paper with Adam eagerly helping. When she pulled out a ruffled yellow parasol, she gasped. "It's so pretty!" She opened it and twirled around the yard.

"And what do we say?"

"Thank you, thank you, thank you!" Sophie ran to Rebecca and gave her another hug. "I love it, Aunt Rebecca."

"My pleasure. Thought you might need a little shade out here."

Sophie took off at a run with the parasol spinning on her shoulder. Adam careened after her, and Jim and Rebecca shared a smile. Jim led the way to the house. "Thank you. That really wasn't necessary."

"I think every little girl should have something pretty. I hope it's all right that I dropped in like this. I know you have a phone now. I should have called."

"Of course it's all right. You're always welcome." He ushered Rebecca into the kitchen and pulled out a chair for her at the table.

"Thank you." She had another small box only several inches long, sedately wrapped in blue and brown paper. She handed it to Jim.

"What's this?"

"It's your birthday too."

"Me? No, I don't need anything." Jim stared at the box, not sure of what to do or say. He put it on the counter and poured Rebecca some lemonade.

"Sure you do. It's just a little something." She sipped from her glass. "Go on. It won't bite, I promise."

Smiling uneasily, Jim sat at the table. He unwrapped the box and pulled off the lid, finding two silver cufflinks inside. He lifted one and saw the faint engraving in the shape of a four-leaf clover. He shifted uncomfortably. It was a thoughtful, personal gift, yet he and Rebecca hadn't spoken more than pleasantries to each other over the years. "I don't know what to say."

She smiled softly. "Well, you can get that panicked expression off your face, Jim Bennett. I'm not looking to be courted."

"Uh…" Jim cast about for a response. Rebecca had always put him off balance somehow, and today was no different. "You're not?"

"No, I'm not." She laughed, raising her right hand with the three middle fingers up. "Scout's honor."

Jim exhaled, laughing himself. "I'm sorry. You're a lovely woman. I'm just…" *Homosexual. Queer. Unnatural.* "Not interested in seeing anyone." He pushed thoughts of Cal away like he was swatting uselessly at flies.

"That's very understandable. You have to move on in your own time, Jim."

Move on. Would he ever be able to move on from Cal? How could he? He looked at Rebecca. Could he ever marry another woman? Have sex with her and be a good husband? For the sake of his children he knew he should, but denying himself again felt like a death sentence.

He realized he was staring when Rebecca cleared her throat and pointed to the gift box.

"Ann wanted to get these for you last Christmas. Remember when she and I went to Poughkeepsie for the day? She spotted these in a window and put them on layaway. She said you didn't dress up very often but the clovers were so perfect. I was there a few months ago and they hadn't been sold."

Jim swallowed thickly. *Oh, Ann.* "You didn't have to do that."

"I think she would like it, you having them. It's for her as much as you. I miss her so desperately sometimes."

Jim could only nod, because God knew he hadn't missed his wife as much as he should have. He'd never loved her like she deserved to be loved. He squeezed one of the cufflinks, the metal cool against his palm.

Rebecca smiled sadly. "I know Ann would want you to be happy."

Nodding again, Jim put the cufflink back in the box and pushed his chair back. At the fridge he poured his own glass of lemonade before gulping it down, willing the nausea to pass.

"Have you heard from Cal? I was sorry he had to leave so suddenly."

Jim tensed, and he took a breath to level his voice. "No."

"It's only been a month or so. I'm sure he'll be in touch soon."

Sophie burst through the door, the parasol still over her shoulder. "Daddy, let's go for a walk."

"I have work to do, sweetie. Mrs. O'Brien will be back from the market soon." He leaned against the counter, gripping his glass so hard he was afraid it would shatter.

Rebecca smiled brightly at Sophie. "There's nothing I enjoy more on a sunny Saturday than a nice walk. If you'd do me the honor?"

Sophie glanced at Jim, and he nodded.

"They can show me around the orchard. It's been a long time," Rebecca said as she stood and smoothed down her dress. "Sophie, go get Adam and I'll be right out."

Jim cleared his throat. "Thank you."

"I didn't mean to upset you. I really would like to be friends."

"Of course. Ann…" Jim took a deep breath. "Ann cared for you very much. I hope you know that. You're always welcome here." He went to the table and picked up the gift box. "This was very thoughtful. You're right, Ann would be glad that I have them."

Rebecca nodded and joined the children outside. Jim listened to their gay singing, fading away as they disappeared into the orchard. He wasn't sure how long he stood there. Finally he took the box and went upstairs.

Standing in front of his dresser, he stared at the single comb and gold watch resting on the dark, worn wood, and at the tangle of his dog tags. Taking the cufflinks from their box, he carefully arranged them beside the watch. The second hand moved faithfully, and he held the watch to his ear to hear the ticking. Although he hadn't worn it but once since Cal had given it to him, he wound it every day without fail.

He placed it back down carefully. It was of the finest craftsmanship, and the thought of damaging it out in the orchard made Jim's mouth go dry. He brushed his fingertips across the glass face. Not a day had gone by that he hadn't picked up the phone and considered dialing the operator to put him through to Manhattan. But it wasn't fair. He had to let Cal go.

His gaze drifted over the cufflinks, and he took a shuddering breath. *God knows I don't deserve him.* He hadn't deserved Ann's love either. Had never been able to be the husband she needed. He'd failed her. Cal. All of them.

With quick movements, he put the cufflinks back in the box and grabbed his tags, stuffing them in as well. But no, that wasn't right. He opened the top drawer and shoved the dog tags behind his socks. After replacing the lid on the box, he hid away the cufflinks as well. His gaze returned to the watch, and Jim knew he should put it in the drawer. Make a fresh start.

He reached for it, but curled his fingers into a fist. As the memories overflowed, he practically ran from the bedroom, his head spinning. In the hallway he leaned over the banister, clutching the smooth wood as he caught his breath. The door to the guest room stood open, and Jim found himself going inside.

The night after Cal had gone, Jim had crept down the hall in the small hours and lain atop the sheets, inhaling Cal's scent. But the traces of him were gone now. Mrs. O'Brien had washed all the bedding before Ron and Lorraine's visit in July, and they'd soon be arriving again to celebrate Sophie's birthday. He felt a ridiculous resentment toward them for being in Cal's space, even though he'd invited them himself.

Jim sat on the side of the bed where Cal had slept. He couldn't hear anyone outside, and so just for a minute, he indulged himself. It was his birthday, after all. Jim closed his eyes and remembered.

"DADDY, I'M GOING to fall."

"I won't let you. Keep going." Jim walked right behind her, hands over her eyes as they entered the barn.

Mrs. O'Brien, Rebecca, Ronald, Lorraine, and Adam trailed behind them. Lunch had been a collection of Sophie's favorites, including potato salad, and macaroni and cheese. They'd had a picnic on the grass by the paddock, and Sophie had held court with her new parasol on her shoulder the whole time. Jim insisted Rebecca stay for the meal, and fortunately she'd softened Ronald's typically surly demeanor.

Jim had milked Mabel in the morning and told Sophie not to go into the barn. Now he led her to the worktable and took his hands away from her eyes.

She gasped. "For me?" Her face was alight, eyes wide.

Jim kissed the top of her head. "Happy birthday."

She threw her arms around his waist tightly. "I love you, Daddy."

With a full heart, Jim hugged her back. "Love you too."

"My goodness, it's gorgeous." Rebecca approached the dollhouse, which sat on the table with the biggest bow Jim could find sitting atop it. "I want to play with it myself."

Sophie opened the doors of the house and peered in the windows. "You can come over and play any time, Aunt Rebecca!"

Lorraine smiled and nudged her husband as Adam squirmed in her arms, reaching out toward the dollhouse. "Isn't it remarkable?"

Ronald frowned. "How'd you afford it?"

"Cal made it. I just finished up the painting and bought the dolls."

Sophie spun around. "Uncle Cal made it? For me?"

"Yep. He'll be very glad to know how much you like it."

"Really?"

Jim smiled. "Really."

She bounced. "Can we call him? I want to say thank you."

"You expect us to believe that city slicker didn't just buy it at one of those fancy stores?" Ronald muttered.

Jim's smile was tight. "I saw him make it, Ron. He worked on it night after night."

Mrs. O'Brien announced, "I think it's time for some birthday cake! Sophie, darling, later you can write Uncle Cal a thank you letter. I'm sure he'll love that. We can put it in the post on Monday."

Sophie glanced up at Jim. "We can't call him?"

"He's awfully busy, sweetheart. I think Mrs. O'Brien has the right idea. You can draw him a picture and make it all nice."

As Ronald opened his mouth, Mrs. O'Brien called out, "Come along, everyone!" She led the way out of the barn.

Lingering, Sophie peeked into the dollhouse again, reaching out to gingerly touch the dolls inside. "Daddy?"

"Yes? Come on, you've got to blow out the candles." Jim ran his hand over her loose curls. "Nine this year. Do you think you can do it?"

She nodded, but still stared at the dollhouse pensively. "Did Uncle Cal really make this for me?"

Jim crouched. "He did. He worked very hard on it. I know he was sorry he had to go before he could give it to you."

"So…he's not mad at me?"

A wave of guilt washed over him. "No, sweetie. I promise he's not mad at you. He had to go back to the city. It was nothing to do with you."

"Is he going to come back?"

"Maybe to visit one day."

Tears welled in her eyes. "Why can't he come back to stay? I miss him. Don't you miss him?"

Jim struggled to keep his expression even. "I do."

"Why does everyone have to leave? Eddie didn't even say goodbye. He was my best friend while you were away. And now Uncle Cal's gone. Why can't they come back?"

He kissed Sophie's forehead and pulled her into his arms. "I wish I knew. Now come on, it's your special day. Grandma brought your favorite—lemon upside-down cake."

"Daddy, it's your special day too."

He smiled as he stood. "I know. You're the best present I've ever had."

She wiped her damp cheeks. "You're the best daddy in the whole wide world."

They left the barn hand in hand. Even if part of him would always be hollow without Cal, he still had this. Jim squeezed Sophie's palm, and she hummed as they made their way back home.

CHAPTER NINETEEN

1944

"YOU AGAIN."

The young corpsman didn't sound particularly surprised, and Cal shrugged with a half-hearted smile as he shook the rain from his hair and wiped his face. "It's my stomach, doc."

"Uh-huh. Go take the cot next to your buddy." He nodded toward the back of the medical tent.

Mud and ever-present water squelching in his boots, Cal passed the rows of cots until he found Jim, who was curled on his side, nodding to something the boy in a nearby cot was saying. When Jim saw Cal's approach, his face lit up—as much as it could considering both his eyes were almost swollen shut.

Before Cal could say anything, the other Marine started chattering. "Hey, pal. So whaddya say? The Golden Gate in forty-eight?"

Cal squeezed Jim's shoulder as he passed by and sat on the cot on Jim's other side. They were all too thin now, but Jim was alarmingly frail beneath his blanket. Cal put on a smile. "I say that it's only forty-four now, and if we have to spend another four years on these godforsaken islands they're going to have to do something about this rain."

Since leaving the safety and comfort of Australia a year earlier, the months had ticked by, a monotony of training and fighting, and the hell of the jungle and the wetness that never went away. Perhaps even more than the enemy, it was the jungle that wore them down, battering them endlessly with bugs and damp and disease.

The boy laughed, a little too manically. "Is it always like this? I dunno, I just got here last month, and it hasn't stopped raining."

"In the summer it's unbearably hot. It's a change of pace, at least."

"Have you killed a lot of Nips? I haven't had a chance to kill any yet. They say it's malaria, and some people just get it really bad. I'm one of them. Boy, I'd hate to be sent home without killing a Jap."

Jim rolled over to face Cal, grimacing. Some of the replacements were okay, but others were like this, still annoyingly gung ho.

"If I can go home without killing another man, that'll be just fine with me," Cal said. The thought of home made him ache unbearably.

The boy's attention was caught by another patient, and Cal tuned him out. "How are you feeling?" he asked Jim.

"Better than I look. I hope."

"Nah, you look fine."

Jim's puffy lips twitched. "If I didn't know you I'd almost believe it. You should have been a corpsman, Cal. You could reassure the dying that everything would be okay. You have that way about you."

"You're not dying." Cal's tone was too sharp, and he forced a smile. "Not on my watch."

"Speaking of which, you must be running out of excuses to get sent to sick bay."

"Don't underestimate me, Jim. There are plenty more where this came from." Cal grinned.

Jim scratched his scalp and ghosted his fingertips over his swollen features. "Every time it starts to go down, it swells right back up. Doc thinks it's some kind of bug or parasite. Maybe an allergy. Who knows."

"Enjoy the rest. Not that we've gone to battle lately. We're coming across fewer and fewer Japs on patrol, which is good because we're low on ammo. Between you and me, I don't think the Japs want Cape Gloucester anymore. Or they've decided to just let the jungle be the end of us. Not a bad strategy."

"I've been resting for months, Cal. They finally released me from the hospital, and here I am in sick bay again. I need to fight. I need to stop letting you all down."

"Hey, you're not letting any of us down. It wasn't your fault you broke your ankle in that damn pothole. Just like it's not Sully's fault he got that infection on top of the malaria flaring up. No one blames either of you. We do blame you a little for the Coca-Cola you got to drink and the nurses you got to flirt with over there on Banika Island."

Jim tried to smile. "You'd suppose it would be great, huh? But I couldn't stop thinking about you here. Wondering if you'd been hit." He paused, taking a shaky breath. "I don't know what I'd do if you'd been gone when I came back. Every day I hated myself for not being here fighting with you. Leaving you all to die."

Cal rubbed Jim's arm. "Don't ever think like that. You couldn't fight. And you can't fight now when you can barely see. We're doing just fine, so don't worry." But he had to admit that as glad as he'd been for Jim to be out of harm's way, he'd missed him fiercely.

"You're doing fine now that it's winding down here. Still plenty of our guys dead." Jim shivered. "Sometimes I hate them so much. The Japs. I hate them so deep down it's like a disease. Maybe that's what this is." He waved a hand at his swollen face. "Hatred."

"We all hate them. We have to. It's war." Cal picked up the blanket from the cot he was sitting on and spread it over Jim.

"I can't remember what it's like to be truly dry. I feel like I'm covered in mold from the inside."

Cal nodded. "My socks are disintegrating again. I only got them last week."

"I tried to write a letter home, but my pen clogged and then the point split in half. I remembered O'Neill over there had a pencil, but it had swollen and burst."

"At least we're out of the rain in here." It battered the large tent's roof endlessly in a constant chorus. "I haven't had a smoke for days. Tried to keep them dry in my helmet, but no dice, as usual."

"We thought Guadalcanal was bad, but New Britain takes the cake."

"Having been to the old Britain, which is damn miserable and damp enough, I have to agree."

Jim sighed. "Melbourne seems like a dream now. Let alone home." He pulled the thin blankets closer around his shoulders. "I don't want to miss another Christmas. Missed two already."

"That's eight months away. Plenty of time for us to win this damn war."

"She's more than four and a half now. Walking and talking, and then some. She'll be old enough to understand Santa Claus. To believe that reindeer landed on the roof when she sees the presents on Christmas morning. Eddie, the man who tends the orchard, made her a little swing set. Ann says he's been a godsend. It should be me doing that. Not him. I should be taking care of my family."

Cal patted Jim's shoulder. What could he say?

"Ann sent a picture from last Christmas, but I can't keep it dry." Jim pulled his arm out from beneath the blankets and handed Cal the small, curling photograph.

Cradling it gingerly, Cal examined the stained picture. Sophie's chubby-cheeked smile was fading already—her dark ringlets and the Christmas tree behind her disappearing as the paper yellowed. He could see Jim in the shape of her eyes and the set of her nose. "She's beautiful, Jim."

"Prettiest girl in the world. I don't want to miss her next birthday."

"I'm sure you'll see her soon."

Jim's voice dropped to barely a whisper. "She won't even know me. I'm a stranger to her. Her whole world is her mother and grandparents, and even Eddie. I bet she can't even remember me."

Cal crossed the narrow aisle and nudged Jim over on the cot so he could perch on the side. When Jim was at his lowest, this was the fear that plagued him. Cal would reassure him as often as he needed to. He squeezed Jim's arm and spoke softly. "Sophie's your daughter. Once you go back home, it won't take long at all before she forgets you were ever gone. I promise."

"What if I never go home, Cal?" Tears welled in Jim's swollen eyes, leaking from the edges. "What if I never see her again?"

Cal hated seeing him like this, and cursed the Japs and a God he didn't believe in. "Hey, hey. Of course you're going home." He smoothed his hand over Jim's shorn hair. "We're going to get through this."

"It's never going to end. After we won on Guadalcanal, and had that break in Australia, I didn't think…I hoped it wouldn't be long." Jim's shoulders shook with a broken laugh. "It just keeps going. One island after the other. Battles that never get us anywhere. Good men dying, and all these new boys coming to replace them. And the rain never stops. I feel like I'm growing vines—like the jungle's consuming us bit by bit."

"I know." Cal wanted to take Jim in his arms. Hold him and make everything better, and take the sickness from him for his own. Instead he pulled a sodden cloth from his pocket and gently wiped Jim's tears from his cheeks. "It'll be okay. It will."

Jim swallowed thickly. "Sorry. You should go back. I'll be fine."

"Can't. My stomach's killing me, remember?" Cal smiled.

As if on cue, the corpsman made his way through the sick bay in their direction, so Cal stretched out on his cot. He schooled his features into a pained expression, shooting Jim a wink. He groaned. "Doc, I think I'm dying."

"Uh-huh." The corpsman shined a light into Cal's eyes and gave him a cursory exam. "It's probably a parasite."

"Is that your answer for everything?"

The corpsman smiled wryly. "Pretty much. This fuckin' jungle's full of 'em. That garbage they're passing off as food is probably gonna kill us before the Japs get a chance."

"Did anyone ever tell you your bedside manner needs work?"

At this, the corpsman grinned. "Yeah, but they're all dead now." He turned to check on Jim—another cursory exam. "You two'll make it. Don't worry." He glanced at Cal. "You can stay the night unless we need the bed for someone worse off." Then he was gone to tend to a man screaming on the other side of the tent.

Cal sat up to yank off his boots. "Stop me if you've heard this one. There once was a man from Nantucket."

Jim smiled—a real smile despite his swollen face. "Thanks for staying with me, Cal."

"You say that now, but just wait until you hear the rest of this joke. You'll be begging to get rid of me."

"Been trying to shake you for ages now, but you're pretty stubborn."

Cal grinned. "Afraid you're stuck with me."

1948

Taking another gulp of whiskey, Cal picked up the envelope again. From the open window behind the couch, the sounds of the street floated up—cars honking and motors humming. Although it was officially September, the oppressive heat of summer wasn't in any hurry to leave. A ceiling fan stirred up the warm air. Cal could have turned on the air conditioning, but he felt too confined with the windows shut.

The ice in his glass rattled, and the condensation wet his fingers. In his boxer shorts, he stuck to the leather couch, and he shifted uncomfortably. After wiping his hand on his white undershirt, he traced the neat, curled script of the return address.

Miss S. Bennett
Clover Grove
192 Green Hills Road
Tivoli, New York

In the envelope was a homemade white card with a drawing in pencil crayon of the doll house. He reread the message.

Dear Uncle Cal,

Thank you for my birthday present. I love it.
    I wish you would come visit soon. We miss you.

From,
Sophie
xoxo

The whiskey burned as it slid down Cal's throat. He'd loved Jim for so long, and had never thought about the possibility of feeling anything so powerful for someone else. But oh, he loved those children. He'd always known he'd never be a father, but for the first time he wished he could be.

Shaking his head, he put the card back in its envelope and dropped it on the coffee table. He hadn't worked for almost two months, and hadn't left the apartment now in a week. He'd shaved that morning for the hell of it, even though he knew he'd spend the day napping and listening idly to the radio. On Jim and Sophie's birthday, he hadn't gotten out of bed at all.

The radio crackled now with big band music that reverberated along with the low beats of the ceiling fan. Cal knew he could only wallow so long before he had to find a way to move on. Perhaps he'd go to London anyway, or travel across Europe. Maybe go to Paris and see what the Germans had left behind.

He took another drink and wished he had some applesauce. Cal would have thought he'd be sick of apples and apple byproducts, but he missed everything about the orchard. He wondered what Mrs. O'Brien was making for dinner.

He dozed, and sweat gathered on his brow. The horns from the street were a strange lullaby, mixing with Benny Goodman's trumpets. Late in the afternoon, a storm rolled by, and Cal slept more deeply, dreaming of Guadalcanal and the tropical rain seeping into his skin, Jim huddled by his side whispering words Cal couldn't make out.

It was evening when Cal woke, groggy and somehow more tired.

The newsman recited the day's events, and after Cal hauled himself up to shuffle over and flick off the radio, he froze with his hand outstretched.

"The heavy storm that swept across New York City intensified as it reached the Hudson Valley, with winds gusting up to sixty miles an hour and producing hailstones as large as two inches in diameter."

Dread uncoiled in Cal's gut.

"Saugerties and the surrounding area received the worst of it with untold damage to property and homes."

Saugerties—right across the river from Tivoli. If the storm had hit the orchard…

"Hudson Valley crops have been seriously affected, and injuries have been reported—several life-threatening."

The newsman droned on as Cal snatched up the keys to the Cadillac, pausing only to tug on slacks and cram his feet into the closest pair of shoes before he was gone.

WITH HIS HEART in his throat, Cal turned off the engine and cut the lights. Clover Grove was shrouded in darkness, and clouds were still heavy overhead. Cal had stopped the Cadillac some distance away, not wanting to wake the kids. No lights shone from the windows, which wasn't surprising since it was after midnight.

Cal walked toward the house, his leather loafers slipping on the sodden grass. He stood in front of the door but didn't knock. *Should just get in the car and go back to Manhattan.* He hadn't stopped to think before rushing onto the road. Now, standing in front of the dark house, he felt unbearably foolish in his undershirt. He shivered in the night breeze.

It had been hard enough leaving in the first place, and even if the crop was ruined, what could he do about it? Jim wouldn't take a handout. Shaking his head and muttering to himself, Cal returned to the

Cadillac. With his hand on the door, he stopped. Maybe he should take a look at the trees and see what the damage was. Perhaps the hail had missed the orchard and there was nothing to worry about. He could go for a walk and stretch his legs, and then drive away long before Jim woke.

At the thought of Jim sleeping—his lips parted, chest rising and falling as he snored softly—Cal had to close his eyes and steady himself, battling the impulse to rush inside and climb into Jim's bed. Knowing that he'd never kiss or touch Jim again had carved a hole inside him that would never be filled.

Sure, he'd lived with it for years, and the pain had been dulled by acceptance. But now that he'd actually *had* Jim, his absence was a fresh wound that Cal feared would never heal.

With a deep breath, he gathered himself and headed down the rise into the orchard. He knew the terrain well enough now that even in the dark he didn't stumble. As he approached the trees, Finnigan's familiar bark echoed in the night, and Cal made out the low shape of the dog racing his way.

Crouching, he scratched behind Finnigan's ears. "Hi, boy. I missed you too." He chuckled as Finnigan licked his face, the dog's tail whipping back and forth.

A flicker of movement caught Cal's eye, and his heart skipped a beat. There was Jim, like a statue among the trees. He appeared rooted to the spot, so Cal approached with Finnigan dancing around his heels.

He stopped several feet from Jim. Perhaps this had been a mistake indeed. "Sorry to arrive unannounced. I can go."

Jim stared for a few more moments. "Are you real?"

Cal took another step. Jim seemed dazed, the way he was sometimes after one of his episodes. "I heard about the storm, and I wanted to make sure everything's all right. Are you okay? The kids?"

Nodding, Jim said nothing else.

Cal gazed around at the trees but couldn't see much in the gloom. "The apples?"

Blinking, Jim seemed to return to reality. "Ruined. More than half from what I can tell." He bent to pluck an apple from the ground. "Can't sell them bruised and dented."

Hating the defeat in Jim's voice, Cal took the piece of fruit, examining the battered skin. "One hell of a storm, huh?"

"I've never seen hail like that. Hope I never do again. Need to rebuild part of the roof on the barn. The house too. The hail dented the heck out of the truck."

"Jesus, I'm sorry, Jim. If there's anything I can do, tell me."

"There's nothing anyone can do." He grimaced. "Mother Nature always gets the last laugh. It's the way of the world."

"You know if you need money, I'll—"

"We'll get by." Jim uttered the words as if by rote.

"How? How are you going to get by with less than half your income? Never mind fixing the damage?"

Pain pinched Jim's expression. "I don't know. I'll figure something out." He squared his shoulders, seeming to give himself a mental shake. "I won't take your money."

"Why do you have to be so damn stubborn?"

Jim shook his head. "It wouldn't be right. You've already given me so much, and what can I give you in return?"

"Jim…"

Of course they both knew what Cal wanted—what they both wanted—and their gazes locked, the heavy, damp air suddenly electric. Cal still had the apple in his hand, and he dug in his nails, resisting the urge to close the distance and wrap Jim in his arms. Then he gave in and took a hesitant step.

For a moment, Jim's resolve appeared to crack. The desire and raw *need* in his expression stole the air from Cal's lungs. He knew all the reasons they'd parted hadn't changed, but he wanted Jim desperately—as much as he ever had, maybe even more. Even if it was only one more night, there was nothing stopping them.

Although they weren't touching, Jim jerked back, shaking his head.

"We can't, Cal. I can't."

With a sigh and a nod, Cal tossed the apple and jammed his hands into the pockets of his slacks. He suddenly felt very foolish, and he backed up. "I should get going. Oh, thank Sophie for the card. Tell her I called or something."

"Wait. It's too late for you to drive back now. I can't turn you out."

Cal tried to smile. "It's okay. You're under no obligation to be hospitable to guests who turn up uninvited in the middle of the night."

"Stay until morning. You can see the kids. They miss you."

"I miss them too."

"Sophie loves the dollhouse. I moved it into their room, and she spends hours with it. Brought over a few of her school friends to see it last week. They said they wished they had an Uncle Cal."

The pang he felt still surprised him. "I really do miss her. Adam too. And I really should go."

"Stay. It's one night."

"I have things I need to do tomorrow."

"Oh. I don't want to keep you from your work. How's it going with your father?"

"Good, good. I might go to London again." The lies slipped off his tongue far too easily. "The bank's doing well, and we're expanding across England and into Wales." That was the truth, at least.

"London." Jim nodded. "That's great, Cal. I'm sure you'll do a wonderful job. You'll have to send the children a postcard." He smiled weakly. "England and Wales will be lucky to have you."

"Thanks. So, I should get going." He turned.

"Cal, wait."

Forcing himself to breathe, Cal circled back around. "Yeah?"

"I'll worry about you out on the road at this hour. Just wait until morning. Please?"

Cal thought of Ann's accident. "All right. How about I stay in the cabin?"

"Don't be silly. You can sleep in your room." Jim's smile was forced, and his tone too light. "I'm sure we can control ourselves for a few hours."

Cal laughed awkwardly. "I'm sure."

They fell into step together and made their way back to the house. As they passed the barn, Cal thought of their last time in there—on his hands and knees with Jim pounding into him. If only he'd known it would be the last time, he would have…what?

Taking a sharp breath, Cal ordered himself to forget it. *This is the way it has to be.*

In the kitchen, Jim poured them each a glass of water. He offered whiskey, but Cal shook his head. There was nothing left to do but go to bed, and they eased up the stairs, even though the children usually wouldn't be woken by anything quieter than a freight train rumbling through the sitting room.

Jim peeked in at the kids, and Cal paused in the guest room doorway. "Good night," he whispered.

Cal's chest ached as they shared another look that said everything they couldn't. Then Jim nodded, and Cal shut the door. He kicked off his shoes and folded his slacks and undershirt over the chair in the corner. Clad in his boxers, he climbed under the familiar sheets.

Despite everything, it felt like coming home.

CHAPTER TWENTY

1944

An explosion boomed across the water, the sound washing over them with a growl as their amtrac approached land. The men huddled together in the floating tank, taking turns peeking at the cloud of smoke hanging over Peleliu. The amtrac gave more shelter than the Higgins Boats, for which Jim was grateful.

"It don't look very big," Sully said, speaking loudly over the roar of another bomb. Overhead, American planes soared, and warships dotted the ocean behind.

"No, it doesn't." Pushing his helmet out of his eyes, Jim smiled. "Remember what the lieutenant told us on Pavuvu before we left. This one should all be over in a couple of days."

"Looks like we've already shelled the shit out of it. Can't imagine there are many Japs left on that miserable rock," Pete added.

The air snapped with the reverberations of more explosions, and flames flickered in the smoke. Then, as the wave of landing vehicles approached shore, the barrage ceased, and there was a sudden, eerie silence.

Cal was pressed up behind Jim, and he leaned in, his breath tickling Jim's neck.

"Here we go. Keep your head down."

"You too."

If Cal said anything else, it was lost in the mortar and artillery that rained down from the island. Their amtrac plowed on, the smell of burning metal mixing with the salt air. As they lurched to shore, the men leaped over the side.

Jim took in the sight of the beach, already a graveyard of smoldering amtracs and bloodied and charred men. The sand was littered with holes, and in many Jim could spot the helmets of Marines taking cover from the barrage of mortars and machine gun fire coming from the headland, which appeared carved out of coral.

Praying he wouldn't hit any unexploded mortars, Jim burrowed into the sand. They were pinned down and had to take out the enemy firing from the headland or they'd never make it across the beach. He glanced about for Cal, breathing in relief as he spotted him digging into his own hole.

The ground shook, and Jim spat sand from his mouth. Sweat dripped into his eyes. He blinked, hoping the Marine tank rumbling out from the trees wasn't a figment of his imagination. He heard Pete's shout, urging on the tank as it took aim at the coral fortress.

Jim followed the direction of Pete's voice and saw him, his arm raised as he cheered on the tank. Then there was a burst of sound and fire, and Pete disintegrated into gore in a plume of acrid smoke that burned Jim's nostrils. He opened his mouth to scream, but no sound came.

Pete was gone.

The tank fired into the hole through which the Japs had been firing, yet the men inside disappeared one by one, jumping out of sight. Somehow they escaped, as if by some sleight of hand—rabbits in a magician's hat.

When the Japanese firing was silenced, Jim and the others abandoned their holes, hurrying into the scrub beyond the beach and sliding into a crater left by a mighty blast in the dry earth. Sully, Joe, and others joined him, and Jim looked back for Cal. For a minute, there was no sign, and Jim craned his neck as his pulse raced. Cal had been fine, but then again so had Pete right up until the last moment.

Jim squeezed his eyes shut as if he could block out the memory. Counting under his breath, he waited. The seconds were like hours. Another Marine scurried toward them, but Jim knew from a glance that it wasn't Cal. "Ninety-three, ninety-four…" he muttered.

"He's coming, Johnny." Big Joe thumped on Jim's back, his preferred method of reassurance.

Just as Jim scrambled to his feet to find him, Cal jogged into sight and dropped into the crater. Jim took a shuddering breath, and his body relaxed just a bit. Around Cal's neck swung four extra canteens. He ducked his head and pulled them free.

"Figured we could use all the water we can get from the looks of this place."

They all drank, passing the extra canteens around and saving their own water for later. The sun scorched them, and Sully huddled beneath his helmet, his skin already reddening. He grumbled, "Never thought I'd miss the fuckin' jungle, but I'm sure glad we ain't gonna be here long."

They were close to the airstrip that made the island valuable, and in the distance, rocky outcroppings rose above the flat landscape. "Japs must be up there," Jim noted.

Joe nodded. "Yep. Should be plenty of fun getting across that airstrip. Not too many places to hide."

They all murmured their agreement.

"Hey, where's Pistol?" Sully gazed around, pushing up his helmet.

"Maybe he found another crater," Cal said, although he didn't sound convinced.

Images of Pete's last moments played out in Jim's mind, the smell of singed flesh making his mouth water as his stomach lurched. He hadn't eaten since they were on the transport ship, and he inhaled deeply through his nose, not wanting to lose what little he had in his stomach. "No."

Cal's hand was warm on his arm. "Jim?"

"He's not coming." Jim cleared his parched throat. "He got it on the beach."

"Pistol got it?" Sully sounded incredulous. "But…ain't nobody who could take down the Pistol. He's tough as nails."

"Not tougher than a mortar," someone said. Jim didn't know him.

Joe swore. "Fucking Nip bastards."

They sat in silence under the blazing sun. What more was there to say? Before long, the lieutenant was barking commands. "Stovepipe boys, your target is the enemy bunkhouse across the airstrip. Move out!"

Soon they found out how thin the cover really was, and how easily the Japs could take them out. Machine gun fire burst endlessly, shells falling as the Marines raced across the airstrip, their equipment an albatross in the unbearable heat.

"Gonna kill us all, aren't they?" Sully winced as they dove into another crater as a shell exploded nearby. "We're sitting ducks here."

Then another Marine skidded into the crater, a radio man this time. "Got any water?"

Jim had drained his canteen already, and he and the others shook their heads.

The radio man swore. "There's no water on this fucking island so they sent some over from the ships in old gas drums. Too bad they didn't rinse them out first. There's men down all over the place, sick as dogs. Like we don't have enough problems with these Jap fuckers in their tunnels."

"Tunnels?" Cal asked, his face grim.

"Yeah, I heard they got this whole island set up with tunnels and caves and hidey-holes while we're running around here in the open like it's goddamn target practice."

Jim's stomach churned anew. "I thought this one was supposed to be easy."

The radio man barked out a laugh. "Story of our fuckin' lives."

1948

THE ROOSTER'S CROWING echoed in the dawn, and Jim rolled onto his back. He hadn't slept a wink, his mind whirling as he imagined the orchard's books and tried to calculate the damage the hailstorm had done to the potential profits.

Of course, the fact that Cal was under his roof again, just down the hall, didn't help to still Jim's restless mind. He'd hoped that after not seeing Cal for more than two months the fever for him would have dimmed. That perhaps Jim's feelings could return to the proper friendship they'd shared instead of the immoral attraction that had burned right through him.

Often during the long summer, Jim's thoughts had gone to Cal, and when Jim's traitorous body responded, he'd refused to give in. He hadn't touched himself even once, knowing the fantasies his mind unspooled would only make Cal's absence harder to bear. And of course it was a sin no matter how right it felt.

But now his body hummed. The thought of Cal so close—oh, the things they could do together; the joy and release he would find in Cal's arms—was intoxicating. He knew it was wrong, but he yearned for it all the same.

Rubbing a hand over his eyes, Jim rolled out of bed and crept to the bathroom. He needed to focus and get a hold of himself. He splashed water on his face and peered into the mirror in the cool morning light. What kind of man would think to do such things when it put his children at risk?

Nothing had changed. Homosexuality was a crime in the eyes of the law and the Lord. Jim stared at his own reflection. How could he even consider it again? He had to close the door on this shameful part of himself. Cal would go to London, and it would all be for the best.

Footsteps creaked in the hallway, and he opened the door to find Sophie in her nightdress by the guest room. Jim whispered, "Shh. Come away from there."

She did as she was told, wiping sleep from her eyes. "Who's in there?"

"Uncle Cal."

Her face lit up and her voice rose. "Uncle Cal?"

"Shh. Yes. He arrived last night. You were already in bed."

"I knew he'd come back!"

"He's not staying, sweetie. He has to drive back to the city this morning. He just…happened to be in the area for business."

"What kind of business? Why can't he stay? I want him to stay."

"Go do your chores, and we'll talk about it later. Mabel's waiting."

"But—"

Jim gave her a look. "*Now.*"

Grumbling, she hurried off, and Jim sighed. He hated lying to her. At least Adam wasn't old enough to really understand or ask questions.

It was almost time for Sophie to leave for school when Cal came down wearing his trousers and one of Jim's dressier shirts. She raced over and flung her arms around him. "Uncle Cal!"

Adam clung to Cal's legs, and Jim could see the emotion in Cal's face before he painted on one of his big smiles.

"If it isn't Sophie and Adam Bennett. I thought I might find you two here. Have you been good for your daddy?"

They nodded in unison, and Sophie said, "We're always good, Uncle Cal."

Jim had to laugh at that, and soon they were all laughing. The happiness glowing in Jim's chest was so bright he had to turn away. He cleared his throat. "Sophie, you'd better go or you'll miss the bus."

"Uncle Cal, will you be here when I get back?"

Cal glanced at Jim. "Not today, I don't think. But I'll try and visit really soon. Thank you for your card, by the way."

"I love my dollhouse so much." She tugged his hand. "You have to come see it!"

"Honey, you're going to be late." Jim picked up Sophie's lunchbox and handed it to her.

"It'll just take a minute!" She scrambled down the hall with Cal in tow and Adam following.

"One minute!" Jim called after them.

The *ring-ring* of the bell on Mrs. O'Brien's bicycle sang out, and Adam changed course, speeding outside to greet her. Jim followed, squinting in the sunlight. "Good morning, Mrs. O'Brien."

She twirled Adam in her arms before resting him on her hip. "Good morning." She glanced at the Cadillac. "I see you have a visitor."

"He stopped by last night. Wanted to see how we were doing after the storm."

"Ah. That was very kind." She gazed at the orchard in the distance, littered with ruined apples on the ground. Many left on the trees were equally bruised. "I wish there was better news. What are you going to do, Jim?"

The knot of anxiety in his gut swelled. "I don't know. We'll get by." *God, please let us get by.*

"If there's anything I can do, don't hesitate."

"Thank you, but you already do more than enough."

As Sophie and Cal came outside, Mrs. O'Brien clucked her tongue. "You'd better skedaddle and catch the bus, young lady!"

Cal hugged Sophie and pressed a kiss to the top of her head. "Go on. I'll see you soon. I promise."

"Okay." She turned to go, but then spun around. "You promised, so you can't take it back now." With that, she shot off down the drive with her lunchbox in hand.

Mrs. O'Brien kissed Cal on the cheek. "How lovely to see you again. I do hope you'll be staying."

"Thank you." Cal glanced at Jim. "Maybe."

Maybe?

"I'll leave you to it then." She disappeared inside with Adam.

Jim cleared his throat. "Cal, we talked about this."

"I know. Look, just hear me out. Let's go for a walk." He started toward the orchard.

Jim had no choice but to follow.

Once they were alone in the trees, sidestepping ruined apples, Cal stopped. He glanced down at the borrowed shirt. "I hope you don't mind. I was feeling a little underdressed. I'll have it cleaned."

Jim shook his head. "I don't care about the shirt. I care about you making promises to Sophie you can't keep."

Cal took a deep breath. "Maybe I can."

"Cal—"

"Let me say this. Please?"

Exhaling sharply, Jim nodded and crossed his arms. Why Cal insisted on making this more difficult was beyond him. He couldn't bear to be near Cal and not touch him much longer.

"I'm not going to London. Or Cardiff. I never was. I quit in July. Or was fired, depending on your perspective. Had it out with the old man, and it's over. I'm never working for him again. I'll never be the son he wants, and I need to stop trying to be, even half-heartedly. I realize I've said it before, that I'm done with the bank. But this time I mean it."

Jim wasn't sure what to think. "I'm sorry to hear that."

"You know, I was sorry for a while. Right up until yesterday." He gazed at the trees. "But now I know what's really important. What I want. I just hope you want it too."

"Cal…"

"You said you'd let me finish." He cleared his throat. "Okay, the way I see it, we both have a problem. You have an orchard full of fruit you can't sell. I have more money than I could ever need, and an acute case of boredom and aimlessness. But last night I realized there's a solution to both our problems."

Jim sighed. "We've been through this. I'm not taking your money, Cal. I won't."

"So make me your partner. All on the up and up. The orchard will be half mine. I won't be giving you anything. It's a business investment."

"An investment in an orchard with a ruined crop that barely keeps afloat on a good year? It doesn't make any sense. I appreciate the offer, but we both know you're full of it."

Cal's face split into one of his beaming smiles. "Me? *Full of it?* Why, Jim Bennett, that's harsh talk coming from you."

Jim couldn't help but smile along. "Stop distracting me. Yes, you're full of it."

"What if we could turn the damaged apples into profit?"

"If we had a magic wand, sure."

"We'll make cider. The hard stuff. I have a buddy in New York who owns three pubs, and I can sell it to dozens more." His eyes were alight. "If there's one product that's a sure thing, it's booze. I'll get my cousin in Philly to make the hydraulic press and we can build a cider house. It could work."

Jim couldn't help but be a little swept up in Cal's excitement, and his heart thumped. "But how long does hard cider take to ferment?"

"A couple of years."

"*Years?* Cal, I don't have years. I don't know how I'm going to get through the winter."

"It's an investment. We harvest the undamaged apples and sell them like usual. The others we'll turn into cider. In the meantime, you'll have the money from the sale. If I'm going to go in fifty-fifty, I need to buy my share."

Jim frowned. "That doesn't seem right."

"Why not? If I buy half this orchard I'm paying fair and square."

"But…" Jim paced back and forth, tugging at the collar of his navy work shirt. "I know you're only doing this for me."

Cal's laugh was unmistakably sad. "I'm doing it just as much for me. Yes, I want to help you, and I'm sorry if that's something your pride can't bear. But I love you, and I love Sophie and Adam. I love this place. I've never been so happy in my life as I have been here. I want a piece of Clover Grove for myself. I want—no, I *need* something to live for."

Jim swallowed hard. "You know I want you to be happy. Of course I do."

Cal stepped toward him, smiling softly. "So say yes. Sell me half the orchard, and let's build something great together. A business that'll be more than just enough to get by on. We can do it, Jim. I know we can."

Despite himself, hope bloomed. Jim tried to tamp it down. "But you know we can't…be together the way we want. It's just going to be harder if you're here. It's impossible."

"It's better than nothing, Jim. I don't have to live here. I can come out every week or so. Every two weeks, or every month. Whatever works. That way I can still see the kids. Can still see you. No matter what's happened, or what will happen, you're my best friend. God, I've missed you." He looked at his shoes and murmured, "Haven't you missed me?"

It took everything in Jim not to go to him. He balled his hands into fists. "Of course."

Cal glanced up, his eyes hopeful. "Really?"

"Don't ever doubt it." He took a deep breath. "Cal, I want you as a friend. But we can't let it go any further. For all the reasons you left in the first place."

"I know. It'll be fine, Jim. We were friends for much longer than we were…" He trailed off, the word unsaid but hanging in the air.

It echoed in Jim's mind. *Lovers.*

"I don't know what to think." He looked around at his trees and the battered, useless fruit. "Harvest should begin in a few weeks, but I've got to start picking up the fallen apples now. And we'd still need to build the cider house, and have the press made."

"Leave it to me. You get some help in and start collecting the apples. I'll do the rest."

"I can't believe I'm even considering this." Jim rubbed his hand through his hair.

Cal smiled. "You're not considering it. You've made up your mind."

"I guess you know me pretty well, huh?" Jim chuckled. He pondered it quietly for another moment, letting the hope run wild. Maybe everything would be okay after all. He could save the orchard, and at least he and Cal could be friends again. "You really want to do this?"

"I'll have a lawyer draw up the papers today."

"All right. Yes."

Cal leaned forward as if to pull him into a hug, but apparently remembered himself. He extended his arm. "Friends. Business partners. Nothing more."

Jim took his hand, ignoring the flare of need that shot through him. "Deal."

CHAPTER TWENTY-ONE

1945

"I THOUGHT YOU Guadalcanal boys were being rotated home." The replacement hurried to keep up with Cal, Jim, and Sully.

"What, and leave all this?" Cal waved his hand to take in Pavuvu, which honestly did seem luxurious after the death and utter desolation of Peleliu. It was safe, at least, and there were some comforts. With the sun setting, it was almost pretty. "Nah."

"Bunch of first battalion went," Sully muttered. "But they couldn't send us all. Someone's gotta teach you new boys the ropes."

In another life, Cal would have laughed at the idea of little Sully, still squeaky-voiced and skinny, being one of the old breed. But he was a veteran now, his sunken, sometimes-vacant eyes telling the story. They'd barely made it through Peleliu, and for what?

"Sergeant, what was it like on Guadalcanal? I read all about it in the papers. I couldn't wait until I was old enough to join up."

It took Cal a moment to realize the replacement was talking to him. "Well, we won. So it was fine."

The replacement chattered until Cal sent him on an errand, and Sully sauntered off with a nod. Cal lit a cigarette and exhaled the sweet smoke, gazing at the pink sky as more replacements ambled by.

"They're so young." Jim watched them go. "They don't know yet."

"They will soon enough."

Sighing, Jim leaned against a palm tree. "Hope Joe's making out all right at home. Wonder what it's like, going back after all this. Might as well be the moon, it feels so far away."

"I could talk to Captain Brown. You're overdue. You and Sully both."

"And you're not? Besides, I heard you already talked to the captain."

Cal brushed it off with a smile. "I'm a sergeant now, Jim. I'm practically planning this thing with Patton these days."

Jim regarded him evenly. "They were going to send you home, weren't they? You've fought three campaigns."

"So have you."

"I was in the hospital for most of Cape Gloucester. So was Sully. But you weren't. I heard you fought to stay. Insisted on it."

Part of Cal had wanted to take the ticket home so desperately, hoping that the war would end before he had to return. For a terrible moment, he'd wanted to go and never look back. But the thought of returning to New York while Jim was still in hell was unimaginable.

The shame that he'd even considered it prickled his skin. He kicked at a stone. "Figured someone had to stick around to keep you and Sully out of trouble. Especially you."

Jim's lips twitched. "Yeah, I'm a real ne'er-do-well."

"A menace. They need me to keep you in line."

"Good thing you're on the job, Sergeant Cunningham."

Cal nudged Jim's shoulder. "Don't you call me that."

"Why not? You deserve it, Cal."

He snorted. "They threatened to send me to Officer Candidate School. Said I should have gone there in the first place."

"They're right."

"Why, because I'm loaded and went to Princeton?"

"Because you're a leader. You're the one who got us through Peleliu. Kept our spirits up. We all looked to you."

Despite himself, Cal basked in Jim's praise. "You know they only promoted me because most of the NCOs are dead, and they can only ship over so many from the States.”

“Even so, you deserve it.” Jim gazed at him intently. “We had a hell of a time on Peleliu, Cal. But you didn’t let us give up. So don’t be hard on yourself.”

He nodded, trying not to smile too widely. “All right.”

A grizzled Marine sauntered by, puffing on a cigarette. “You guys hear the reports from Iwo Jima? They’re in tough.”

Cal said, “Sounds like Peleliu all over again.”

The Marine grunted. “Ain’t that the truth. But we’ll be moving out soon enough ourselves with all this training we’re doing. They’ve got another battle planned for us, that’s for sure. Another one of these fucking islands. There’s a million of ’em.”

Puffing on his cigarette, Cal tried not to think about it. He and Jim watched the sun dip below the horizon and slapped at the mosquitoes as they buzzed to life.

When they returned to their tent, the mail was being delivered. Each man with a letter from home read it eagerly while the others asked what the notes said. There was nothing for Cal, which was expected. He’d received a perfunctory Christmas card from his parents, and likely wouldn’t hear from them again until the next December.

A land crab scuttled by, and he smashed it with his bayonet. “Damn things won’t get the hint.”

But Jim didn’t reply. He sat on his cot, his eyes roving over neat script that Cal knew from a glance was Ann’s. He swallowed down his unfair resentment and spoke up. “How are things at Clover Grove, Jim?”

His expression blank, Jim didn’t answer as he folded the letter neatly and stowed it back in its envelope. Cal sat beside Jim and gave him a nudge. “Everything okay?”

“My father died.” Jim’s voice was flat.

That caught everyone’s attention, and the chattering in the tent stopped. Cal gave Sully a look, and Sully gestured to the others.

“It’s almost chowtime. Let’s get a good spot in line.”

When he and Jim were alone, Cal murmured, “I’m sorry.”

Jim nodded, his throat working. "It shouldn't be a shock. He's been sick. First he broke his hip, and then his heart started to give out. You know how it is."

"Still is a shock though, huh?" He rubbed Jim's back.

"Yeah. Silly, isn't it?"

"Not at all."

Jim swallowed thickly. "He was a good man. Had a good life. He was the best father I could have asked for. When my mother passed, he took on so much. I was such a burden."

"You were no such thing, and he'd tell you the same."

Tears glistened in Jim's eyes. "I wish I could have been there with him."

"He understood you had to do your duty. He was proud of you."

A sob escaped Jim's lips, and he hung his head. Cal pulled him closer, murmuring to him as Jim slumped against his shoulder. He let Jim cry, and when there was nothing left he urged him back onto the cot and pulled the blanket over him. Jim was asleep in minutes, his breath still hitching. Cal skipped dinner and watched over him, ready in case Jim woke again.

As Cal drifted off to sleep later, he said a silent prayer to any deity listening that no matter what horrors they had to face in their next blitz, Jim would make it home in one piece.

1948

LEANING AGAINST THE paddock fence, Cal watched the last wall go up on the cider house with a deep sense of satisfaction. They'd decided to situate it near the top of the rise, but far enough away from the house that any noise wouldn't be heard. His cousin had come through with the press in only a month, and Cal had made sure the extension on the electricity line had been finished in time. Of course, when you had enough money, miracles were infinitely possible.

"Look at this, Uncle Cal!"

Cal turned and watched Sophie trot around the paddock on her horse, Trixie. "You're a pro. Make sure you hang on tight."

She rolled her eyes artfully. "I'm not a baby."

"You should still hang on tight no matter how grown-up you get."

Sophie giggled and continued prancing around. Cal glanced back at the cider house to watch the progress. They were building it around the press after laying the foundation and putting on the floorboards. One side would slide all the way open if they ever needed to replace the machinery, and storage for the fermenting barrels had been built into the ground to keep them cool all year.

As the wall went up, Cal squinted at it, deciding it looked decidedly upside down. Sighing, he headed over, muttering, "If you want something done right…"

The workmen were heaving the wall back down when Sophie's scream pierced the air. Wheeling around, Cal saw Trixie sidestepping in the paddock, her nostrils flaring. Cal was moving already, legs pumping as he raced across the grass. He vaulted the paddock fence and almost landed on Sophie where she was crumpled on the ground.

He thought his heart might beat right out of his chest as he crawled to her. "Sophie!"

Screaming, she clutched at her left arm, tears streaming down her cheeks. "It hurts!"

Relieved she was still breathing and talking, Cal glanced up as Mrs. O'Brien appeared. "I think it might be dislocated."

"Oh dear. You'd best drive her to the hospital in Rhinebeck. I'll get one of the workers to fetch Jim from the orchard. He can meet you there."

Mrs. O'Brien hurried off, and Cal lifted Sophie as gently as he could. "Shh. It's all right. You're going to be all right."

She clung to him, whimpering with her face pressed to his neck as he carried her to the Cadillac and eased her down onto the back seat. He drove quickly, careful of any potholes in the road. The whole time he kept up a monologue. "They'll fix you up lickety split, don't worry. When I was a kid I was in the hospital every other week. You'll be right as rain, I promise. Everything's okay, Sophie."

The admitting nurse assumed Cal was Sophie's father, and he didn't disabuse her of the notion. After Sophie was settled on a bed in the emergency room, Cal sat and took her good hand in his. "It's okay, honey."

She clung to him, blinking away tears. "I'm sorry, Uncle Cal."

"It was an accident." He brushed her hair back from her forehead.

The doctor arrived a minute later and examined Sophie gently. "The shoulder's dislocated. We'll have to reduce it. Don't worry—we'll give her something for the pain first."

Cal nodded and hoped Jim wouldn't be long.

He still hadn't arrived by the time they forced Sophie's shoulder back into its socket, and Cal held her still, wishing it was him as she screamed in agony. Then it was done, and they bound her arm in a sling.

"You'll have to follow up with your doctor to ensure it's setting properly. She's young, and it should heal quickly." The doctor signed off on the chart and was gone, his lab coat fluttering behind him.

Jim finally rushed in. He peered at Sophie anxiously and caressed her damp cheek. "Are you all right, baby?"

She nodded, sniffling but clearly trying to put on a brave face. "I'm okay, Daddy."

The older nurse on the other side of the bed frowned at Cal. "I thought you were her father?"

"I'm her uncle."

"Oh." The nurse nodded. "All right. I'll be back with the prescription and then you can take her home."

"Thank you," Jim said.

The woman smiled. "Maybe I'll come back with a lollipop too. Would you like that, Sophie?"

Nodding, Sophie managed a smile of her own.

Cal recognized the tense set of Jim's shoulders. "It was dislocated, but the doc says she'll be just fine. No need to worry."

"You were supposed to be watching her." Jim faced him, clearly struggling to keep his tone in check. "How did this happen?"

"I'm not sure." Cal's ears were hot.

"Why weren't you watching?"

"The workmen made a mistake on the cider house. I was only gone for a minute." The excuse was pitiful to his own ears. "I'm sorry, Jim."

"Daddy, stop. It was my fault."

Jim and Cal turned their attention back to Sophie. Jim brushed at her cheeks where fresh tears spilled. "Of course it wasn't."

She nodded. "It was! He told me to hang on, but when he wasn't looking I let go. I made it all the way around three times, and then I wanted Trixie to go faster. She did, and I fell. Please don't blame Uncle Cal."

"It's okay, Sophie. I should have been watching." Cal hoped his smile was reassuring. "It's not your fault."

"Yes, it is! And if Daddy's mean to you, you're going to go away again!" To Jim, she pleaded, "I don't want him to leave. Why can't he come back and live with us?"

Jim opened his mouth and closed it, and Cal jumped in. "Hey, I've been back every week to visit. I'll be back next week, too, I promise."

"Why can't you just stay? Why do you like the city more than us?"

Cal walked around the bed and pulled a chair up to the other side. "I don't like the city more than you, but there are things I need to do there. Believe me, whenever I'm in Manhattan I'm counting the hours until I can come back to Clover Grove and see all of you." It was the truth, but he avoided Jim's gaze.

"Really?" She swiped her sleeve across her nose.

"Really." Cal leaned over and pressed a kiss to her forehead.

Once they had her settled into Jim's pickup, happily sucking her lollipop, Jim closed the door and spoke quietly.

"I'm sorry. I overreacted, and I was wrong."

"No, I got distracted. I shouldn't have."

Jim sighed. "She's growing up, and we can't watch her every second. I know she's going to fall off more than one horse in her life." He frowned. "I hope not literally."

Cal couldn't help but smile. *We.* "It's still awful seeing her hurt. I've never felt so powerless. Not since what happened on Okinawa."

Jim winced, his eyes clouding over. Before he could say anything, Sophie's muffled voice came from inside the truck. "What happened on Okinawa?"

They answered in unison, "Nothing," and hurried out of earshot toward where Cal had parked the Caddy.

"I'd better get her home," Jim said. "Are you still driving back to the city?"

"I suppose so. Unless you want me to stay tonight." *Say yes.*

Jim shook his head. "We're fine. I don't want to keep you."

"I was thinking I could come back in a few days and we'll put the new press to the test."

"Sure." Jim smiled. "Sounds good."

They stared at each other for too long, and finally Cal climbed into his car. "See you."

Jim stood there for a few moments, before disappearing back to the truck.

Cal followed Jim out of the parking lot and onto the main road. At the juncture, Jim turned left back toward Tivoli, and Sophie waved in the back window with her good hand. Cal made his right turn and watched them getting smaller and smaller in the rearview mirror, until the road curved and he was alone.

"SEE, SO WITH this part, the apples are scratted. That means ground down."

Jim's lips quirked. "Yes, I know what it means. You've certainly gotten up to speed on cider making, haven't you?"

"Of course I have." Cal grinned. "I don't do anything halfway." He walked around the machine, swiping his arm across his forehead. Indian summer was in full swing, and they both wore only white T-shirts and jeans although it was October. "And here's where we squeeze the juice out."

"It's huge. Your cousin did an incredible job."

"Only the best for Clover Grove. I made sure of it." And paid dearly for it, but Cal didn't mention that since Jim hadn't. "Come on, let's test out a batch."

The press whirred to life, and Cal pulled the door to the cider house shut, even though there was nobody to disturb since Sophie was at school and Mrs. O'Brien had taken Adam to the market. He wanted Jim to have the whole experience and flicked on the overhead light. It was only a single bulb, but it shone brightly enough that workers could safely operate the press even at night.

They watched in easy silence as the machine did its work. Cal asked, "When are you going to start harvesting the rest of the apples?"

"Next week. There are some that weren't damaged. Not enough, but at least we're ready with the press now. Even if they're bruised, they'll work fine here."

Cal watched the first juice squeeze out with satisfaction. "I think we should toast. Make it official now that the paperwork is done."

"All right. To the new and improved Clover Grove." Jim smiled widely. "You get the glasses, and I'll collect the juice."

Cal was about to open the door when Jim sputtered and swore. Spinning around, Cal found Jim with one of the press receptacles in his hand and juice splashed all over him. Cal couldn't hold it in, and his laugh echoed over the hum of the press. Jim glared, but couldn't stop from smiling, and soon they were both laughing so hard Cal had to hold onto the wall.

"You have to hit the release button instead of just yanking on it."

Juice dripped off the end of Jim's nose. "You don't say?"

Giggling helplessly and in a most undignified manner, Cal peeled off his T-shirt over his head. "Here. Let me help." He blotted at Jim's face with the cotton. "How's it taste?"

"Not bad. Not bad at all." Jim grinned, still laughing. "You sure we should make hard cider out of it?"

"Booze is where the money is, my friend. Of that, I'm sure." Jim's hands were dripping, and without thinking, Cal lifted one to his mouth. "Let me taste." He sucked Jim's finger between his lips, his tongue swirling around it to gather the sticky, tangy juice.

As he came back to his senses, Cal froze. Jim was staring at Cal's mouth. Then he slowly eased out his finger, and Cal waited to be pushed away. Instead, Jim pressed his next finger to Cal's mouth, and Cal bit back a groan as he took it between his lips. He licked and sucked Jim's skin clean finger by finger, both of them breathing shallowly. Jim's eyes were riveted to Cal's mouth.

When Cal released Jim's hand, their gazes locked, and they clutched at each other, hands scrabbling and mouths open. They stumbled to the wooden floor, the press still humming. Jim tore off his T-shirt, revealing his lean muscles and the fair hair sprinkled across his chest.

Cal rolled on top of him. Jim's skin was damp from the juice, and Cal licked, circling his tongue around one nipple and then the other as Jim moaned, his fingers digging into Cal's bare back.

Shifting down, Cal lapped at Jim's bellybutton, the tang of apple and Jim's sweat sweet on his tongue. He was afraid to talk and break the spell but couldn't stop the words from flowing out. "Missed you. Missed this. Jesus, you taste so good. I want you so much."

Jim's fingers tangled in Cal's hair, and he panted, lifting his hips in invitation. "Don't stop."

Cal made quick work of Jim's belt and unzipped his fly. He mouthed at Jim's hardening dick through his shorts, inhaling the musky scent deeply. His own cock was aching in his jeans, and he rutted against the floorboards.

He gripped the waistband of Jim's drawers, and—

Daylight flooded the cider house as the door slid open. Cal sprang from Jim, scrambling to his feet as he blinked at the doorway, the adrenaline of desire crystallizing into icy terror. He made out Mrs. O'Brien's silhouette as she backed away and was gone.

Chapter Twenty-Two

1945

"T HIS WILL NOT be an easy operation."

Shoulder to shoulder with the other men on the deck of their transport ship under a cloudy night sky, Jim and Cal shared a look.

Cal leaned in, muttering, "At least they're giving it to us straight this time." His breath tickled Jim's ear.

The lieutenant went on. "This island is only a few hundred miles from the Japs' home islands. They will defend it with as great, if not greater, tenacity than they have shown before."

There was no sound, but Jim could sense the ripple of unease and dejection that traveled through the troops.

"We expect heavy casualties on the beach."

While Jim, Cal, and Sully listened impassively to talk of the seawall they had to scale and the threat of Japanese paratrooper attacks, the squad replacements shifted from foot to foot, their eyes growing wider and wider. When the lieutenant was done, he dismissed the men, and most milled about on deck.

One of the new boys, a blond barely old enough to shave more than a single whisker, approached Jim. "Corporal Bennett?"

Sully glanced over. "Nah, that's Johnny."

Jim had to smile. "What is it, Tim?"

Tim swallowed convulsively. "It's just…it sounds like a suicide mission. Something the Japs would do, whaddya call it…"

"Kamikaze."

"Yeah, like that! Eighty to eighty-five percent casualties on the beach? Even if we make it, how the hell are we supposed to fight the Japs by ourselves?"

Cal appeared. "It's just like your card games, Gambler. You win some, you lose some. Worrying about it won't do a lick of good."

Tim nodded. "Okay, Sarge."

"But from what I've seen, you win a hell of a lot more than you lose. Don't worry."

Jim smiled to himself as he leaned against the railing and turned to the sea. As always, Cal had a way of putting the men at ease, whether it was with a joke or a smile or a kind word. Jim was still smiling when Cal took a spot at the rail, brushing against him. A shiver flashed through Jim's body.

"Are you cold? My God, have we finally sailed far enough north that we need our field jackets again?"

Jim chuckled. "Not quite yet, but close. I'm sure I'll change my mind soon enough, but I welcome the chill."

"Amen." Cal peered at the sky as the ship powered onward, and then pointed to the horizon. "The Southern Cross is almost gone."

Indeed, the constellation hung low in the sky. Soon it would slip away completely. "I'll miss it."

"Yeah, it's just about the only thing. The southern hemisphere can keep everything else. Especially the mosquitoes. Sully's doing well, though. Maybe being out of the heat helps?"

"Maybe. It's a strange disease."

After a minute of comfortable silence, Cal spoke. "I hate lying to them."

Jim inched closer to Cal, pressing into him. "We have to. They'll learn for themselves soon enough. But you were right—there's no sense in worrying. It won't help. This ship'll get us there whether we worry ourselves sick or not. Landing should be in what—two days, you reckon?"

Cal nodded. "I wish it was tomorrow and we could just get it over with. Hell, eighty-five percent."

The thought that this really could be it—that he and Cal and the others would likely be dead soon—sent a fresh tendril of dread spiraling through Jim. "It's in God's hands now."

"I suppose it is." Cal blew out a long breath. "You know, Jim…if I don't make it…" He seemed to be battling with himself, the words lodged in his throat.

"You're going to make it. We both are."

"Okay, it's a deal. Neither of us buys it on this Jap island." Cal extended his hand.

With a smile, Jim took it, shaking firmly. "Deal."

On the morning of April first, they devoured steak and eggs in the mess, the nervous energy palpable. That it would be the last meal for many of them was something Jim tried to keep from his mind with limited success. After chow, they dressed in their battle gear and organized their ammunition and combat packs. Jim hefted his mortar ammunition bag as dawn broke. Up on deck, they milled around, their squad sticking together.

A command rang out. "To your quarters! On the double! No troops topside."

Squeezed back into their tiny compartments wearing all their battle gear, they waited. As time ticked by, the heat climbed. Jim whispered to Cal, "So much for the cooler weather."

"Yeah, it's null and void when we have to wait down here like we're in a can of human sardines being roasted." Sweat beaded on Cal's face.

Tim cleared his throat. "Why can't we wait up top?"

As if in reply, the firing began.

"Don't want us to get strafed on deck, Gambler," Cal said. "Those Jap planes get awfully low, and their machine guns can nail us right here on board."

When the sailors finally opened the hatch, the men streamed out, and Jim gulped in the fresh air. They went to their assigned area on deck, and Jim couldn't help but marvel at the sight unfolding before him.

What appeared to be hundreds of Japanese and American planes droned overhead while the massive fleet of US ships assaulted the beach. The noise was incredible, a cacophony of manmade thunder and lightning. The fleet stretched as far as Jim could see. Maybe they'd get through this.

When H-hour arrived, they were keeping low in their amtrac, full speed toward the beach. Soon a strange sound floated back to the troop compartment. Jim looked at Cal. "Is that…?"

"Laughter." Cal shouted to the machine gunners up top. "What's so funny?"

"They ain't fighting! Barely fired at us at all. We're walking across the goddamned beach like it's Sunday on Cape Cod."

With Cal in the lead, they all climbed out of the troop compartment to sit on the edge as their amtrac—and hundreds of others—sailed on, unopposed. As Sully led the men in a round of "Back in the Saddle Again," Jim breathed deeply, the tension draining from his body. The spray of the ocean was cool, and as the others whooped and laughed, for a moment he allowed himself to believe they truly were conquering heroes.

Ahead, the other troops landing were cool as cucumbers, taking the beach in combat formations but dodging no enemy fire. The odd shell exploded in the distance, but nowhere near them. Dotted with lush farm plots, this island was a stark difference from the lunar surface of Peleliu.

Cal leaned in to be heard over the raucous singing. "Seems like they mixed up their battles. They said the last one would be easy and this one would be a killer. But I'll take easy any way we can get it."

Jim nodded, gazing around in wonder. A dark thought skidded into his mind. "Think the Japanese know about April Fool's?"

Although he laughed, Cal's expression was pinched. "I sure hope not."

"You know they're not going to just let us take this island. Not this easily."

But then the others were poking them, and they joined in the singing again.

On shore, Gambler grinned as they shouldered their gear and clambered easily over the seawall, which had been blasted down to little more than rubble. "This isn't so hard."

Jim said a silent prayer as they moved inland and left Okinawa's gentle beach behind.

1948

HIS HEART THUMPING painfully, Jim buckled his belt and yanked his damp T-shirt over his head before racing out of the cider house. Mrs. O'Brien was striding toward the paddock, her green dress fluttering. Jim called out, "Wait!"

She stopped but didn't turn. When he reached her, Jim realized he had no idea what on Earth to say. He swallowed down a surge of bile. "Please…"

Amazingly, when Mrs. O'Brien faced him her eyes were as kind as ever. She touched his arm briefly. "Oh, child. I'm sorry to barge in like that. I should have thought."

"But…" Jim struggled to make sense of her words. His skin prickled hotly. "Why would you think that I…that we…?"

She smiled sadly. "You've never looked at anyone the way you do him. When he left, you were so brokenhearted. It was plain as day."

Panic flapped its wings against Jim's ribcage. "You knew? Does everyone?" He thought he might be sick on the grass.

"No, love. Don't fret. I'm sure no one else gave it another thought. But they don't know you the way I do. Since you were a little boy at my skirts asking for another cookie when you and Stephen would play."

Clenching his hands to keep them from trembling, Jim took a shaky breath. "When? Just when Cal left—that's when you knew? Or before?"

"One day I brought Adam out to the orchard to say hello since he was missing you. You and Cal were there—not doing anything, just sitting under a tree. But your head was in his lap."

Jim cringed. "I'm sorry."

"No need to apologize. I just turned back and announced our arrival so we didn't startle you. Can't get much by me, I'm afraid." She smiled. "Don't look so frightened. I won't tell a soul."

"But it's wrong! It's a sin!" Didn't she understand that?

Mrs. O'Brien sighed. "There was a time I would have agreed with you. Would have blindly condemned you without another thought, the way many people would. But after Stephen died, the world became a different place. I began to question many things I'd taken for granted. Happiness can be so fleeting, Jim. We have to take it where it comes and be grateful for it."

She can't mean it. "But it's unnatural."

Mrs. O'Brien snorted. "Says who? Not the ancient Greeks, if I recall. Homosexuals have been around since the dawn of time. Does it feel unnatural to you?"

His cheeks flaming, Jim struggled to answer. "I don't know." *No.*

"Forget about what anyone else thinks. If it were just the two of you on a deserted island, would you give it a second thought?"

He rolled around the idea of being truly alone with Cal. No fear or shame. Complete freedom. "No. I wouldn't."

She nodded encouragingly. "There's your answer."

"But I'm a sinner!"

"We're all sinners, Jim. Each in our own way."

"Not you."

She laughed and brushed away a strand of hair that had slipped free of her bun. "Why not me? It may not look like it now, but I was young once." Her face took on a wistful expression. "Oh, the trouble I'd get up to as a girl in the old country. Paddy McFarrell used to brew a wicked *poitín* out in his granddaddy's barn on the sheep farm. You've never had moonshine until you've had Irish moonshine."

"You were young. All kids get up to that kind of trouble. It's not the same. It's not against the word of God."

"Don't kid yourself. We were breaking commandments left and right."

Jim struggled to find the right words. "These feelings I have…I shouldn't have them. They aren't right."

"Have you seen Trevor Turner lately?"

Jim blinked at the abrupt change in subject. "I don't think so."

"I saw him last week at the market with his parents and his new wife. She's pregnant with their first."

"Oh. I've been so busy here I haven't been paying attention to the neighbors. Uh, I'm glad to hear it."

"Are you? I wasn't, you see. Do you know what I thought, when I saw them all? Joan and Lewis, and Trevor and his new bride? I thought, I wish that was me. Me and Gerald, with Stephen and poor dear Rebecca. I hated that it wasn't. I stood there in that marketplace with a smile on my face, and the feeling in my heart was sheer jealousy. Hateful jealousy and a bitterness that I don't think will ever truly leave me as long as I live."

Jim tried to think of what to say. "I'm sorry."

"Why them? Why are they the lucky ones? Why didn't *my* son come home? Why is he in the ground across the sea with a million other boys like him while Trevor Turner gets to live? Why should Joan's son return without a scratch while Stephen was blown to bits? It isn't fair, Jim. It isn't fair."

"I know." Tears gathered in his eyes.

She rubbed a hand over her face. "It's a terrible thought, isn't it? To be jealous of my friends' happiness? To begrudge them their son and their future grandchildren? To want them to share my loss? It's cruel, and the very meaning of sinful."

"No." Jim shook his head emphatically. "It isn't. It's human. We've all felt things like that. No one would ever judge you for it."

She reached for Jim's hands. "So why should anyone judge you for your thoughts? For your feelings? Feelings of *love*, not resentment and anger. Yes, some would judge you, but to the devil with them. Don't ever hate yourself for loving."

Jim had to swallow hard over the lump in his throat. "It's not that easy. I wish it was."

"What worth having is ever easy? Not much in my experience. Does he make you happy?"

Jim nodded. "But—"

"But nothing! I've watched you grow into a fine young man. You were always a good friend to my Stephen. He never got the chance to have his own family, and I'll be damned if I watch you throw away your happiness. The people we love are what matters in this life, Jim Bennett."

"What about the children?" Jim clung to Mrs. O'Brien's weathered hands, her wedding band digging into his finger. "Don't they deserve a mother?"

"They had a mother, Jim. Ann was a good soul, but she's gone. Nothing will bring her back."

"I could remarry. Sophie needs a mother. She needs a woman to guide her."

"What am I, chopped liver? I'll be around until you get sick of me and tell me to shove off."

Jim had to laugh. "I would never do that."

"Besides, it's not in you to marry some poor girl knowing you'll never really love her. Is it?"

Thinking of Rebecca, Jim sighed. "No."

"Cal's a good man. He's mad about you, that's for certain."

Jim's stomach flip-flopped foolishly. "You think so?"

"For God's sake. Of course! Came rushing back here when you needed him, didn't he? He'd do anything for you and those children."

"But what would we tell Sophie and Adam? No one could know. Can you imagine what people would do if they found out? We'd go to prison. I'd lose my children."

She sighed. "Yes, I'm afraid this will have to be your secret. You and Cal must be very careful if you decide it's worth the risk."

"I don't want to live a lie."

She squeezed his fingers. "Either way you have to lie. Be happy with Cal and lie to the world or find another woman and lie to her. Or be alone and miserable, lying to yourself. I wish it didn't have to be so. You have a difficult choice to make, and whatever you decide, I'll be here."

Nodding, Jim took a shaky breath.

She pressed a kiss to his cheek and let go of his hands. "Now you'd better go talk to Cal, and I should make sure Adam is still napping and not burning down the house."

As she walked away, Jim blurted, "I don't really remember my mother."

Mrs. O'Brien turned back, her lips pressed together.

"But you always made the best cookies and kissed my knee when I scraped it falling off the handlebars of Stephen's bike. I haven't thanked you enough for…all of it. Everything."

"No need for thanks."

"I can't imagine a finer mother than you've been to me."

Tears shimmering in her eyes, Mrs. O'Brien returned and threw her arms around him. She was warm and smelled faintly of cinnamon, and Jim clung to her.

"Thank you. Thank you," he repeated.

She kissed his cheek again. "Go on now."

When Jim returned to the cider house, Cal was dressed and pacing back and forth, looking for all the world like a man awaiting the executioner. Before Jim could reach for him, Cal spoke.

"I'll go. We can talk on the phone about business if we need to, but I'm sure you'll have it all under control."

Jim blinked. "Is that what you want?"

"God, of course not."

"Mrs. O'Brien said…" Jim's mind still spun like he'd been riding the tilt-a-whirl at the county fair.

"Look, people might think it's wrong, but that doesn't mean we have to listen to them."

"She doesn't." He could still hardly believe it.

"She doesn't what?" Cal hesitated. "She doesn't think it's wrong?"

"No. She said you and I should be happy together."

Cal's eyebrows shot up, and he grinned. "She's a hell of a woman."

"She'll keep our secret." It felt strange saying the words aloud. Someone had found out, and the world hadn't ended. Jim wanted to give in to the elation, but worry still churned his gut. "But others won't. We can't expect this from everyone. It's still illegal. Sophie and Adam, they…" He took a deep breath, trying to calm himself.

Cal's smile faded. "I know. We were reckless. I'm sorry."

Jim ran a hand through his mussed hair. Mrs. O'Brien's words of encouragement warred with the voice telling him to put an end to it now once and for all. "I don't know what to do, Cal."

"Neither do I." He smiled softly. "I wish I did. I wish there was some magic solution to all of this. But there isn't. I'm supposed to leave today anyway. I'll come back in a week. We can think about everything while I'm gone."

Jim nodded, even though he ached to beg Cal to stay. Was this how it would be between them forever? Furtive encounters followed by separations with neither of them ever truly happy?

"If it had been someone else, this could have ended very differently. I'm sorry I let things get out of control."

Jim had to smile at that. "As I recall, you weren't acting alone."

"I suppose not." Cal glanced at the press. "Well, it's up and running now. Let me know if there are any problems and I can talk to my cousin."

"Okay. Sure."

They stared at each other. Then Jim squared his shoulders and turned away. As they walked back to the house, Cal fell into step with him, easy like always. Jim missed him already and knew that nothing about their situation had really changed.

Yet he couldn't stop the hope from blooming.

Chapter Twenty-Three

1945

"DO YOU THINK it's true, Sarge?"

"What's that, Gambler?" Cal led his squad down a ragged ridge as part of a bigger convoy as their company moved across the island. He leaped over a gap in the rocks at the bottom.

Still clearly delighted by his nickname, a flash of a smile brightened Tim's face. He fell into step beside Cal as they neared a green farmer's field. "About the fighting down south? The trouble the army's having?"

"Yes."

Gambler blinked. "Oh."

"I know you new boys can't believe it given how our company's had pretty much a walk in the park the last month, but our luck's going to run out."

"Didn't you hear it last night?" Sully asked.

"The thunder?"

"That wasn't thunder." Jim spoke quietly, his attention on a plow horse tethered to a low fence.

The horses they'd come across had all looked similar, more like over-grown ponies. Jim had an affinity for them, and Cal watched as he pulled out a lump of sugar from his rations.

"Here you go, boy." Jim scratched the horse's muzzle, murmuring to it.

A Marine called Husky passed by with his squad. "Gonna make your getaway, Johnny? Don't think that beast'll go fast enough."

"Fast enough to outrun you, Husky," Jim replied with a smile.

Cal joined him, patting the horse's flank. "You know between the horses and the kids, you're not going to have any rations left."

"Like you're one to talk. You gave away your last candy bar days ago."

Cal shrugged. "Damn kids with their big eyes. We're all going to be starving by the time this battle finally finds us."

"Or we find it."

"Either way." Cal stepped away from the horse. "Let's get moving. Have to keep up."

After climbing another small ridge, they came across a group of Okinawans. Of course the young men had been pressed into service, so the company had only encountered women, children, and old men. The locals watched them silently. They were being put into internment camps, which Cal understood the need for. Yet whenever he saw them, bedraggled and seemingly shocked and confused by the invasion, his stomach tightened.

A lieutenant called out, "Take ten!"

Sully and some of the men from other squads pulled out rations, and after a bit of hesitation the children gathered around. Cal walked to a small stone well, aware of the uneasy gaze of the women and old men. The water was cool, and he filled his canteen, breathing deeply.

Next to him, Jim dipped his canteen. "Nothing quite like the smell of pine."

"God, I missed it. I was actually cold last night. Was confused for a minute by the unfamiliar sensation."

Jim smiled softly and watched Sully and the others playing with the children, who laughed. "It's strange, isn't it? The only soldiers we've seen have been dead by the roadside. But there are civilians everywhere. Makes me think of…"

Cal screwed the lid back on his canteen. "What?"

"Home. Of what it would be like if war came to Tivoli. To Clover Grove. If I was herded off my land and put in a camp."

"I hadn't thought of it that way." Now that he did, Cal felt decidedly uneasy. The idea of foreign troops marching up Fifth Avenue seemed impossible, but surely the people of Okinawa had never expected Americans on their doorstep.

"All this time we've been fighting the Japs, but it was so far away from Japan. Now that we're getting close it just…it changes things." Jim shook his head as if casting off the thought. "I guess they're used to it over in Europe. Civilians everywhere there."

Cal followed Jim's gaze to a giggling little girl. "The kids must make you think of Sophie."

Jim gulped from his canteen before wiping his mouth with his sleeve. "Yeah." He seemed to want to say more, and after a few moments, he did. "Guadalcanal and Peleliu—they were like something out of a horror story. The heat and the bugs and the death. But this place…it's a home."

They stood in silence, watching the children until they moved out.

A day later, they were back in the thick of it. Eyes wide, the replacements panted, cringing as rifles popped and the whine of incoming artillery reached their ears. Cal thought grimly to himself that at least the new boys finally knew what real battle was like. He scooted next to Gambler, who struggled with his mortar base. "You're pushing too hard. Ease up."

Shaking, Gambler nodded. "Yes, Sarge." He ducked as another shell exploded nearby. "How long?"

Cal helped the ammo carrier, a trembling boy they called Winnie, with his load. "How long until what?"

Gambler swallowed hard. "Until it stops?"

"When we're off the line, and not even then. Stay sharp. All of you. Just remember your training. Do your jobs and we'll get out of here." They all knew it was a lie, but he had to say it. He forced a smile. "Think of the stories you'll have to tell your girls back home."

Crouching, he rejoined Jim and Sully. The shellacking from the Japanese continued, shells and artillery beating back the rifle squads that tried to push forward. With bullets tearing up the ground at his feet, a Marine carrying an injured man on his back came into sight on the field.

"Can we send up a smokescreen?" Sully asked.

Jim shook his head. "We're too close to our troops."

"Come on, come on," Cal muttered, eyes glued to the staggering man.

One of the replacements cried out, "Jesus, can't they let the injured go through? Ain't there rules about that?"

"The Japs don't follow any rules except their own, and their number one rule is to kill us at all costs," Cal answered.

Struggling with the weight of his injured comrade, the Marine pushed on. A burst of machine gun fire peppered the air, and he toppled to the ground. Cal's breath lodged in his throat as he willed the fallen man back to his feet. Then in a blur, Jim was gone, racing out from behind the relative safety of their foxhole before Cal could even blink.

Swearing, Cal grabbed his rifle and went up on his knees, targeting the Jap machine gunners. There was a flicker of movement, and he fired, taking the gunner down. Another appeared, and Cal got him in his sights.

Dragging the two fallen men across the field, Jim struggled back.

The Japs' attention was now on Cal, and he flattened as they returned fire. But he refused to retreat into his foxhole and shot repeatedly as Jim and now Sully and a few others rescued the downed men, finally able to haul them to safety.

A cheer rose up from the other Marines, and Cal shimmied back, pushing with his elbows. Saliva filled his mouth as nausea reared up, thinking of how easy it would have been for Jim to be cut down. Cal squeezed his eyes shut and fought to breathe. When Jim slid into the foxhole beside him, Cal raised his head.

Some men would be proud as peacocks after such heroics. But Jim's gaze was on the enemy's position, and he acted as if he'd only left to relieve himself, and that nothing unusual whatsoever had happened.

Cal's voice was hoarse. "Are they going to make it?"

"Don't know. Pray to God they will."

Cal gripped the front of Jim's jacket. "You ever pull a stunt like that again, and I'll kill you myself."

Blinking, Jim stared. "If it was me out there injured, I'd want the help. Wouldn't you?"

"Christ, of course. That doesn't mean you go barreling into enemy fire. You can't risk yourself like that!" He leaned close to Jim, tightening his fingers in the neck of Jim's jacket. "Not you."

Jim frowned. "I'm no better than anyone else out here. Besides, it was your sharpshooting that saved the day. You were just as much at risk."

"That's not the point!" He gave Jim a shake. "Just be careful."

Jim's expression softened. "Is that an order?"

Cal huffed out a laugh as he let go. "Yes, it's a goddamned order."

Another round of shells screamed toward them as Sully dove back into the hole, and they ducked their heads, helmets clanging together as another wave began.

1948

"FOR GOODNESS' SAKE, Cal. It's one evening. Surely you can carve some time in your busy schedule to celebrate your parents' anniversary. Your father and I want you to be there."

Cal wedged the phone between his ear and shoulder and lit a cigarette as he sat back on the couch. The late-afternoon sunlight dappled the walls of his apartment. "Did Dad say that?"

His mother huffed. "Of course he wants you there. You're his only son, and this is an important event. Thirty-five years together is nothing to sneeze at. Everyone will be there. I'm sure you'll have a lovely time."

"I'm sure."

"Darling, would you please cease with the cynicism? I realize you and your father are not on the best terms at the moment."

"What did the old man have to say about that?"

"He told me you quit." She sighed. "With no notice, I might add."

He blew out a stream of smoke. "I had another commitment."

"Your friend with the little…what is it? A farm?" She pronounced the last word as if it had stuck to the bottom of her suede peep toe pumps.

Cal wondered whether Victoria Cunningham, *née* Withrow, had ever stepped foot on a farm.

"Apple orchard."

"Yes, well. It sounds charming. But really, you can postpone whatever it is you're doing by a few days and come to the party this weekend. You cannot expect your sister and Charles to do all the work representing the next generation of the Cunninghams. Besides, I haven't seen you since my charity ball in the summer, when you graced us with your presence for barely more than half an hour. Your sister has taken on the planning of this party, and your support would mean the world to her."

"I'm sure Laura will survive just fine without me. As will you."

There was a long pause, and then his mother's voice softened. "I do miss you, Cal. I hope you know that."

Resignation washed over him. "All right. I'll be there."

"Excellent. Kiss, kiss."

He listened to the dial tone until it began beeping and returned the phone to its cradle. After stubbing out his cigarette and pouring himself a finger of whiskey, he picked up the phone again. On the fourth ring, a breathless voice answered.

"Hello, this is Clover Grove. Sophie speaking."

Cal smiled, and the burn of the whiskey disappeared into gentle warmth. "Hi, Sophie." It had only been five days since he'd seen her on his weekly visit to the orchard, but he missed her so damn much.

"Uncle Cal?" She squealed. "I missed you!"

"Me too, kiddo. How's your shoulder?"

"Lots better. Dr. O'Brien says I can take the sling off soon."

"That's great. How's everything else going?"

"Good. The harvest is starting, so there are lots of people around to help pick. Daddy's really busy. He's tired. I wish you were here every day."

"I wish I was too." Worry mingled with the residual guilt from his conversation with his mother. "Your daddy's okay, isn't he? He's not sick or anything?"

There was a pause. "Not sick. Just sad the way he always is when you're not here. And…"

After a few moments of silence, Cal asked, "And what? What is it, hon?"

Her voice was hushed. "I don't know if I'm supposed to say anything. It might be a secret."

"You can tell me. Your daddy and I don't have any secrets." His pulse galloped. "Did something happen?"

"Last night he was yelling."

"That doesn't sound like your dad. Did he yell at you? Were you naughty?"

"No! Besides, it wasn't at me. It wasn't at anyone—it was in the middle of the night. I heard him yelling, and I went to his room. He was asleep. I had to shout for him to wake up. He said it was just a bad dream."

Cal closed his eyes, steeling himself against the urge to get in the car and drive to the orchard right away. "I'm sure that's what it was. We all have bad dreams sometimes."

"I know, but Daddy's are worse. I heard Mommy talking about it once with Aunt Rebecca."

"It's true, your dad has some bad nightmares sometimes."

"Because of the war."

"Yes. Because of the war."

"Do you have nightmares, too, Uncle Cal?"

He sighed, rubbing his face. "Sometimes."

"Is it because of Okinawa? I don't understand what it means. Is that a bad place?"

Cal wanted to say yes—that it was a terrible place. Yet there had once been beauty there, and good people. But the war had turned it all impossibly ugly. He kept his tone light. "Don't worry about any of that. We're both fine, and I'll be there to see you soon."

"Tomorrow, right? Daddy said you're coming tomorrow."

"Actually it's going to have to be Monday. There's something I need to do this weekend that's really important."

"More important than *us*?"

He could practically see Sophie's pout through the phone. "Never. But I have to go see my mom and dad. Can you tell your daddy to call me when he gets back from work?"

"Okay." There was a muffled noise, and then, "Adam, don't! Uncle Cal, I have to go. Bye!"

Cal smiled to himself as he hung up. He couldn't wait to get back to see the kids—and Jim. Even if Jim hadn't changed his mind and it was only a visit. Now Cal just had to get through the weekend. He poured himself another drink.

"CAL, YOU REMEMBER the Thorngoods?"

He pivoted on the smooth marble of the great hall, his best dress shoes not even making a squeak. Hundreds of guests crowded under vaulted ceilings and Impressionist frescoes. His mother placed a diamond-encrusted hand on his tuxedo sleeve. Her anniversary bracelet was a perfect complement to her engagement ring.

A smile in place, Cal nodded. "Of course. Eva, Michael. It's been too long." He kissed Eva's cheek and shook Michael's hand.

Aging gracefully, Eva was as coiffed and perfectly presented as ever, the emeralds sparkling in her ears accenting the green shimmer in her black gown. "Cal. How lovely to see you again."

"What are you up to these days?" Michael asked. "I hear you've quit the family business like any good prodigal son should. I thought when you joined the *Marines* it was the height of your youthful rebellion." He was grayer on top and bigger around the middle, but he was still a handsome man. "You know you can always come work under me. I'm sure I could find a place for you."

Cal returned the smile genuinely. "I'm sure you could. You always were a mentor, Michael. But I'm a business owner now." From the corner of his eye he saw his mother jolt ever so slightly.

She laughed softly, pressing one hand to the scalloped neckline of her satin blue gown. "No tall tales tonight, Cal."

"Didn't Father tell you? I was sure he would. We share an accountant, after all."

His mother's smile tightened. "Eva, Michael, would you excuse us? I see the Edwardses have arrived and we must greet them." She threaded her hand through Cal's arm and tugged gracefully.

As they wove past Cal's sister speaking in hushed tones with the butler, Cal wheeled, giving his mother no choice but to follow. Laura beamed and planted a kiss on his cheek.

"Don't you look handsome, big brother?"

Cal grinned. "Always." He nodded to her upswept hair and gown of deep purple. "And don't you look ravishing?"

"Always." She winked.

Cal felt like a heel for how long it had been since he'd seen his sister. She was eight years younger, and they'd never known each other particularly well what with boarding schools. Perhaps it was something he could change. He glanced toward the disappearing butler and snagged a glass of champagne from a passing tray. "Everything all right?"

Laura groaned. "Total disaster. The oysters haven't arrived yet." She shook her head. "Mother, I don't know how you plan these parties all the time. I haven't slept for days!"

"Years of experience, I suppose." She tightened her hand on Cal's arm. "Darling, you must come along. Laura, we'll see you shortly before the speeches."

They smiled and chatted with a dozen guests before they were able to escape into the corridor to the east wing. His mother picked up her pace and ducked into one of the day rooms, closing the door behind them.

"All right, what is this talk of a business? What don't I know?" She frowned, clearly puzzled and possibly a little hurt.

"I honestly thought Father told you. I'm sorry."

"Your father has been very busy with the bank, and of course I've had luncheons and my ladies' clubs, not to mention running this house. Laura's tried her best this week to lend a hand since it's my anniversary, but it's all very involving. So please tell me what's going on."

Cal leaned against the floral wallpaper with one shoulder and ran his finger around the rim of his champagne flute. "I bought half the orchard. Went into business with Jim."

She blinked and was silent for a few moments. "Jim? That fellow from the war?"

"Yes, Mother. My best friend, Jim Bennett."

"But…why on Earth would you do that? What do you know about fruit?"

"I've learned a lot, actually, but Jim knows apples. I know business. We're expanding. I had Milton in Philadelphia make an apple press so we can start brewing cider. It was a good business opportunity for me."

"I didn't know you were interested in having your own business." She smiled uncertainly. "You never mentioned that."

Cal shrugged. "It never came up."

"I wish it had. I know you don't believe it, but I'm interested in your life, Cal. I'm your mother."

Before Cal could respond, the door opened and his father entered, wearing a perfectly pressed tuxedo that stretched across his broad shoulders. He closed the door behind him and wore an unnervingly calm expression on his face. Cal's mother stood up straighter.

"Our son was just telling me about his new business venture. You never mentioned it."

"No. I didn't." He fixed Cal with a glare.

Cal forced a smile. "Mom, we can talk later. I'll tell you all about it."

"Not much to tell." His father's face was stony. "Not much at all."

She raised a smooth eyebrow. "Well, your father started the bank as a business venture and look at it now."

Cal's father practically growled. "There's a hell of a difference between the bank and growing a few apples. It's a passing fancy. He'll come to his senses any day now."

"Will I?" Cal clenched his jaw.

"I might even take you back one more time."

"How kind. But it won't be necessary. I'm not coming back."

His father went on as if he hadn't spoken. "George Jackson was just telling me about his daughter. She's twenty-one now. He said she was asking about you."

His mother clapped her hands together. "She's a lovely girl, Cal. I admit I've had my eye on her for a little while now. I know, I know, you want to choose your own wife. But time marches on, my dear."

"I'm queer, Mom."

The words were out of his mouth and fracturing the air, all sharp edges, before Cal could call them back.

She stared, her jaw scraping the plush carpet, and his father's face went dark red.

In for a penny... "Jim's not only my best friend. He's my lover. I want to make a life with him. I'm *going* to make a life with him, one way or another. I'll never marry George Jackson's daughter, or anyone else's. The life I want is with Jim on our orchard."

Tears shone in his mother's eyes, and she peered at him as if she'd never seen him before. He supposed she hadn't.

She shook her head. "How could you say such a thing? It sickens me."

"It's the truth. This is who I am."

"No. It was that war. The *Marines*," she spat. "If you'd joined the navy and been an officer like you were supposed to, this wouldn't have happened. They clearly warped your mind. You're confused."

"I'm not confused. This is who I've always been."

She laughed wildly. "You most certainly are not! Not my son. My son is not…a disgusting *perversion*."

Cal thought he might snap the stem of his champagne glass. "It's not disgusting to me. That's my real life, and you need to know. I guess I need you to know it. Even if you can't accept it."

A discreet knock at the door was followed by the butler's low tones. "The speeches are to commence in two minutes."

Cal's breath was stuck as he waited, listening to the butler's footsteps receding. A clock ticked in the silence.

Finally his father cleared his throat. "I think it's time for you to leave."

Blinking furiously and dabbing at her eyes, his mother wouldn't meet Cal's gaze. "Yes. I think it is. We'll make your excuses."

Laughing hollowly, Cal nodded. "You've been doing it for years, so why stop now?" He raised his glass. "Here's to you, Mr. and Mrs. Cunningham."

After tossing back the champagne, he made his way through the east wing and out the servant's entrance. The valet jumped up to retrieve the Cadillac, and Cal waited in the cool night, watching his breath cloud the air.

He'd actually done it. He didn't know whether to laugh or cry.

"I REALLY WISH you'd have come inside."

Cal shrugged as he and Jim strolled between the trees. The midafternoon sun beamed down, and crickets sang. He wished he could bottle the tranquillity of the orchard and bring it back to Manhattan. He didn't miss the honks and clamor even a little.

"Nah. It was the middle of the night. I was afraid I'd wake you all on those creaky stairs. It was easier to just sleep in the car."

"Next time wake me up, okay?"

"Sure." Cal couldn't resist twisting an apple off a low-hanging branch. He bit into it, savoring the sweet tang. "I tell you, they do not make apples like this in the city. Nothing like fresh off the tree."

"Uh-huh. Are you going to tell me why you showed up here in the middle of the night in a tuxedo? I thought Sophie was seeing things this morning."

"Yeah, I'll tell you." The thought of his mother's reaction sat in his gut like an unexploded mortar. "Just not right now, all right?"

"All right."

"Good thing I still have a few duds here." Cal fiddled with one of the buttons of his plaid shirt.

"Yeah." Jim stopped by the cider house. "About that…" He licked his lips.

Desire like a rocket shot up Cal's spine. God, he wanted to kiss those lips. Wanted to pull Jim to the ground and lose himself in him.

"I've been thinking about it."

"About my clothes?" Cal half smiled, butterflies swirling in his stomach. "I am a dapper dresser, whether it's for evening or apple harvesting."

Jim laughed. "No. About…everything. Our situation."

"Right." Cal's heart thumped. *Please say you want me, no matter what.*

He took a deep breath. "Cal, I—"

The low rumble of an approaching vehicle reached them, and Jim glanced toward the laneway. Cal followed his gaze, and a moment later a truck came around the bend. Jim made a noise of surprise, blinking as if he couldn't believe his eyes.

Cal peered at the pickup. "Who is it?"

A tall man with light brown hair stepped out, wearing the same kind of casual jeans and work shirt Cal and Jim did. He raised his hand in a tentative wave.

"Eddie."

CHAPTER TWENTY-FOUR

1945

"AW, COME ON, Husky. You finally found an excuse to go home, huh?" Cal said, clearly putting on a smile.

Slipping in the mud, Jim rushed over to join Cal as he walked alongside the stretcher. "Take care of yourself, buddy," Jim added. "You'll be fine."

Ashen and somehow smaller than Jim had ever seen him, Husky smiled weakly. "I sure will, Johnny. Finally going home. Tell Sully he'd better keep his scrawny ass out of trouble. Same with you, Hollywood."

"Since when is my ass scrawny?" Cal feigned offense as he patted his rear end with both hands. "This is one hundred percent prime beef right here."

Then the corpsmen were loading Husky into the transport, and he was gone, the truck rattling over the uneven road. Jim rubbed his face. He felt as if he hadn't slept in days. "Think he'll make it?"

"Fifty-fifty, I'd say." Cal's smile and jocular tone had vanished.

"At least it's over for him now. One way or the other."

They watched the truck go.

When Sully found out Husky was hit and already evacuated, he disappeared into his foxhole by the gun pit and curled in on himself. The rest of the squad sat on a cluster of rocks and ate cold K rations. The canned beef loaf was gelatinous and mercifully tasteless as Jim forced it down. They were off the line for the night, at least.

After dinner, Cal left to get briefed by one of the new replacement lieutenants. Along with the enlisted men, officers were getting killed left and right. Captain Brown had gotten nailed a week before, and there seemed to be a new officer every other day. Jim watched as Cal and the other NCOs nodded, their faces grim.

"That doesn't look so good." Gambler jerked his chin toward the huddle.

"No."

As the rain began again, Gambler pulled his field jacket tighter around him. "God, I wish the rain would quit."

Jim resisted the urge to snap that they'd lived through the rainy season twice already, and that this was nothing. But the rain had indeed been getting heavier and more frequent, so instead he just chewed on a biscuit that crumbled like dust on his tongue.

After a minute of silence, Gambler suddenly shook with a sob.

Jim perched on the rock next to him and patted his back. "It's all right. You'll be okay."

"No, I won't, Johnny!" Gambler shook his head, trembling. "I'm so scared. Marines aren't supposed to be scared."

"We're all afraid. Every last one of us."

"Look at them." He nodded to Cal and the other NCOs. "The brass is sending us back in. All these weeks it's just nonstop. Even when we're off the line, it still doesn't ever stop."

"I know." It was quieter in their camp, but in the distance the rumble of battle continued unabated. Army and Marine divisions made painfully slow progress against the Japs, who true to form were not giving up the island without a brutal fight. Even off the line they had to constantly be on guard for flanking Jap attacks or paratroopers plummeting from above.

Resting now at the edge of a small forest, they were all worn down—thin, hollow, and battered. Two of their squad's replacements were dead, and now Gambler and the others knew for themselves the hell of battle.

Gambler sniffed quietly. "I'm never going home, Johnny. I'll never see my folks or my little sister again."

"We all feel like that." Jim had to tamp down a swell of emotion as Sophie's little face filled his mind. "All we can do is keep our heads down and pray we're one of the lucky ones." He didn't feel very lucky at the moment.

Gambler swiped at his red eyes. His shorn blond hair was splattered with mud. "There's a girl. Prettiest girl in all of Rhode Island. I was going to ask her to marry me."

"What's her name?"

"Louisa. Hair like coal and big green eyes like a cat's almost. All the boys were after her in high school, and senior year she picked me. Said I made her laugh. She writes me letters and says she's waiting for me to come home. She'll be some other fella's wife. Won't even remember me."

"Of course she will. Besides, you'll be there. You'll make it." Jim put his arm about Gambler's shivering shoulders.

When Cal returned, he roused Sully and sent him and one of the new boys on patrol. Jim offered Cal the candy bar from his ration, grateful their supplies had been refreshed at least. "You look like you could use this."

Cal sat next to Jim on the rocks. "Thanks." He unwrapped the chocolate and snapped it in two, handing half back to Jim. Nodding to Gambler's foxhole, where the boy had settled into a fitful, sniffling sleep, he asked, "He all right?"

"As he can be." Jim sighed. "Are we making a push?"

Shoulders hitching up with a deep breath, Cal nodded. "Heading south."

"Think it'll be bad?"

Cal met his gaze. "Yeah. We should get some sleep."

It was almost dawn when Jim stirred in his foxhole. The rain had let up, although he was still soaked to the skin, cold and clammy as he stretched his aching limbs. The fighting had quieted in the night, and it was almost eerily calm as he shuffled toward the trees to piss. As he passed the rest of the sleeping squad, he blinked at two empty muddy foxholes.

Without another thought, he raced into the forest with his rifle at the ready. He was already too far gone when he realized he should have woken Cal and the others. He followed the route Sully and the replacement would have taken, darting his eyes left and right in the gloom. Everything faded away behind him and he listened intently.

Stopping in his tracks, he peeked around a large patch of scrubby bushes. Ahead, two figures sat against the wide trunk of a tree. Adrenaline bursting through him, Jim raised his rifle and fired as he dropped to his belly in the muck. The shot echoed through the leaves, but the two men didn't so much as flinch. As his heart clobbered his ribs, Jim got them in his sights again.

It was as though time stood still, everything silent but for the blood rushing in his ears. Jim stared at the unmoving men, and finally realized what he was looking at.

Who he was looking at.

He blinked, certain his eyes were betraying him. He pushed himself to his feet and took a tentative step. Then another, and another, until he stood trembling in front of the bodies.

Sully's red hair was almost the only distinguishable feature left. Where his hazel eyes had been were now empty, bloody sockets. His mouth was horribly stretched around a hunk of flesh. As Jim tried to make sense of the gore and slashed uniforms, he realized it was Sully's penis that had been shoved into his mouth.

The replacement was equally brutalized, and Jim choked on a scream and surging bile. He looked down and realized he was standing in the blood and guts that had been strewn across the forest floor.

By the time he registered the footsteps, they were right behind him. Jim yanked his Ka-Bar knife from his belt as he lunged around. Cal raised his arms as he barely dodged the blade.

"Whoa! It's me!"

Cal. He'll fix it. He'll make everything okay. Jim lowered his arm and swayed on his feet. Cal caught his shoulders, and his fingers dug into Jim's flesh.

"It's okay. You're okay. Come on, let's get back."

"We can't go without them. Did you see? Do you see them?" Jim felt as though he would disintegrate if not for Cal's grasp.

"I see them, Jim."

"Sully…and…I can't remember his name. Lord, I should know his name!" Jim forced his lungs to expand, and a sob escaped his lips. Sully's voice echoed in his head—the twang of his accent so familiar. He'd never hear it again. Jim tried to remember the last thing he'd said to his friend. He couldn't.

"It's all right." Cal's voice caught as he peered at the carnage. He cleared his throat and urged Jim to take a step. "Davis. His name was Davis."

Gambler was on his knees heaving, and the others clearly struggled with the urge. One of them cried, "Sweet Jesus, look at them."

Despite himself, Jim's gaze returned to Sully and Davis. Davis's hands and feet had been chopped off, along with his ears. Rage boiled up in Jim's gut, and he'd never hated the Japanese more than he did in that moment. "I'll kill them all."

Cal's breath was warm on his cheek, his arm steady around Jim's shoulders as he urged another step. "Okay. Let's go. We'll come back with stretchers and make sure they have a proper burial."

Gambler wept. "They were supposed to wake me and Logger up when it was our turn. I should have woke up myself and realized they weren't back. I should have looked for them. Maybe—"

"It would have been too late." Cal's voice was thin, but even. "If it's anyone's fault for not realizing, it's mine." He turned Jim around and prodded him back to their camp. "We have to go."

Jim shuffled through the leaves and dirt, telling himself not to look back.

Hours later as the sun set and the skies opened, Jim huddled behind a boulder on the outskirts of a village as bullets ricocheted overhead. The war waged on, indifferent and relentless.

Gambler was beside him swearing under his breath, cursing the Japs for surprising them, and the women and children for being in the way. "Why the fuck aren't these people cleared out? And what the fuck are the Nips doing here? We aren't even at the ridge!"

The rock was rough against Jim's cheek, and he closed his eyes, seeing not the blackness he craved, but Sully's final empty, terrible gaze. He opened his eyes again, wishing the noise would just stop. He was so tired. He vaguely remembered packing his gear that morning and moving southward with Cal at his side, murmuring words Jim didn't understand.

Now he was here in the growing darkness with the rain pouring into his eyes. He closed them again.

"Jesus Christ! Help me with this mortar! The riflemen can't do it all, Johnny!"

Jim opened his eyes again to find Gambler shaking him roughly.

"Snap out of it! Please! I can't do this by myself."

The fear in Gambler's voice penetrated the fog in Jim's mind, and he focused on what Gambler wanted him to do—set up the gun. He'd done it a million times, even blindfolded back in training, and Jim readied the mortar as the world continued exploding around him. When he was finished, he closed his eyes again.

Then someone was slapping his cheek, and he blinked to find Cal a few inches away, holding Jim's face in his palms. Jim tried to make out what he was saying.

"Don't leave me now, Jim. It's going to be okay. We just have to get through this ambush. We're pinned down. Are you hearing me? Jim!"

Jim hated seeing Cal upset, and the haze began to dissipate. He had to do his job. His buddies were counting on him. *Cal* was counting on him. "I'm here."

Cal uncovered the ammo while Jim peeked out from behind the boulder to aim. All he could see were several ramshackle huts, but the

Japs had to be on the other side. Movement caught his eye, and he squinted. Cal was about to drop in the shell, but Jim grabbed his wrist. "Wait."

The woman staggered into view from behind a hut, her belly heavily swollen. Jim heard Cal shout, "Hold your fire!"

Enemy machine gun fire and artillery still came, and the woman wept, shaking her head as she stumbled toward them in the darkness. Jim inched to the edge of the boulder, crouched and ready to move. The poor woman didn't belong here. He had to help her.

Cal's fingers were tight on Jim's shoulder. "Jim, stay right here."

"Good God, she's pregnant. The Japs may not care, but we should!"

They watched as she came closer, shaking her head rhythmically, a sob ripping from her throat.

"No," Cal said sharply. "Something's wrong."

Jim moved before he knew what he was doing. He needed to save her. He couldn't fail this woman the way he'd failed Sully. He slipped in the muck, staying low and lurching forward. He was reaching for her, getting closer, closer—

Strong hands dragged him back, hauling him through the mud.

Cal yelled, "Stop!"

Jim thrashed, kicking and scrabbling at Cal's grip. "We have to—"

Hot gore exploded over them as a blast tore the night. Jim choked on charred flesh, certain it was his own, or Cal's. He screamed, and tasted blood.

Then there were hands pulling him through the mud, and he blinked the singed mess from his eyes. He screamed, "Cal!" The hoarse voice at his ear was the sweetest sound he'd ever heard.

"I've got you."

They reached the relative safety of the boulder. Cal was covered in blood and guts, and Jim grabbed at Cal's arms and legs, making sure he was whole. Jim miraculously had all his limbs, too, but—God! The woman! He had to go back.

He tried to scramble around the boulder again, but Cal held him down. "Bastards strapped her with explosives. It's over."

Jim could do nothing but spit the metal of her blood from his mouth, too much of it already swallowed deep inside him. He thought of the terror and sorrow in her eyes, and Sully's empty sockets.

And he knew it would never be over.

1948

BESIDE JIM, CAL tensed. "Eddie? The Eddie who used to work here?"

"Yeah. I guess it's a day for unexpected arrivals." Jim put a spring in his step and met Eddie by the paddock fence.

After an awkward beat, Eddie extended his hand. "Jim. How are you?" He smiled tightly, the dimples in his cheeks barely making an appearance.

"Just fine. Thank you." Jim took Eddie's hand. "This is Cal Cunningham."

The two men shook, and Cal smiled, although it didn't reach his eyes. He asked, "What brings you back to Clover Grove?"

"I know harvest is almost here," Eddie said. "I thought I'd see if you could use the help. I'm visiting my folks in town."

Jim wanted to say that it was too little, too late for Eddie's help now, but he pushed the unkind thought away. "How are your parents?"

"They're good. How are Sophie and Adam?"

As if on cue, Sophie's voice rang out, and she burst from the house with Adam at her heels. "Eddie!"

A genuine smile lit up Eddie's face. "There's my girl!" He lifted Sophie into a big hug.

Resentment flared in Jim. It was completely irrational and unfair—he should be glad Sophie was seeing her friend again. Cal squeezed his elbow for a fleeting moment, and Jim inhaled deeply. Of course Cal understood without him needing to say a word.

Eddie placed Sophie back on the ground and bent to hug Adam.

"Look at how much you've grown! Both of you."

"I'm a big boy now," Adam said.

"He's a goober," Sophie added.

Laughing, Eddie ruffled Adam's light curls and straightened. To Jim, he said, "I can't believe it. It seems like just yesterday I saw them last."

"It was almost a year ago," Cal noted. "Kids grow. It's what they do."

His tone was jovial, but Jim could sense the surprising hostility beneath it.

Eddie nodded. "True enough. Jim, the place looks great." He laughed incredulously. "Is that a cider house?"

"It is. Cal's co-owner of the orchard now, and we're expanding the business. Making hard cider," Jim said. "I'm afraid we're all hired up for the harvest, though."

Eddie's smile was tight again. "I figured you might be. I wanted to stop by anyway and say hi. I guess I should let you get back to it."

"But you just got here!" Sophie grabbed Eddie's hand. "You have to stay for a little while at least! I'm making shepherd's pie for dinner. Mrs. O'Brien taught me."

Eddie smiled. "That sounds delicious, Soph. If it's okay with your dad I'd love to stay."

"Of course." Jim smiled, too, although he had to force it. He wasn't sure why he was so unsettled by Eddie's sudden reappearance. "We have some work to do, though."

With a furrow in her forehead, Sophie looked back and forth between Eddie and Jim. "That's okay. Eddie can play with us. Oh! You should see the dollhouse Uncle Cal made me! Come on!" She tugged on him impatiently, and off they went.

Cal laughed darkly. "Too bad you didn't go to church today. I could have run him off before you got back."

Since it was Sunday, the pickers had the day off, but Jim hadn't felt like dressing up and going into town. It wasn't the first service he'd skipped lately, although he knew he should take Sophie and Adam. But listening to the minister talk about living a Godly life filled Jim with confusion and shame. He needed to get his head on straight before he returned to church.

"I'm sorry to say I wouldn't have minded if you had. Seeing him again like this, it's...I don't know." Jim scrubbed a hand through his hair. "It's strange, is all. I should be glad he's all right, given the way he disappeared."

Cal snorted. "You don't owe him anything, Jim."

"Why do you say that? I know he left suddenly, but he was a big help to Ann and my father while I was gone. And when I got back. He was a good worker. That's what made him taking off like that so upsetting."

Cal plucked a blade of grass and rolled it between his fingers. "I just don't like him." He glanced up. "You didn't seem too happy to see him either."

"All right, I'm not. It's silly, really."

"What? Tell me."

Jim put his hands on the fence and watched Mabel graze, her tail flicking rhythmically. "When I got back, it was...difficult. Sophie didn't know me. She was so little when I left. When I came home, she was six. I was a stranger, and it was Eddie she knew. At first she clung to him. How could I blame her?"

"But it still hurt."

Jim sighed. "It did. But I was so messed up then. The nightmares were terrible. Poor Ann didn't know what to do."

"Sophie told me you had a nightmare recently."

His pulse spiking, Jim took this in. "She told you that?"

"Don't look so guilty. It's not your fault." Cal reached out.

Jim sidestepped. "Of course it's my fault. I shouldn't still be having nightmares. Lord, it's been years."

Cal grabbed Jim's hand. "*It's not your fault.*"

"How can you say that? You were there, and you're fine. What's wrong with me?" He pulled free and began pacing.

"Fine? None of us are fine, Jim. Some of us just hide it better."

"I'm weak. I've always been weak."

"Weak?" Cal exhaled sharply. "I don't ever want you to talk that way. *Feel* that way. I know you think you failed them somehow. Sully and Davis. That woman."

Jim squeezed his eyes shut as the memories reared up. "I should have saved them."

Cal's hands were gentle as they rubbed up and down Jim's arms. "You couldn't save everyone. None of us could."

Thoughts of Sully and the nameless woman flowed into memories of Ann, and of that other terrible night. Jim pushed them away, wishing he could erase them from his mind forever. He opened his eyes and focused on what Cal was saying.

"We all came home with scars. We do our best every day to go on with our lives and put it behind us. That's what you're doing. Your best. It's all we can do."

Cal was right, of course. Jim knew it, but he couldn't help the shame and powerlessness that still lived deep within. He wanted to fall into Cal's arms and lose himself in the warmth and strength.

Sophie's laughter rang out in the distance, and Cal's hands fell away. Jim felt bereft, and he watched Mabel munch. There was so much he wanted to say to Cal, but he needed to gather his thoughts. He had to say it right.

"Let's do some work and get through today. Once Eddie's gone, we can talk."

Cal's eyebrows raised. "About everything?"

"Everything."

THE STARS WERE bright as Jim and Eddie wandered near the paddock. Cal had volunteered to help Sophie clean up, and Jim knew he had to go ahead and get it over with. He didn't even know what *it* was, this strange string of tension wavering between him and Eddie. He hadn't held a grudge when Eddie left, or he hadn't thought so, at least.

Jim breathed deeply. He loved the ripe, heavy smell of the apples after a sunny day near harvest. The air was rich and soothing, and he steadied himself for what was to come.

Eddie leaned against the fence and lit a cigarette. "He's good with the kids. Your friend Cal."

Jim bristled already. "He is. We're lucky he's here."

"Looks like he'll be sticking around, huh?" Eddie motioned to the cider house. "Glad to see you finally decided to expand. I always thought there was an opportunity there."

Jim shifted uncomfortably. "You did. I should have listened. I was a bit stuck in my ways."

"I suppose we all are sometimes." Eddie cleared his throat. "Look, I shouldn't have left you in the lurch the way I did. I'm sorry. But…"

"But what?" Jim almost held his breath.

Something caught Eddie's eye, and Jim glanced over his shoulder to find Cal approaching with two glasses and a bottle of beer tucked under his arm.

"The kids are taking a bath." He passed one glass of whiskey to Eddie and then the beer to Jim.

Jim took a long sip, trying to quell the growing dread. The three men drank in strained silence until Eddie stubbed out his cigarette on the fence. He handed his empty glass to Jim.

"I suppose I should be going."

Cal laughed bitterly. "That's it? Nothing else to say?"

Eddie stood up straighter, his jaw tight. "What's that supposed to mean?"

"You know what it means." Cal balanced his glass on the fence post. "Jim deserves the truth. He beat himself up all through the war for not being here. But Ann was no saint. She was getting on just fine without him. Wasn't she?"

Jim gripped the glass and bottle in his hands. "What does that mean?"

Eddie's nostrils flared, and his gaze was intent on Cal. He spoke as if Jim wasn't even there. "He already has more than he deserves. He has *everything*." Eddie flung his arm out. "All of this. The kids. What do I have?"

Cal looked ready to punch Eddie's lights out, and Jim felt like he was coming late to a conversation. "I don't understand. Eddie, it was your choice to leave."

"How could I stay without her?"

As if he was underwater and finally struggling to the surface, the pieces fell into place. Jim was silent for several heartbeats before finding his voice. "Ann? You and Ann?" His mind spun, and he felt unbearably foolish. Had he really paid such little attention? He dropped the glass and bottle, and they thudded on the grass.

Eddie jabbed a finger at his own chest. "*I* loved her. More than anything. More than you ever did. Ever would. But she wouldn't leave you. No matter what you did to her."

Jim's face flamed, and he had to look away.

"Jim would never have hurt her," Cal gritted out.

Eddie's laugh was harsh. "That's what she said. That it was an accident. Always making excuses."

Jim swallowed thickly. "It was a nightmare. I lashed out. I wasn't in my right mind." He cringed at the memory of waking to Ann trembling beside him, her eyes wide, holding her palm to her tear-streaked face. The terrible bruise that marred her pale cheek in the morning. "I never meant to hit her. To hurt her." He chanced a glance at Cal.

Cal watched him with soft eyes. "Of course you didn't."

Eddie snorted. "I see you're the same. Making excuses. When her mother visited I hoped she'd talk some sense into Ann. But it always came back to the children. She wouldn't leave them. Knew she'd never be able to take them away from you, even though—" He broke off.

"What?" A terrible thought whipped through Jim's mind, and his stomach lurched. "You and Ann… Is Adam…? No, Adam is my son."

He wouldn't let himself make it a question. "He's mine."

Something flickered across Eddie's face. Regret? "Yes. He's yours. She ended it with me the minute she got the letter saying you were on your way home. You were here a week later."

Relief flooded Jim. If Adam hadn't been his... He couldn't bear to think of it.

"How noble," Cal muttered.

Eddie clenched his jaw. "She was a good woman. But she was lonely. We didn't plan on it, believe me." He looked at Jim. "She didn't betray you easily. I never thought she'd love me back. I was happy just to be near her. To help her any way I could. But she needed something more than a friend. She said—"

"What?" Jim's voice was hoarse. "What did she say?"

"Even before the war, you know it wasn't right between you."

Jim swallowed roughly. "I know." He thought of Ann, good and kind, yearning for something he could never give her. The words scraped out of his throat. "I don't blame her."

It was silent but for the crickets and Trixie's nickering from the paddock. In the distance, Finnigan barked.

Then, Eddie's anger seemed to drain away. His shoulders slumped, and he sounded weary. "I know it was wrong. I should have left when you came back. But even if I couldn't have her, at least I could be near. At least I'd have something." He shook his head. "But there's only so long you can go, being close to the person you love without having them."

The heat of Cal's stare flushed Jim's cheek. He waited for Eddie to go on.

"I begged her to run away with me." Eddie ran a hand through his hair. "I know it was wrong, but I was desperate. She would never leave her children. She knew there was no way you'd give them up. But it got harder and harder, and that night, I—"

Eddie took a ragged breath. He stared off into the distance as if he was watching it unfold. "You were asleep, and we argued. I told her I was leaving. For good. Got in my truck and drove away. Didn't even make it to the end of the lane before I knew I was coming back the next day. I would never have really left her."

"But she followed you," Cal said quietly.

Eddie nodded. "If I'd come back right away, she never would have gotten in the car. Or I'd have found her in the ditch. Instead she died out there. Alone. I could have saved her." Tears glistened in his eyes. "I should have saved her."

"It was an accident. It wasn't your fault." Jim glanced at Cal. "Some things we just can't prevent, no matter how hard we try."

"I should go." Eddie closed his eyes briefly. "I don't know why I came here. I don't know what I expected. It's not as if anything will bring her back. I thought I could outrun it. That if I ran and didn't stop, it couldn't catch me. I went all the way out to California. To the edge of the ocean. But she was still just as gone there as she is here."

Jim ached to hear Eddie talk of it. He'd never loved Ann that way. But he shuddered to think of what he'd do if anything happened to Cal. There would be no place far enough to escape. He wanted to take Cal's hand right then and there and squeeze tight.

Eddie squared his shoulders. "I guess I needed to come back before I could finally move on. I'm sorry, Jim. I know you must hate me for what I've done."

"I don't hate you."

Eddie blinked. "You don't? How's that?"

"We can't change the past. We can only go on and do our best."

Cal smiled softly. "Sounds like a good plan to me."

"This was your home, Eddie. You're always welcome here." Jim extended his hand.

Eddie swallowed thickly and clasped Jim's palm. "Thank you." He glanced at the house. "Can I tell them goodbye this time?"

Jim nodded. "I hope you find what you're looking for."

With a sad lift of his lips, Eddie walked away, and Jim leaned against the fence. He and Cal didn't say anything as the minutes ticked by.

When Eddie left the house, he climbed into his truck with a final wave.

Jim watched the taillights disappear. The rumble of the engine faded away until there was only the crisp breeze rustling the drying leaves, and Cal's warmth at his side.

CHAPTER TWENTY-FIVE

1945

Pink, red, and orange reflected off the scattered streaks of cloud as the sun disappeared beyond the waves. Cal inhaled the salty air. The troop ship cut through the sea cleanly.

Wiping sleep from his eyes, Jim joined Cal at the railing. Cal nudged him. "You almost missed the sunset."

Jim was still groggy, but he returned the smile. "Guess I needed that nap."

"Guess so. That's the whole point of sending us home, right? We need all the rest we can get."

Cal tried to ignore the worry nagging him. Even though the battle for Okinawa was over and they'd been rotated home, Jim wasn't back to normal. Not that Cal knew what normal was now. They were all utterly exhausted and shell shocked. Haunted by the things they wished they could forget.

But Jim slept day and night, refusing to come ashore when they were given leave in Hawaii. Cal had hoped Jim would begin to come around as they left the fear of having to invade Japan—and the carnage that would mean—behind. But Jim rarely roused himself from his rack. He hardly shaved and only wanted to sleep. When he did, he often screamed and whimpered from nightmares, lashing out blindly when Cal shook him awake.

Jim stared at the sea. "Do you think we'll have to come back?"

"God, I hope not. With the war over in Europe, the Japs have to know they can't win. Not with all the Allied forces turning their attention to the Pacific."

Jim's voice was flat. "I don't think they'll ever surrender."

Cal gave him another nudge. "Come on, let's get some grub. Just think, before too long we'll see California on that horizon. We can't worry about what'll come down the road. It'll come either way."

Jim nodded, and they headed down to the mess hall and got into line. They'd just picked up their trays when the loudspeaker crackled.

"Attention. This is the captain."

The chattering ceased as the men froze. Cal prayed fervently that it would be good news.

"On the sixth of August, American forces dropped an atomic bomb on the Japanese city of Hiroshima. The destruction and loss of life has been great. We await further news and will pass it on when it comes through. At ease."

The speakers went silent, and the men stared at each other for several stunned moments. Then a murmur swelled.

Jim shook his head. "My God. The atomic bomb."

"If this doesn't make them surrender, I don't know what will," Cal said. "Must be a lot of civilians dead, hitting a city." He shuddered. Yet to his shame, the greatest emotion he felt bubbling to the surface was relief.

As the days went on and they neared the States, the men could talk of little else but the possible surrender and an end to the war. The thought that they might really be going home for good was almost too much. Cal was afraid to get his hopes too high.

At least it roused something in Jim, and he was more alert than he'd been in a long time. Cal stayed close to him, the relief warring with the profound sense of loss he already felt.

One morning, Cal leaned against the ship's rail, smoking cigarette after cigarette. Of course he'd always known Jim would go back to his wife and child. To his life. It was as it should be. Yet the dawning reality of it as they neared the mainland choked Cal a little more with each passing mile.

Even if they remained friends, they'd never have the closeness they'd shared at war. The closeness Cal had allowed under his skin, burrowing so deep that he felt its loss already. The idea of returning to Manhattan, knowing Jim was only a few hours away was unbearable.

"Penny for your thoughts."

Cal smiled, jumping slightly as Jim leaned next to him. "Sorry. You'll need at least a dollar to capture everything going on up here." He tapped his head.

"I think I can afford it. Maybe fifty cents."

It felt like so long since Jim had laughed and joked, and Cal fought the urge to throw his arms around him. "You can give me a down payment."

Jim gazed out. "Almost there. I feel like…" He paused. "Like we crossed an imaginary line, and as we get closer to home the air is easier to breathe. It's silly."

"It's not. I feel it too. The surrender has to be coming. It has to be."

"If it's not…we can't go back there, Cal. I can't."

Cal leaned closer. "We won't. You'll be home with your little girl before you know it."

Jim closed his eyes for a moment. "I just want to hold her again. Lord, I want that." He breathed deeply and smiled. "I can't wait for you to meet her. You'll have to come visit once we're back. We're not that far from the city."

"I will. Of course." But in his heart, Cal knew it was a lie.

They woke on the morning of August fifteenth to another announcement. In their bunks, the men blinked awake, instantly alert. Cal imagined the whole ship held its breath, with even the engines going quiet.

"On August ninth, we dropped a second atomic bomb on Japan. Today, Emperor Hirohito issued Japan's unconditional surrender to the

Allied forces."

After a moment of stunned silence, shouts of joy echoed throughout the ship, drowning out the captain's remaining address. Cal leaped from his bunk, Jim meeting him halfway as they embraced tightly. All around them, men whooped and hollered, hugging and slapping each other's backs in a chaos of celebration. A few men wept, and their buddies comforted them.

Cal held onto Jim for longer than he should have, but Jim didn't pull away.

When they prepared to dock the next day, packing up their sea bags for the last time, Cal reached into the bottom of his and pulled out a slender box about six inches long. He cleared his throat. "Hey, Jim. Here's a little something."

Jim blinked. "Huh?" He took the box with a puzzled smile. When he saw the gold watch nestled inside, his jaw dropped. "But...*Cal.*" He lifted the watch carefully. "When did you get this?"

Cal shrugged. "Picked it up in Hawaii. You're always complaining about your watch not keeping good time. It's nothing."

"Nothing? It's gold! It must have cost a fortune."

Cal waved his hand dismissively. "Nah, I got a great deal."

"I don't know what to say. I don't have a gift for you."

"I wasn't expecting anything. I just thought you might like it."

"We still have a long train ride home, you know. You're not getting rid of me just yet."

"I know. Just a little something to remember me by. Wanted to give it to you before I forgot." He picked up his sea bag and went through the motions of stowing his gear while he spied Jim from the corner of his eye.

After turning the watch over, Jim traced his fingertip over the engraving on the back. Cal knew what it said, of course. He'd kept it simple.

C.C.

J.B.

1948

As Jim put the children to bed, Cal re-dried the dishes he and Sophie had left in the rack. Listening to the low murmur of Jim's voice as he read a bedtime story, Cal swiped the cloth uselessly over one plate and then another.

When Jim returned downstairs, their gaze locked, and without discussion they grabbed their jackets and headed outside. Cal expected to stop by the paddock, but Jim walked on. Cal followed, staying quiet as they made their way past the cider house and down into the orchard.

Among the trees, Jim stopped. Finnigan was barking again in the distance, and Cal shifted from foot to foot. He blurted, "I'm sorry."

Jim frowned. "What could you be sorry for?"

"For not telling you about Ann and Eddie. I had my suspicions."

"I didn't." Jim laughed hollowly. "Isn't that ridiculous?"

"She was your wife. You loved her."

"I did. She was…" Jim's voice broke, and he paused. "She was a kind soul, and I could never love her the way she deserved. Is it strange to be *glad* to discover your wife had a lover while you were off at war?"

"Not in this case. Maybe you'll stop hating yourself. Take her down off that pedestal." Cal raised his hands. "I'm not saying she was a bad woman. But she wasn't perfect, and her death wasn't your fault. We all do the best we can."

"When she was pregnant with Adam, I could barely bring myself to look at her. As her stomach grew, every time I saw her I thought of Okinawa. Of that night." Jim's breath stuttered. "I shut myself away from her. Even after Adam was born. We slept in the same bed, but we were strangers. I cringed away from her whenever she reached out."

"The war left you broken. Left us all broken in our own ways."

"Lord, Cal. I *struck* her. I didn't mean to. I was still asleep. But I did it all the same. She should have left then. She'd still be alive."

Cal stepped closer, yearning to touch. "There's no way to know what might have been."

Jim went on, his eyes unfocused. "It must have been plain as day, Ann and Eddie. But I didn't see it. I didn't see a lot of things. I wouldn't allow it. All these feelings I tried to hide, even from myself. I couldn't see myself clearly, let alone anyone else." He looked at Cal. "You must think I'm such a fool."

"I'd never think that. *Never.*"

"Of course you wouldn't." The branches waved gently in the breeze, dappling the moonlight over Jim's face. "You've always loved me for who I am, good and bad."

Cal took a shaky breath. "I always will."

"And I haven't loved you well enough at all." Jim raised his hand when Cal would have interrupted. "I hope you'll let me make up for it. I hope you'll stay. Because I love you and I don't ever want you to leave again."

As relief and joy coursed through him, Cal laughed. He took Jim's face in his hands and kissed him soundly. "Say that again."

Jim chuckled unsteadily, his voice thick with tears. "Which part?"

"All of it."

Then Cal was kissing him, and they wrapped their arms around each other. Cal inhaled Jim deeply, licking into his mouth and holding him close. He would have climbed into his skin if he could.

Jim pressed kisses to Cal's cheeks, forehead, chin, and nose. "I love you," he murmured. "I love you."

The ground was damp with chilly evening dew that would soon be frost as the harvest ended, but Cal didn't care as they tore off their clothes. He clumsily spread his jacket and shirt and stretched out on the ground as Jim covered him. They both groaned, kissing deeply. Rocking together, they were already hard.

"I need you." Cal urged Jim to straddle his chest so he could take Jim's cock into his mouth. As Jim moaned his name, Cal sucked messily, getting Jim as slick as possible. They were almost frantic as Jim licked his fingers and reached down to open Cal's ass, making Cal groan wetly and spread his legs. Jim shimmied down between them.

Cal held his knees to his chest as Jim pushed into him. It burned like hell, and it was the greatest thing he'd ever felt. Jim was inside him again, and nothing else mattered. Not the hard ground, or the rock digging into his spine, or the brisk breeze scattering goose bumps over his flesh.

Tipping his head back, Cal moaned as Jim began to fuck him. It felt as though it had been years since they'd touched, and he met Jim's thrusts, threading their fingers together on the grass by his head as Jim leaned over with a smile dancing on his lips.

"I dreamed of you like this." Jim's eyes were bright, and his hair stuck up. Sweat beaded on his lip. "Out here in the orchard, naked in the moonlight."

Cal drew him down for a deep kiss. He panted. "How did it end?"

"However we want." Jim kissed him again as he angled in deeper and hitched Cal's legs higher.

They strained together, grunting as their flesh smacked in the calm of the orchard. Sparks of pleasure flickered through Cal's body as Jim brushed the perfect spot inside him. "God. There. Harder. I need—" He pulled Jim's head down and kissed him.

Reaching between them, Jim stroked Cal's cock. "I want this forever. Want you."

Cal had to shut his eyes as the pleasure thundered through him, his throat closing as he came. Tingling from head to toe, he gasped and clamped down on Jim's cock. Jim thrust wildly, his arms shaking. Cal felt the heat of Jim's seed deep inside him, and Jim buried his head in Cal's neck as he cried out.

As he softened inside Cal, Jim pressed their foreheads together. His lips parted as he caught his breath. Cal kissed him gently, and wished they could stay forever.

Of course, they had to get dressed eventually, the night chill catching up with them as they pulled on their clothes and boots. Laughing, Jim licked his palm and ran it over Cal's unruly hair. Cal did the same to Jim with a smile.

The question tumbled from Cal's lips before he could stop it. "What changed?"

"Nothing. I've always loved you." With an achingly serious expression, Jim brushed his thumb over Cal's bottom lip. "Always."

"What about everything else? The kids?"

"We'll be careful. We'll keep what's private between us private. We'll come out here or go to the cabin. I wish I could go to sleep with you every night and wake up with you every morning. But we can still love each other. We can still make a life together. Even with our secret." He exhaled a shaky breath, clear anxiety creasing his face. "It's not perfect, I know."

"I don't need perfect." Cal rubbed their noses together. "Just you."

SOPHIE TUGGED CAL'S hand. "We're going to miss it!"

"Okay, okay."

She huffed. "Uncle Cal, would you hurry up?"

"Yes, ma'am." Cal increased his pace as they wove their way through the crowded main street. The Harvest Festival was in full swing, and tables of crafts, baked goods, and produce lined the street.

The autumn sun was high in a blue sky, and it looked as if almost everyone in the county had come out. The hailstorm had hurt the region badly, and the community was banding together. It made Cal smile.

In the field beyond the street, a few carnival rides creaked and played tinny music as the children laughed in delight. Cal spotted Adam chortling as he and Mrs. O'Brien rode the carousel. Mrs. O'Brien waved as they passed, but Sophie clearly had another destination in mind and tugged Cal toward a gathering crowd.

On a wooden platform, a man in a suit waited. Cal frowned. "Who's that?"

"It's the mayor." Sophie squeezed into the crowd, her face alight.

She wore a dress with a wool cardigan, and pushed her sleeves up to her elbows, her cheeks rosy. In the warmth of the crowd, Cal was glad he'd left his jacket with Jim.

"What's he waiting for?"

She giggled. "You'll see!"

A moment later, a woman stepped up with a cream pie in her hand. Cal laughed. "Don't tell me she's going to—"

The crowd roared as the pie landed on the mayor's chest, splattering cream all over his suit. Two more people stepped up for their turn, the last landing their pie squarely in the mayor's face. For his part, the man simply licked his lips. "Strawberry cream. My favorite!"

Everyone laughed, and then the show was apparently over. Sophie beamed. "Wasn't that funny?"

"Sure. But why do they do that?"

She shrugged. "I dunno. Because it's funny."

When they made their way back to the Clover Grove table set up on the street near the bakery, Jim glanced up from a piece of paper. "Did they get him good this year?"

Sophie grinned. "Uh-huh."

Cal took his seat beside Jim. "Why exactly does the mayor of Tivoli agree to this ritual?"

"People bid money on the pies and it goes into the town's coffers. It's a tradition. The bidding wars can get pretty darn fierce."

"I'm glad it's not me with a pie in my face. Although…" Cal examined their table. "If there are any of Mrs. O'Brien's apple pies left at the end of the day, I'm eating one."

Sophie plopped onto Cal's lap. "You can't eat a whole pie."

Jim snorted. "Oh, he could. Believe me."

"I won't even use a fork."

She poked him in the stomach. "You'll get fat."

"It's true. I will. Let's hope I don't get hungry enough to eat you." He tickled her as she squirmed and squealed.

A little girl in pigtails appeared. "Sophie, come ride the tilt-a-whirl!"

With a quick glance at Jim, who nodded, Sophie disappeared into the crowd. Cal tapped the piece of paper in Jim's lap. "What's that?"

Jim passed it over. "I picked up the mail. There was a letter from Joe. He got married." Jim held up a small black and white photo of big old Joe with a tiny blonde on his arm.

"First Gambler and now Joe?" Grinning, Cal read the letter, scrawled in Joe's messy hand, telling of how he'd made foreman at the mill and that Miss Lydia Rogers had agreed to become his wife. "We should invite them to visit." He glanced at Jim's unreadable expression. "Unless…I guess we shouldn't." Cal folded the letter and handed it back.

"No. We should. Definitely. I'll write this week."

"Okay." Cal smiled and felt that silly flip-flop of his stomach that hadn't gone away yet. He wondered if it ever would. He and Jim sat in companionable silence, watching the townsfolk go by.

"Hello, Clover Grove." Rebecca approached the table. "I'll have a glass of cider, please. I'd prefer the alcoholic kind, but I suppose it's not ready yet."

"I'm afraid the regular old cider will have to do for now." Jim poured her a glass and waved off her offer of money. "It's on the house."

"All right, if you insist. How did the harvest go? All finished?"

Jim nodded. "We are. Still lots of work, but the picking's done for the year."

"Good." Rebecca smiled at Cal. "And I hear you're staying on permanently."

"That I am." Cal could still hardly believe it was true.

"Welcome to Tivoli, Mr. Cunningham. Officially, that is."

"Thank you kindly." Cal stood and walked around the table to kiss Rebecca's cheek.

They were jostled suddenly, and Cal looked down to find Sophie scowling at them. "Say hello, Sophie."

"Hi, Aunt Rebecca," she muttered.

"Hello, honey," Rebecca said. "Are you having fun?"

Sophie only nodded.

"Well, I should get going. I'll see you all soon." Rebecca waved and moved into the crowd.

Staring after her, Sophie's frown deepened. Jim and Cal shared a glance as Cal sat down again. Jim looked just as lost as Cal felt.

"What's wrong, sweetie?" Jim asked.

"Nothing." It was a half-hearted response at best.

"*Sophie.*" Jim gave her a stern look. "Come on, now. Did something happen with Jane? Did you bicker?"

"No." Sophie peeked at Cal. The next moment she exclaimed, "Are you going to marry her?"

Cal couldn't have been more surprised if he'd gotten a pie in the face. "Who? Your pal Jane? She's a little young for me, don't you think?"

Sophie huffed. "You kissed Aunt Rebecca." Her eyes narrowed. "I saw."

"I was only being nice. She's my friend. Your daddy's friend too. Not to mention yours. I'm not going to marry her."

Sophie's lip trembled. "Promise?"

"I promise." It would certainly be an easy one to keep.

"Sweetheart, what's gotten into you?" Jim asked.

"Uncle Cal said he's going to stay with us. For good."

Cal opened his arms and beckoned Sophie onto his lap. "I'm staying. For good."

She glanced back and forth between Cal and Jim. "Okay." She relaxed against him. "I believe you."

Holding her close, Cal pressed a kiss to her head, and Jim rubbed her arm gently. He and Jim looked at each other, and Jim smiled softly.

The sun was setting as they packed up the truck with the table and chairs and leftover apples and cider. Sophie and Adam were already slumped together in the middle of the cab, fast asleep. Cal had the keys in his pocket and got behind the wheel as Jim climbed into the passenger side.

Even when the engine rattled to life, the kids didn't so much as twitch. Jim flicked on the radio, keeping the volume low as Art Mooney crooned about his four-leaf clover. Cal sang along softly as he pulled onto the road, and Jim reached over the kids to rest his hand on the back of Cal's neck.

Cal came to the crossroads and turned toward home.

EPILOGUE

1957

SOPHIE INHALED DEEPLY as she walked around to the kitchen door with her suitcase in hand. Clover Grove was just as she'd left it.

Well, almost.

Most of the leaves were off the trees, and a thin layer of snow clung to the roof of the barn. The orchard extended for another twenty-five acres now, and the young trees were ready to give fruit next year. The demand for Clover Grove hard cider had grown steadily through the years, and the cider house hummed with activity near the ever-expanding storage and fermentation shed.

She breathed in the sweet, fresh air again. It was good to be home. Her oxfords slipped in a puddle of slush, and mud splashed her stockings. Her knee skirt wasn't quite as practical here as it was at school.

The rich smell of Sophie's favorite beef casserole wafted out as she opened the door. Her dad spun around from the counter, dropping the knife he was using onto the cutting board with a clatter. "Sophie?"

"Hi, Dad." She put down her case and hugged him tightly, relaxing into his warm, familiar embrace as she rested her head on his shoulder.

When she pulled away he checked his watch. The face was scratched and the gold worn, but he'd shrugged her off when she'd suggested getting it fixed or buying a new one.

"I thought you were coming in on the later train?"

"I finished early so I decided to surprise you. Dr. O'Brien gave me a ride on his way home. He said Mrs. O'Brien wants us all to come for lunch on Saturday, and to invite Grandma and Grandpa too."

"Sure. That'll be nice. Grandpa might not want to come, but if you give your grandmother a call, you can convince her. What time's the train on Sunday? Can you stay for church?"

"Of course." Sophie secretly hadn't been to a single service since going to college, but she knew it would make her father happy.

"Oh, were you able to meet up with Aunt Rebecca in the city last week on your class trip? I forgot to ask."

Nodding, Sophie smiled at the memory. "We went for lunch near Central Park, and then took the kids to FAO Schwartz. It was really fun. They've gotten so big now. Stephen's almost seven and Lucy's five already. Uncle Luke's got a new job on Wall Street. Aunt Rebecca said he likes it a lot."

"I'm glad to hear it." Dad took hold of her shoulders, smiling the way he did when he got sentimental, the little wrinkles deepening around his eyes and mouth. He asked, "And how are you? How are your classes?"

"Since we talked on Sunday night? They're still good, and yes, I'm still studying hard."

"I know you are, sweetie. Look at you. A college girl." Something flickered across his face. "Your mother would be so very proud."

The old familiar sadness flowed through Sophie for a moment. "I know she would." She smiled. "Geez, don't make me cry already. I've only been home for five minutes."

"Sorry." He ran his hand over the short waves of her hair. "You cut it. Looks beautiful."

Sophie beamed and patted where her hair curled just under her ears. "Thanks, Dad. Where's Uncle Cal?"

"In the barn. Why don't you say hello while I finish up dinner?"

She grinned. "You made my favorite."

"Of course. Mostly because it's one of the only things I can cook, and Cal's making the Thanksgiving turkey tomorrow. He says I'm allowed to mash the potatoes and that's it."

"A wise move after last year."

Dad picked up a dish towel and snapped it at her playfully before she escaped outside, squinting at the sun disappearing beyond the treetops. She thought about going to change into her old overalls as she hopped over a puddle of slush, but didn't want to take the time.

From the paddock, old Trixie nickered, and Sophie called out softly as she passed, her breath clouding the wintry air. "I'll see you soon, girl."

The barn was still green, but a deeper shade that had been freshly painted that summer. She admired it as she drew near, smiling as she remembered how they'd all ended up splashed in green after Adam decided to splatter Uncle Cal and their dad with his paintbrush. Sophie hadn't gotten it out of her hair for days.

Inside the barn, Uncle Cal looked up from where his head pressed against Gretchen's flank as he milked her. "Would you look at what the cat dragged in."

In the corner, Finnigan raised his head as well, his tail wagging. He trotted over slowly. Sophie bent low and scratched behind his ears. He was too old to chase deer now, and she was relieved to see him again, knowing it wouldn't be much longer for him. "Hi, Finnigan. Are you keeping Uncle Cal out of trouble?"

"Never. Trouble's my middle name." Uncle Cal hauled her up into his arms and gave her a spin.

Her laughter echoing in the rafters, she clung to him.

Uncle Cal placed her gently on her feet and brushed back her coiffed hair. "Very stylish, Miss Bennett. You're early. Eager to leave the bright lights of Ithaca behind?"

She grinned. "Something like that." Reaching up, she touched the hair by his temples. "You didn't have gray in September. Must be because you miss me."

He nodded seriously. "It must be. Or I'm getting old, and it can't be that."

Laughing, Sophie went to Gretchen and gave her a pat. "You're only thirty-nine. It's not *that* old."

"Thank you. That's very reassuring. You want to take over? I'm sure Gretchen won't mind. She's never kicked anyone—not even me."

They shared a smile as Sophie took the stool. She leaned down and pulled gently. The rhythm of milking was strangely comforting. After a few moments of peaceful silence, she gathered her nerve. "I met a boy," she blurted, and then mentally cringed. This wasn't at all how she'd rehearsed it.

"Did you?" Uncle Cal didn't sound too thrilled. "All right, tell me more about this boy."

"His name's Matthew, and it's not like that. We're just friends. We sit together in American lit." She pulled steadily, the milk squirting into the bucket. With a deep inhale, she rushed on. "He's a homosexual." Holding her breath, Sophie dared a glance back.

Uncle Cal was frozen in place where he stood leaning with one shoulder against the wall. He cleared his throat. "Is he?"

"Uh-huh." Sophie's pulse zoomed as she went back to milking, watching the bucket fill. "I don't really see what the big deal is. Doesn't bother me."

"It doesn't?" Uncle Cal's voice was strained.

"Nope." There was no milk left, so she stood and backed out of the stall. Sophie shrugged and forced herself to meet his gaze. "Not at all."

Slowly, a smile lit up Uncle Cal's face. "That's good to know."

"Maybe…" Her nerve faltered.

"What, sweetheart?"

"Maybe you could tell my dad some time. Or I could. *We* could. I think it would be good. For him to know."

Nodding, Uncle Cal swallowed hard. "It would."

Finnigan barked as Adam burst into the barn, dropping his bike with a clatter. His jeans were splattered with mud and getting too short for him. He was even ganglier than she remembered, all awkward limbs and pimples, and his hair had lost all its blondness now. Sophie grinned. "Hey, goober."

Adam rolled his eyes. "Aren't you too old to call me that now?"

"I'll never be too old to call you goober." She pulled him into a hug. He pretended to be reluctant the way he usually did now, but he still held her close. She leaned back. "Christ, you're almost taller than I am already."

"Whoa, is that the kind of language they're teaching you at Cornell?" Uncle Cal chuckled. "Don't let your father hear you talk like that."

Dad's voice floated down from the house. "Dinner's ready!"

Adam patted his scrawny belly. "Thank God—I'm starving." He took off at a run. "Come on!"

Uncle Cal put his arm around Sophie's shoulders and pressed a kiss to her temple. "Good to have you home."

She wrapped her arm around his waist tightly, and they made their way back to the warm glow of the house as the night settled in, laughing as they puddle jumped.

In the kitchen, they took their regular seats at the battered old table. Sophie's chair still tilted when she leaned to the left, but she'd probably miss it if her dad or Uncle Cal fixed it.

After only a few bites, Adam flung a pea at her. Dad said that was enough, so of course Uncle Cal tossed a pea at him. Dad retaliated, and Sophie launched her own attack, and soon peas flew off their forks every which way. They laughed so hard that dinner took forever to eat, but she didn't mind at all.

The End

About the Author

Keira aims for the perfect mix of character, plot, and heat in her M/M romances. She writes everything from swashbuckling pirates to heartwarming holiday escapism. Her fave tropes are enemies to lovers, age gaps, forced proximity, and passionate virgins. Although she loves delicious angst along the way, Keira guarantees happy endings!

Find out more at: www.keiraandrews.com